TRUE SELF

THE SOUL MAGIC SERIES

BOOK TWO

ANNE WILLIAMS

THE PNEUMA PROJECT

Printed in the United States of America

Published by The Pneuma Project

www.ThePneumaProject.com

Identifiers:

LCCN: 2020946177

ISBN: 978-1-7357237-0-9 (paperback)
ISBN: 978-1-7357237-1-6 (hardback)
ISBN: 978-1-7357237-2-3 (ebook)

Available in paperback, hardback, e-book, and audiobook.

Book design by JetLaunch. Cover design by Debbie O'Byrne.

ACKNOWLEDGMENTS

There is so much more than you can imagine that goes into writing and publishing a book. So many people have contributed in various ways. I'd like to start by thanking my children (who are teenagers now!). I've always thought it was my job to support them and their life goals, but they have been the ones who have helped me with mine. My parents have been behind me, cheering me on as I reach higher and higher to achieve my dreams. Their support has meant more than words can express. Next, I'd like to thank my WoW family. I've never been so awed by the genuine support and encouragement than I've been by what they've shown me. Who says virtual friends aren't real friends? Not I. And finally, I'd like to extend a heartfelt thanks to all the readers of The Awakening who have given me such positive feedback. I hope you enjoy this book even more than the first!

PROLOGUE

Perspective is how we see and judge the world based on our own experiences. It is, in essence, a person's truth. It is also how we identify our "self." Rene Descartes spent a portion of his life devoted to understanding what truth was outside of personal perspectives. What is truth, and hence what is permanent in our world that is fluid and forever changing?

People with old souls see the world differently, and perhaps have a better grasp of what it means to be truly oneself. After all, it is the ones with old souls that have experienced many different perspectives and can call upon them all to judge people and circumstances. However, when you've lived hundreds of lifetimes and had so many experiences, you tend to believe your perspective is a universal truth rather than an opinion. More often than not, though, when you try to force people to live up to your view of them and your truths about the world, they will fall short.

Let's return to Descartes and his famous "I think; therefore, I am" statement. It becomes difficult to accept personal perspective as truth and apply it fairly to one's identity in the world no matter the age of the soul or how many—or few—lifetimes they've existed. So how does one identify their true self? Is it the diligent worker who dots their i's and crosses their t's? Or is that same person who drinks too many beers after work and yells profanities at his wife and children? How can different versions of the same person all be labeled as "true"?

When an affinate completes the Awakening, they face these conflicting thoughts. How can you live the life of the mortal body when your soul has an opposing perspective? How can you be suddenly thrust into the world as a mortal being and be expected to abide by its laws when your soul tells you that you're so much more? It's utterly exasperating, to be honest. I said it before, and I'll say it again—being a teenager sucks, but being an Awakened affinate teenager comes with a whole new definition of suckiness—and maybe a few really cool perks.

Balance in all things,
Adya

CHAPTER ONE

"I don't know," Ashley said hesitantly. Her right eye narrowed and twitched slightly. "It's going to be weird calling you Adya. I mean, you still *look* like Emily." The two roommates took time to catch up after their summer apart while the new Abecedarians were getting placed in their elemental residence halls. Ashley had written Emily letters during the summer, but since she was in the wilderness of Alaska, Adya didn't have a way to write back.

Adya laughed. "You can call me Ady; it's close to Emily. I promise I won't hold it against you if you slip up occasionally. Besides, I still *am* Emily. Only I'm more than *just* Emily now."

"I wish I could've stayed for you after you-know-who did those awful things. You looked dead when I saw you last." Ashley frowned.

"This isn't *Harry Potter*, Ash. You can say Myra's name." Adya chuckled.

"Yeah," Ashley said. "Saying her name makes me want to puke, though."

Adya rolled her eyes and laughed. "Speaking of vomiting—or hopefully not—we have a new kitchen staff this year, including a woman head chef, Chef Caroline." Adya filled her roommate in on the Lucas situation, how he made a deal with Myra to poison the students at the End of Year

Celebration in exchange for, presumably, getting his affinity returned. "Yeah, apparently she was former Elder Eli's chef. When Eli disappeared with Myra, the remaining Elders went through his house and belongings. That's when she requested to remain in the service of affinates. Ted immediately offered her the position here."

"Do you think she'll let us sneak in for snacks?" Ashley asked.

Adya fondly recalled the memories of visiting with Lucas in the kitchen and felt his betrayal and loss deeply. "She seems cool, but I haven't needed comfort food lately."

"Speaking of the need for comfort food. . . did you talk with Brandon over the summer?" Ashley hung up her last shirt and sat on the edge of her bed, perched to hear real gossip.

"Yeah, we talked a bit. Brandon's dating this girl back home now. But things are good between us. We're back to being just friends," Adya said with a smile.

Ashley furrowed her brows and frowned. "That's it? So, you didn't have any wonderful soul memories of past lives with him? No hot affairs?"

Adya laughed. "Well, you know about the one in the desert. His and my life have touched many times in the past. Things between us may change when he finishes his Awakening. For now, I'm grateful for Brandon's friendship in this life, regardless of whether he and I end up together."

Ashley stewed in silence. She was both jealous and dismayed by her roommate. Adya seemed noticeably different than the Emily she knew before her Awakening, coming across so mature in thought for a thirteen-year-old. Ashley would've been devastated to learn that Xander—now known as Calder after he completed his Awakening and broke Ashley's heart just before the end of the school year—had a new girlfriend, let alone a non-affinate girlfriend. "Fine," she resigned. "What about Lir? Have you heard from him?"

2

Adya still hadn't told anyone about her kiss with Lir, but Ashley had always been aware of "something deeper" between her and their water elemental healing teacher. "He flew back when he heard about Myra's attack. He was there when I woke and was the first one to see me after I completed the Awakening. We spent some time together, but it was mostly talking about how we could help restore the knowledge in the books destroyed by the fire in Maggie's office."

"Ugh!" Ashley protested and threw her hands up in the air. "You've gone full-blown boring. Give me Emily back."

Adya scrunched up her face. "Gee, thanks. I don't know what you want me to tell you. I've been working with the Elders and doing things by myself all summer. There wasn't much opportunity to even think about dating."

"Fine," Ashley submitted. "Can you at least reassure me that we've always been best friends?"

"You know I can't tell you about *you*, but I know you already understand we have a deep-rooted friendship." Adya smiled and skillfully changed the topic. "So, tell me all about Alaska."

Ashley sighed and rolled her eyes in dramatic exasperation, but as she told her stories—some of which she'd already shared with Adya in letters—her eyes lit up, and her voice became animated. No matter how much Ashley detested roughing it, being in nature for the summer suited her well.

"It's almost time for dinner, ladies," Greta interrupted as Ashley was nearing the end of the story about a momma bear and her two cubs.

"Thanks," Adya replied. "How many new water affinates do we have this year?"

"Just one in our house," Greta said with slightly slumped shoulders, sounding somewhat deflated. "So, I'm sure she could use some water elemental friends." She motioned to someone outside the girls' room. A girl with dark brown hair, big glasses, beautiful ebony skin, and braces appeared beside

3

Greta. "Girls, I would like you to meet Sierra. Sierra, this is Adya and Ashley."

"Nice to meet you," Ashley said with a warm smile.

The girl smiled shyly. "Hi," she said, and then immediately looked down at her well-worn sneakers.

"We're about to go to dinner. Want to join us?" Adya asked as she stood from her bed.

Sierra shrugged and looked up at Adya briefly. "Sure."

Greta's shoulders relaxed, and she breathed a small sigh of relief when they offered to help the new Abecedarian. "I will see the three of you later," she said and continued down the hall to let the others know it was dinner time.

"So, what do you think of it so far?" Brandon asked Sierra as the four of them ate their first course.

"It's nice," Sierra replied.

Everyone nodded in agreement. "Yeah, and in case you were wondering, all the residence halls are elemental themed," Brandon added astutely, obviously remembering the previous year's humiliation by Titus.

"Oh," the girl said.

Adya couldn't tell if Sierra's short responses were because she was intimidated by Brandon, was attracted to him, or if she was just timid.

"I remember how nervous I was last year," Ashley said. "I'd never been away from home before, at least not without my family."

"Yeah, I've never even gone on a vacation," the quiet girl admitted.

"North Shore Academy feels like a resort, at least when you're not in class, but you have to wear uniforms," Brandon added.

"If she's never been on vacation, how would she know what a resort was like?" Ashley's head made a small circle as she dramatically rolled her eyes.

Like Sierra, Adya remained mostly quiet during the meal. She found herself struggling with how to interact with the three who hadn't completed their Awakening. It felt like she was an outsider, like when she went home for the previous winter break and tried to hang out at the mall with her old friends. Having been caught up in her thoughts, Adya suddenly interrupted her friends mid-conversation. "How's your girlfriend, Brandon? Angela, isn't it?"

Ashley and Brandon simultaneously raised a brow in surprise by the seemingly random question while Sierra remained quietly picking at the wild rice and chicken dish that had just arrived.

"Yeah, Angela," Brandon said and shifted in his seat uncomfortably. "She's okay, I guess."

"How'd you meet her," Ashley asked enthusiastically, preparing herself to hear some good gossip finally.

"Dad got me a job at the country club for the summer. She was there with her family a lot. We just got to talking, and it was cool." Brandon shrugged. He glanced at Adya, presumably to see her reaction, but Adya gave no indication that she was unhappy, or uncomfortable, hearing about his new girlfriend.

"Aww, that's sweet. It sounds like it should be a movie," Ashley gushed.

Brandon chuckled uneasily. "It wasn't that interesting. We had fun together over the summer. Don't know how well a long-distance thing is going to work out, but we said we'd give it a shot." Brandon glanced at the clock on the wall. "Speaking of which, I need to go call her. It was nice meeting you, Sierra."

The Abecedarian flashed a shy smile as Brandon left.

As soon as he walked away, Ashley huffed. "He didn't even say it was nice to see *us* again." Her deep blue eyes rolled in annoyance. "Boys."

As Sierra left for the library for orientation with Adamina and the other Abecedarians, Ashley returned to the common room in their residence hall. Adya decided it was a beautiful night for a walk, and while she didn't have a specific destination in mind, she needed to get a grasp on her out-of-place feeling.

Adya was passing by the old main hall—which was still under reconstruction from the fire—when Calder unexpectedly jogged up beside her. "Hey."

"Oh, hi," Adya said as the boy's pace slowed to match hers. "Is everything okay?" She looked to make sure Ashley wasn't around. Despite not having any hard feelings towards Calder, she knew it would hurt Ashley's feelings for Adya to be chatting with him.

"Yeah, I mostly wanted to thank you for saving us at the celebration and apologize for making you feel like you were insane about your dislike for Myra," Calder explained.

"You're welcome, and it's okay." Adya smiled. "Although 'dislike' is putting it mildly. I have a question for you, though."

Calder shrugged. "Sure, what is it?"

"Why did you end things with Ashley?"

Calder's eyes widened, and his cheeks flushed subtly. "Because she—"

Adya held up her hand, cutting him off immediately. "Don't feed me the bullshit you fed her. I know you, and I know what you two have meant to each other in past lives. Tell me the truth."

The boy paused, looking thoughtfully into the distance. Finally, he looked back to Adya and said, "Why haven't you told Brandon the truth?"

Adya narrowed her eyes, replying somewhat defensively. "He deserves to make his own choices no matter what lifetime it is. I didn't see any good that would come of me telling him before he completed his Awakening."

Calder nodded. "My reasons were similar. I didn't want Ashley to feel manipulated. I want her to decide where her future lies and with whom. Besides, you know how many times I've hurt her." His expression darkened. "Maybe it's time she doesn't suffer."

Despite Adya knowing intimate details of Calder and Ashley's past lives—both the good and bad—she couldn't help but turn his words internally. She felt the sting of the suffering she'd caused Lir for lifetimes. "You've also been responsible for lifetimes of her happiness. Pain is always a part of life, and it's the reason why we can appreciate love and happiness so much. I don't think the struggles of your past lives with Ashley are enough to break ties with her completely in this life, but I do understand what you're saying," Adya added. "Can I ask you another question?"

Calder nodded. "Fire away."

"Do you feel out of place among all the people who haven't completed their Awakening yet?"

"A little. Seeing people for who they've been for lifetimes when they don't know who that even is yet can be a bit of a mind fuck," he admitted.

"How do you cope with it? I mean, I've been around Awakened people since it happened. Seeing everyone again and knowing who they are without them knowing is harder than I imagined," Adya admitted.

"Lir helped me out before he left. He reminded me that the un-Awakened version of ourselves is still us. I don't know. It made a lot of sense the way he said it." Calder shrugged. "It was more difficult when I was home over the summer because my family expected me to be the same Xander as when I started school. I just had to learn how to be both. I guess that's why we have a class on being Awakened this year."

Adya hoped the class would help. "Thanks for talking with me, Calder. I think I just needed to talk with someone else who's dealing with this weird limbo of Awakened and un-Awakened people."

"No problem, Adya. See you in class tomorrow," Calder said as he walked towards his residence hall.

"See ya." Adya waved and continued her thoughtful stroll. She hadn't seen Maggie in a few days and decided to join her in her new temporary office.

"Do you think she'll try another attack?" Adya asked Maggie as they drank some tea in her closet-turned-office. It felt unnatural to be in the windowless room, and she knew Maggie didn't like being so out of touch with the earth.

"I wish I could tell you, Adya. From what we understand of Myra and Eli's plan, it seems more self-serving than vindictive. We have people keeping an eye out for the two of them and Lucas."

Adya could see the pain in Maggie's eyes that remained after her old lover helped Myra poison them. While they never had a conversation about Lucas specifically, Adya knew from the depressed energy around Maggie that her legal guardian felt the loss deeply. "If there's anything more I can do, I'm happy to help."

"You've done more than anyone could've ever asked of you already. Until we can locate them, we just have to keep our guard up." Maggie reached into the drawer of her desk and pulled out a large envelope. "Lir sent me one of his old journals. He said you guys uncovered it in New Orleans along with a faded picture. Since these are partially yours, too, I wanted you to read through it before I scan it into the new digital archive."

CHAPTER ONE

Adya took the envelope with a soft smile. "Thank you. I'll read through it tonight and let you know tomorrow if there are any parts of it I don't want in the archive. I'm sure it'll be fine, though." Adya felt some comfort in being able to escape from her current life—even if only for the night—before she was thrust into the start of classes the following day.

CHAPTER TWO

Adya awoke the next morning with a tight grip on the photograph Lir sent Maggie. She had a long, restful night of vivid and beautiful dreams of a time long ago. But with the dawning of the sun came the transition back to her current life and new classes. Most of her classmates went to History of the Academy class with Adamina again. Adya, Calder, and several others who recently completed their Awakening went to a separate class subtly named Psychology of the True Self.

As she settled in her seat, Adya's eyes roamed over the faces of the other students. She recalled soul memories with many of them—some were acquaintances, and some were friends of friends, but others simply hadn't touched any of her lives significantly.

"I haven't seen you in lifetimes, Adya. How are you?" Coro, a third-year air affinate, greeted Adya when they took their seats.

Adya smiled at the girl who had kept her Native American roots in her current life. "It has been too long, Coro. I'm doing well. How are you?"

"Happy to be here, thanks to you," the girl said sincerely. "When did you get your third affinity? I still can't believe it."

Adya looked down at her hands. Despite everyone being unconscious when she'd used her earth affinity—the only one that wasn't publicly known—news of it had somehow spread to most of the students over the summer, and the secret she'd kept for the previous year was out in the open. "My twin brother passed it to me when he died in the womb," Adya explained. "He would've been an air affinate."

Coro nodded thoughtfully. "Yes, I recall your earth abilities when you were with us in the Arizona Territory. That's really cool, though. Maybe we could do a ritual to the wind god, Niltsi, together."

"Of course," Adya said amicably but noticed six other pairs of eyes on her—her heroics the previous year made her somewhat of a celebrity. Adya offered a polite smile to her onlookers just before class began.

"Good morning," the teacher began. The woman's hair was the same shade of champagne blonde as Ashley's, and it was pulled up into a tight, slightly off-center bun. She looked over the rim of her stylish, mauve cat-eyed shaped glasses as she addressed the class. "I'm Dr. Ilene, and I've spent lifetimes studying what 'self' means. In this class, we will spend several months studying each of the qualities of 'self.'" Dr. Ilene turned to the whiteboard and began writing as she continued, "The seven qualities we will focus on are spontaneity, reasoning, creativity, free will, spirituality, discernment, and love." She set the marker down and turned back toward the class. "My goal is to help you successfully transition to your new, Awakened life while understanding how the 'you' of this lifetime fits into your soul's life."

The structure of the class felt precisely like what Adya needed. She settled in, blocked out all the soul memories that persistently flashed in her mind, and listened to the first lesson on spontaneity.

"But how do we express ourselves when we have to keep our true selves—our soul selves—from everyone who hasn't completed the Awakening?" Adya argued as she stayed after class to talk with Dr. Ilene.

"Why do you feel you have to hide your soul self from anyone?" Dr. Irene replied as she leaned against the side of her desk, listening to Adya. "No one has ever said that you have to pretend to be someone you're not."

"That's true," Adya agreed, "but I can't go up to, for example, my best friend and say, 'Remember when we tried this same thing three lifetimes ago?' can I?"

Dr. Irene shook her head. "No, but would you approach someone with amnesia and boast about a situation she couldn't remember? Having a moral code not to cause harm to people doesn't exclude you from being yourself. That code inside of you is part of your true self as well, isn't it?"

"I suppose," Adya resigned with a defeated exhale. "It's just very confusing to try to be a part of two worlds, I guess."

"You have forever been a part of two worlds, though, Adya. And if you think about it, most humans are a part of two or more worlds. Let's take a typical, non-affinate man, for example. He goes to work, goes out with friends, and goes home to his family. Do you think that the same 'self' exists in those three places and that he acts the same regardless of his environment?"

"Well, no. I would guess that man acts differently in each place," Adya said.

"Does that mean only one of those 'selves' is his true self, or can all versions of himself be genuinely him?"

"I guess all versions could be parts of his true self," she admitted.

Dr. Ilene nodded. "Exactly. Just because you choose to express parts of yourself differently to different people doesn't mean that you aren't acting as the authentic you. Spontaneity is allowing yourself to accept your emotional spectrum in different situations and express those feelings, just like you're doing now. Sometimes it means that you accept the emotions, but don't necessarily act on them immediately, too."

Adya's stomach rumbled in hunger. Her cheeks flushed, and she reflexively moved her hands to cover it.

Dr. Ilene laughed and pushed herself away from her desk. "It seems that your true self is self-expressing right now. Go and enjoy your lunch. I'm always happy to delve into these topics with you anytime."

"Thank you. I know I'll have a billion more questions before the course ends." Adya smiled and left to join her friends at lunch, thinking a lot about how to express her true self to her un-Awakened friends.

"That's not so bad," Adya interjected. Sierra had been admitting how much trouble she had with Maggie's first meditation class. "I went back to my room and started packing after that first class. I swore it was a mistake that I was here." The group of friends laughed, nodded, and once again, Adya felt in touch with the part of herself that her friends knew.

"Yeah, she was pissed!" Brandon agreed.

"I even hid her duffle bag for the longest time just in case she tried to leave again," Ashley admitted.

Sierra giggled, too, and was starting to relax and talk more around her new friends. "So, did you focus on the water fountain in the back of the room?" she asked her friends.

Brandon shook his head. "No way. I didn't even know there was one in there until Ashley told me. It was a candle for me."

Sierra's big brown eyes appeared to get even wider behind her glasses in response. "Really?"

Adya smiled. "You naturally gravitate toward your element, like you did when you chose your residence hall."

"But I didn't choose." Sierra's head tilted slightly while her brows furrowed.

"I know it's hard to understand now, but trust me, it'll start to make more sense. You are a water affinate, and you'll work closely with that element. Brandon is a fire affinate and is very good with his element."

Brandon smiled. "And Adya is very good with three elements."

Adya furrowed her brows at Brandon but quickly softened her features as she turned back to Sierra.

"Three elements?" Sierra's eyes widened again, and her mouth hung open.

"Yes, I'm a novelty. I'm a tri-affinate and work with the elements earth, air, and water." Adya still wasn't comfortable with this being common knowledge. She didn't desire to be a celebrity—or to be detested—for her extra abilities, but judging by the scathing and awed looks she sometimes noticed, that notion was far out of her control.

"How do I learn that?" Sierra asked.

It was good that the Abecedarian was opening up to them. Still, without her knowing that she could manipulate the elements yet, some of the conversations were more difficult to navigate.

"You're born with it," Ashley stated matter-of-factly.

"Oh," Sierra replied, looking a bit disheartened.

None of the three wanted to bring up Myra or the unnatural way she got her bi-affinate status, so they all resumed eating their meals.

All the second year affinates had civics class after lunch. As explained by the teacher, Huo, civics was akin to an alternate history taught in the History of the Academy class. In essence, it was an introduction to how elemental affinates controlled governments, laws, and economies around the world.

"Every child in the United States learns about democracy and the forming of our nation and its laws. But they only learn part of the truth," Huo began. "While the government provides people with a sense of fairness and balance, it is the affinates' influence that assures those external, visible stabilities balance the elements."

This class meant something more to Adya than it would have to Emily since the soul she now fully knew had been responsible for ensuring the world stayed in balance for over a millennium. While Adya was never an Elder—nor did she aspire to be—she knew that she was among the oldest souls still around. Not to mention she was a very close friend to Ava, who was the last *Primum Vivere*, or original soul. Adya witnessed firsthand the difficulties the Elders faced in modern times to preserve the balance in a world that was hell-bent on destroying itself, and still profoundly felt the absence of Ava, who had grown tired of fighting against the changing world.

"I know some of you are already thinking, 'But what about all the wars and injustices around the world?'. The full answer is an essential topic we'll cover thoroughly in this class. The short answer, though, is that free will trumps even our elemental abilities. Open your books to chapter four. Yes, I realize we're skipping the beginning, but it will make more sense to circle back to it once you have a better grasp of the topics."

The class opened their books while exchanging questioning glances with each other. The first chapter they were covering included the era of Adya's original lifetime. She allowed herself to be enthralled by the breadth of knowledge presented, learning about what happened outside of her community on the Nile River.

"What was it actually like?" Ashley asked Adya as they dressed for bed. "I mean, it seems like such a simple life, but a hard one, too."

Adya smiled, happy to share some of her earliest memories with her roommate. "We kept mostly to ourselves. A few of the members of my tribe would travel down the river to trade with other tribes, but most of us stayed at the oasis. I was in charge of making sure our water was plentiful and clean. Essentially, I was the water shaman and held a high place in society because of how precious water was for life in the desert."

"Were there other affinates in your tribe?" Ashley inquired, now sitting on her bed, leaning back against the headboard.

"No, and I didn't know at the time why I could do what I did. There weren't Academies back then for us to retreat into to help us understand. I acted on instinct and trusted my soul to guide me."

"That's crazy. Do you think you would've figured out your affinities in this lifetime if they hadn't recruited you to the Academy?"

Adya shrugged. "I'm sure my life would be vastly different without the Academy, but I have always been able to understand that I have affinities in each lifetime, and eventually, I have completed the Awakening in each, even without help or guidance. I was probably seventeen when I Awakened in my second life, but then again, we didn't keep track of ages the same way back then."

Ashley listened to her roommate in awe. "I can't wait until I can recall all my lifetimes. I wonder how long ago my first life was."

Adya scrunched her nose. "You've already told me how different I am. I'm going to suggest that you enjoy—and learn about—who you are now before all your lifetimes merge." Adya spoke kindly, not trying to dissuade Ashley, but instead was hoping to prevent Ashley from being frustrated if it took her longer to complete the Awakening.

Ashley yawned. "I really like the new you, Ady. I just hope you'll indulge my need for romantic gossip."

Adya muffled her yawn with a hand. "I'll do my best."

"Night, Ady," Ashley said.

"Night," Adya replied and fell asleep, remembering the rippling sounds of the river in her first life.

CHAPTER THREE

B etween learning about the characteristics of the true self and studying what seemed to be her personal history, the first month and a half of school flew by.

"Look what I can do!" Sierra burst into Ashley and Adya's room one afternoon. She proudly showed off her ability to make ice cubes in a glass of water.

"Wonderful, Sierra!" Adya encouraged.

"We're getting in line early for dresses for next weekend's Harvest Festival Masquerade, right?" Ashley said, not intending to overlook Sierra's new talent.

"We get dresses?" Sierra said with wide eyes, apparently not offended that Ashley didn't praise her new talent.

Ashley's grin grew as she started to explain the formal gowns the alumni gifted the students and the magical dance they would attend.

"I've never worn a fancy dress or even gone to a dance before," Sierra admitted and chewed on her bottom lip. "Do we have to dance with boys?"

"*Have* to dance with them? More like *get* to," Ashley replied.

"But it's also okay if you don't want to dance with a boy," Adya added. "I'm going to dance with my friends and enjoy the night. Besides, more often than not, boys ruin the evening."

Ashley rolled her eyes. "Agree to disagree, but I understand why you'd say that. I'm not going with a boy to this dance, either, although I'm hoping *someone* will ask me to dance there."

"Oh? Who's this new interest of yours?" Adya asked.

"I'm not gonna jinx myself. If you do see me dancing with a boy, *try* to be happy for me, okay?" Ashley pleaded.

Adya narrowed her eyes. "It better not be Titus."

Ashley held out her right pinkie finger. "Swear to me that no matter what, you will just be happy for me."

Adya glowered, but reluctantly locked pinkies with Ashley. "Fine. As long as you're happy, I'm happy."

Sierra looked dizzy after the exchange between the two roommates. "And I thought my sisters were crazy."

The night of the dance arrived, and Sierra looked stunning in her shimmery blue dress that brushed the top of her knees. Her mask was adorned with blue and green feathers and fit perfectly over her glasses. Adya and Ashley—well, mostly Ashley—had finished Sierra's look with neutral tone makeup that accentuated the girl's maturing bone structure. Sierra's dark, naturally curly hair sat atop her head, pinned up with sparkling clips, with a few locks of hair cascading to the tops of her shoulders.

Ashley picked a full-length gown that faded from a deep blue on top into a light blue that swept against the floor. The sleeveless, partially backless dress framed her spiral-curled honey-blonde hair that bounced between her shoulder blades. Adya knew that whomever the boy Ashley wanted to dance with that night would be a fool to say no.

Somehow, Adya managed to get to the gown selection on time and found a beautiful dress made of iridescent material. Anytime she moved, a multitude of blue and green hues reflected through the fabric of the long, flowing skirt. Adya felt that it nicely represented all three of her elements. Her chestnut hair was pulled back and clasped on the sides with a pair of blue and green rhinestone hairpins, a gift from Maggie.

After the homage to the elements, the affinates retreated into the hall. The beautiful dance performed by the previous year's graduating students was still enchanting to Adya. She mentally left the Harvest Festival Masquerade for a moment, revisiting a soul memory of dancing with Lir in the French court. Thankfully, wigs were not in style anymore because the birdcage she wore on her head back then gave her a sore neck for weeks. As Adya returned to the present, she reflectively rubbed her neck.

"Who do you want to dance with?" Sierra whispered to Adya as they adjusted in their chairs.

Adya shook her head. "I'm just hoping to have fun dancing with my friends," she whispered back just before Adamina thanked the dancers for their performance.

"I think you should dance with Brandon," she said.

Adya smiled and waited for Adamina to finish with the mic before replying. "Brandon and I are just friends. If you wanted," Adya added while recalling her initial instinct that Sierra might be attracted to Brandon, "you could ask him to dance with you, though."

Terror briefly flashed across Sierra's visible features. "Nuh-uh. No way. I couldn't. Besides, he has a girlfriend."

"Then why would you say you thought I should dance with him?" Adya shook her head and laughed. "Never mind, if you want to dance with him, you could—and should—ask him. He's actually a pretty good dancer. I don't think his girlfriend would mind if you shared one dance with him," Adya added with an encouraging smile. Honestly, Adya didn't know if Brandon's girlfriend would mind or not. She hadn't spent much time with Brandon lately. It had been over a month since he ate a meal with the group, and Adya couldn't remember the last time they shared a conversation outside of an in-class assignment. He had a lot of new fire elemental friends thanks to his heroic fire consumption half a year prior and was even eating his meals with them. Almost all of the fire affinates, even the older students, hadn't learned how to absorb fire yet.

Most of the returning students reused their masks from the prior year, so it was relatively easy to identify who everyone was. Adya saw the boy, Griff, who had asked her to dance as an Abecedarian. She still really liked his lion mask. She also noticed Brandon was wearing the same fire mask as last year. He was standing with a group near the cider bowl when Adya decided to wander over and chat with him for a moment.

Even though Adya was wearing the mask he gave her last year, Brandon didn't notice her as she politely pushed past him for a drink. He and his friends were too enthralled in sharing underage driving stories to pay much attention to others around them.

Adya waited for one of the boys to finish his story before she interrupted. "Ahem."

"Oh, hey, Emily—errr, it's Adya now, isn't it?" A third-year fire affinate was the first to acknowledge her presence.

"Yeah, it's Adya," she said with a smile.

The guys stared at her and then looked to Brandon. They collectively decided to return to dancing with the rest of the school. "I'll catch up in a minute," Brandon yelled after his friends before turning to Adya.

"You seem very popular this year. Do you have a spare minute to talk with an old friend?" Adya asked sweetly.

Brandon shrugged his right shoulder and followed Adya out to the balcony. "What's up?"

"Hello to you, too," she replied with a frown. "It's been a while since we talked, and I just wanted to see how you're doing."

"I'm fine," he said while glancing over his shoulder at the dance.

"Cool," Adya said and nodded slowly before drilling into him. "Are you avoiding me for some reason?"

Brandon laughed without the emotion behind it. "No, why would you think that?"

"Because," she drew out the word dramatically, "you *have* been avoiding me. Right now, you won't even look at me. What's going on?" Adya demanded. The tapping of her foot on the wood floor was almost louder than the bass from the music inside.

A sigh of exasperation escaped Brandon. "Look, Adya, I didn't want this to be a big deal. I should've known you'd make it into something, though." Brandon folded his arms defensively and took a deep breath. "My girlfriend doesn't think it's cool for me to have female friends here, especially the ones I used to date."

Adya blinked in surprise. "So, what you're saying is that you can't hang out, talk, or even *look* at me specifically because your *girlfriend* says so?" She shook her head with a clenched jaw. "Fine. Have a good life, Brandon." Adya pushed past Brandon and through the door. She returned to her table, where she stewed alone for the next five songs.

Finally, Ashley came over and dragged Adya back outside by her arm. "You look like you're going to erupt. Spill," Ashley demanded and impatiently drumming her fingers against her crossed arms.

Adya exploded at Ashley. "You'd *think* that he would at least *know* that we're important to each other, even as friends. But nooooo. He's letting his un-special girlfriend decide who he can and can't speak to. Why are they even talking about me? I've been nothing but supportive of him and his new fling. I didn't think it could be worse than Myra, but here we are." Adya flailed her arms frequently during her outburst while Ashley watched and waited for her friend to take a breath.

"Wow," Ashley started, but then was immediately interrupted by Adya.

"I know, right? Wow is exactly how I felt when he slapped me with that crap." Adya huffed and glowered.

"Well, no, I was saying 'wow' to you and your outburst. Although I'm pleased that it didn't involve deck chairs flying or rain dumping down on us. Why are you this upset? You've been happily doing your thing, and he's been doing his for months. Why did you pick tonight to blow up?" Ashley's tone went from sarcastic to annoyed. "I swear, Ady, it's like you're determined not to have a good time at dances."

Adya was still breathing hard from her emotional outburst but sighed and hung her head. "You're right. I don't know how to do this."

"Do what?" Ashley asked. "Dance? Have fun?"

"Yes, no—I don't know. I guess I don't know how to be normal anymore."

"I'm telling you this as a friend, so don't explode on me. You seem to expect people to be the version of themselves that you knew in other lifetimes. We're not those people yet, and I don't know if we'll ever be. We're just us, take it or leave it. I like gossiping about boys. Brandon likes having a normal relationship with a normal girl. Sierra just wants to feel pretty and have fun. What do you want, Adya?"

It amazed Adya how Ashley's soul-self could shine through in random moments. Of course, just as she thought this, she realized that Ashley was right; Adya expected everyone to act like the person she knew them to be from past lives. With her head still hung in shame, Adya replied, "I just want my friends to be happy. I'm sorry for ruining another dance, Ash."

"Don't be so dramatic. You've hardly ruined the entire dance, and it's long from over. Maybe you could give this another try and actually have some fun?" Ashley suggested while tugging on her friend's hand.

Adya forced a smile. "I will, but give me a minute to collect myself."

CHAPTER THREE

Ashley released Adya's hand and nodded. "You have three songs to get back inside, or I'll make it rain on you or something," she said with a grin.

"Thanks, Ash. I'll be in soon."

After Ashley returned inside, Adya turned and rested her arms on the wood railing, looking out to the west and the fading light of the sun.

"You have a passionate soul, Adya," Dr. Ilene said as she occupied the space beside Adya at the railing.

Adya cringed. "How much of that did you hear?"

Dr. Ilene smiled. "Most, if not all. Don't worry, though. We've all been there. No one ever said it was an easy transition into your new life."

"That's just it, though. The transition was easy, well except for the almost dying part. The summer was great. But I can't seem to find my place between the two worlds, in this lifetime more than any other. I feel like I know Adya completely, but I don't really remember who Emily was or how she would act at a school dance."

"To be completely honest, not many thirteen-year-old girls know who they are yet. Emily *is* still a part of you, but it seems like you're trying to completely erase her and who she wants to be."

Adya considered what Dr. Ilene was saying and nodded. "I suppose you're right, but I don't know how to be Emily anymore."

Dr. Ilene looked thoughtfully at the horizon. "You're aware that we've known each other in a few lifetimes. You have had differences in who you were in each. For example, do you remember being a rebellious party girl during Prohibition?"

Adya smirked, recalling the fun times she'd spent with Lir in New Orleans during that era.

"But do you also remember the proper girl in London who would rather hang in the gallows than sip alcohol, even at a wedding?"

Again, Adya nodded.

"If your soul dominated every one of your lifetimes, why are there stark differences between them?" Dr. Ilene didn't wait for an answer. "It's because you allowed your mortal self the chance to be who they were."

"So, what you're saying is that I should allow myself to let Emily be who she wants to be and not try to control her despite having so many lifetimes of experiences to guide her?"

"Yes! That's precisely what I'm saying. So be thirteen for a night. Go dance with your friends, flirt with boys, and enjoy the loud music. Otherwise, you'll—"

"I'll end up yelling at my friends and stealing away all the joy and happiness I could be enjoying. I get it. Putting it into practice might take time, but I understand. Thank you, Dr. Ilene."

"Anytime, Adya. Now go and enjoy your night."

Adya managed to compose herself after the talk with Dr. Ilene and enjoyed the rest of the night dancing with her friends. It still wasn't easy to allow herself to be a thirteen-year-old kid, but she made improvements that night. Her friends all danced together during the upbeat songs, and she and even asked an Abecedarian air affinate to dance when she saw him sitting at a table by himself. Despite his awkwardness and her greater height, she enjoyed slow dancing with the boy whose soul was new to her.

Towards the end of the night, Adya saw Ashley dancing with someone. It wasn't Titus—for which she thanked the elements—but she wasn't sure exactly who it was. Regardless, when she caught Ashley's eye, Adya smiled and flashed her friend a thumbs-up sign.

Ashley apparently had fun with her mystery-guy and didn't walk back to the residence hall with Adya and Sierra when the dance ended.

"Did you have fun?" Adya asked the girl who was smiling from ear to ear.

"Everything was so beautiful, and Steve asked me to dance with him. I can't wait to write home to my sisters. I had my first dance with a boy!" Sierra spun in a circle gleefully.

Adya smiled. "I'm so happy for you."

"When's the next dance?" the anxious girl asked.

"There's one in December before winter break where everyone gets to participate in the winter solstice ceremony before the dance. It's unbelievably wonderful."

"And we get new dresses for that dance, too?" Sierra asked enthusiastically.

"No, we have to wear white robes to that ceremony and our dance clothes underneath," Adya explained.

"Oh. I don't know if I have any dresses to wear to it," Sierra said sullenly. "I guess I could wear this one again."

"Between all of us in the dorm, I'm sure we can put together a new outfit for you and make sure you look and feel just as beautiful as you do tonight," Adya assured Sierra as they walked towards their room. "Sweet dreams."

"G'night, Ady."

CHAPTER FOUR

"**Y**our sister?" Adya asked in surprise as she helped Maggie carry boxes from her closet-turned-office into her newly renovated one. It had taken over six months for the reconstruction project to be completed, but Adya could see the relief in Maggie's face once she saw her old office again.

"Yeah, she said my dad died a few months ago and would like us to get together over Christmas," Maggie clarified. "I wasn't going to go, but I've reconsidered. I'm sure that I can count on you not to get into trouble over winter break, can't I?" Maggie eyed Adya suspiciously.

"Hey, I've been good this year! No surprise affinities, no eruption of powers, no new mortal enemies acquired. I think it's safe for you to leave and reconnect with your family. Besides, Greta is staying here over the break. Maybe I can help her redecorate the residence hall or something." Adya smiled as she placed a cardboard box on Maggie's new desk. "They did a good job restoring this. Aside from the smell of fresh paint, you'd never know this was practically reduced to ashes half a year ago."

"Besides the volumes of irreplaceable books missing," Maggie sighed but seemed to appreciate the effort that was put into the restoration.

"Okay," Adya plopped down on the new sofa and gave Maggie a knowing look, "what's wrong?"

Maggie furrowed her brows. "Who said anything was wrong?"

"You sighed. You never sigh," Adya pointed out as she patted the sofa cushion beside her.

"Lucas wrote to me," Maggie began as she tucked her legs under herself on the couch. "He said that he has elemental abilities again and wants me to join him."

"How did he—" Adya cut herself off, knowing that wasn't the critical part of the story. "I mean, how do you feel about that?"

Maggie chuckled lightly. "It's tempting; I'm not going to lie. And if it was anyone other than him asking, I would've shredded the letter without another thought. I know I shouldn't consider it. I know that what they did to us was unforgivable, but—" Maggie sighed again and turned her gaze to the window. "Maybe it's from being stuck in a windowless office for so long—I don't know. I've just been feeling so depressed about not having my affinity."

"Have you talked with Ted about this?" Adya asked.

"No. If I did, the Elders would have the means to track them down, and then I wouldn't get to make this decision for myself," Maggie admitted.

Adya turned her gaze out the window, too. "If you do this," Adya said, "you wouldn't be able to teach here anymore. I don't think even Ted would be okay with you accepting whatever technology they're using to give affinities."

"I know. There's another thing, too. Lucas doesn't have an earth affinity now. He says his gift is with air." Maggie twisted her hands.

"Would you be happy with another elemental gift? I mean, you miss your earth affinity. If you got air or fire or water, wouldn't you still be in the same state of mourning?" Adya was pulling on her lifetimes of knowledge to try to logically say what her heart was feeling: don't do this.

"That's still another issue I'm trying to reconcile. I love my gardens; I love my students. I don't want to lose that." Maggie trailed off and played with a strand of her hair.

"I can't imagine how hard this is for you." Adya was at a loss for words.

"I don't think I'm going to write him back yet, but I'm going to take the time at my sister's house over winter break to think it over."

"I've been told that I need to allow Emily to grow and not block her out with all my Adya memories. So, in the spirit of that, Emily is saying that you can't leave, that she would miss you too much, and that anything that Myra has a hand in is bad news."

Maggie returned her gaze to Adya and laughed genuinely. "I'll keep that in mind, *Emily*." She took a deep breath and looked around her office. "I honestly don't think I could leave here. North Shore has been my home for a long time."

"It's my home now, too," Adya reminded her. "I have no idea what I'm going to do with myself this winter break. It'll be my first Christmas without my mom." The sudden realization hit Adya with an unexpected swell of emotion.

"Maybe something unforeseen will pop up, and you won't spend all break thinking about what you're missing," Maggie suggested.

"Maybe," Adya replied distantly, trying not to focus on the ache in her chest. She shook the fog from her head and returned to their conversation. "Anyway, I should probably go and get ready for the winter solstice ceremony." She hugged Maggie before standing.

"I'll see you there and at the dance."

"Yeah, fingers crossed that I manage to enjoy myself this time. At least I'm not recovering from a seizure and confined to a chair this year," Adya joked as she left the office.

At this year's winter solstice ceremony, the heads of the earth and air elemental groups invited Adya to participate with their reverences along with her water one. It was still very reflexive for her to shy away from publicly using her air or earth affinities, and as a result, she almost declined to participate. Fortunately, she was able to make peace with her insecurities and agreed to join in with all three of her affinities' homages to the elements.

Openly embracing her gifts made the ceremony more special to her. She remembered looking on in awe as the other elemental groups spoke to their element the previous year, and getting to be a part of three this year left her feeling whole.

"So now we go to the dance?" Sierra asked as they handed their white robes to Greta.

"Yes," Adya replied and then turned to Ashley. "Are you going to dance with Cal again?" Adya found out it was Calder that Ashley was dancing with at the previous dance. While they had agreed it didn't mean they were getting back together, it at least opened communications between them again—unlike Adya with Brandon. Calder rejoined them at meals, and besides the bonus of Ashley being happy, Adya was glad to have someone else who completed the Awakening in their group.

Ashley smiled at Adya. "It's possible," she said, trying to sound mysterious, but the answer was in the grin on her face.

"Joe asked me to dance as we were leaving History of the Academy class today," Sierra beamed.

Just as Adya promised, all the affinates in the water elemental house worked together and designed an outfit that looked stunning on the Abecedarian. One of the girls had a black and white dress that was Sierra's size. Because it was sleeveless, they found a white button-up long-sleeve shirt to go underneath. Ashley donated a pair of red tights to go with

Sierra's glossy black flats, while Adya let her borrow a necklace and earring set with crystal snowflakes.

"He'll be the luckiest guy there," Adya said as they walked into the banquet hall. It rivaled the beauty of the year prior.

As Adya danced in her silver dress, she wanted to make actual snowflakes fall but figured Adamina would probably send her off to dust the library or something. After about half an hour of fast songs, the DJ slowed it down. Eventually, both Sierra and Ashley joined their partners on the dancefloor, so Adya excused herself to grab some punch. She watched her friends—and all the dancers—with a smile.

A quick tap on the shoulder sent a shock up Adya's spine. She instantly whipped around and accidentally sent her drink flying towards the person who startled her. In a reflexive action, she froze the liquid mid-air, so when it collided with Lir's chest, it hit with a thump instead of a splash.

"Oh my god! What are you doing here?" Adya cried out as she tossed her empty cup aside and wrapped her arms around Lir in a giant hug.

"It looks like I'm narrowly avoiding a dry-cleaning bill," he chuckled and squeezed her back.

"What happened to Greenland? Did you finish your project already?" Adya asked, refusing to release her old friend. She deeply inhaled his unique watery scent from his dark blue dress shirt, where her head rested against his shoulder.

Lir laughed. "We'll talk about that later. I came here to ask you for a dance."

"Liar," she declared and stepped back to eye him suspiciously.

Lir held up his hands in innocence. "I swear it's the truth. Although, I thought there'd be a line that I'd have to wait in."

"You're a terrible tease," Adya huffed, crossing her arms.

"Hey, Adya," Brandon said as he stepped past Lir, almost bumping into him as he grabbed a cup of punch.

Adya barely suppressed the need to sneer at Brandon and took Lir's hand. "I'd love to dance with you." She tugged Lir onto the dance floor and placed her free hand around his neck.

"Uh-oh. Adya is spiteful tonight, I see. What did I step in the middle of?" Lir asked as he placed a hand on her waist.

Adya was quite clearly leading the dance as the two swayed in a single spot near the side of the dance floor. "We'll talk about that later," Adya replied, obviously mimicking what Lir said moments earlier.

Lir smiled. "Feisty as ever. Nothing changes, does it?"

A small frown marred Adya's features. "I'm supposed to be allowing Emily's personality a chance to shine through. I thought that's what I was doing."

"So, what would Adya have done differently in that situation?" Lir inquired.

"Something. . ." Adya thought for a moment and smirked, "much more dramatic."

The slow song came to an end, and Lir stepped back to bow at his partner.

"We should go for a walk so we can talk about the *real* reason why you're here," Adya suggested and reached for his hand.

Lir smiled as he briefly squeezed Adya's hand before releasing it. "We'll talk tomorrow. You should enjoy the rest of your dance."

Adya glowered at him. "You *are* a horrible tease. But fine, we can talk later. Are you staying on campus?"

"No, I have a suite nearby, but I'll be back in the morning. I've heard the new chef is even better than Lucas." Lir winked and pressed a kiss to Adya's temple. "Enjoy your night, Ady."

Adya shook her head and laughed as Lir walked toward some of the teachers, and she found her way back to her friends who were dancing to a pop song.

"Who was *that*?" Sierra yell-whispered to Adya.

"An old friend and former teacher here," Adya said.

"Do you think he'd dance with me, too?" the wide-eyed girl asked. The boy she had been slow dancing with elbowed her, but they all ended up laughing.

The girls had a great time together at the dance and were laughing and talking loudly on the way back to the water elemental residence hall.

"Yeah, you would've had Lir for a class after winter break if he still worked here," Ashley told Sierra as the group continued towards their dorm.

"I wouldn't have learned anything in his class," the girl admitted with a dreamy look in her eyes.

Several other girls in their group nodded in agreement. "I heard Lir is off modeling in Europe now," one fourth-year girl said.

Adya shook her head with a slight smile. "He might be in his mind, but he's just doing a research project in Greenland."

"He came here just to dance with you, Ady?" Sierra asked.

Before Adya could reply, she felt a tug on her arm. "We need to talk."

"Yes and no," Adya replied before motioning for the girls to go ahead. She turned to face Brandon with an annoyed expression. "I thought talking to me was against the rules," she said flatly.

"Why are you acting like this?" Brandon asked, looking sincerely confused.

Adya stared dumbfoundedly at him. "You're not serious, are you? We haven't spoken in *months* per your insistence, and just because you said hi to me, I'm supposed to be all friendly with you?"

Brandon shrugged. "I just thought—"

"No. You didn't think at all. Your girlfriend does that for you now, remember?" Adya crossed her arms and continued to scowl.

"Ouch," he replied.

"Is this your way of saying you two broke up, and now you have permission to breathe the same air as me again or what?" Adya felt justified in her anger.

"Well, no. We didn't break up," Brandon admitted, but still seemed genuinely confused as he fumbled with his hands. "I don't know. I saw Lir talking to you, and something inside me compelled me to say something."

"So, you're jealous?" Adya blinked furiously. "I swear to the elements, Brandon. I'm nothing but supportive of your relationship, and you treated me like a plague. But then I talk to one of my oldest friends, and now you feel you have a right to say anything to me?"

Brandon shrugged. "I can't explain it. I just feel—I don't know—threatened by him."

"Not that I owe you any explanation, but Lir is, and has always been, my *friend*. He is seven years older than me, and we're just friends. Unlike us," she added, motioning between herself and Brandon.

"It's not how I wanted it to be," Brandon said, his slumping shoulders mirrored the sound of defeat in his voice. "But you're right. We aren't friends anymore. I don't know what I was thinking."

Adya knew precisely what he was—unconsciously—thinking, but it didn't excuse his behavior. "If you wanted to be my friend," Adya said more calmly, "you need to approach me as a *friend* and not a jealous ex-boyfriend. Enjoy your winter break, Brandon." Adya turned away from him and started back to her residence hall.

"I remember us, Ady," he yelled after her.

Adya stopped in her tracks and closed her eyes. She felt and heard him approach her again.

"I have many soul memories of us together from different lifetimes," he said as he placed his hand on her shoulder.

CHAPTER FOUR

"That's just it, Brandon—they were different lifetimes. You've made your choice for now, and I've done nothing but respect it. You don't owe me anything in this lifetime," Adya replied with a tired voice. Her eyes were still closed, but she could feel the heat from his touch penetrate her body. It amazed her that the fire within him could completely freeze her in place.

Brandon pulled Adya's shoulder to turn her to face him. Before she could protest, his lips were melting against hers.

Adya had waited over a year for that kiss, and while she was confused and angry, she kissed him back passionately. Her hand grasped the back of Brandon's neck as their lips and tongues met with the passion of lifetimes of intimacy. Hot tears streamed down Adya's cheeks, and despite her old soul desperately wanting to hold onto that moment, she felt Emily regain control and tore herself away—this wasn't what she wanted.

Brandon fumbled for her hand, tried to explain what prompted that moment, but Adya had already backed away and was wiping the tears from her cheeks.

"Have a nice winter break, Brandon, and happy birthday," she said and briskly walked back to her residence hall without looking back.

In the sanctuary of her room, Adya flopped on her bed.

Ashley was waiting inside, eagerly anticipating the impending gossip. "So? What did he want?"

Adya buried her face in her pillow. "He kissed me," she said with a muffled voice.

"He *kicked* you?" Ashley asked with a horrified expression.

Adya sighed and pushed herself up, "No, he *kissed* me."

Ashley looked stunned. "I don't know whether to say yay or to call him a jerk." She looked to her friend for clues about how to react.

"I'm debating the same thing, Ash."

"Did you—you know—kiss him back?"

Adya nodded.

"Wow. Okay, did Brandon say anything, or did he just assault you with his lips?" Ashley asked, still trying to get a full understanding of the situation.

"He said that he's jealous of Lir, but nothing has changed. He's still with his girlfriend. We still aren't friends."

"Does that make you like, frienemies with benefits?" Ashley asked and couldn't hold in the giggle.

Adya smiled, too. "Maybe, but at least I won't have to deal with it for the next two weeks."

"But you'll be thinking about it the entire time."

"Maybe, but then again. . . maybe Lir will make me forget all about Brandon." Adya wiggled her eyebrows suggestively.

The two girls collapsed into a fit of giggles. "In both of our dreams. Oh, Ady. I hope you have a good break."

"You, too, Ash. Goodnight."

CHAPTER FIVE

The dining hall was practically empty the following morning. Lir and Adya had an entire section of the room to themselves as they ate breakfast and chatted.

"Did you enjoy the rest of your dance?" Lir asked while seated across the table from Adya.

"Yeah, I had fun with the girls." After a small pause, Adya added, "And Brandon kissed me." Adya's eyes dropped to her plate, and she shoveled some eggs in her mouth so she couldn't immediately answer the question that she was expecting Lir to ask.

Seemingly unaffected by the news, he simply responded, "Figures."

Adya immediately looked up and eyed Lir suspiciously. After swallowing her bite, she asked, "What's that supposed to mean?"

"Nothing," Lir replied innocently and then mirrored Adya by filling his mouth full of eggs. "Mmmm," he commented.

"No, you don't get to be so cavalier about this. What do you mean by 'figures'?" Adya pulled Lir's plate away from him so he couldn't avoid the interrogation with another bite.

Lir twirled his fork in the air and stared at Adya. "Not that you would remember because they aren't your soul memories, but he and I have had—let's say a very competitive past. There may have even been a duel over you at one point."

"A duel?" Adya blinked several times in a row. "Over me?"

"You seem surprised, although I'm not sure why. You are quite aware of our feelings for you in past lives, Ady."

Adya nodded. "So what? Now you both pee on me to mark your territory?"

"I can't speak for him, but I have never peed on you." Lir smirked and took his plate back from the bewildered Adya.

"Jokes on you both. I've already accepted a marriage proposal from someone else," Adya said smugly.

Lir raised a brow. "Oh? And who's the lucky guy or girl?"

Adya made up a story on the spot. "His name is Pierre, and he's a sexy French bazillionaire internet guy."

"That's not even a real word, Ady." Lir rolled his eyes at her.

"So?" she said. "It still sounds better than having two guys who aren't even interested in me fighting over me."

"I'm not even going to bother to correct you," Lir groaned.

"Good because you know I'm right."

Lir sighed. "So, with all this drama in your life, does it mean you're not curious about why I'm here?"

"Not in the slightest," Adya lied with a taunting smile and stole a grape from his plate.

Lir chuckled. "Fine, then I *won't* tell you that I came here to take you to Switzerland for winter break."

Adya nearly choked on the grape. "We're going *where*?"

"To the land of hot chocolate and bank vaults," Lir replied and stole the last strawberry from Adya's plate.

"I'm on board for the hot chocolate, but bank vaults?" Adya tried to recall any lifetime where she would've banked in Switzerland. In fact, her memories of Switzerland weren't pleasant at all. "I don't get it."

"Maybe I should keep it a surprise," Lir teased.

"Or maybe you should tell me, so I don't ditch you with the yetis in the Alps."

"Wrong continent for yetis, but fine. After you died in 1801, I collected some of your journals and belongings and put them in a vault in Switzerland. The Elders had just created the bank, and while it ended up being a huge economic boost for the country, it also stores lifetimes of memories for many affinates."

"So, we'll be able to give some of our lifetimes back to Maggie?" Adya asked.

"Yes, that's the plan. There are other things besides journals in there, too." Lir added.

"Maybe it'll cheer Maggie up to fill some of her shelves," Adya said thoughtfully.

"What's wrong with Maggie?" Lir looked genuinely concerned.

"Ask me again when we're not here," she replied mysteriously.

Lir looked at her, blue eyes bright with curiosity, but nodded.

"Now, tell me more about this supposed duel."

"Do you know how long it's been since I was here?" Adya asked Lir as their private jet touched down in Geneva.

"A few centuries, if I recall correctly," Lir replied.

"It was just after the ordered killings of the Roma in 1510. My tribe fled to England," Adya said with a hint of sadness. "Such beautiful people and so much senseless killing."

"Yes, but it was in England that we met in that lifetime," Lir reminded her.

Adya's smile returned. "You were fishing near Dover when we crossed. With your help, my people didn't suffer public beatings for being vagabonds," she recalled. "Someday, we should revisit some of those places together."

"The world is forever changing. I doubt there's much left that we'd remember," Lir commented as he grabbed his and Adya's bags.

"It doesn't have to look the same to feel the same. Besides, I wouldn't give up modern beds and return to sleeping on straw mattresses and dirt floors for anything." Adya stretched her arms and legs as she stood to disembark the aircraft. When the door opened, an icy breeze blew in, tousling her loose hair. After a shiver, Adya raised her hand to push the cold air back. "Brrr," she said. "I'm going to have to pull out my winter coat when we get to the hotel. I can't believe I've already gotten used to the mild Louisiana winters."

"I guess I won't be taking you to work with me in Greenland any time soon," Lir teased. "This practically feels like summer."

It was nightfall on Sunday when they arrived at the airport. Beautiful lights decorated the entire city for the season. "It's like a Christmas fairytale here," Adya commented as their chauffeur held open the door of the waiting limousine. Adya slid in and gazed around the interior in awe. "I've never been in a limo before."

Lir followed her inside the car, and the driver closed the door behind him. "It amazes me that you still have a list of things you've never done." Lir picked up the white carafe from the beverage console and poured two mugs of steaming liquid. "Is drinking authentic Swiss hot chocolate also on that list?" He handed Adya a cup and then picked up the other for himself.

Adya inhaled the aroma while her hands cradled the warm cup. "That depends. Does Swiss Miss count?" She held in her giggle and took a sip.

"Not even remotely." Lir joined her in drinking the hot beverage as the car started towards their destination.

"Mmmm," Adya said. "This trip was worth it for the drink alone."

"I thought it was worth it for the company," Lir teased. "We're going to check-in at the hotel first, and then we can visit the Christmas Market if you'd like."

"So, this isn't just a business trip?" Adya asked.

"The bank isn't open until the morning. I thought you might like to enjoy yourself a little before returning to the Academy. But if you just want to visit the vault and return home—" Lir trailed off as he sipped his hot chocolate.

"Of course, I want to see more than just the inside of a bank vault," Adya declared.

"Good. I had a fun trip planned, but if you weren't up for it, the plane could be ready to take you home tomorrow afternoon."

"You planned a fun trip? Hmmm, well, who am I to ruin your plans. Just promise you won't parade me around like your kid sister," Adya added with a playful nudge.

Lir rolled his eyes at her. "Would I ever do that?"

Adya glared, and her playful demeanor dissipated. "You would and have. Remember New Orleans last summer?" She breathed out a frustrated sigh. "It's fine; I get it. I guess it doesn't matter. I appreciate you planning something fun for me." She settled back into the seat and attempted to look like she wasn't pouting.

Lir tipped his imaginary hat at Adya, and they rode the rest of the way in silence until the car stopped in the front of the Hotel de la Paix.

Adya stepped out of the car and could feel the energy of her elements calling to her. She'd traveled to enough places in the past year to be able to appreciate how different the elements in each place could feel. The nearby lake spoke to her first, followed by the cool breeze that swirled around her in greeting. While she couldn't see them at night, she knew the majestic mountains were nearby.

"You should probably come in out of the cold," Lir suggested as the doorman held the door open for them.

Adya closed her eyes, breathed in deeply, and smiled before entering the grand hotel. The staff treated them like royalty, politely bowing their heads in acknowledgment to the two affinates as they were ushered to the elevators and up to their suite.

"I could get used to this," Adya commented, feeling her new self take in the luxurious accommodations.

The two entered the suite, followed by the bellhop with their bags.

Adya knew her smile was as grand as the room that felt both modern and historic. Silver, white, and blue couches, chairs, and drapes complimented the light wood floors. In the bedroom, a fire danced in the black fireplace. A giant bed with a fur comforter draped across the end was next to the fireplace. She giggled like a thirteen-year-old girl as she jumped onto the bed. "This is incredible!" she exclaimed.

Lir watched her and laughed. "Yeah, a little nicer than the Academy beds, huh?"

Adya warmed her hands by the fire but suddenly had a sobering realization. "There's only one bed?"

"Don't worry, Ady. I'm sleeping on the sofa," Lir explained. "They don't have two-bedroom suites, so I'll rough it."

"Are you sure? I can take the couch," Adya offered, although she really wanted to sleep in the bed next to the fire.

"I'm sure. Besides, we're only here for a night."

Adya frowned. "I thought you said we were staying?"

"In Switzerland, yes. We'll be taking a train somewhere else after the bank tomorrow," Lir said mysteriously.

"Will the next place have a fireplace in the bedroom?" Adya asked.

Lir chuckled. "Yes, I believe *both* bedrooms have fireplaces. Why don't you find something warmer to wear, and we'll head out to the Christmas Market?" he suggested and turned away from the bedroom and Adya to tip the bellman.

Adya hadn't realized how much she'd grown. It had been a year since she last needed her winter coat when she was with her parents over the last winter break. She stared at herself in the full-length mirror and scrunched her nose in distaste when she noticed the sleeves of her coat only covered three-quarters of her arms. She was tempted to toss it directly into the fire but opted for throwing it near the trash can. She had to settle for doubling up her sweaters to go along with her blue jeans and boots that thankfully did still fit.

"I'm ready," she announced as she exited the bedroom.

"You're going to be really cold. Where's your coat?" Lir asked as he zipped up his thick leather jacket.

"Doesn't fit," Adya shrugged. "I'll be fine, I'm sure. Hopefully, they'll have one I can buy at this market of yours."

Lir shrugged and opened the door for Adya. "They'll have hot chocolate and warm mulled wine, for sure, to help keep you warm in the meantime."

"Mmmm. . . I still have fond memories of drinking *hypocras* in France," Adya mused.

"I'm sure you do," Lir smirked. "But you'll be enjoying the non-alcoholic version this year."

"And so it begins," Adya grumbled as they rode the elevator down.

"If that's a shot at me treating you appropriately for you age, then get used to it," Lir insisted and stepped out of the elevator.

Adya hung behind, feeling the full frustrations of a hormonal thirteen-year-old.

"Are you coming?" Lir asked as the elevator attendant held the door open for Adya.

"Fine." She huffed out of the elevator, stomping her feet like a pouting child. "But I don't know how you expect me to have fun if you're gonna play big brother all trip." Adya walked past Lir and out of the hotel lobby. It was frigid outside, making it difficult to push aside the longing to have Brandon with her if for no other reason than to keep her warm. She was incredibly frustrated with Lir at the moment, so she'd be damned if he was aware of how cold she actually felt.

"Should I let you lead the way?" Lir asked when he caught up to Adya. He was mindful of Adya's annoyance and didn't blame her, but it didn't change anything as far as their friendship was concerned.

Caught up in her sudden burst of anger, Adya traipsed down the beautifully lit street for several long minutes until her temper ebbed.

"I don't know where I'm going," she finally admitted and tugged her sleeves down to cover her hands.

"If you'll allow me to guide you without throwing a tantrum, I'm happy to show you the way." Lir tucked his hands in his pockets, protecting them from the biting cold.

"Yeah, that would be okay," Adya conceded and stopped walking so Lir could catch up.

The two walked side-by-side down the icy sidewalk towards the festively lit market. Lir finally broke their long period of silence. "What do you want from me?" he asked pointedly.

Adya shuffled along the sidewalk with her arms wrapped around herself to conserve what body heat she had left. Finally, she stopped and faced Lir and let her frustrations out. "I want you to see me as *me*, not this body I'm in. I don't want to be your student or your little sister. I want you to be the version of *you* that threw all the constraints of this timeline out the window to give me my first kiss." She tried to take back some of the emotion by shrugging, but the longing in her voice gave away that she cared more than the shrug indicated.

"This is hard for me, too, Ady. Did you ever stop to think that I want the same, that it takes every ounce of my moral fiber to keep the deep-seated love I have for you locked away?" Lir's eyes flashed wildly between Adya's as he shrugged out of his coat and wrapped it around her.

She was momentarily startled by the warmth that surrounded her, but then very appreciative. "Thank you," Adya said humbly, the angst faded from her voice. "It's just you make it seem like it's easy to treat me like just another kid." She stepped closer to Lir, trying to share warmth.

"You'll never, in any lifetime, be just another kid to me." Lir linked hands with Adya in the pocket of his jacket that she was wearing. "C'mon. After our visit here, I have a theory I'd like to try with you. Let's get some wine for now."

Adya looked at Lir curiously but followed along while trying to share her warmth with him.

"*Deux hypocras,*" Lir said to the vendor.

Adya wrapped her hands around the warm cup of alcohol when Lir handed it to her. "What's your theory?" she asked as they both sipped the warm spiced wine—the alcoholic kind. She could feel the warm liquid coat her throat and caress her stomach while she internally celebrated the small victory.

"Let's find you a jacket and scarf, and then we'll talk about my theory," Lir said with a grin.

Adya pulled Lir's free hand back into his jacket pocket with hers, and they strolled through the booths taking in all they had to offer. "Oh! Look at this one." Adya released his hand and felt the plush fur lining the hood of a white jacket.

"Try it on," Lir offered and held her drink while she took off his coat and tried on the white one. "It looks nice on you," he said.

The kiosk host pointed Adya towards the mirror to see for herself. "It's cozy and warm," she commented, but Lir was already paying the merchant when she looked back. A subtle frown took over her features. "I guess this means we won't keep each other's hands warm now."

Lir laughed and tugged Adya by the hand.

Adya squeezed his hand as they walked together for a while through the maze of Christmas themed booths.

"How are you feeling?" he asked after they'd sampled many foods and drinks.

"Less cold and more relaxed," she smiled. "I'm sorry about earlier. Emily is pretty strong-willed, and I've been encouraged to let her shine through," Adya said. "Years of living in the home of an oppressive father can do that to a girl, you know."

"It's not like he's the first oppressive father you've had," Lir reminded her.

"True," she replied and recalled past lives. "How are *you* feeling? Warmer with your jacket back?"

"Yes, but it has this earthy aroma to it now. Can't figure out where it came from." Lir nudged Adya.

Adya rolled her eyes and laughed. "So, are you ready to tell me this theory of yours?"

"Let's grab another spiced wine and head back to the hotel, okay? We'll talk when we're out of the cold."

"Sure," Adya replied and followed Lir's lead.

Adya giggled as Lir pointed out people and things the entire way back to the hotel room, all the things she was too angry to pay attention to on the way to the market. She considered that maybe Lir had been right about her not having alcohol, but her insides were warm, and she was happy, albeit a little tipsy. Besides, she couldn't let Lir know he was right.

"I take it by your smile that you enjoyed the night?" Lir asked as the two entered the hotel room and sat on the sofa.

"It was magical. I don't know why there aren't Christmas markets in every city," Adya said happily.

"It wouldn't be the same in most other places, but I'm sure they're around outside of Switzerland," Lir commented. "So, are you ready to hear my theory?"

Adya adjusted herself to face Lir and nodded. "You haven't had a theory that hasn't completely fascinated me. So, let me have it."

"You know how to share soul memories, but only the ones shared with the person, and only from your perspective of that memory, right?" Lir began. He continued after Adya nodded. "What if there is a way to share a personal soul memory that didn't include you?"

Adya tilted her head thoughtfully. "So, it would be like a Vulcan mind-meld or something?"

Lir laughed. "Something like that. I got to thinking after our conversation at breakfast, about you not knowing the extent of the rivalry between Brandon and myself over the lifetimes, and I started wondering if there was a way for you to see those memories."

Adya bit her lip as she considered this idea and slowly nodded. "You mean like using something like water memory in some way?"

Lir nodded. "Yes, that's what I was thinking. I wasn't sure I was going to share this theory with you, but after the whole 'you treat me like a child' rant you went on, I thought maybe it was time you had some insight on things."

"You want me to see your memories?" Adya asked in surprise.

"I want you to understand why I feel the way I do about you, and words don't seem to be reaching you," Lir explained.

Adya frowned. "It's not your fault. It's completely mine. This body, this life—" She paused and breathed out a sigh. "This body is so far behind where my soul exists. I don't recall having this problem in any other lifetime. I'm sorry if I doubt your intentions." Adya's gaze shifted from his face to the sofa. "You shouldn't have to give up your soul memories to console me."

"I don't *have* to do anything. I didn't need you here to retrieve the items from the vault, but I *want* you here, just like I want you to know my memories. Come with me." Lir took Adya's hand and led her to the bedroom where the fire was still burning. "Have a seat," he suggested as he guided her to the foot of the bed.

Adya perched on the edge of the bed, both nervous and excited, not quite sure what Lir was planning. How would he share his soul memories? Was he going to kiss her again? Was he going to try something more? She anxiously rubbed her hands together while she watched him go to the bathroom and heard the shower start a moment later. Lir returned to the bedroom and opened the window. A frosty breeze pushed its way in as he joined Adya sitting on the foot of the bed.

"The elements have joined us," he said and took Adya's hands as he did on the first day of their elemental healing class almost a year prior. "Let them speak to you and give us balance as we try this."

Adya closed her eyes and heard the water in the shower falling like rain, the wind embracing them, the fire warming them, and the mountains grounding them. "I feel their balance," she stated.

"I'm going to recall a memory, and I want you to concentrate on the water element in my body. Ready?"

Adya nodded and felt Lir's body relax. It took her several moments to redirect her attention from the living elements surrounding them and focus on the water within Lir. She could feel the slight imbalance in him from the wine but remained determined to find the memories contained within the water. Her palms pressed harder against his as he continued sitting there silent and relaxed.

"It's not working," she whispered after a few minutes.

"Release your sense of control and allow the memory to flow to you," he said quietly.

Adya tried again but couldn't forego the instinct to bring balance to his body rather than allow the elements to exchange his memory. Finally, she sighed and let her hands fall. She looked at Lir with disappointment. "I'm sorry," she said. "In this position, my instincts are to heal you."

"I felt that, too. Let me think." Lir stood up to pace while he thought aloud. "What if this is less about balancing the elements and more about controlling them?" Lir walked over to the window and closed it before shutting off the shower in the bathroom. When he returned, he switched off the gas to the fireplace and closed the bedroom door. "Do you trust me?" he asked as he hovered near the wall.

"With all my soul."

"Lie down on the bed," he instructed.

Adya unzipped her boots before scooting back on the bed. She propped herself up on her elbows as she reclined on her back with her head hovering over the pillow and her eyes watching Lir with curiosity. "Okay, now what?"

"I'm going to turn off the light and join you on the bed. Okay?" Lir slid his shoes off and waited for Adya to reply.

Adya nibbled her bottom lip as she let her head fall back against the plush pillow.

The room went black, and Lir laid beside Adya on the bed. "Do you recall after our first class together when I asked you to describe the room with your eyes open and then with them closed?"

"Yes," Adya said, her voice sounding shakier than she would've liked.

"So, let's try this again without the noise of everything else around us. Place your hand here," Lir said and found Adya's hand on the bedspread.

Adya allowed her body to relax while Lir guided her hand to his chest. She fondly recalled how incredible Lir's bare chest looked during their swim at the lake and felt her heart race as her palm pressed against him. Adya was surprised to feel Lir's heart beating rapidly, too.

"Are you still okay?" he asked in a whisper.

"Yes," Adya replied and focused on the warmth of his chest beneath her hand.

"Now open your mind to my memories," he said softly.

Aside from his heart beating, Adya could feel Lir's breath as he rolled to position himself on his side to face her. She turned, too, so they mirrored each other and threaded the fingers of her free hand with his.

"Slow down your breathing, slow down your heart," Lir whispered as the two remained unmoving on the bed.

Adya didn't know if he was talking to himself or her, because she felt his body relax and his heart rate slow. A wave of dizziness overtook her. As Adya was about to sit up, a memory played out for her.

A sad melody extended from inside his body onto the ebony and ivory keys at his fingertips. Adya sat behind him in her blue silk dress, enjoying the music that he would always play for her, but utterly unaware of the ache she'd caused in his heart. He should be happy for her; he knew she loved Paxton but kept hoping that maybe in this lifetime, she would choose differently. As the music carried on, Lir's thoughts lingered on the sunset picnic he'd planned for her, of the tree beyond the grasses where she loved to sit, of the ring he was going to give her. A tear trickled from his cheek to the white keys, and his back imperceivably shook as he entertained his glowing guest who was too intoxicated with joy to comprehend his mourning.

Adya gasped and tore her hand away from Lir's chest. As her hand brushed her cheek, she felt a tepid tear rolling down her face. Her chest was tight with emotion; there were no cohesive words that formed in her mind, only the deep sadness of his that she felt from his memory. It was her first soul memory she experienced with him in this lifetime, but it was *his* version of the events. It was *his* heartbreak she felt, not her exuberance that she'd felt before from her memory.

Adya rolled onto her back and released Lir's hand as she stared up at the barely visible ceiling in the room. Lir allowed her space, but remained on his side, watching her closely.

"You were going to propose?" Adya finally asked. When Lir said nothing, she continued. "I'm such an idiot. I'm so sorry." She rolled back on her side to face him and wrapped an arm around his waist while resting her cheek against his chest.

Lir stroked her hair as he held her against him. "I didn't share that with you to make you feel bad or sorry for me, Ady. I did want you to understand that loving you is always balanced with heartache. So, when you accuse me of treating you like you're a child, it isn't as simple as you make it sound to shut out the constraints of this lifetime. It's damn hard, but it's also a way for me to protect myself. . . and you."

"I understand," Adya began and tilted her head up to look at Lir. "But you kissed me, and you brought me to this fantastical, beautiful place. I don't believe that you really want to protect either of us, and I know for certain that I don't need protecting."

"No," he said lightly and stroked her cheek with his thumb. "You are a fierce soul that doesn't need protection. But that won't stop me from trying to do it anyway."

"I know. Because you're a stubborn soul," Adya replied, smiling again. "Do you want to try to see one of my memories?" she offered.

"Not tonight, Ady. I'm going to get the couch ready so I can sleep. We need to get to the bank early in the morning." Lir kissed the top of her head and started to roll off the bed.

Adya grabbed his hand before he got out of reach. "It would probably be okay if we both slept in the bed. It's big enough," she said. When he hesitated, she added, "It's not like we're naked or are even going to do anything remotely unsavory. It's just sleeping, and I think I'll sleep a little better tonight knowing you're not stuck on an uncomfortable couch."

Lir sighed in resignation and sat back on the bed. "Fine. You win, but I'm not lighting the fireplace again. It's not one of my favorite elements," he admitted.

"Gee, I wonder why?" Adya released his hand and slid over to allow him ample space on the side of the bed opposite the fireplace.

"Goodnight, Ady," Lir said while yawning and tucking himself in under the covers.

"Goodnight, Lir," she replied, adjusting herself in a cool spot on the bed.

As she started to drift off to sleep, Lir reached over and intertwined his fingers with hers.

CHAPTER SIX

T he next morning, the two showered—separately—and
packed their belongings before leaving the hotel. It was
busy with suited men conducting business inside the
bank lobby. Adya took the time while they waited to admire
the building that affinates in another lifetime created.

"Right this way." A slender woman with platinum blonde
hair wrapped in an elegant bun led the two through a discrete
door. She reminded Adya of Dr. Ilene, only perhaps a little
younger.

Adya followed Lir and the bank manager through coded
doors, down sterile hallways, and finally down a stone staircase
to the subbasement of the bank. Not only did it look old, but
it smelled old, too, but the nice kind of old like Adya had
smelled in the small house on Elder Tama's estate the year prior.

Lir shifted a folded box he was carrying to his left arm
and retrieved a key from his pocket, which he handed to
the banker. With her key inserted in the lock above Lir's,
the woman turned the keys and opened a heavy door to a
bedroom-sized vault. "*Merci*," he said and took Adya's hand
as they walked into the vault together. The bank manager lit
several lanterns on the walls of the room before leaving the
two to their business.

Pinching the bridge of her nose to suppress a sneeze, Adya looked around at the priceless heirlooms in the room. Stacked through the vault was everything you could imagine: from clothing to books to works of art to furniture to photographs. "Oh my god, is that—"

"Your wedding dress? Yes. I told you I brought some of your belongings here," Lir reminded her. He moved from watching her look at remnants of past lives to searching for the journals he originally came to retrieve.

Adya lowered her hand from her nose and marveled at various items from her past. She admired the things from Lir's in past lives, too. "I can't believe you never told me that you saved all these," she said.

"It never came up in conversation," he replied nonchalantly while rummaging through old books.

Adya threw him a dubious look, but Lir was too busy carefully turning the pages of an old journal to notice. When she returned to her browsing, her eyes settled on a covered painting. This time, she couldn't stop the sneeze from erupting when the thick coat of dust scattered as she removed a sheet to reveal a painted portrait.

"Bless you," Lir said, but didn't look up from what he was reading.

"Wow," Adya breathed as she looked at the beautiful artwork. "Who painted this?"

"Hmmm?" Lir pried himself away from his reading long enough to glance over at the painting. "Oh, right. I painted that of you. I told you about that, didn't I?"

"No," she replied dreamily. Adya lightly touched the soft blonde curls that framed the woman's face. "My hair was so different then," she said with awe. "You captured me so perfectly, but I don't remember posing for you. I didn't even know you could paint."

Lir finally put the journals down and joined Adya in front of the painting. "I didn't need you to pose for me—I always see you clearly in my mind." Lir smiled at his work and then turned back to the stack of books.

Adya followed him. "How have I known you for so long but not know that you're a gifted artist?"

Lir shrugged. "It's always been something I've done in private for reasons of my own. I never felt comfortable sharing something so intimate with the world. Besides, you don't know *everything* about me."

Adya stared at him with confusion, shook her head, and then resumed browsing. "You're so weird, Lir."

"Ah-ha!" he exclaimed. "This is what I was looking for. Here," he said and handed Adya an old leather-bound journal.

She took the book from Lir and opened it up. "My diary," Adya said with a small smile. "Wait, did you read this?"

"Maybe," Lir replied with a sly grin.

"Talk about not wanting to share your intimate things with the world. . ." Adya grumbled and glowered at the man beside her. "I guess there isn't any recourse with knowing this now. How many are we taking for Maggie?"

"There are about a dozen journals to send to the Academy," Lir said while placing a stack of books in the shipping box. "You never told me what's going on with Maggie."

Adya sat down on an antique wooden chair and frowned. "She got a letter from Lucas. He said he has an affinity now and wants her to join them."

"Join him? With Myra and Eli? She's not considering it, is she? They're monsters," Lir said.

"I know this, and you know this, but think about it from her perspective. Everything that connects Maggie to her past lives, and to knowing our souls, is gone thanks to the fire. She feels a huge loss, and it's making her feel the absence of her abilities, too. They're offering Maggie a chance to get it all back." Adya frowned, still concerned, realizing there were so many reasons why Maggie would choose to leave.

"What does Ted think?" Lir asked.

"He doesn't know. I'm the only one who knows, and I told Maggie that I'd keep it to myself until she comes to a decision. She wants a chance to decide this for herself. I told her how I felt, and I know this is a hard decision for her to make."

"When's she going to decide?"

"She told me she was going to think it over while she visited her sister for winter break." Adya looked sadly on the books they'd gathered, knowing it wouldn't replace even a fraction of what she lost.

Lir rubbed his forehead as he processed the news. "We should tell Ted," he concluded.

"No! She'll never forgive me if we do." Adya jumped up out of the chair, feeling a pain in the pit of her stomach.

"Will you forgive her if she joins with Myra?" Lir fired back.

Adya toyed with a strand of her hair as she considered the question for several long moments. "I thought about that when Maggie first told me about the letter and decided that if I ever lost my gifts, I might do horrible things to get them back. So yes, I would forgive her. Myra and Eli? Never. And I swear I will bring them down eventually."

Lir couldn't suppress his smirk while listening to Adya. One of the things he loved about her was her passionate soul. "I'll get in touch with Maggie and try to persuade her to stay at the Academy."

"She's gonna be pissed that I told you," Adya remarked.

"She knew I was taking you on this trip. I don't think she expected you to keep this from me." Lir shrugged and took the journal back from Adya to place it in the shipping box with the others. "There's one more thing I want to show you while we're here," he said and walked towards an old jewelry box in the corner. He opened a drawer and withdrew something small. "This," he said as he brought the item to Adya, "is the ring I was going to give you that day."

Adya took hold of the ring and marveled at the exquisite craftsmanship. It was a delicate gold band with diamonds ornamenting the sides and led to a large blue sapphire paired with a pearl on top. "It's—wow—this is beyond beautiful." She looked up from the ring to Lir. "But you were married in that lifetime. Why didn't you give this to her?"

Lir gently clasped the outside of Adya's hand and looked deep into her eyes. "Because this was meant for you, representing your two affinities at that time. I never considered giving it to anyone else—ever."

While Adya rolled her eyes to try to minimize the gravity of it, she was, in reality, fighting off tears. "You're a sentimental old fool," she said and lightly pushed his chest, but the shakiness of her words expressed her genuine feelings. In a whisper, she added, "I would've said yes."

Lir chuckled and motioned to take the ring back. "Another life, my sweet Ady. But maybe some lifetime will give me another opportunity." Lir returned the jewelry to the box, pausing for a moment before securing the jewelry box again. "Now, we have a train to catch soon, so let's lock up and get the box mailed to Maggie."

While Lir was on the phone with members of his research team, Adya spent most of the three-hour train ride to Lucerne staring out the window at the snowcapped mountains and glistening rivers and streams, while she savored several cups of hot chocolate. In all her lifetimes, she had only spent a couple of decades in Switzerland. Much of those years was spent trying to keep herself and her tribe alive, which didn't leave much opportunity to appreciate the scenery.

The surrounding majestic mountains shimmered in the afternoon sun as the two departed from their train car. The air was crisp and clean; Adya genuinely admired her new surroundings. "I love the elements here," she said as Lir stood with her to admire the scenery.

"There isn't a season when it's not beautiful here. You should consider visiting in the summertime. I can see you enjoying hikes in the mountains," Lir remarked.

A man holding a sign with Lir's name was waiting for them on the train platform. He took their bags and ushered them to the awaiting car.

"Is it just me, or do cars seem out of place here?" Adya asked as the car drove them to the hotel.

"It certainly has a timeless quality to it—like you," Lir added with a smile. His eyes lost focus as he gazed out the window while the car drove next to the lake.

Adya admired the light dusting of snow on the roofs of the old buildings and the cobblestone street they were driving on. "Oh, look!" Adya exclaimed and tapped Lir's knee to get his attention. "It's a horse-drawn carriage!"

Lir chuckled as he watched the couple being pulled in an open carriage by two white horses. "We can do that later if you want."

Adya nodded enthusiastically. "I want to."

The car stopped in front of the Grand Hotel National, a hotel that looked like a verifiable stone castle, overlooking Lake Lucerne. A cool breeze from the lake greeted the affinates as they stepped out of the car. Adya had packed her new coat in her suitcase but enjoyed the shiver her element caused.

While Lir checked them in, Adya sauntered through the red-carpeted lobby, admiring the artwork displayed and the warm sun shining through the windows.

Lir walked behind her as she admired the lake through the window. "Grab your coat from your bag. We're going to go for a walk while they ready our residence."

"I could use a walk after that long train ride," Adya admitted and retrieved her coat.

Lir left their bags with the bellhop stationed by the front desk before the two exited the hotel and walked along the shore. "I'm surprised the lake isn't frozen," Adya commented.

"It hasn't frozen in fifty years," Lir said. "But I'm sure it's plenty cold."

Adya smiled and agreed with a nod. "When was the last time you were here?"

"About fifty years ago," Lir replied with a grin. "I may or may not have had something to do with the lake freezing," he said mischievously.

"I remember you left the States around then," Adya recalled. "We didn't see each other again until last year." Adya frowned as she contemplated the passage of time in her mortal body. "Has it really been more than fifty years?"

"More or less," Lir said. "Things never felt the same anywhere in America after Ava Ascended," he recalled, "so I returned to Europe. I spent several years in Ireland and Scotland before I came here in the summer of '63."

"I would like to know more about that time we spent apart," Adya admitted. "Did you marry a Scottish lass and paint pictures of the Alps?"

"With some more work on sharing personal memories, maybe we can both share our time apart," Lir said distantly.

"Maybe I'll even share some of my Woodstock memories with you," she teased.

"Mmhmm," Lir replied but was obviously still lost in another thought.

"Hey," Adya said and stopped in front of him, looking up into his blue eyes. "Where'd you go?"

"Sorry," he said, shaking his head and returning to the present. "Just thinking about the last time we were with Ava."

Adya tried not to visit that soul memory too often. It still made her feel sad even though Adya had continued afterward to have a fulfilling life. "I bet she would've loved Lucerne."

Lir took Adya's hand, and they continued walking, turning right at a corner to head down a street away from the lake. "She spent a lot of time in Geneva. Most of her belongings are in the bank there."

Adya blinked in surprise, looking over at Lir as they walked. "Why didn't we get some of her books to send to Maggie?" In truth, Adya would've loved to have spent time going through Ava's collection of heirlooms and journals.

"I don't think the Elders would give either of us the key to that vault," Lir replied with a chuckle, "let alone allow her memories to be on a shelf in an office at an Academy."

"The 'real history of the world' kept in a flammable office. . . yeah, probably not a good idea," Adya acquiesced. "Do you think you'll ever get tired of what this world does to itself and choose to Ascend?"

"Maybe after I complete my bucket list," Lir grinned. "But that's likely a long way off still."

"Good, because I can't imagine not having you in my lives, Lir," Adya said as she playfully bumped into him.

"Same with you, Ady," Lir said, but squeezed her hand instead of bumping against her. "We're here," he said as the two walked up to a pond in a small park. A few people were observing the stone wall behind the water from a bench that faced it. "Welcome to the *Löwendenkmal*," Lir said as the two neared the water's edge.

"The Lion Monument," Adya replied as she gazed at the massive stone carving of a dying lion. She started to take a step onto the seemingly frozen pond when Lir pulled her back.

"It's not safe to walk on," he warned and looked around.

Adya glanced at all the people milling about and decided she wanted a little more privacy. She called upon the cold air from the mountains with a slight flick of her wrist and brought a gust of arctic wind blowing through the park. Immediately, the people who were enjoying the almost-comfortable afternoon tightened their arms around their body and started to leave.

"That was mean," Lir said with a smirk and crouched down to put his hand on the ice. The color of the ice became whiter, indicating it had thickened, and the two stepped onto it together.

Adya shrugged and then almost slipped with her second step, but Lir grasped her arm and saved her from the embarrassing fall. "Thanks," she said as she tried to compose herself.

As they slowly and carefully neared the lion, Lir read the inscription carved in the rock above it, *"Helvetiorum fidei ac virtuti."*

"For the loyal and brave Swiss," Adya effortlessly translated as she admired the French and Swiss coat of arms displayed with the lion. "Was this to honor the Swiss who fought in the French Revolution?" Adya looked at Lir for answers. With the revolt brewing in the streets of Paris, Adya and Lir managed to escape from France before the Revolution began, taking sanctuary in England.

Lir nodded. "Lucas Ahorn finished this in 1821. I knew him as a young stonemason in Germany long before he created this. We met not too long after your death and not much before my own. He tried to teach me sculpture, but stone was not a good medium for this water affinate." Lir smirked as he continued to admire the art.

Adya looked around to see if the park was vacant before she called upon the wind to lift her. She hovered by the lion's enormous head. "It's remarkably sad," she commented as she touched the lion's face, running her fingers over the exhausted and pained features.

"It is, but you should probably come down before someone sees you," Lir warned while acting as a lookout man.

Adya stayed levitating for a moment and then caressed the stone paw on her descent to the ice. "A bit of hypocrisy there, Mr. Freeze-an-entire-lake."

Lir shrugged as he retook hold of Adya's hand. "What can I say? I was trying to impress a woman."

Adya eyed him curiously. "Did it work?"

That was not the question he was expecting to answer, but liked Adya's ability to shift from total revere to a playful old soul in a matter of seconds. "For quite a few exhausting days, yes." Lir winked at Adya, and they both laughed.

"I recall a few of those exhausting days with you myself," Adya added with an entirely wicked grin. "And I didn't even need to make you freeze large bodies of water."

Lir cleared his throat. The light flushing in his cheeks was a clear indication that he recalled those times with Adya, too. "Yes, well, that was an entirely different life, now wasn't it."

"Mmmm," Adya replied, thoroughly enjoying teasing Lir. "Feels like it was only yesterday."

Lir looked at her sternly. "Yeah, I definitely need to protect you in this life—from yourself."

Adya smiled angelically at him, and the two walked back to the hotel.

Their room was more exquisite than the one in Geneva. Scents from the vases of blossoming flowers on display throughout the main room greeted them as they entered, while colorful rugs decorated the polished hardwood floors.

Adya placed her hand on the silk-covered walls as she saw the lake out the balcony doors shimmer in the late afternoon sun. "This room reminds me of that villa in France," she said while Lir walked past her to the room on the left. "Do you remember the one with the vineyard and the pigs?"

Lir chuckled, obviously remembering. "This is my room," he commented as Adya joined him in the doorway.

Adya's eyes roamed from the red wall behind the bed to the stunning crystal chandelier hanging from the ceiling. There were French doors set against the far wall that led out to a balcony with a view of the lake. "Why is this one your room?" Adya asked, feeling like she'd be quite comfortable in that room.

"Because yours is over here," Lir said and walked back through the living room area, down the hallway just inside their entrance door, and into a small sitting room with an attached bathroom.

"Wow, just because I'm smaller, you're sticking me in the bathroom?" The bathroom was nothing to complain about, though. Adya admired the marble floor and counters with shiny gold fixtures and a giant glass door shower.

"Would I ever stick you in the bathroom?" Lir said with an eye roll before he opened the door in the back of the sitting room that opened into her bedroom.

"Probably," she replied with a grin and then moved to join Lir.

In Adya's lifetimes, she had been privy to the luxuries of royalty, and this room was reminiscent of some of the grandest estates she'd visited. Gold silk covered the walls of the lavish bedroom. A white king size bed was against one wall, with a red sofa opposite it. Like Lir's room, a pair of doors led out to a balcony.

Adya pulled out her phone and snapped a few pictures. She would be sure to text them to Ashley when she settled into bed for the night.

"And just like that, you switch from being an elegant lady from the past to a modern teenager," Lir commentated with a chuckle.

Adya shrugged off his remark. "I have to have proof to show Ashley where I spent my winter break." She switched her camera to selfie mode. "Can I take one of us with the lake in the background?"

Lir eyed her suspiciously as Adya opened the door to the balcony. "Did you tell her about—?"

Adya looked back at him. "Our kiss? No," she said, but then realized she didn't know if that would bring him relief or hurt him, so she added, "It was something special to me that I didn't want to share with anyone except you." It reminded

Adya of the conversation she had with Brandon following their first shared soul-memory. He didn't tell Myra or anyone for the exact reasons. Adya quickly pushed thoughts of Brandon aside and returned to the present with the man in front of her.

Lir smiled, which eased Adya's concern. "I wasn't accusing you of anything. Honestly, I expected that you would, but I agree. It was something special." He joined Adya on the balcony, where they stood with their backs to the lake.

Adya smiled at Lir. "I'm glad it was special for you, too." She looked at her phone that she held at arm's length and counted down before snapping a picture of the two of them.

Lir glanced at the time and ushered Adya back inside. "You have an appointment at the spa downstairs, and I have some work I need to get done."

Adya's eyebrows furrowed with confusion. "I'm going to the spa?"

Lir nodded and repeated what he just said. "And I have some work to get done. We'll eat dinner when you get back. Have fun," he said as he nudged her to the door.

"Oh, okay. Well, you, too!" Adya laughed and left the room. As she meandered to the elevator, she realized she didn't know where the spa was. Thankfully, once she stepped inside, the floors were named, and the second was labeled "spa."

The woman at the desk greeted Adya by name when she walked in the door. "I am Elena," the tall, slender woman said with a German accent. "Come with me, Adya."

She almost told Elena that she could speak German, but Adya noticed in the lobby when they first arrived that their dialect was a bit different than the German she knew. She followed Elena down a hallway with white marble floors and black marble walls to a sizeable room with a rack of dresses on one side and a three-way mirror on another. It reminded Adya of the gown selection at the Academy before the Harvest Festival Masquerade.

"What's this?" she asked. At the mention of "spa," Adya automatically imagined a massage or maybe a manicure, not trying on gowns.

"You need a gown for your evening, yes?" Elena asked while motioning Adya towards the dresses.

"I—uh—I guess?" she replied and started sliding the dresses down the metal bar as she looked at them. After careful consideration, she selected a long, soft black gown. "Can I try it on?"

"Of course," Elena replied. "I will return in moments to check the fit."

After the door closed, Adya undressed. The A-line, off the shoulder suede dress cascaded to the floor as she slipped the gown over her head. She admired herself in the mirror, while her hands moved down the sides of the bodice to the comfortably cinched waist, feeling the long sleeves of the gown move effortlessly with her arms. A smirk grew on Adya's lips as she turned to preview all sides of her attire, appreciating that the mature dress made her look more like her old soul felt.

Adya continued studying herself from varying angles in the mirrors until there was a knock at the door. "May I come in?" Elena asked.

"Yes, of course," Adya replied and smiled at the woman's reflection as she approached. "What do you think?"

"*Wunderschönen*. You are beautiful, Adya. Are you happy with this?" she asked.

"Very much so," Adya said as her hands caressed the soft material wrapped around her body.

"Good. Now let's go style your hair," Elena said and guided Adya to a pair of silver kitten heels, which she slipped into, before walking her to a chair in the salon.

Elena wheeled over an adjustable sink and washed Adya's hair. The scalp massage relaxed her and let her mind wander to what the night had in store for her.

When Adya sat upright again, there was a bag with her clothes lying on the counter. "Do you mind if I text my friend while you dry my hair?" she asked.

"That will be no problem," the woman replied.

Adya retrieved her phone from her belongings and texted Ashley while Elena combed and blew out her hair.

Hey, Ash. You'll never guess where I am, she messaged and then attached the pictures she took of her room.

After several minutes, Ashley texted back: *That doesn't look like the Academy. Where the hell are you?*

Just took a little trip to Switzerland, Adya replied.

The response back was quicker this time. *You jumped on a plane and flew to Switzerland by yourself?!?!?!*

Adya grinned. *Nope. Not by myself.* She sent the picture of her and Lir and waited for Ashley's reaction.

Ashley didn't bother to text back. Instead, she FaceTime called her friend.

"Umm, my friend is video-calling me. Is that okay?" Adya asked Elena.

"Sure, fine," the woman replied politely and continued to blow dry sections of Adya's hair.

Adya accepted the call, but before she could even say 'hi,' Ashley began talking.

"You ran away to Switzerland with Lir? Tell me everything!" Ashley was walking around her house, presumably away from her brothers, who seemed to be intensely playing a video game in the background.

Adya told her the basics of the trip so far, about getting journals for Maggie in Geneva and about the train ride to Lucerne. "I think he needed a break from Greenland," Adya explained.

"Uh-huh. More like Lir needed to see you again. So, are you guys sharing that bed you showed me?" Ashley accused.

Adya laughed. "No, definitely not. He has a separate bedroom. We're just two old friends enjoying a break from work and school."

"I think you make a cute couple," Elena interjected.

Adya blushed.

"See? I'm not the only one that sees through this 'we're just old friends' façade. Who's that, by the way?" Ashley asked as she sat on her bed.

"This is Elena. She helped me pick out a gown and is doing my hair now," Adya explained.

"And makeup, too," Elena added.

"Hi Elena," Ashley said and waved. "What are you getting all dressed up for anyway?"

"Hi Adya's friend," Elena said and reached over to turn on the curling iron.

"I honestly don't know. Lir told me to come to the spa, and here I am."

"I'm coming!" Ashley yelled to someone outside her room. "I'm gonna need to hear more about this trip, but I have to go virtually kick my brothers' asses. Text me later, okay?"

"I will. Have fun with your family," Adya said.

"Haha. It's you who needs to have fun. Talk to you later, Ady," Ashley said.

"See ya," Adya replied and hung up the call before tossing her phone back into the bag with her clothes.

Elena styled Adya's hair into soft curls, partially pinning up some strategic pieces, and then did her makeup. When Elena finished, Adya could barely recognize her thirteen-year-old self. "Wow," she said as she stood transfixed by her reflection. She looked like an older, more mature—and more suited to her old-soul—self.

"You like?" Elena asked as she dusted a little bit of silver glitter into Adya's hair.

"I love it. You are amazing, Elena. Thank you."

As Adya walked the hallway to the room, she felt the spiral curls in her hair bounce with every step. When she entered, the floral aroma had given way to the scent of food that beckoned her empty stomach to join Lir in the dining room.

"Wow," Lir breathed in awe as he stood to greet Adya. While Adya was enjoying her pampering in the spa, he'd changed into a black suit with a white button-up shirt, and a deep blue tie adorning his neck. She thought he looked as if he had just stepped off the red carpet in Hollywood at a movie premiere. "Where'd Ady go, and who are you?"

Adya narrowed her eyes at him. She suddenly wished she had a folded fan she could smack him with. "Very funny," she said snidely. "I could ask the same about you. Who knew you cleaned up so well?" she teased.

Lir took Adya's hand to guide her to a seat at the table and then kissed the back of her fingers as she sat. "I couldn't take you to the symphony looking so good without putting on a clean pair of slacks, now could I?"

The smell of Lir's cologne lingered in his wake as he took a seat across from Adya at the table. "It makes sense now," Adya said.

"What does?" Lir inquired as he motioned for Adya to begin eating.

"I was hoping you weren't planning on a hike tonight after you had me get all dressed up."

Lir laughed. "No, no hiking tonight."

During the meal, Adya noticed Lir watching her often, and not just when she was talking with him. "What's wrong? Do I have lipstick on my teeth? Or food in my teeth?" Adya picked up a spoon from the table to inspect herself.

"Put the spoon down. I'd tell you if you had something in or on your teeth," he said.

"What is it then?" Adya asked.

Lir shook his head. "There's nothing wrong. I swear."

Adya took the last bite of her tiramisu, eyeing Lir doubtfully.

Lir sighed and stood up, offering Adya his hand. "The truth is," he paused and shook his head. "It's nothing bad; I just am awed by how beautiful you look."

Adya felt her cheeks heat up with a blush, and she smiled suddenly, feeling a bit shy. "It's probably the makeup. But Elena gets all the credit for this."

Lir shook his head and handed Adya her coat. "No, she just accented the beauty I've always seen in you." He held out his bent arm to Adya. "Are you ready to go?"

Adya was still tingling inside from Lir's compliments when she hooked her arm through his and nodded. "I'm looking forward to tonight," she said, and they exited the room.

Adya let out a small squeal when they were greeted at the door by a horse-drawn carriage. The driver assisted Adya up, and Lir covered their laps with the warm, woolen blanket from the seat. The entire way to the concert hall, Adya pointed out all the spots decorated with Christmas lights. She didn't feel a hint of cold air but snuggled up against Lir anyway as they made their way through the cobblestone streets.

Inside the hall, they took their seats in a private box that looked down at the stage and audience. "Maggie will never let me travel with you again when she hears how much you're spoiling me," Adya said as they waited for the performance to begin.

Lir grinned in response and squeezed Adya's hand as the lights dimmed. "Let's hope you're wrong about that," he said in a whisper.

Adya didn't restrain the rush of soul memories that danced in her mind as the familiar melodies played. Occasionally, she glanced at Lir to see if he was joining her on their musical chronicle through lifetimes. His beautiful blue eyes were lidded as the music entranced him, too, and he absentmindedly traced his thumb against the soft skin of her hand.

Toward the end of the performance, the orchestra began playing a waltz. Lir leaned in to whisper to Adya, "Would you like to dance like we used to?"

Adya glanced around at the audience, who were all in their seats. She really wanted to say yes but was concerned they would draw attention to themselves.

"Come on. No one will even notice us in the back of the suite." Lir stood and urged Adya to join him.

Adya allowed herself to be pulled up to him, glancing discreetly around to see if they'd drawn any eyes to them. In the back of their private box, they couldn't see the other suites, so she felt comfortable with his proposed idea.

Very formally, they placed their hands in their respective dancing positions and began waltzing to the symphony's melody just like they had done in the soul memories Adya experienced.

Adya's tiny heels raised her to a height to be able to rest her cheek against his. "You've never looked better in a suit than you do tonight," Adya whispered to his ear as they danced.

"That's not saying a lot about my past lives," he whispered back jokingly.

It was saying a lot more than Adya could admit to him. She had loved him in so many lifetimes, but there were only a couple of times when she'd fallen in love with him, or rather allowed herself to fall in love with him. In their first lifetime together, the two fell fast in love, but circumstances forced them to love each other in secret. Adya was already married in that first lifetime together, and when her husband discovered their affair, Lir was promptly "encouraged" to join the army, separating the two until the next lifetime. The other times, it was something similar and always ended in heartbreak. Maybe she unknowingly put up defenses to spare herself that disappointment. It was the only conclusion she could come to as she recalled their lifetimes together.

Adya knew it was different for Lir, that he not only loved her in many, many lifetimes but also was in love with her for most of them. He never put up the defenses to protect his heart. Maybe it was this realization of her defensiveness, or perhaps it was the music, their attire, or the land they were in together. Whatever way she looked at it, though, she could feel her defenses faltering—she was falling for Lir, and none of the voices of reason in her head could persuade her otherwise.

The carriage was waiting for Lir and Adya after the concert ended. With the wind having picked up, the two huddled together during their ride through Lucerne. When the carriage stopped at a bridge over the lake, Lir helped Adya down, and together they walked under the thousands of twinkling Christmas lights.

"It's been a magical night," Adya admitted as they kept close together with joined hands.

"It's brought back many wonderful memories," Lir admitted as they stopped to gaze out over the water at the festively-decorated city.

"We should come back in a few years," Adya suggested, "and do this again."

"We're not halfway through this trip yet, and you're already planning another?" Lir teased.

Adya was grateful for his lighthearted response. "I just figured you wouldn't be able to top tonight, so yeah, I'm planning to do this again." She hoped her reasoning didn't sound as forced as it felt.

"You have so little faith in me, Ady," Lir replied with a laugh. "Let me see your phone," he said.

Adya cautiously handed it to him, not sure what he had planned. "Please tell me you're not going to throw it into the lake."

"No, I just thought we could take another picture so you can remember this night that you don't think I'll be able to top."

Adya laughed. "That's an excellent idea. I'm not sure when I'll get the chance to see you this dressed up again."

Lir held out the phone and snapped a picture while Adya was looking at him with adoring eyes.

"I think you're supposed to look at the camera, Ady," he said, apparently unaware of the reason for her gaze.

"Oh, right," she said and smiled at the camera for a second one.

"That's a great picture of you," he said as he inspected the last one taken.

"You don't look too bad yourself," she replied and tucked her phone back into her coat pocket. "You know," Adya began without thinking, "Elena says we make a cute couple."

Lir raised a brow at Adya. "Who is Elena?"

"The woman responsible for this look," Adya paused and gave a small twirl, loving the way she felt. "She saw the picture of us from earlier when I sent it to Ash. I hope you don't mind. Ash gets on me about how boring I am because I never have any good gossip to share with her. Not that you're gossip. Oh, never mind." Adya turned to face the city again as she blushed.

Lir laughed. "I don't mind. It's not like it's a secret that we're on this trip. Besides, I agree with Elena."

As she fumbled for words that would even remotely come close to explaining how she felt, Adya decided just to show him. She spun to face him, pushed up on her toes, and kissed him.

Lir was startled by her action and froze for a moment as Adya pressed her lips against his. As Adya started to pull away in apparent rejection, he brought her in closer and kissed her back.

For Adya, kissing Lir felt so different than when Brandon had kissed her only a few days prior. While there was a fire in

CHAPTER SIX

Brandon's kiss, there was fluidity with Lir's and a feeling of being completely safe and protected.

Their lips eventually parted, but they remained close enough that they still shared each other's breaths. "I'm so sorry," Adya said. "That was stupid of me. Maybe we should—"

Before she could finish her sentence, Lir pulled Adya's lips back to his, like he was starving for the old soul in front of him. In a moment of unbridled passion, Lir's lips parted, and he caressed Adya's lips with his tongue, as though he needed to commit every touch to memory. He turned their bodies, so her hips pressed against the handrail.

Adya returned Lir's kiss with matched passion, grabbing at the front of his coat before threading her fingers into the hair above the back of his neck. Time and space disappeared as the two got lost in their private moment. Lir's hand caressed Adya's cheek and then made a slow descent down the side of her neck to her side, where he grasped her hip and pulled her body impossibly closer so even the cold breeze couldn't penetrate the barrier of heat radiating from them.

It felt like Adya was going to float away, so she held onto the back of Lir's neck tighter. Magical tingles spread throughout her body, like all the molecules of water within her were dancing. His lips overwhelmed all her senses, and the only thought that came to her mind was the absolute realization that she was in love with him.

It took Adya a moment to realize when Lir's lips retreated from hers, but her eyes eventually fluttered open.

Lir remained standing where he was, looking at her with what seemed to be confusion. "You're in love with me?" he asked, bewildered and a bit breathless.

"I—I didn't say that," Adya replied, blinking faster than usual in an attempt to collect her scattered thoughts. She bowed her head to avoid his gaze, not entirely sure what she would find there.

Lir put a finger under her chin and raised her eyes again. "But I *heard* you in my mind. Did you think that?"

Adya was thoroughly embarrassed now but nodded. "How did you—was that—like a soul memory exchange or something?"

"A thought transfer, maybe? I don't know. I didn't think that was even possible," Lir laughed and squeezed Adya in a hug.

Adya hugged him back but without his enthusiasm, confused by whether it was her actual thoughts or him hearing those thoughts that was making him so happy. "Lir," Adya didn't know what to say, "I would've never told you that. I know we can't—I mean that it's an impossible thing for us right now." Adya frowned darkly and released Lir from her embrace.

Lir took a moment before he managed to compose himself. "You're right." He took Adya's hand and guided it to his heart. "I struggle every moment of every day to push back those same thoughts. Seeing you tonight, looking like an older version of yourself, I let my guard down, too. At the symphony, I couldn't stand to be so far away from you, so I asked you to dance. You don't have to tell me how impossible this is, but my heart—no, my soul doesn't seem to care what it should or shouldn't feel."

Adya could feel Lir's heart racing as her palm pressed against his chest. She felt the weight of their impossible situation coming down on her. "Maybe," she started, "we can just be as we want to be while we're in this timeless place."

"And when we have to leave? What happens then?" Lir asked.

"You return to Greenland, and I go back to the Academy, the same as before. We step back into the lives we have to live for now." Even saying the words made Adya's heart ache with sadness, but it wasn't as if they could go back and reverse the last ten hours of their lives that led them to this moment.

"Is that what you truly want?" Lir asked cautiously.

"I'm not looking forward to this trip being over, but that's how it will have to be."

"Adya?" Lir asked and paused for her to respond. "May I kiss you again?"

The dread that threatened to creep in and ruin Adya's night melted away. With a quick nod, the two made an intimate pact with their lips to forego all barriers and impossibilities and just be their authentic selves for the remainder of their vacation together.

CHAPTER SEVEN

Adya awoke early the next morning and got dressed. The two stayed up late after returning from the symphony, chatting about other lifetimes together, and generally enjoying each other's company until they were both too tired to stay awake and retreated to their respective bedrooms. She left a note for Lir, who was still asleep, before she hurried down to the spa. She was grateful to see Elena at the desk when she arrived.

"Adya," Elena said with surprise. "Did you enjoy your night?"

Adya smiled. "Yes, and that's the reason I'm here. Could you teach me how to put on makeup?" As she was drifting off into a blissful sleep, she concluded that if they were genuinely going to try to exist as their soul-selves on this trip, Adya wanted to look the part. She never bothered with makeup at home and only succeeded in wearing it to the dances at the Academy with Ashley's help. It had never been necessary in her past lives, either, except for those rare occasions when they would apply copious amounts of white powder to their faces and bosoms, and bright red pigment to their cheeks and lips. Thankfully in those times, Adya already had her earth affinity and steered clear of the toxic and often lead-based makeups that were so popular.

Elena smiled kindly and walked Adya to her station. "Is this for a special event?" she asked as she placed various kinds of makeup on the counter.

"No, nothing like last night. I just want to learn how to apply makeup for everyday wear," Adya admitted. "My mom died before she could teach me, and I don't bother wearing it at the Academy."

"You have natural beauty and do not need it," Elena said, "but I will teach you."

Elena explained the purpose of all the makeup and then showed Adya how to apply it to herself. The result surprised Adya; she looked so natural, but also much older.

After paying for the new makeup, Adya thanked Elena.

"I am happy that you are happy," Elena replied. "If you have questions, I am here."

"Thank you, Elena. You're a miracle worker." Adya hugged Elena before returning to her room.

"Good morning," Adya said as she entered the room with a bounce in her step and saw a shirtless Lir pouring himself some tea.

"Good morning yourself," Lir said and set down his cup. He walked over to Adya and kissed her gently before tilting his head to inspect her. "You look different today," he commented.

Adya giggled and rested her palm on his left peck. "It's possible that I'm still glowing from last night."

Lir laughed. "Well, that and you're wearing makeup now?" He caressed Adya's cheekbone with his thumb.

"Yeah, I just thought since we're throwing caution to the wind, I could at least look less like your kid sister," Adya admitted.

Lir shook his head and smiled. "You've never needed makeup to be beautiful. And I have always seen through your outward appearance to your soul."

"So, I'm an old lady in your eyes?" Adya teased.

Lir smiled. "More like an ageless beauty," he replied. After a moment of admiring her, he asked, "What would you like to do today?"

"Hmmm," Adya said thoughtfully. "Elena was telling me of a few places we should visit. There are museums and chocolatiers and parks. Oh, and we can go up into the mountains and maybe ski." Adya got momentarily lost in Lir's eyes as he watched the ideas pour from her. "Or we could stay in and enjoy each other some more." Adya brushed her nose against Lir's and placed a hungry kiss against his lips.

"Mmm," Lir replied to her seductive gesture. "You are entirely too tempting, my dear Ady. But I don't think we should let ourselves get *that* carried away on this trip." Lir cleared his throat to compose himself again. "We can do *most* of your ideas, and there will still be time for us, too. How would you feel about enjoying a day on the lake?"

"I didn't think the boat tours ran this time of year," Adya said. "Well, at least according to Elena, they don't. It was one of the first things I asked her."

Lir smiled. "The tours don't run, but what about taking a private boat out?"

Adya's eyes lit up, and she nodded enthusiastically. "I'd love that."

"Good, I thought you would." Lir parted from Adya to answer the knock at their door and returned with a covered tray of food. "Let me make a quick phone call. You can start eating, and I'll join you in a minute when I'm done with the call and get dressed." He placed a kiss on her cheek in passing as he walked towards his room.

"You could leave your shirt off for a bit longer," Adya called out after him. She heard him chuckle as he closed the door. She fanned herself with her hand, feeling a little flush from finally allowing herself to appreciate Lir's toned body fully.

As she ate her eggs and fruit, Adya could hear Lir's muffled voice in the bedroom. It sounded like he was speaking Gaelic, but it was hard to hear anything clearly. While she waited for Lir to return, she sent a text to Ashley. Adya knew Ashley would still be sleeping but would be happy to receive the first of the two photos that Lir had taken of them the night prior, the one where Adya was gazing up at Lir. With the picture, she included a message that said, "Just wanted you to know that I'm thoroughly enjoying myself." In truth, Adya didn't know how much of the intimate side of the trip she would end up sharing with her roommate but knew Ashley would appreciate the hints of romantic gossip that she always tried to pry out of Adya.

Lir soon joined Adya at the table—fully dressed, to Adya's dismay. "We're all set to go out on the lake today. How's breakfast?"

"Not bad," she said as Lir sat in the chair beside Adya. "It's just eggs, so I suppose it's difficult to make them taste as amazing as, say, our dinner last night was."

Lir nodded and began eating his simple breakfast. "The weekend breakfasts are more elaborate. They usually serve *zopf*, a kind of bread they only make and serve on the weekends. It goes wonderfully with jam and honey."

"I look forward to trying it," Ady said as she stood up from her empty plate to pour them fresh cups of tea.

It didn't take long for the two to finish their breakfasts and embark on their adventure for the day. Adya and Lir walked a short way down the lake to a small dock that had seven rather large boats anchored to it. "Care to guess which one we're taking?" Lir asked as they neared the first yacht.

Adya didn't know how she was supposed to guess until she read the name of the third boat in the line. "Belisama," she said with a growing smile. "Is this—?"

Before Adya could finish her question, Lir jogged ahead. He greeted the man that had just climbed off the Belisama with a giant hug. "It's been too long, old friend. You'll never guess who's with me," he said and motioned towards Adya.

The middle-aged man with a well-groomed black beard that had streaks of age in it squinted towards the approaching girl. "That isn't Ady, is it?"

Adya immediately had confirmation of who it was when he spoke and held out her arms to greet the man. "Murchadh," she said, embracing him warmly. "What are you doing in Switzerland?" Adya kissed the man's cheek and smiled into the face of a man who would forever carry the pain of true love lost. She was genuinely surprised to see that he had continued for so many lifetimes after his love Ascended centuries prior. Belisama was a *Primum Vivere*, like Ava, and a water and fire bi-affinate.

"Ahh, I wanted to show my *cuisle mo chroidhe* all the waters of the world," Murchadh explained as he helped Adya climb on board the ship that carried his love's namesake.

"I'm not sure Bel would've enjoyed it here," Adya said and turned to watch Lir climb aboard after her. "Last time we were all together, she was rather enjoying the warm sun and clear blue waters in the Caribbean."

"Aye," Murchadh replied. "She was as stubborn as she was beautiful and stayed far 'way from the cold."

"I'm not sure I can blame her," Adya replied as she shivered from the cold wind sweeping across the lake.

"Why don't you head inside, Ady. I want to catch up with Murchadh and maybe convince him to let me drive this beauty a bit," Lir said kindly while looking hopeful at his old friend.

"Aye, just be careful of Muriel. She's a wee bit protective," Murchadh warned as he started up the stairs to the ship's helm.

"Muriel?" Adya asked, but Murchadh was already out of earshot.

Lir shrugged unknowingly at Adya and then followed Murchadh up the stairs.

Adya slowly opened the glass door leading to a large interior cabin. "Hello?" she called out cautiously. She half expected to see a red-headed woman wielding a broom. Instead, an orange and white striped cat jumped up on the couch and meowed at her. "Oh," she said in surprise and held out her hand for the cat to smell. "You must be Muriel," Adya said, although she found it odd to be having a one-sided conversation with an animal. Adya's father had never permitted her to have pets, and they weren't allowed at the Academy, so her interactions with them in this life had been somewhat limited thus far.

Muriel stared at Adya but didn't move, so Adya slowly sat on the far end of the couch from the cat. "I'm Adya, an old friend of Murchadh," she continued. When the engine started up, Adya jumped a little, startled by the sound, but Muriel didn't seem affected by the noise or the motion that followed as the men above guided the craft onto the lake.

After recovering from the jolt of the boat moving, Adya relaxed and stared out the windows at the lake and mountains. It was so peaceful and beautiful, and now that she was warmer, she recanted her thought about Belisama not enjoying it there.

As Adya relaxed, the cat did, too, and walked towards Adya without her realizing. Muriel sniffed Adya and then meowed at her for attention. "Well, hello there," Adya said and once again held out her hand to the cat. Muriel sniffed Adya's fingers and then rubbed her face against them.

The boat circled half the lake before coming to a stop far away from the shore. Muriel was curled up in Adya's lap and was purring almost as loudly as the engine when Lir and Murchadh entered.

"She's taken a'liken to ya," Murchadh said as he came over to rub the cat's head.

"Aye," Lir said, "I feel jealous of a cat right now." In the hour or so that Lir and Murchadh were steering the ship, Lir's Irish accent had grown thicker.

Adya smiled and patted the couch beside her. "You should be jealous. Muriel and I are best friends now." But as soon as Murchadh sat down, Muriel jumped down from Adya's lap and up into his. "Hmph, and I thought we were friends," she said, playfully sounding offended.

"That's okay. You still have me," Lir said and held Adya's hand.

Murchadh laughed as he stroked Muriel's orange fur. "Dontcha take it to heart, Ady. Muriel's been my *companach* for lifetimes. She's an old soul fer a cat."

Adya looked at him with furrowed, confused brows. "What do you mean she's been your companion for lifetimes?"

"Jus'that," Murchadh explained. "She found me after Bel Ascended, a gift from her, I b'lieve. Muriel finds me in all 'er lives an' mine." Murchadh continued to stroke the cat's orange fur. "When she stops coming 'round, it'll be time fer me to Ascend."

The story genuinely moved Adya. She wondered if Belisama really did send the animal to be her lover's companion after she Ascended or perhaps the cat was a part of Belisama's soul. "I read a book like that a couple of years ago," Adya said. "It was about a dog whose soul would reincarnate and would come back as a different dog to find his owner. I never thought animal souls could actually come back, too." Adya realized after the words escaped her that there was one other person she'd known who had an animal companion for centuries.

"T'is true," Murchadh said with absolute certainty.

The three—or four, if you counted Muriel—of them spent the afternoon and a good portion of the evening sharing adventures they'd had in their lives apart and reliving the memories they'd experienced together. Lir and Murchadh shared a bottle of single malt whiskey, and by the end of the evening, they were both singing old Irish folk songs. Adya joined in on a few and sang some of her own but had no interest in drinking the whiskey.

"I bet'er be gittin us back," Murchadh said as he turned his glass upside down on the bar. "S'pose to snow t'night," he said and walked out of the cabin.

Adya looked at Lir with concern. "Is he okay to drive the boat?"

Lir smiled at Adya and traced the rim of his glass with the tip of his middle finger. "Aye," he replied. "He's been much drunk'r." He reached into his pocket and pulled out his phone.

"What are you doing?" Adya asked with a laugh. She walked over and stood next to Lir while he searched for something on his phone.

"I have one m're song for you, *mo ghaol*." Lir hit play on his phone and set it on the counter before offering his hand to Adya.

Adya wasn't sure if he was sober enough to stand but helped Lir to his feet regardless.

While the intro played, Lir explained, "I 'erd this song decades af'er we parted last lifetime. All my 'appiness, all my desire I've known o'side of yew has fall'n short of what I 'eel 'ith yew."

Adya's brows furrowed. Between Lir's now thick accent and his intoxication, she didn't know if what she understood of what he was trying to say was the truth.

And then he began singing with the song:
"We were born before the wind
Also younger than the sun"
Adya smiled as he sang the old Van Morrison song and swayed with him to the music.

Lir caressed her face and didn't break his gaze into her eyes as he sang, "*I wanna rock your gypsy soul, just like way back in the days of old... and then together we will float into the mystic.*"

Adya was utterly flattered, feeling like Lir had written the lyrics himself about her. She laughed when he twirled her around and then caught her in his arms.

"*C'mon girl, too late to stop now.*" Lir rested his forehead against Adya's as the song ended.

Within moments, their silent revere into each other's eyes turned into a passionate embrace. Lir lifted Adya onto the edge of the counter and positioned his body between her legs. His hands caressed her face while his lips feverishly captured hers.

Adya found herself lost in the moment, too. Whether it was because of the intoxicating taste of whiskey in his mouth or from the very heart of her soul's desires, she did nothing to dissuade him. She caressed his jaw as it moved while he kissed her and knotted her other hand into the bottom of his shirt.

One of Lir's hands moved from her cheek and threaded into the hair at the base of her neck. With a gentle tug, Adya's head tilted back, and her lips pried from his. Within a breath, his lips were leaving a trail of hungry kisses down to her neck. Lir's free hand left her face, too, tracing over her shoulder and down her arm that was grasping his shirt. At her wrist, his hand left her arm and tugged up on her shirt. The material was lifted just enough for his fingers to caress her bare abs and the bottom of her rib cage.

Lir's hands were both hot and cold, and combined with the sensual kisses on her neck, Adya breathed out a soft moan. No longer was the mortal body in control of her actions—it was Adya's soul that took over with her countless lifetimes of sensual experience. Her legs tightened around Lir's waist and tugged him hard against her body. Her breath was heavy as she tugged his shirt up and pressed her palm against his skin.

As they approached the crescendo, when things were about to escalate even further, the boat jolted and came to a halt. The glasses on the shelf rattled, and Muriel jumped up onto the bar and meowed at the pair. Adya's legs released Lir, and both their hands instantly fell to their sides.

Murchadh burst through the door just as the two had created a small space between their bodies. "Made it!" he announced proudly.

Muriel jumped off the bar, and Adya followed the cat. She flashed Lir a brief confused look before walking past him.

"It was so good to see you again, Murchadh," she said and tried to smooth her tasseled hair. She hugged Murchadh and then turned back into the cabin. Lir's back was to her, barely having moved since their embrace lurched to an end. "It was nice meeting you, too, Muriel."

The cat responded with a meow.

"Are you coming, Lir?" Adya said, trying not to sound impatient with his odd behavior.

Lir cleared his throat and turned around, careful not to meet her eyes. "Yes, it's always good to see you, Murchadh. We'll talk again soon." The drunken Irish accent had faded; Lir apparently sobered in those few moments apart.

"' ill do, Lir." The two men shook hands, and Lir descended to join Adya on the dock.

Adya and Lir walked without talking or touching. Adya kept looking over at Lir, but his gaze didn't waiver from the ground. Even in the elevator, they stood silently apart and walked into the hotel room in the same uncomfortable silence.

Adya followed him into the main room where she paused, but Lir continued towards his room. "Umm, goodnight?" she asked, feeling thoroughly rejected.

Lir paused at his bedroom door but didn't look back as he spoke to Adya. "I think I just need to sleep this off. Goodnight," he said and closed his bedroom door behind him.

Adya stared at his door with a dumbfounded expression. Tears pooled in her eyes as a wave of complete humiliation washed over her. Angry, hurt, and confused, she turned on her heel, marched to her room, and slammed the door shut. Although her entire body felt heavy, she somehow managed to make it to her bed before she collapsed. The cascading tears soaked her pillow.

The following morning, there was a soft knock at her door. "Breakfast's here," Lir's muffled voice came through the closed door.

Adya didn't respond. She hadn't moved from the spot where she collapsed the previous night and laid there hugging a pillow, feeling as if she hadn't slept a wink. What was she supposed to say to him? Should she apologize? She had been completely sober. At least he had an excuse. What was he going to tell her? Was he even going to look at her again? Was he going to pack her onto the plane and send her back to the Academy? All the worst-case scenarios whirled in her mind, leaving her paralyzed on the bed.

The slow-moving shadows in the room had shifted considerably before Lir returned to her door and knocked again. "Adya? Can I come in?" When she didn't respond, he opened her door enough to poke his head inside. He saw her lying on the bed, still dressed in her clothes from the night before, clutching the pillow. With a heavy sigh, he invited himself in and sat on the edge of her bed. "I'm sorry," he began.

Adya squeezed her sore eyes shut and hugged her pillow tighter, waiting for the worst that was sure to follow.

"Not about kissing you, but I'm sorry about how I treated you afterward."

Adya turned her head slightly and peeked at him with one eye.

"I could make the excuse that I was drunk and didn't know what I was doing, but that's only partly true. Yes, I had way too much whiskey, but my actions that followed—the song, the kissing, all of it—was the very truth of how I feel about you. My soul stripped down of all its caution and defenses, just—" Lir paused for a moment and looked into the one eye of Adya's that he could see. "I love you, Adya. I know I've told you that before, and it always seems to lack the gravity of how I truly feel." Lir sighed again and stood. "I wanted you to know that and that you deserve better than to be assaulted by some drunk fool no matter how much he loves you."

Lir started to leave Adya's room when she finally spoke. "I love you, too," she whispered just loud enough for him to hear.

Lir paused and looked back at Adya, who was finally sitting upright in her bed.

"Will you please stop walking away from me?" Adya asked.

A pained expression marred Lir's handsome face. "That's the last thing I want to do," he admitted and sat down on Adya's bed again.

"You have an odd way of showing it," Adya replied with a hint of playfulness in her tone. She took a cleansing breath and continued. "Last night," she began and rested her hand on top of his, "you might've been drunk, but I was completely sober. Everything I participated in with you came from my soul. Do you think I could've confidently done what we did last night if the desire didn't come from the heart of my soul? If you say last night was assault, then it's only fair to say I assaulted you right back." Adya paused for only a second before continuing. "Dr. Ilene has been teaching us to find our true self by understanding the seven qualities that define self: spontaneity, reasoning, creativity, free will, spirituality, discernment, and love. With you on this trip and last night, I finally understand what those mean to me. Last night was not a mistake for me—it was my true self expressing herself." Adya surprised herself with how well she expressed her thoughts despite all the doubts and insecurities she had been drowning in from before their talk.

Lir flipped his hand over and held Adya's in his. "I'm still in awe of how much you can amaze and surprise me. You possess a gift, Adya, one that isn't attached to any element. My mind is constantly trying to make logical choices. I create excuses and constraints to try to justify everything. And you just express your truth without any apology."

"Apparently, all *you* need is a whole lot of whiskey to do that, too," Adya said with a smile.

"Yeah, well, my overly-analytical mind thinks the whiskey was a terrible idea and is making me pay dearly for it today," Lir replied and rubbed his aching forehead with his free hand.

"But you were so cute with your full Irish accent," Adya teased and moved closer to Lir. "Will you let this bonnie lass help?"

Lir chuckled. "I don't think I deserve not to feel this one," Lir admitted, but turned his body to face Adya, "but if you can forgive me for hurting you, then I suppose I can forgive myself, too."

Adya released Lir's hand and caressed his face with both of hers. "I forgive you." With her hands resting on his face, she closed her eyes and drew on the elements to help bring balance back to Lir's body. Within moments, she could feel Lir relax, and his body returned to a more balanced state. Her hands remained on his face when she opened her eyes. She caressed his skin with her fingertips, appreciating the man who had captured her soul's heart. "Do you know what will make us both feel better?"

"A swim in the indoor pool here?" Lir asked.

Adya laughed. "That sounds nice, too. But I thought a visit to a chocolatier today would cure anything I wasn't able to heal."

Lir smiled and kissed the palm of her hand. "You're all the cure I need, but the chocolate sounds pretty good, too. I think it's Christmas, though, so nothing will be open. We'll do that on another day before we leave, okay?"

"Promise?" Adya asked and hovered her lips over his.

"Promise," Lir replied as his lips met hers.

CHAPTER EIGHT

"I haven't been ignoring your texts," Adya explained to Ashley when she called her later that evening. Lir had gone to the lobby to secure their plans to go skiing the next day, and Adya decided it was an excellent time to reconnect with her friend.

"You sure as hell haven't been answering them. I sent you like fifty in the past day. I thought maybe you were dead or something!" Ashley berated her friend on the other end of the phone line but was more interested in finding out the meaning of the picture Adya had texted her. "So that picture—was there an invisible alien on Lir's head, or were you just staring at him with lust in your eyes?"

"It was an alien. Definitely," Adya replied dryly.

"I'm calling bullshit on that. What's going on between you two? And I want the truth," Ashley demanded.

"The truth is. . . it's complicated. I don't know much at this point except that we both love each other."

"Oh. My. God! Did you just say you loved him or was that a bad connection?"

"You heard me right," Adya admitted and felt her cheeks warm with a blush. "But as I said, it's complicated. This trip is a break from reality, and in a little over a week, he returns to his research in Greenland, and I go back to the Academy."

"Couldn't you just, I don't know, do the long-distance thing?" Ashley suggested.

Adya glowered, even though her friend couldn't see it. "Haven't we had this conversation before? He was my *teacher*. His body is seven years older than mine, and that's all anyone is going to see. No one, not even other Awakened affinates, will appreciate or even fully accept that our old souls want to be together. Maybe in a few years, things will be different. I don't know."

"Does that mean you're going to be in a constant state of moping for the next few years?"

Adya sighed. "No, I think it'll be different this time than when he left school last year." She didn't know if that was true but was hopeful that her fully Awakened soul would be able to weather this storm better than her un-Awakened self had.

"I know you'll never admit it, but I was right about you two last year, wasn't I?" Ashley wasn't bragging and sounded genuinely concerned about her friend.

"We just spent a lot of time sharing soul memories. Yes, I started to feel something more than our teacher-student relationship, and it hurt me a lot when he left. Now that I'm Awakened, I can appreciate that the feelings I felt were coming from my soul. I just wasn't capable of processing them."

"Thanks for finally admitting that, although it was obvious with your fake sickness and sad music all the time," Ashley said.

"Yeah, sorry about that and for not telling you about it then. I need to ask a favor of you now, though."

"Let me guess. . . don't tell anyone about your torrid romance with your former teacher, right?"

"Yeah, like I said, maybe in a few years things can be different, but for now, we're going to leave everything here in Switzerland," Adya explained, although in the back of her mind, she was already trying to find an alternative to just dropping things cold turkey. She gazed at her reflection in the mirror. Even without makeup on and her slightly stringy hair from swimming earlier, Adya could see the change in her appearance; she could see the maturity of her old soul reflected in her once adolescent features.

"Aside from falling in love, tell me all about Switzerland," Ashley said, bringing a happier tone to the conversation.

Adya walked around their apartment-esque hotel room while she told Ashley all about what she'd seen on her trip. Lir returned while she was still on the call and kissed Adya's temple before going to his room to give Adya her privacy.

After half an hour of hearing all about Ashley's Christmas and sharing her adventures, Adya hung up with her friend. She approached Lir's door and knocked softly, but he, too, was on a call.

"You know why that isn't possible," Lir said to the person on the other end of his call. He looked frustrated as he paced back and forth in front of his bed but motioned for Adya to come in. "Take some time off, then."

Adya entered and sat down on the foot of Lir's bed.

"Yeah, I'll talk to him," Lir said, sounding defeated. "Call me again before you make any final decisions, okay?" Lir nodded to whatever was said to him. "You know I'm here for you no matter what. Talk to you soon." Lir ended the call and joined Adya on his bed, his legs flush against her own.

"That didn't sound good," she commented and repositioned herself behind him. Adya placed her hands on Lir's shoulders and started rubbing them. He was definitely tense.

"It'll be alright," Lir replied and then relaxed into Adya's massage. "Mmmm, that feels wonderful."

Adya smiled behind him and leaned in to pepper the back of his neck with small kisses. "And now?" she whispered.

Lir shook his head. "You'd better be careful doing things like that," he warned.

Adya bit her bottom lip and grinned. "What if I don't want to be careful?" she asked as she traced the skin of his neck with the tip of her nose before pressing an open-mouthed kiss under his ear. She could feel a low growl vibrate in his chest when her hands circled him, and she raked her nails against his chest.

Barely a moment passed before Lir pinned Adya to the bed. "I warned you," he growled and leaned in to capture her bottom lip in his teeth.

Adya stared into his wild eyes that stared back into hers and felt her entire body tingle with excitement. The same instincts from the night before took over her, and she hooked one leg around Lir's waist and pulled his hips down to hers. Adya lifted her head to satisfy her hunger for his kiss.

Lir released one of Adya's wrists and captured her face as they kissed, and their bodies pressed together. Her free hand clasped the back of his head, and her fingers tangled in his hair while their mouths fought for dominance.

Adya gasped for breath when Lir's lips broke free, and his teeth nipped at her jaw. With his eyes trained on hers, Lir moved his hand to her waist and paused. She unconsciously arched her back and breathed in sharply when he tugged her shirt up, exposing her stomach.

Adya's mind flooded with sensual memories of a time when they were together in the Caribbean. *The strong wind from the threatening storm bent the trees to their will, but it was nothing compared to the explosive encounter she and Lir shared that night.*

Adya returned her mind to the present when Lir freed his hips from the constraint of her leg and ripped off his shirt. She gazed at the magnificent, half-dressed man before her, eyes lingering on the faint red scratches on his chest, with a hunger she had only felt in lifetimes long passed. Adya only guessed that he remembered the same things from the way he was looking at her, but then bowed his head and kissed her exposed abdomen with the same fervor as her lips moments before. With her heightened senses, Adya could feel herself spiraling out of control. She reached down and grabbed Lir's bicep while her eyes fluttered and closed.

Lir's kisses trailed lower, threatening the waist of her jeans when suddenly the doors leading to the balcony burst open, and a rush of cold air pushed forcefully into the room, startling the pair.

In the moments that followed, Adya felt Lir's cheek rest against her stomach as he wrapped his arms tightly—almost protectively—around her torso. She looked down past her heaving chest to the top of his head, and her body relaxed. The wind in the room subsided as Lir continued to hold Adya.

A long while passed—maybe ten minutes—and the two remained unmoving except for their breathing, which eventually returned to its regular cadence. Lir shivered from the cold outside air touching his bare back and finally broke the silence. "I should probably close the doors," he said in almost a whisper. As his arms snaked out from underneath Adya, he kissed her soft stomach softly once more before rising.

Adya scooted herself backward on the ruffled red bedspread and laid her head on his pillow while she watched Lir secure the balcony doors. "Leave it to me to ruin a moment," Adya said lightly, only half-joking.

Lir sat on the edge of the bed and traced the palm of Adya's hand with his fingertips. "I wouldn't say you ruined anything. More like you saved us both from doing something we really can't allow to happen."

Adya smiled sadly and motioned with her head for Lir to lay down beside her. "My true self sometimes forgets that this body may not be ready for everything that my soul has already experienced."

Lir relaxed on the bed beside Adya and brushed strands of her hair from her cheek. "I should've had more control," he admitted, sharing her lamenting smile. "Did you know that I'm afraid I'll do something and lose you again?" he admitted.

Adya's hand touched Lir's chest and traced over his muscles while she looked with concern and confusion into his eyes. "Why do you think you'll lose me? I'm not going anywhere."

His fingers softly traced Adya's face as if they were trying to memorize her features. "We'll be leaving all of this behind in very soon. We will be living our separate lives again, and Paxton will be returning to yours again soon, too."

At the mention of Paxton, Adya's heart wrenched painfully. Lir wasn't wrong; in the year and a half she'd known him in this life, her and Brandon's relationship had revealed signs of the passion that still existed between them. Soon Brandon would complete his Awakening and fully become the soul of the man who had always won Adya's affections over Lir. "We have a choice in every lifetime. What if in this life I want that choice to be you, Lir?"

Lir's eyes darted around the room, not meeting hers, and he chuckled darkly. "Everything in this life seems to be conspiring against you making that choice."

"I'm here now, aren't I?" Adya pointed out but knew that wasn't enough. She removed Lir's hand from her cheek and placed it on her heart. "I want to share a memory with you."

Although still looking defeated and a bit hesitant, Lir gave the nod.

In truth, Adya didn't know if this was the best memory to share with Lir or if it would hurt him, but it was the only way she could think of to console the heartbreak he had already started preparing for. Adya closed her eyes and recalled a recent memory, the night of the dance just before winter break when Brandon kissed her. She replayed those moments in her mind, focusing on the moment when her new self abandoned everything her old soul was telling her about that embrace and rejected Brandon. The short memory replayed over and over in Adya's mind until Lir's hand retreated from her chest, and she opened her eyes to see if he saw her memory.

"You craved that moment for so long," Lir began, his brows drawn tightly together in confusion. "Why did you push him away?"

CHAPTER EIGHT

"You know why," Adya said and then explained further, possibly realizing it for the first time herself. "I spent a long time insisting that he should make his own choices, encouraging Brandon to do what was right for him in this life despite knowing that I've loved him as Pax in many other lifetimes. I think in all my stubborn insisting, I was trying to tell that to myself, too, that I needed to be free to choose for myself in this lifetime, just like him. Why can't my choice finally be you—be us?"

"That won't be the easy choice, Ady. There's already so much stacked up against that happening," Lir said.

Adya nodded. "Yes, but I don't have a father or husband in this life, preventing me from deciding my fate for myself."

Lir finally smiled. "No, you just have an ocean and about four and a half years separating you from really making that choice."

Adya wrinkled her nose. "I suppose it's true that you could return to Greenland and find your soul mate in a polar bear."

Lir laughed, and the light returned to his eyes. "There aren't any polar bears where I am in Greenland, silly. Besides, I like my girlfriends to be less hairy than me."

Adya smiled and stroked his smooth chest. "Is that your way of asking me to be your girlfriend?"

Lir chuckled. "I overheard you talking to Ashley about me. I figured if someone besides us knew about us, it kinda made it official by default."

"How very romantic," Adya said with a roll of her eyes.

"Is that a yes?" Lir asked.

Adya smiled as she grabbed the back of Lir's head and pulled his lips to hers. "Yes," she whispered.

"We should probably get some sleep. We have to be up early to catch the tram to the mountains," Lir said as their faces remained close.

Adya kissed Lir softly once more. "Goodnight, then," she said and snuggled up to his chest.

"Does this mean you're sleeping in here with me tonight?" Lir inquired.

"Yes," she replied, smiling against his skin.

"You are a force of nature, *mo ghaol*." Lir chuckled and kissed the top of her head. "Goodnight, Ady."

CHAPTER NINE

"I swear I'll be fine," Adya insisted as Lir hovered over her. "If I could do this on the cobblestone streets in Lucerne and up and down the aircraft stairs *twice*, I can definitely manage on the ground here."

"I carried you in and out of the plane both times," Lir reminded her. "Besides, it's my job to worry about you." He winked at her as they slowly made their way to the water element resident hall.

"They still won't let you inside, even if you are a former teacher and helping a cripple back to her dorm," Adya said as she tilted her head up to kiss Lir softly.

Lir looked around hesitantly to see if anyone was around before he kissed Adya back. Despite her New Year's resolution to not pretend their relationship didn't exist, Lir still felt the need to be discreet. "I'm going to go talk to Ted, and then I'll be back to say goodbye."

Adya shook her head defiantly. "Not 'goodbye,' and don't think of pulling an 'Irish goodbye' with me, either. You have fifteen minutes—maybe twenty—and I'm going to hobble over and pull you out of Ted's office myself."

"You're not going to hobble anywhere. You're *supposed* to be resting that leg." Lir wrapped his arm around Adya's waist and kissed the top of her head. "I'll be back soon."

Adya felt Lir watching her as she ascended the stairs to the resident hall. While she didn't look back, she smiled, knowing that his protection was coming from a place of love.

Adya broke her ankle while skiing in the Alps with Lir the day after Christmas. "I leaned to go one way," she explained to Greta as the older woman helped her to the couch in the common room, "but my right leg had different plans altogether."

"Oh my goodness," Greta said as she sat down beside the second year affinate. "I've heard the ski patrol in the Alps is very responsive."

"You'd think so," Adya explained, "except we weren't exactly supposed to be on the part of the mountain we were on. It was three long hours of cursing in every language I know before the helicopter arrived and took me to the medical center."

"I should've guessed," Greta said with a laugh. "So, you and Lir, huh?"

Adya blushed and nodded.

"It's about time. I shouldn't say this, but—" Greta paused and looked around discreetly. "I've been secretly rooting for you and Lir to get together," she said with a wink at Adya.

"We have quite a bit of history, for sure," Adya said. "I just hope I don't screw it up this time."

"How long have you two known each other?" Greta asked.

Adya thought for a moment, counting back. "Two thousand years, give or take a century. I lived in the Rome area from the time when Romulus first established it until the building of the Colosseum. I met Lir for the first time between Caesar and Octavius's rule."

"It boggles my mind sometimes when I think about how many lifetimes you've lived. And you knew Ava, too, right?" Greta asked.

"Yes, I knew Ava longer than I've known anyone else. Until she and I met, I didn't know that there were others; she was the first affinate I'd ever met. It was my sixth lifetime, and I lived in a small community south of hers on the Euphrates

River in Mesopotamia. Ava had lived so many lives before I met her, more lifetimes than I have even now." Adya smiled as she revisited memories of Ava. "Did you ever know Belisama?"

Greta thought back for a moment. "I never met her, but she was an Elder when I attended the Academy in Ireland in my second life."

Adya nodded. "I caught up with her soul husband while we were in Switzerland. I couldn't believe he hadn't Ascended yet, but apparently, he has a cat that he believes was sent to him by Bel and says the cat finds him in all his lifetimes. I never knew animals had soul lives like us."

Greta nodded thoughtfully. "I've heard of that before, but I've never known anyone who has one. That's really incredible. Maybe we should teach a class here about that."

"I was thinking the same thing," Adya said. They both smiled. "Did you have a nice winter break?"

"Honestly, it was pretty quiet around here. I should've taken Ted's advice and gone on vacation," Greta said.

Adya nodded in agreement. "I love the Academy, but a vacation away from here was very good for my soul."

Greta chuckled. "Yes, I can see that, although not so good for your body."

"It wouldn't be Switzerland if it didn't threaten me in some way," Adya chuckled darkly and then glanced at the clock on the wall. "Hmm, Lir was supposed to be back by now. I should probably go check and make sure he didn't leave without saying anything." Adya pushed herself up and positioned her crutches under her arms. "Don't give me that look, Greta. I'm perfectly fine to get around with these."

"Okay," Greta said while holding her hands up in defeat. "I won't try to stop you, just be careful, okay?"

"I will, I promise," Adya said as she hobbled towards the door.

It took about five minutes for her to go from her dorm to the main building where Ted's office was, a trek that would generally take just a minute. She took the familiar, albeit freshly redone, hallway towards his office and heard him and Lir involved in a conversation.

"She has to make this choice for herself," Adya heard Lir say.

"If you'd come to me earlier, we wouldn't be in this position," Ted replied.

Adya knocked on the door to announce her presence. "Are you talking about Maggie?" she asked with furrow brows and a voice filled with concern.

Ted sighed. "Yes, Lir just told me that her time off request is so she can decide whether or not to have Eli's procedure done. Why didn't you tell me about this?" Ted demanded of her.

Adya frowned. "Maggie isn't back?"

"No, and answer my question," Ted insisted.

Adya hobbled over to stand next to Lir. "Because this needs to be her decision, not one you or the Elders force upon her." Adya looked at Lir and spoke, "Did you know she wasn't going to be here?"

Lir nodded, his face filled with concern. "She asked me to be your interim guardian while she took time to make the decision. I told her that wouldn't be possible."

Adya's eyebrows drew together in thought. "That was Maggie on the phone on Christmas, wasn't it?"

Lir nodded. "I was hoping she'd reconsider and make her decision to stay here before we returned. I didn't want you to worry."

"Well, she didn't, and now I have to contact the Elders and let them know that Eli and Myra are actively recruiting for their insane experiments," Ted said in complete frustration. "And you two. . . that's a whole other topic that I have to deal with."

Adya frowned darkly. "Anything between Lir and me is none of your business," she stated flatly. "Lir isn't a teacher anymore, and you don't have a say about my personal life." Adya sounded much older than her body appeared.

Lir took Adya's hand and squeezed it, proud of her for standing up for herself and them the way she did. "I'm not trying to cause problems for you, Ted. Adya's right, though. Anything between her and I isn't your concern."

Ted pinched the bridge of his nose. "Just. . . be mindful of your age difference, please?"

"Despite being young in this life, I'm actually older than both of you. I can manage to take care of myself quite well," Adya reminded them.

That was apparently not the right thing to say to Ted at that moment. "You are still a student at my Academy. I'm responsible for you, Adya, so please don't fight me on this. Lir, can you contact Maggie and find out if she's considering their offer?"

"Of course, Ted. I've got to catch my plane, but I'll be in contact with you as soon as I have any news," Lir said.

Adya and Lir started to leave the office when Ted added, "And Adya, you and I will be having a conversation in the next day or two."

Adya cringed internally but continued heading back outside with Lir. "I didn't think you were going to tell him about us," she admitted to Lir when they were out of Ted's earshot.

"He's not blind, Adya. He noticed my Claddagh ring almost immediately."

The days following Adya's skiing mishap, they two spend a lot of time relaxing in the hotel. In the spirit of Adya's New Year's resolution, they came up with the idea together to make a stop in Ireland on the way back to the Academy to pick out authentic promise rings to help them feel more connected when they returned to their regular lives. They both wore a subtle silver ring on their right hands with the heart facing inwards. "I'm positive it wasn't hard to put two and two together since he was aware you were with me in Switzerland."

Adya nodded. "I suppose you're right, but it's still none of his business who I do or do not choose to love." She flashed a smile, full of adoration, at Lir.

Lir smiled back. "Yes, but who you love and how others treat you because of it is of great concern to me." Lir sighed and stopped next to the car that had been waiting for him and wrapped his arms around Adya, "I'm gonna miss you, *mo ghaol.*"

Unexpectedly, Adya didn't feel any sadness, and her smile was genuine when he said he was going to miss her. "I'm going to miss you, too. I'm going to fly to Greenland the second the semester is over, and we can spend the summer together." Adya allowed her crutches to fall to the ground as she wrapped her arms around Lir's neck. "Promise you'll call me when you get there and when you talk to Maggie and any other time you're thinking about me."

"It's gonna be one hell of a phone call, lasting for five months," Lir grinned.

"You can be so cutely cheesy," Adya said with complete adoration. "I love you, Lir. Thank you for a magical trip."

"I love you, too, Adya, more than you know." Lir kissed Adya fiercely before he picked up her crutches and handed them to her. "Remember, don't open the gift until I call you. Promise me," he said as he hovered in the doorway of the car.

"I don't know why I have to wait, but fine. I swear I won't open it until you call. Be safe and stay warm, okay?" Finally, Adya could feel the emotion pooling in her eyes.

"Stay true to yourself, *mo ghaol.* I'll talk to you soon." Lir slid into the backseat and closed the door.

Adya stood and watched until the car disappeared before returning to her resident hall to unpack and resettle into her life as a student at North Shore Academy.

"Are you sure you're alright?" Sierra asked as she joined Adya on her bed. Sierra arrived before Ashley and noticed Adya hadn't seemed like her usual self when Sierra told her all about her Christmas with her family.

"Yeah, I'm going to be fine," Adya said with determination as she somewhat anxiously twisted her promise ring on her finger. While this parting from Lir didn't feel as heartbreaking as their previous one had, Adya felt a different kind of sadness in knowing that the soul she loved was going to be absent from her life for months. She took a cleansing breath and said, "I got something for you in Switzerland."

Sierra's worried eyes lit up. "You bought me a gift?"

"Of course. You didn't think I could go to a faraway winter wonderland and not think about my friends at all, did you?" Adya opened her desk drawer where she had placed Sierra and Ashley's gifts, as well as the one she promised Lir she wouldn't open until he called. "I hope you like it."

Sierra accepted the small rectangular gift from Adya and quickly tore off the wrapping paper. When she opened the box, her eyes sparkled. "Oh, Ady. It's beautiful."

Adya smiled as Sierra pulled out the silver and blue necklace. "That's a real snowflake from Switzerland in the heart-shaped charm," she explained. "It will help you with your affinity to have a part of your element from another place."

"Can you help me put it on?" Sierra asked, too excited to keep her hands steady.

Adya nodded with a chuckle. "Of course." She hopped around on her uninjured foot to stand behind Sierra and clasped the necklace around her neck while Sierra held up her hair.

"I'm never taking it off. Thank you, thank you, thank you!" the Abecedarian squealed.

"What's all the noise in here?" Ashley said as she entered the room.

"Ash!" both girls said in unison.

Sierra ran over to hug Ashley and to show off her new necklace while Adya reached for her crutches to join her friends in the doorway.

Ashley shook her head in disbelief as she watched Adya crutch over to her. "I half expected this whole broken ankle thing to be a hoax so you could spend more time in Switzerland with Lir."

"That would've been a good cover," Adya agreed and gave her old friend a tight hug. "I've missed you," she said softly, full of sincerity.

The girls spent the rest of the evening catching up and recanting their holiday away from school. Ashley loved the necklace that Adya picked out for her, a delicate silver and onyx beaded necklace with a captured snowflake in a heart in the center.

"Who's the other gift for?" Ashley commented after Sierra had gone to her room for the night.

"It's for me from Lir. But he said I couldn't open it until he calls me," Adya explained.

"So why isn't it opened now?" Ashley prodded.

Adya laughed. "I promised him I wouldn't," she replied with a shrug and then threw a warning look at her roommate. "And I keep my promises."

"But if I open it. . ." Ashley's eyes gleamed wickedly while she wiggled her fingers. "And if you happen to see what it is, you technically wouldn't be breaking your promise," Ashley suggested and started moving towards the drawer.

Adya stopped Ashley with an outstretched crutch. "Don't even *think* about it," she warned.

"Alright, alright. Fine. But we're opening it as soon as your phone rings, okay?" Ashley insisted as she reclined back on her bed.

"As soon as he calls," Adya confirmed.

Almost on cue, Adya's phone beeped with a text message, and Ashley jumped up. "A text counts, too, right?" she said, creeping towards Adya's desk again.

Adya picked up her phone and frowned. "Calm your horses, Ash. It's from Brandon. He says we need to talk." Adya tossed her phone on her desk and relaxed back onto her bed.

"Oh," Ashley replied. "Aren't you going to text him back?"

Adya shrugged. "Probably not. Our 'talks' never go well, and I'm already in a questionable mood."

Ashley rolled her eyes at Adya. "If I were you, I'd go talk to him and show off your new ring."

Adya laughed. "You are so spiteful, but that's actually a good idea." With a sigh of resignation, Adya texted him back to meet her out by the tree in ten minutes and then gathered her crutches. "Wish him luck," she said.

"Why him?" Ashley asked.

"Because I might beat him upside his head with my crutches if he tries to kiss me again." Adya smiled cheekily, and Ashley's voracious laughter followed her out of their room.

Brandon was already waiting at what used to be their tree when she hobbled up.

"Whoa, what happened?" he asked and then moved to help Adya.

"I don't need your help," she insisted and stopped when she was within five feet of him. Her eyes narrowed as she looked at him. "What do you want to talk about?"

"Do you notice anything different about me?" he started.

With the tree branches shading most of the artificial light, she hadn't paid much attention to how he looked. "Did you get a haircut?" Adya asked vindictively but already knew what was different about him from the first words he spoke.

"'I will always find you in every lifetime,'" Brandon recited as a quote.

"Your promise to me on your first deathbed," Adya said without much emotion. She felt a pang in her heart despite being resolved in her choice for this lifetime. "Do you expect me to throw you a party now, Paxton? And then continue where we left off?"

The boy faltered and then shrugged. "I don't know about the party, but yeah, Ady. I thought that maybe we would keep that promise."

"It was your promise, not mine," Adya replied coldly, but sighed. "I'm sorry. I just don't know how you expect me to react to this after all the fighting you did with me as Brandon."

"Well," Paxton began and walked towards Adya, which was quickly countered by her with a step backward. He sighed and didn't bother to finish his sentence.

"Just because we've loved each other in other lifetimes doesn't mean that's going to be true in every one. Maybe because we met before we Awakened in this lifetime, or maybe there's more to love than fate. I don't know, but as I told you before, we all have to make our own choices in every lifetime. I've made a different choice this time," Adya said with all the inner strength she could muster.

"Oh," he replied, sounding deflated. Paxton nodded his head and walked past Adya.

Adya closed her eyes and breathed a sigh of relief but immediately tensed again when Paxton turned back around and continued.

"I don't give a damn about fate or choices. A part of me has always known that I love you, Ady, and I acted in stupid ways before I Awakened. I can't apologize for being a fourteen-year-old kid and not seeing the bigger picture. It's a real shitty trick that Lir pulled by manipulating you to him before I Awakened and could know what I was fighting for. No, I'm not going to give up fighting for you or us in this lifetime."

Adya spun around and practically fell over. "The two of you have played this childish game every lifetime since you and I first met, and it's getting old. I'm not an object to be won or lost, nor does anyone have a claim on my soul. I am my own person in every lifetime, and I get to make my own choices." Adya noticed the shock and dismay in Paxton's eyes, and she tried to calm herself down a little by taking a deep breath. "Lir didn't manipulate me. His actions had nothing to do with you or what you and I have shared in past lives. I have loved him for longer than you've been alive in any of your lifetimes."

"I never said you didn't love him," Paxton interjected.

The frustrations in Adya started to build again. "If you hadn't been such an asshole to me for most of the time we've known each other in this lifetime, maybe you would've had a chance. You and I—that would've been so easy. We go to the same Academy, we're in the same class, and no one would even bat an eye at us being together. I will *not* apologize for giving you the chance to show your true self in this lifetime, nor will I change my mind about who I choose to love. I'm in love with Lir, and as soon as this body ages appropriately, *he* is who I will spend this life with." This time it was Adya who stormed—or rather angrily crutched—her way past him back to her dorm.

The only thing Adya needed at that moment was thousands of miles away on a plane to Greenland. She stared at her phone, willing it to ring until she passed out from sheer exhaustion. But she didn't sleep soundly that night. Adya awoke nearly every hour and checked her phone, but there weren't any missed calls or text messages from Lir. She would've thought he would've at least texted when the plane stopped to refuel.

The following morning, Adya's foul mood was even worse. While the other students happily chatted about their winter breaks with their friends in the dining hall, all Adya could feel was a desperate need to talk to Lir and the palpable tension that hung in the air between her and Paxton. She barely touched her breakfast, and Ashley, Sierra, and Calder sat in uncomfortable silence around her, afraid to be on the receiving end of the wrath they could feel boiling in their friend.

At the end of the meal, Calder had finally worked up enough courage to speak to Adya. "Need any help getting to class?" he offered.

In a surprising tone of calm resolution, Adya replied, "I'm not going to class. Excuse me," she said and stood from the table, leaving her bewildered friends behind.

Adya checked her phone every minute, but there was still nothing from Lir despite her more than numerous texts and phone call attempts. The insides of her arms ached from aimlessly walking all over campus while the other students were in their classes. She wanted to scream in frustration, but mostly, she needed to hear Lir's voice and to tell him about Paxton and how she had said to him that she was choosing Lir. Adya was so proud of herself for that, but also angry that Lir seemed to be ghosting her. She wondered if the gift was some kind of break up façade and was on the verge of opening it up several times, but her heart knew that Lir was sincere when he said he loved her, and he certainly wouldn't break up with her like this. So, she left the gift wrapped in her desk and found other outlets for her wild emotions.

Sitting on the dock at the lake, she switched between freezing the body of water and making it boil. When she grew tired of that, she forced gusts of wind to break off dormant tree branches and blow them into the water.

By lunch, Adya had drawn a small crowd of onlookers who finally dispersed when Ted walked out to her.

"Something is obviously bothering you, Adya," Ted began with his calm and collected tone. "Why don't we go to my office and talk?"

"Why? So you can berate me some more for my relationship with Lir?" Adya fired at him. "No, thanks."

Ted took a deep breath and tried again. "Actually, I wanted to give you a chance to express yourself healthily before you took out half of New Orleans with a tornado."

Something in Adya's erratic mind heard reason in Ted's words. "Fine," she growled and pushed herself to stand. When Ted tried to help, she shot him a direct glare. "I can do this myself."

The two walked in civil silence to Ted's office, where he immediately closed his door after she'd entered.

"You don't have to tell me what's flared this destructive mood of yours, but I'll listen if you want to talk." Ted calmly took a seat in his chair behind the desk while Adya stood uncomfortably, balancing with her crutches.

"What I really need is to talk to Lir," Adya stated flatly.

"He's likely still on his way to Kangerlussuaq. It's a pretty long flight, and he's been gone for barely twenty-two hours. If you factor in the time to refuel the aircraft, I will guess he should be contacting you shortly," Ted said calmly.

"The texts I've sent him have gone through. He knows I need to talk to him, but he hasn't even messaged back." Adya finally sat down and sighed. She knew she sounded like a crazy stalker, but between her encounter with Paxton, the lack of response from Lir, and her sleep-deprived mind, Adya had nearly convinced herself that something was wrong.

"I haven't heard from him, either, but if I do, I'll make sure he's spoken with you or will speak with you after we talk. There aren't reports of missing airplanes or anything out of the ordinary, so try relaxing. If you'd like, I can try calling him now," Ted offered.

Adya couldn't decide if it would be better for Lir to answer Ted's call or if it would only make her worry more. In the end, she shook her head. "No, I'm sure you're right. I'm just tired and in a bit of pain."

"Why don't you go see Gaia. She can help with the pain and maybe give you some tea that will help you get some sleep," Ted suggested.

His phone started ringing, and Adya decided that his suggestion was better than her torturing her elements, so she stood and briefly thanked him before exiting his office.

"*Hello?*" Adya heard Ted answer his phone as soon as she was in the hallway.

"*Thank you for calling. Yes, I wondered why we didn't see him back at the Academy. No, I understand. We'll definitely miss him.*"

Adya wasn't trying to eavesdrop, but with her slow-moving self, she understood the gist of the phone call Ted accepted. She thought back to her first day at North Shore when he said they never had any students voluntarily leave, and realized that someone not returning after winter break had to be significant for some reason, but she couldn't fathom what that could be.

Visiting Gaia turned out to be precisely what Adya needed. Not only did she help with the pain, but she gave her something to help her bone mend faster. Adya was sent back to her dorm to drink some sleep-inducing tea and to rest.

While waiting for the tea to kick in, Adya turned up the volume of her phone and laid it on the pillow beside her head so she wouldn't miss Lir's call. Within minutes, Adya's body finally relaxed, and she drifted off into a much-needed sleep.

CHAPTER TEN

Adya yawned and stretched when Ashley's piercing alarm woke her. Although a bit groggy, she felt remarkably better than she had when she'd fallen asleep.

"Good morning," Adya said with another yawn.

"Oh my god. You're finally awake!" Ashley said with way too much enthusiasm for the early morning.

"Yeah, well, your alarm made sure of that." Adya tapped her phone to check for missed messages, but there weren't any. She sighed with frustration but didn't feel a fraction of the anger or worry as she had before the sleep.

"You've been asleep for like two and a half days!" Ashley said.

Adya blinked and rubbed her eyes. "Two and a half days?" She shot up into a sitting position ignoring the lance of pain in her ankle, "What?!"

"Yeah. I've never even slept that long, although I know I felt like I could've before. You scared me half to death, you know. Gaia said you were fine, though, and that your body just needed to heal. How are you feeling?"

"There's no way I was asleep for that long. Lir would've called. This isn't a funny joke, Ash." Adya could feel the panic rising inside her.

"No one called that I know of," Ashley said with a frown. "Maybe he thought you'd be better off without him?"

Adya defiantly shook her head. "No, Lir wouldn't just ghost me. Something's wrong." Adya tried to stand, but nothing in the room would stay still. She fell right back onto her bed with a frustrated, "Ugh."

"Yeah, what did you expect? You haven't eaten in like three days. Stay there. I'll go grab some food for you and let Gaia know you're finally awake," Ashley suggested.

Adya ran her fingers through her greasy hair while trying to make sense of things. She picked up her phone again but found no messages still. When she attempted to call Lir, the call went directly to voicemail. She tried texting, but it didn't notify her that it was received. Looking back at her other texts that were received, none of them were marked as "read." Restarting her phone didn't yield any different results; Adya didn't know whether to cry or scream.

Ashley returned shortly with some fruit for Adya. "Gaia will be right here. Are you feeling any better?" she asked cautiously, taking a seat next to her friend.

Adya tossed her phone to Ashley. "No. His phone is going straight to voicemail, and he hasn't read any of the messages I texted him." Adya didn't care if her friend read the crazy texts she'd sent her boyfriend, and Ashley didn't give any indication that she cared what Adya had sent.

"This is really weird, Ady. I'd be flipping out, too," Ashley consoled. "Maybe he lost his phone?"

Adya shrugged in response. "I don't feel good about this, Ash. I'm terrified that something's wrong."

Ashley rubbed Adya's back, allowing her roommate to lean on her as they sat huddled on Adya's bed. "It's gonna be okay." She didn't know if that was true, but what else could Ashley say at that moment that would be of any help.

"Could you give us a minute alone, Ashley?" Ted asked as he entered their room with Gaia.

"Yeah, sure," she replied and left the room after giving Adya a comforting squeeze.

Adya looked between the adults that entered her room and closed her door. She'd never heard of a guy coming into a girl's dorm before—even Ted. Something was very wrong.

"Have you heard from Lir?" Adya asked the pair.

Gaia moved to check Adya while Ted patiently waited.

"She's fine, just her heart rate is a little on the high side," Gaia confirmed.

"I'm freaking out, so yeah, my heart rate is high," Adya said.

Gaia nodded at Ted before slipping out of the room.

"To answer your question, no, Lir hasn't called. But we found out that when the plane stopped to refuel in New York, he rented a car at the airport. The pilot says he was going to be gone for about an hour, but Lir never come back," Ted began.

"What happened to him?" Adya felt the blood drain from her face.

"We don't know," Ted admitted and placed a calming hand on Adya's forearm. "The rental company tracked the car; it was abandoned at a diner off the highway outside of the city. There were no signs of struggle, no signs that he was injured or anything like that."

"But you don't know where he is now?" Adya was already blinking in a sad attempt to keep tears from forming in her eyes.

Ted shook his head. "When the Elders sent investigators to the diner, only one person recalled seeing him. He was chatting with a woman that matches Maggie's description. I know he was trying to convince her to come back to the Academy."

"And you think they just took off together? Lir wouldn't just disappear with Maggie. They were friends, but nothing romantic, if that's what you're trying to suggest," Adya said defensively.

Ted shook his head. "I'm not suggesting that at all. I don't doubt how Lir felt about you. One of the reasons he accepted the project in Greenland was because he was concerned about his feelings for you and knew that it would be a conflict of interest for him to stay. No, he didn't leave with Maggie for romantic reasons, but I'm not sure you're going to like my theory either."

Adya frowned darkly. "What's your theory?"

"We know that Eli and Myra have been recruiting. Aside from Maggie, we have ten students that have opted not to return. Some of them have said they are attending another school, while others just said they were not coming back. So, my guess is that Maggie recruited Lir." The stress of the situation was showing on Ted's face. He looked older and wasn't his usual optimistic self.

"Lir wouldn't have allowed them to recruit him," Adya said confidently. "And I don't believe Maggie would've taken him by force. Is it possible they both just fled to protect themselves from Myra or Eli or whatever recruiting tactics they're using?"

"It's possible, but as time passes and neither of them has contacted the Elders or us—" Ted sighed. "The Elders are meeting tonight to discuss what our strategy will be. The technology that allowed Myra to have her second affinity wasn't some kind of magic; there's a method the machine uses to extract a soul from another person. In Myra's situation, there was another affinate who was injured and declared brain dead. His family permitted us to do the procedure."

"Myra threatened to steal my soul," Adya recalled. "She said she wanted my two affinities because they were the ones she was lacking. Obviously, this was before Myra knew about my earth affinity, but that's not important. My point is that she's a monster. I have to believe if Eli has been encouraging and helping her, that he's a monster, too, and will steal affinate souls without hesitation." Adya felt sick to her stomach with the thought of them taking Lir's soul. "What happens, you know, to the body when they remove a soul?"

Ted shrugged. "We don't know. The boy who donated his soul was brain dead, so after the procedure, he was taken off life support and died just like he would've if his soul was still within him."

Adya's jaw clenched. "I want to talk with the Elders. I want to help find Lir and Maggie and stop Myra."

Ted shook his head. "You are a student, and you'll remain safely here."

"I wasn't asking for permission. They've taken *my* family, *my* boyfriend, and I'm the only one that's ever fought against Myra and won, I might add. I'm the only tri-affinate, and I'm damn near the oldest soul left on this earth. I've battled people more formidable than Myra and won."

"And you've lost battles, too," Ted reminded her. "And for the very reason that your soul *is* so old, and you *are* the only tri-affinate—we hope—is all the more reason to keep you far away from them."

"I can't just sit around and hide." Adya glowered darkly at Ted. "At least let me be a part of the conversation with the Elders."

After a moment of considering, Ted nodded. "Your insights on Myra could be helpful," he resigned. "Be in my office at five. I must address the rest of the students and apprise them on some of what's going on. They already see the decline in student population, and rumors are spreading."

Adya spent the day trying to figure out a way to find Lir and Maggie before the meeting with the Elders. Her ideas weren't great, but she was able to locate Lir's phone with GPS tracking. At least she would have this to present to the Council as a possible lead.

The office was noisy when Adya entered just before five, but it was only Ted and Adamina in the office itself; everyone else was on speakerphone.

"Yeah, well twelve are gone from my Academy," one man insisted.

"My seven missing aren't any less important than your twelve," another said.

Adya frowned as she looked between Ted and Adamina.

"Students have left every Academy in North America," Ted explained to Adya in a whisper.

"What is the Council doing to stop this so-call recruiting?" a woman interjected.

"If everyone will quiet down, we can get started with answering all your questions." Adya recognized the woman speaking as Elder Tama. She gave a brief rundown on everything they already knew, including information about the soul transfer project that Eli spearheaded. Most of the other headmasters on the call were learning about it for the first time. "Ted? Is Adya there with you? I'd like for her to give everyone information about Myra and her abilities."

Adya was genuinely surprised by the request but stepped up and filled everyone in with hopefully valuable information, including Myra's abilities and what she did with those abilities at North Shore. "I think the most important thing to understand about Myra is that her goal isn't to balance the elements; she only wants power. She craves it, in fact, and will destroy anyone and everyone who gets in her way if they aren't strong enough to counter her." Adya looked pointedly at Ted when she said the last part. "I've located Lir's phone in a town called Dobbs Ferry in New York, so maybe Myra and Eli have taken people there."

"The diner where Maggie and Lir left together is in Dobbs Ferry. My guess is that they ditched their phones there before running off to wherever Myra and Eli have made their base." Adya recognized the man's voice from when she visited Elder Tama's estate and assumed he was an Elder.

"They didn't run-off to join Myra and Eli," Adya retorted. "They were taken," she insisted.

Ted interjected while Adamina rested a warning hand on Adya's shoulder. "What Adya is trying to say is that we can't assume everyone who's left the Academies did so willingly."

"We do know that all of the students who left traveled to New York, New Jersey, or Connecticut during winter break. We have teams of investigators working on pinpointing their location. Once we know where they are, we can come up with a plan to safely extract the students and subdue Eli, Myra, and whatever adults they've recruited," Elder Tama stated. "Additionally, Eli has withdrawn all his funds from his accounts, so we can't track him by tracing his transactions. All we know is that his final withdrawal was from a bank in Massachusetts."

Muffled conversations transpired between several of the call participants, talking with people in the same room as them. Ted and Adamina had a side conversation, too, that didn't include Adya.

When most of the side chatter had settled down, Elder Tama continued, "You have all received emails on how to address the students at your school. If anyone gets a suspicious text, call, or email, I want it reported to the Council immediately. If no one else has any questions, let's break and take care of the students at our schools. Go with balance, everyone."

The call ended, and Adya sulked in a chair. "So that's it? We go about our lives like nothing is wrong and *hope* that they can somehow locate Myra and Eli? That's bullshit."

"Our priority, Adya, is to keep you students safe. The Elders have resources to find and deal with them," Adamina explained as if Adya was a child that didn't understand the scope of the situation.

"When you have people you love being held captives by psychopaths, then you can console me with the administrative crap. I'm not going to sit here and do nothing." Adya stood with the help of her crutches.

"Adya," Ted warned.

"You heard them, Ted! They think Maggie and Lir joined with Myra. Do you think it'll be 'safe' for them when and if the Council finds them? Not to mention what is *actually* being done to them while we sit here being 'safe.'" Adya started for the door. "You guys go ahead and keep us safe. I'm going to figure out a way to find them and make sure *they* are safe." She stormed out of Ted's office.

"Let her go," Adya heard Ted instruct Adamina.

Adya didn't know where she was going, though. She didn't have a plan, only her determination to save the two people in the world she loved most. Suddenly she realized she needed someone's help, and not just anyone's—Paxton's.

I know I'm the last person who has any right to ask anything from you, but can you meet me by the tree? I need your help. Adya read over the text about fifty times before she finally hit send and waited. She obsessively checked for replies, clicking and re-clicking the phone screen just as it was about to turn off. After several minutes, Adya raised her arm to throw the device into the lake, frustrated by the days of waiting for replies that never came, when she heard someone approaching.

"You're right. You have no right to ask me for anything," Paxton began stiffly as he walked up behind Adya. Almost immediately, he relaxed slightly. "What is it?"

Adya filled him in on everything from the letter Maggie received from Lucas to Lir and Maggie's disappearance from the diner. "And there are students all over the country that left their Academies over winter break. No one *ever* leaves voluntarily, or at least that's what Ted told us our first day."

Paxton stood quietly with his hands in his pockets and listened, nodding occasionally. "I get why you're so upset about this, but why should I care and what do you think I could possibly do if I did care."

Adya took several deep breaths. She knew she couldn't afford to blow up at him if she had any hope of him helping her. "Because I know you still care about me regardless of how awful I've been or how much I've hurt you with my choices."

"I have zero desire to help Lir no matter the situation," he began. "But you're right. I do still care about you." Paxton sighed. "I know how important Maggie is to you, too. So, what do you need from me?"

It wasn't the exact offer Adya wanted, but with his help to find Maggie, she knew she'd discover Lir, too. "I need to know everything you know about Myra, anything at all that could help me find her and ultimately defeat her. You were close to her for months. Did she ever mention anything about running away somewhere with you or anything like that?"

Paxton took a seat on the ground with his back resting against the trunk of the tree like he used to do when they would share Saturday brunches there. It felt strange to Adya to be there with him again. They were different people than those kids who played with their new elemental abilities.

"She never mentioned anywhere specific, but there were a few times when she said that she and I should just run away together and start a new school," Paxton said with a shrug. "But you already know that most of our time together was focused on making her stronger."

"I know, and I know she's strong," Adya nodded. "But Myra doesn't know how to absorb fire like you," she admitted. "When you were unconscious, she tried to drag you away with her. That's when I unleashed on her." Adya didn't know why she was telling Paxton this. In truth, she would've fought the devil himself—if he was real—to save Paxton at that time.

"Thank you," Paxton said. "And for what it's worth, I'm sorry about how I've treated you this year. I think the part of me that was Brandon just wanted to hold onto 'normal' a little longer. I didn't want to feel like I was fated to live a life from the past. The more of our soul memories I experienced, the more I fought to have my own life. I didn't fully understand the gravity and scope of it all until I completed the Awakening."

Adya rested her crutches against the tree and lowered herself down to sit beside Paxton. "As Calder once described it to me, it's a real mind fuck." That was the first time in what felt like ages that Adya chuckled. "You know I still love you,

Pax," she admitted. "I always will, even if you didn't come to help me with this. I know it's not the same love that we've had in the past, but that doesn't mean I wouldn't face-off with Satan to save you again."

"I'd do the same for you, too, Ady," Paxton replied. "But I don't know how much help I can be right now. I don't have any idea where Myra could be."

Adya thought for a minute and then pulled out her phone. She brought up a map of Dobbs Ferry and shrunk the map to show the surrounding areas. "They are somewhere around here," Adya said as she handed her phone to Paxton. "We know that Myra had no desire to balance the elements, so what if we could use the elements to 'feel' where they were most unstable around this area?"

"How could we do that from here, though?" Paxton asked as he zoomed in and out of the map to see different areas.

Adya furrowed her brows as she tried to think of a solution. "Will you take me to the make-out spot?" she asked suddenly.

"What?!" Paxton exclaimed. "You want to go make out with me, that's your solution? You've gone insane, haven't you?"

Adya glared at him as she used the tree as leverage to stand again. "I didn't say I wanted to make out with you," she sighed and shook her head. "Ash told me that it's a spot that's out of view of all the windows here. What I *want* to do, I don't necessarily want people to see. Do you even know where it is?"

Paxton glowered back at Adya, but stood, too. "Everyone knows where it is. Where have you been?"

"Oh, I don't know. . . maybe spending half a year getting over my boyfriend dumping me, dealing with my mom's death, and fighting off Myra kept me too busy to find time to go off and dry hump someone," she replied tartly as they walked past the dock and down the shoreline away from the buildings.

"You sure had a lot of time to spend with Lir, though," Paxton grumbled from a couple of steps ahead, walking a little faster than Adya because of her handicap.

Adya growled and caused vines to extend from the ground, rooting Paxton in place. "Just because I need your help doesn't give you the right to act like an asshole to me," she explained as she crutched past him.

"Not cool, Ady. Let me go. I thought you needed me to show you where this place was," Paxton leveraged.

Adya rolled her eyes, and with a flick of her fingers, the plant released Paxton and disappeared back into the earth. "I don't have to justify myself to you, but there was never anything going on between Lir and me last year. He was my teacher and just wanted to help me learn to use all of my affinities."

Paxton quickly caught back up with Adya. "Whatever you need to tell yourself," he said with a hint of playfulness. "C'mon, Ady. We used to take shots like that at each other all the time. When did you lose your sense of humor?"

Adya looked over at him and sighed. "When two people you love are being held captive by your ex's maniacal ex, having their soul sucked from their bodies. . . you tell me what kind of joking mood you're in."

Paxton held up his hands in defeat. "Fine, fine. Nothing but seriousness from here on out. The spot is just over there," he motioned with his hand. "So, what's this big secretive plan?"

Adya looked around before responding. "If we work together, we might have enough strength to channel out through the elements to find them. I know it's a long shot, but I don't have any other ideas aside from jumping on a plane and flying there."

"How exactly would you be able to jump on a plane? Don't you need money for a ticket? Or were you planning on committing acts of terrorism and hijacking one?"

"I have access to some of my old accounts," Adya said as she settled on a spot to stand and let her crutches fall to the ground. As she balanced on her good foot, she motioned for Paxton to join her. "C'mere and help me take off my shoe," she instructed.

"Take off your shoe?" Paxton blinked incredulously but sighed and did as she asked. "Do I need mine off, too?"

"Yes, please," Adya said, still trying to figure out if what she wanted to do was even possible. The cold soil under her foot helped ground her in her thoughts.

"You realize it's the middle of winter. The ground is freezing," Paxton complained.

"So warm up your feet then," she suggested. After a moment and Paxton's hopping back and forth between his feet had calmed down, she said, "Now take hold of my hands." Adya held her hands in front of her with her palms facing upwards.

Paxton stood in front of Adya and placed his hands on top of hers. "Nice ring, by the way," he added snidely.

Adya threw him a warning glance. "Do you think that maybe for just a second, you could set aside your jealousy to help me?"

Paxton shrugged. "It was a compliment. What do you need me to do?"

Adya was winging it and didn't exactly know what to do but tried to sound confident regardless. "Close your eyes and think about that map," she started.

"Okay, the map of Dobbs Ferry. It's next to the Hudson River, and a highway runs through it. There are parks all around it, but I didn't see a good place to harness fire there," he said and opened his eyes.

"Fire is everywhere, even when you can't see it," Adya reminded him. "Close your eyes again and call upon the fire to create a circle around us here while picturing a ring of fire around the area we're searching. Got it?"

Paxton focused, and within a moment, the two were standing on the inside of a ring of fire. "I've pictured it," he said, and then suddenly, his feet sunk slightly into the ground. "What the hell?"

"You called your element. I called mine. I figured pulling water from the ground was preferable to making it rain on us. Please stay focused. I need your strength for this."

Paxton settled again, although his tone indicated that he was clearly not happy about standing in a puddle of muddy water. "I'm doing my best."

Adya called upon the wind to move around them, and finally, she was satisfied with their elemental harmony. "We call upon our elements to guide us to the places where you are most unbalanced." Adya thought of the map from her phone and waited for any sign from the elements of imbalance. Anxious, she pleaded, "Please help us restore the balance."

Abruptly, images flashed through Adya's mind. She traveled above a muddy river and felt a hint of disharmony that seemed to grow stronger the further north on the river she moved with her mind.

"Yes," she whispered, "it's working."

The elements shifted to the left, and she was over land with the earth guiding her towards buildings when someone walked upon the ritual. "What's going on here?" It was Gaia, and she wasn't happy to see the students working with the elements outside of the classroom.

Paxton and Adya's hands dropped, and the elements they'd called around them faded back to their original places. "We were just, um, trying to f—" Paxton started.

Adya immediately interrupted him. "We were trying a new ritual I learned in Switzerland. We just wanted to bring harmony back to the Academy with all the students missing and whatnot," Adya improvised. She shot Paxton a knowing look, encouraging him to go along with the scenario she was weaving.

"Yeah, I was telling Ady that everyone seemed a bit off with everything going on. We were just trying to help," he lied.

Gaia seemed doubtful and still not pleased. "I usually find students out here kissing when I'm gathering herbs, not doing unauthorized rituals. You both need to return to your residence halls. I don't want to see you out here again."

"Yes, Gaia," the two said together.

"And Adya, you need to stay off your foot if you want it to heal," Gaia added.

Adya nodded at Gaia while Paxton handed Adya her crutches and shoe before picking up his own. After they were out of earshot from Gaia, Paxton stopped to put on his shoes. "Did you see anything?" he asked, looking up at Adya, who was content feeling the ground on her bare foot.

"Not enough. I felt like I was getting close to seeing where Lir and Maggie were when Gaia found us," Adya sighed.

"Well, close to where they were or maybe just to where there's a major elemental imbalance in the area. We don't even know if it was leading us to Myra and Eli." Paxton's words were tinged with skepticism.

"I was pulled north of Dobbs Ferry on the Hudson, and then I was following it to the west of the river onto land. It was still pulling me west, but even when we got interrupted, I felt I was getting close."

"New City," Paxton said as he stood up from tying his shoes. "I recognized New City when the fire was pulling me towards the imbalance. My dad took us there one summer because he was going to buy some real estate in the town. I'm positive it's what I saw."

Adya dropped her shoe and pulled out the map on her phone again. "Yes, this could be what I saw, too. I don't think that's where they are, but they're definitely close. Thanks for your help, Pax. I really appreciate it."

Paxton picked up Adya's shoe again but didn't release it when he handed it to her. "You're going to tell Ted about this, right?"

"Oh, yeah. Sure. I'm going to go tell Ted about it right now," Adya said dismissively. "Goodnight, Pax," she said but didn't move to leave.

Paxton grabbed Adya's upper arm and sternly looked down at her face as they stood close together. "You can't go there by yourself. You'll end up getting nabbed by Myra and won't be able to save anyone. Let the Elders handle this," he warned.

"They think Maggie and Lir joined with Myra. If I let them handle this—"

"We don't know that they *didn't* voluntarily join with Myra and Eli," Paxton insisted.

"And that's exactly why I have to do this alone." Adya stared up at Paxton, filled with determination and resolve. "Go back to your dorm and believe that I am going to tell Ted what we know."

"How am I supposed to do that?" Paxton said. His eyes flickered with passion as he looked down at Adya. "I told you that I would fight for you."

"Then buy me some time. If I get into trouble, you'll know exactly where I'll be. I'll text you, and you *will* know that I need help. Talk to Ted then," Adya pleaded.

"I can't just let you go," Paxton insisted.

"You have to," Adya replied and maneuvered away from him. "I'll see you again soon. I promise."

"You have twenty-four hours. If I don't hear from you, I'm going to Ted. For the love of the elements, Adya, be careful, and be safe." Paxton sighed and took a step backward towards his residence hall.

Adya watched him for a moment before turning towards the gates that led out of the Academy.

CHAPTER ELEVEN

I n an attempt to stay off the Elder's radar, Adya withdrew a small amount of cash from random ATMs in New Orleans before making her way to Louis Armstrong International Airport. She bought the cheapest flight to the airport closest to New City, New York, and within a couple of hours of leaving the Academy, she was on a plane to Teterboro Airport in New Jersey.

While her cast and crutches helped her gain the sympathy of the airport staff, as soon as she landed in New Jersey, she ditched them both, thinking they would only slow her down. It was painful to remove the cast with her ankle still mending, but she had faith that Gaia's concoction, along with her own elemental work on her body, would be enough to allow her to walk close to normal.

In the taxi from the airport, Adya turned her phone back on. She had seventeen missed text messages, fifteen from Ashley alone demanding to know where she was. Thankfully, none of them were from Ted, but two were from Paxton. "24 hours" was the first, and "Be safe" was the second. Adya didn't send anything back to either of them and hoped her friends believed that she was capable of this.

Adya arrived in New City almost an hour after touchdown at the airport. She tipped her cab driver well and told him to tell anyone that might ask that his fare was a businessman returning home after a trip. It was nearly midnight when she set out on her slower-than-normal walk through the quiet streets of the city. Adya was exhausted, but her determination to find Lir outweighed any other feelings.

It was a cold night, and there was old snow on the ground. Adya shivered as she found her way to a place called Demarest Kill Park. She chuckled darkly at the name and then found a quiet spot near a frozen pond to channel her elements. It was brutally cold, and while the wind was calm, she could feel the heat rapid escaping her body. Adya wished at that moment that Paxton was there to bring fire, but then recanted and desired Lir to provide her the warmth she craved. After all, Lir kept her warm in Switzerland, and it was much colder waiting for the helicopter on the mountain. Adya was more determined than ever to find him.

With a book of matches she bartered from the cab driver, Adya lit some leaves and sticks on fire after extracting the moisture from them. She called on her elements to protect her, protect the fire, and to guide her to where the balance was most needed. Even without the elements' help, she could feel the imbalance in the air; she knew she had to be close but didn't know which direction to explore. A profound meditation with the elements would help bring her the clarity she needed.

"I call on the elements to—" Adya began saying the words to the ritual that she and Paxton did at North Shore. "Just please help me find Lir," she begged.

This time the elements didn't guide her on a journey, but rather directly to a destination. There were old buildings that looked like they had been vacant for decades. A nearly collapsing chain-link fence surrounded the desolate buildings with "No Trespassing" signs halfway falling off. Adya followed the path the elements guided her down—through a hallway, out a door, and into another building. There were a few people that looked to be standing guard in the hall, although they looked more like the palace guards in London with their expressionless faces and icy blank stares than regular security guards.

The invisible force guiding her out-of-body journey transformed into a trickling stream. Adya followed it as is seemed to beckon her around the corner and to the end of the adjacent hallway. Two of the stone-faced guards were outside the room standing beside the door imbedded with a safety glass window and iron bars to see through. Without a physical body to stop her, Adya flowed with the water into the decaying room. Peeling white paint flecked from the walls, exposing the aged drywall beneath. Near the barred window was a stained mattress placed on a rusty bed frame. And in the center of the floor sat a man slumped over, imperceptibly shallow breaths making his shoulders rise and fall.

Adya's heart raced as she moved around to see the man's face; it was her love. "Lir!" she called out, but without physically being there, no sound made it to his ears. Perhaps it was the water that led her to him that helped them communicate because he looked up from his meditative pose when she called to him.

"Adya," he whispered, but he looked defeated. The scruff that would have taken days of him not shaving to appear on his beautiful face was well-grown in. Both of his eyes were bloodshot like he had been crying or hadn't slept for days, and his left eye had a mottled black circle around it.

"I'm close. I'm coming," Adya told Lir, wanting nothing more than to press her hands against him and heal him.

"Don't come," he whispered.

"Don't be such an impolite guest, Lir," a female voice behind him said.

Adya felt the tension in the room rise.

"Go away," Lir instructed the intruder.

"Now, now, don't be like that, my darling pet. I've been waiting for you to call out to our friend. Lucky me that I happen to be walking by when you said her name." Myra stroked Lir's cheek as she circled him. "Funny thing about elements. . . when you're strong enough, you can feel even their subtle shifts."

Lir turned his head sharply away from Myra's touch but remained silent.

Adya could feel her anger rise in her corporeal body, and it threatened to pull her away from Lir. She calmed herself with deep breaths while trying to focus on clues about the location.

"Now be a good boy and invite Emily—or Adya—or whatever she's calling herself now—to join us here. I have so many new things to show her." With a flick of her wrist, the window in Lir's room opened. Snow carried by a strong wind swept into his room and onto him.

Adya watched in horror as Myra tormented Lir. He shivered as the cold air surrounded him, and then he was suddenly clasping his neck, trying to gasp for the air that should've been readily available around him.

Within a moment, Myra released her torture and allowed Lir to breathe again. The window closed, and Lir drew his knees to his chest, huddling as he shivered on this floor.

"Don't keep us waiting. This room seems a bit—" Myra paused with a thoughtful expression before smirking maniacally. "Suffocating." Myra left the room, but Adya suspected she was still listening for Lir to talk.

"Don't say another word, my love. I will get you. Don't give up." Adya watched Lir tenderly for another moment before she allowed the elements to restore her thoughts to her body. In a teary homage, Adya thanked the elements for their help and left the park to find a place to sleep for the night. She would need all her strength if Myra was going to be waiting for her.

It wasn't long before she came across a shady-looking motel on the outer edges of the town. She bribed the less-than-attentive desk clerk to give her a room for the night. Without much effort, she was asleep on top of the dingy comforter that smelled like stale cigarette smoke.

The faint morning sun woke Adya in her motel room, and while she was still a bit tired, her foot felt markedly better. She showered quickly and was at the front desk when the morning attendant arrived.

"Did your family enjoy their stay?" the elderly man asked her as he was printing out her bill, clearly eyeing her suspiciously.

"It was fine, thank you," Adya replied. "Hey, do you know of a bunch of old abandoned buildings around here? Maybe an old insane asylum or something?"

The man chuckled. "Why is it all you kids want to go snooping around creepy old places? Yeah, Letchworth Village is down the road about eight or nine miles. Rumor has it some billionaire guy swooped in about nine months ago and paid cash for it. The town's been tryin' to sell that place for decades. I dunno why anyone would want it." The man shook his head in dismay. "I've heard it's guarded now, so you might want to be careful if you decide to head that way."

"Hmmm?" Adya said absently. She was already pulling up Letchworth Village on her phone. "Oh, yes, I'll be careful. Thank you," she murmured as she walked out the door, eyes trained on the information displayed on her phone.

A couple of miles into her walk, Adya sent Paxton a text. *"Myra and Eli have taken over a place called Letchworth Village just north of New City. In an hour, tell Ted to let the Elders know that's where they've taken everyone. I'm almost there and should be out with Maggie and Lir before the Elders' team arrives."* With her current walking speed, Adya calculated that she should arrive at the compound right around the time Paxton informed Ted and hoped that her speculations were accurate. *"Oh, and Myra has air affinity now, too, so tell them to be careful."* With the messages sent, she forced herself to quicken her pace. "I'm coming, Lir," she said aloud.

Within five minutes of sending the texts, Adya's phone rang. She considered not answering it, but on the fourth ring, she picked up the call. "Don't try to talk me out of this," Adya began.

"How do you know she has another affinity?" Paxton asked without bothering to respond to Adya's assertion.

"The elements took me inside her nuthouse. I saw her using air affinity to torture people. She's got these creepy looking guards outside the rooms where she's keeping affinates captive," Adya explained.

"Did you see Maggie?" Paxton asked.

"No, I didn't have time to explore everywhere. Myra knew I was there. She said she was waiting for me." The anger rose in Adya's voice as she recalled Myra torturing Lir.

"You saw Lir, didn't you?" Paxton guessed. He sighed and continued. "You can't go in there alone if she's waiting for you. It's painfully obvious what both of you are doing. And you have a distinct disadvantage hobbling around on those crutches."

"I got rid of the crutches and cast," Adya admitted.

"For fuck's sake, Ady," Paxton began but was interrupted by Adya almost immediately.

"I really don't care how obvious this is. I'm going to get Lir out of there before she kills him. She almost did last night, and he's already been beaten up pretty badly. I know you could care less about what happens to him, but it's my fault he's there. I have to fix this."

"It's not your fault, so quit acting like a damn martyr. If you go to Lir now, she's going to capture you, too, and then you won't be able to save anyone. C'mon, Ady. You're smarter than this," Paxton pleaded.

"What is the 'smart' thing to do, then? Hmmm?"

"Wait for the Elders to send people, but I already know you're not going to do that. So, you have to do something that Myra isn't expecting."

Adya's mind swam with ideas. *What would Myra not expect?*

"Are you still there?" Paxton asked after several minutes of silence.

"Yeah, yeah. You're right. I have to do something Myra won't expect. Thanks, Pax. Thank you for everything," Adya said sincerely. "I'm glad to have known you in this lifetime."

"Known?" Paxton asked, but Adya ended the call before he could say anything else.

While Adya had no intention of dying, she knew that her new plan put her at a higher risk of not making it out, and she sincerely felt happy meeting Paxton again in this life.

If Adya was going to ignore his warnings completely, Paxton wasn't going to honor her request for a delay before he told Ted. He tucked his phone into his pocket and headed straight to the headmaster's office.

"The elements guided us here, to New City, last night," Paxton pointed to a map that Ted brought up on his computer. "She took off there last night and said the elements showed her where Lir was locked up. . . there," Paxton pointed again to Letchworth Village. "Adya said Myra knew she was elementally there and had been waiting for her. Adya also mentioned something about Lir being tortured and that Myra has air affinity now, too."

"How long have you known about this plan of hers?" Ted demanded as he dialed someone on his phone.

"Last night, but I told her I would give her twenty-four hours before I said anything to you," Paxton admitted shamefully. "She's hell-bent on saving Maggie and Lir before the Elders condemn them for being wrapped up in this."

"And what do you think about their involvement with Myra and Eli?" Ted asked as he waited on hold.

"I don't have many nice things to say about Lir, but I trust Adya and her instincts," Paxton conceded.

The phone clicked off hold, and Ted spoke to the speaker. "I apologize for interrupting your morning meditations, Tama. We think we've uncovered where Eli and Myra have taken the affinates." Ted and Elder Tama had a brief discussion while he filled her in on how they'd been located. "And I'm sure you've guessed by now, but Adya is on her way there as we speak. It's critical that we get some people there, but there are innocents in the area that need to be protected."

While Paxton had never met Elder Tama or even talked to her before, he could tell she was not happy with the current situation. "I will pass along your warning, Ted. This is the situation we were trying to avoid." The Elder stopped short of blaming Ted for allowing a student to go astray, but the tension in the air suggested that a private conversation would be forthcoming. "Take care that none of your other students go missing. I'll call you back as soon as I have any pertinent information to share."

Ted massaged his temples in frustration and worry while Paxton looked on feeling helpless and a bit guilty. Paxton knew he couldn't have stopped Adya from leaving, but he should've insisted harder that she wait or at least allow him to accompany her.

"Tell me more about this ritual you and Adya did last night. I haven't heard of anything like that before," Ted said as he motioned for Paxton to take a seat.

CHAPTER TWELVE

A fter an unexpected but smart delay at a local farmer's market, Adya arrived at Letchworth Village. A spray-painted wood sign that read "The Institute" welcomed her.

"Charming," Adya murmured sarcastically under her breath as she stood in the shadows of an oak tree on the outskirts of the compound, out of sight of the nearby buildings. She watched as some affinates milled around the campus and recognized a fourth-year student from North Shore manipulating the air around her to make snowflakes fall around herself and her companion. Adya could have sworn the girl was a fire affinate and frowned as the two friends laughed.

Beyond those two, there was a group of seven standing around a ruined building. They linked hands and plants sprouted out of the frozen ground around the structure. The vines twisted their way up the walls and joined on the crumpled roof to create a new one made from the earth itself. There was beauty in their work, Adya thought, but even in her simple observations, she could tell the elements weren't in harmony in this newly claimed place. Shortly after that thought, the building next to the one they restored caught fire. Even from her distance, she could feel the intensity of the heat. About twenty affinates ran towards the flames in an attempt to control it. She took this as her opportunity to move in closer.

Adya hurried through the trees, ignoring the dull ache in her ankle, and approached the building that she thought most like the one she visited with the elements the night before. As she expected, there were guards positioned outside the large, slightly worn-looking wooden doors. From her pocket, she retrieved a powdery substance she created from a particular strain of cherries and common herbs she procured at the market, and with the help of her air affinity, delivered the concoction to the sentries. While she waited a few moments for the powder to take effect, she silently gave reverence to her elements.

As soon as the guards' bodies slumped peacefully to the ground, Adya slipped inside the building. As expected, several other guards and affinates greeted her. The sleeping powder quickly filled the room, and Adya covered her nose and mouth with her elbow to protect herself against the effects. Bodies fell limp to the floor before the air was clear.

Confidence was coursing through Adya until she walked into a wall of wind mid-hallway. As the wind calmed, Adya heard clapping and footsteps approaching her.

"Well done, Emily," Myra said as she stood between Adya and the hallway leading to Lir. "Although just as stupid as ever, coming here alone. Did you really think you could put everyone to sleep and march out of here with your boyfriend?"

"It's Adya now," she reminded the model-esque young woman who addressed her. "And I never said I was alone. Others are waiting for my signal before they come in and shut you down," Adya lied. If her timing was correct, though, Paxton would've told Ted everything about thirty minutes prior, and the Elders would no doubt be sending people in to put an end to Myra and Eli's fantasy world.

Myra frowned as though she pitied Adya. "You're as naïve as you are predictable. Do you really think I'm the only person who's tired of living under the Elders and their rules?" Myra laughed. "I think if you opened your eyes a bit, you'd see there's quite a bit of discontent in our little elemental community that extends far beyond the school I've created here."

Adya eyed Myra. "You're so full of shit, Myra. The only thing you can see is your own thirst for power."

"It's Dhruva now since we're correcting each other's names. And what you see around you is a gift for all the people you treat inferiorly, you with your three affinities. Yes, I saw you look down on all your classmates who struggled with their one while you were off playing with your teacher—the special child with three. And the fact that Ted and the teachers chose to keep that a secret from the other students only emphasizes the elitism that plagues our community."

"You were always jealous of me, always having to pretend you were the most powerful." Adya scoffed. "So, this is you selflessly wanting to even-out a playing field you created in your narcissistic mind?" Adya laughed with contempt.

Dhruva shrugged indifferently. "Does it matter? I didn't create the feelings of these affinates. I only gave them the means to do something about it."

"By stealing affinates and forcing their souls into others?" Adya asked.

"It's a give-and-take scenario. Some give for the greater good so others can take and make something better. I don't know why you're struggling to understand this." Dhruva and the two guards that flanked her began walking towards Adya.

"How can you just discard lives so frivolously?" Adya held her ground.

"No one is discarded. All the affinates that have given are still very important to me," Dhruva motioned her head towards her guards. "They can fight for what they believe in without suffering from the constraints their souls burdened them with." Dhruva smiled and caressed the cheek of the guard to her right. "They're loyal, brave, and selfless soldiers.

If only the Elders had listened to Eli, they could have this force for themselves."

"They are husks of people, Dhruva. Do you really think they chose to be like that? To feel nothing?" Adya was horrified.

"They still feel," Dhruva corrected Adya and caused the guard's hand to light on fire.

Adya watched in horror as the man screamed in pain, but a moment later, Dhruva took the flame away, and the guard resumed his post beside her as if his hand didn't have fresh third-degree burns.

"Mmm, the perfect soldier. The perfect man, too, if I might add." Dhruva's smile grew even more wicked. "So now that you understand the scope of The Institute, what are we going to do with you?" The blonde tapped her cheek thoughtfully.

"I'm giving myself to you," Adya said unexpectedly. "In return, you will release Lir and Maggie."

Dhruva's expression betrayed the surprise that her voice wouldn't admit. "You aren't going to put up a fight? You'll just give yourself over to whatever lies before you in these walls?"

"In return, you release Maggie and Lir. Yes." Adya was feeling less confident about this plan if what Dhruva said was correct, and the Elders' reinforcements weren't coming.

"Well, I'm going to take you regardless," Dhruva said confidently. "But Lir is free to leave if he chooses. Consider it a gift to you for not causing more destruction to my school."

Adya felt the fury of her elements rising. She didn't like the way Dhruva was so quickly conceding to her offer. "Let him go *now*, or you will see your precious school reduced to a pile of rubble that even the elements couldn't mend."

"Come now, Ady—that is what your friends call you, right? We were off to such a good start without empty threats." Dhruva sighed dramatically. "Fine, the guards will go fetch your boyfriend, and we'll see what he decides."

Adya twisted the ring on her finger as she anxiously waited to see Lir.

A minute later, a guard returned with Lir beside him. Both took their places just behind Dhruva. "Lir, dearest. Adya here is sacrificing herself so that you can leave. What is it you would like to do?" Dhruva stepped aside to allow Lir to go.

Lir stood up straight and stared absently at Adya with the same blank stare on his face as the other guards.

"Lir," Adya begged. "Leave," she insisted but could feel the dread in her chest, and the unshed tears burned in her eyes.

Unmoved, Lir remained with the other guards.

"No!" Adya cried, and the door behind her burst open with gale-force wind.

"Well, there you have it. Lir's become quite fond of this place and our hospitality, it seems." Dhruva lifted her hand and instantly calmed the air. "And now it's time for you to live up to your end of the bargain. Guards?"

Adya couldn't tear her eyes away from Lir. She was stunned in place and felt her world closing in around her. The light in Lir's eyes was gone. As the man Adya loved approached her, he injected a shot in her neck with no sign of emotion.

"Show our new guest to her room," Dhruva instructed Lir.

Lir forcefully grabbed ahold of Adya's bicep, emptied her pockets of her phone and the little bit of money she had remaining on her, and pulled her down the hallway past Dhruva and the other guards.

"No, no, no," Adya pleaded with him. "You're still in there. Fight this. Please," she begged with tears streaming down her face.

Lir deposited Adya into a room resembling the one he was in the night prior when she visited. As he walked away from her, she tried to root him in place, but her abilities didn't work.

Dhruva appeared from the hallway. She looked in at Adya and smiled. "Oh, right. That little injection temporarily neutralized your affinities. Enjoy your stay. I'll be back to visit. . . eventually." Dhruva waved before she exited the room, followed by her two guards.

Lir was left behind to close the door. A single tear trickled down his cheek, but there was no other sign of emotion or humanity noticeable in him.

When the initial shock wore off, Adya was suffocated by her grief. The man she loved was an empty shell, and his soul was in someone else's body. She grieved the loss of her elements, too. She felt like Dhruva's guards looked—soulless—only she felt every heartbeat with an intense pain deep inside her intact soul.

For the entire first day in her cell, Adya cried, screamed, and beat the walls and window with her fists, but no one came except one guard twice a day to give her another injection and a minimal amount of food. The only upside to the whole situation was that Dhruva didn't continue to torture her by having Lir's body deliver those things.

The one thing the injections couldn't take from Adya was her memories—and her soul, too. She often sat in a lotus position on the floor under her window for long hours and revisited soul memories. This life wasn't her first, after all, when she'd been made a captive, and was she quite adept at temporarily escaping the horrors that others could inflict on people. Delving into memories of happier times helped to keep intact any sanity that was left and to deflect attention away from her broken heart.

After several days of the routine, Adya could predict the guard's arrival by the slight tingle she felt when her affinities started to become conscious again. While Adya was smart enough to know that she couldn't escape out the door without easily being captured again, she also understood as the days dragged on that no one was coming to save her. Dhruva had been telling at least one version of the truth; her insane revolution extended far beyond the chain-link fences and decaying buildings of her Institute. So, in the time between guard visits, Adya began fashioning a weapon out of the crude objects in her room. If she wasn't going to be able to escape, she was determined not to allow Dhruva to steal her soul. Adya would die before she allowed that.

The days in her cell turned into weeks, and eventually, Adya stopped trying to count the individual days. A guard would come, inject the blocker, and go. After eating the scraps of food they delivered, Adya would return to her work of creating an appropriate weapon. The rest of the time was spent blocking out her reality and escaping to other lifetimes.

One afternoon, Dhruva entered Adya's room in place of the guard. Adya remained sitting on the floor under the window, her breathing slow and calm.

"You have quite a few people worried about you," Dhruva said as she held Adya's phone in her hand.

"'I miss you so much, but I'm gonna kick your ass when you get back,'" Dhruva read. "Tsk, tsk. Your best friend in the whole world is threatening violence to you. You seem to bring out the worst in people, Ady."

Adya refused to look at Dhruva as her captor continued to bait her. "And our dear Brandon is quite a mess now that you're gone. He apparently blames himself." Dhruva cleared her voice and tried to mimic Paxton's voice as she read his text to Adya. "'I promised you I wouldn't stop fighting for you, and I haven't.' I might've dodged a bullet getting away from him, with all this lovey-dovey nonsense. Didn't he know that you and Lir had a thing?" she mused. "Whatever. I do admire the strength in his fire affinity still. Is there anything you want to say back to them before we continue with our arrangement here?" Dhruva looked at Adya while holding the phone in her hand, ready to text.

"Go to hell," Adya growled.

"Not the final words I was expecting. Are those for our dear Brandon or Ashley?"

While Dhruva fluttered her eyelids mimicking sweetness, Adya slid the metal shank she'd created from the springs of the mattress from her sleeve and plunged it into her own throat. Warmth spilled over her hands and then down her arms as they fell to the floor beside her. Adya felt herself become faint as a burning, consuming pain radiated from the wound, and blood pooled around her prone body.

Shock rooted Dhruva in place, but the wet thump of Adya's hand falling to the ground broke the momentary reverie. "Guards! Stop the bleeding and get her to the infirmary immediately! Don't let her die!"

Adya's body had gone limp, and she was struggling to keep her eyes open as one of the guards scooped her up out of the rapidly spreading puddle of blood on the floor. As the guard whisked Adya past Dhruva, she drew what little breath she had remaining and whispered, "Fuck you."

Ted frowned darkly as he read the numerous emails Elder Tama forwarded him from political, business, and military leaders from around the world. Eli and Myra had skillfully plotted with non-affinates in positions of power to band together and reject the influence of the Council of Elders. "And this takes precedence over recovering the students?" Ted asked, knuckles white as he held the phone against his ear.

"We are still trying to figure out who is on our side and who's against us. The students that went to the Institute did so willingly, so no, our priority isn't on getting them back," Elder Tama explained shortly over the receiver.

"Including Adya, who went there to *save* these people you've dismissed?" Ted argued.

"She wasn't authorized to go in there. At this point, Ted, we have to assume that she's one of them. I'm sorry. I know that's not what you want to hear. It hurts me to have to tell you that."

"Darius received a text this morning from someone whom we believe to be Maggie. He said that she was trying to find a way to get Adya out, but couldn't do it alone," Ted admitted.

"I have no one I can send on a suicide mission, Ted. I need you to focus on keeping those kids at the Academy safe," Tama countered.

"The students are safe here," he assured her. "But I'm not going to give up looking for ways to save the students who aren't so lucky. Let me know if there's anyone I can contact to help with the bureaucratic situation." Ted sighed as he hung up the phone. "Come in, Paxton," he called out to the boy who'd been standing by the door for half of the conversation with Elder Tama.

"The Elders aren't going to go after her, are they?" Paxton stormed into the room.

Ted sighed. "The last thing I need is for more students to go barging into that place. I'm sending Darius there to extract Maggie and Adya. I need for you to trust me on this, Pax."

"Adya would risk everything to save any one of us," Paxton said.

"Adya *did* risk everything and saved no one. Thank the elements that Maggie still cares about Adya enough to help her escape."

Paxton nodded. "Fine," he said in frustration. "But it's been three weeks, and this is the best plan anyone can come up with?"

Ted nodded sadly. "There's been enough chaos that's erupted since Adya got captured to keep everyone busy elsewhere, exactly how Myra and Eli want it, I'm sure." Ted frowned. "As you know, Adya is a very old soul, and with it comes a power that she hasn't even tapped into yet. If Myra and Eli steal her soul—"

Paxton nodded as Ted trailed off. "I understand. I'm glad you can find some reason to justify saving her," Paxton said sourly.

Ted narrowed his eyes at the boy. "That's not a fair assessment. Adya means a lot to a lot of people regardless of any of that. She has touched so many of our soul lives in different ways. Her soul, along with Emily's mind and body, has made her a bit—" Ted paused to think of a politically correct way to describe Adya's disposition, "—hastier in this life. She is strong enough to get through this, though. That I have no doubt."

"But you're still worried," Paxton remarked. "I can see it in your face."

"Yeah, I am worried," Ted admitted. "I don't know what to expect from Myra. As far as I know, her soul has only lived a couple of lifetimes, and all of them have left unanswered questions lingering with her deaths. Eli is a bit more predictable, but I don't believe he's calling any of the shots. He is a scientist and always wanted to do good for the affinates and bring balance to the elements. This project and Myra have brought out a side of him that I have to believe scares even himself."

"I'm going to tell Ash what you told me. I promise we'll stay here, but she's been barely eating since Ady left. She deserves to know," Paxton explained.

"That's a good idea. And with the elements' help, Adya will be back home with us soon."

"Adya told me that Myra knew when she visited Lir through the elements. So, if we're going to try this, we have to be really careful," Paxton told Ashley as they walked towards the trees that had been burned by Myra the prior year. Knowing that Gaia frequented the area around the make-out point, Paxton didn't want to risk doing another ritual there.

Ashley nodded. Her face had been in a constant state of frowning since Adya went missing. "What are we even going to say to her?"

"I don't know. Keep her morale up? Let Ady know that we're still fighting for her?" Paxton sighed. "I just want to do something, so she knows she's not alone."

Ashley touched Paxton's arm and smiled slightly. "That's a good idea. So, what do we need to do this?"

"First, take off your shoes," Paxton told her.

"What?!" Ashley exclaimed. "The ground is *freezing*!"

"I know, but we need all four elements for this to work. So, take your shoes off while I create fire around us," Paxton ordered.

"Fine," Ashley grumbled.

"Next, you need to draw up water from the ground, so we're standing in puddles."

Ashley scrunched her nose. "Ady's gonna owe me a pedicure for this."

"I'm sure she'll be happy to buy you a whole spa treatment as soon as she's back," Paxton quipped. "Okay, now all we need is wind."

The two looked at the trees, hoping a breeze would pick up, but the air was still in that late morning hour.

"Damn, this was so much easier with Ady," Paxton complained.

"Sorry that I can't be as wonderfully gifted as her," Ashley replied defensively.

Paxton sighed. "I'm not blaming you, Ash. Maybe the elements will take pity on us and work together with what we can do. Do you recall the pictures of Letchworth Village we looked at?"

"Yeah, they're like a bad scene from a horror movie." Ashley shivered.

"Pretty much. Okay, concentrate on those while I speak with the elements." Paxton took Ashley's hands, and they both closed their eyes. "We call upon our elements to join with those of Adya so that we may try to bring our friend balance and harmony."

The two waited patiently and calmly for the elements to guide them to their friend. After a couple of minutes, a gust of wind blew around them, and the two minds joined as the elements led them to the dingy room where Adya was sitting.

"*We're here*," Ashley whispered but didn't know if Adya heard her because at that moment, the door opened, and Myra walked in.

"*Don't give in to her*," Paxton encouraged, but then they both watched in horror as their friend suddenly stabbed herself in the neck with a twisted piece of metal.

The brief connection, although likely one-sided, ended abruptly, and the elements retreated from around Paxton and Ashley before they could open their eyes.

Ashley was grateful that Paxton still had her hands because she was shaking so fiercely from what she just witnessed that she probably would've collapsed onto the ground.

Paxton was shaken up by it, too, and choked out, "Did she just—"

Neither of them wanted to say the words, but both knew that Adya had taken her own life.

"She had to be compelled or something!" Ashley shouted as they gave the news to Ted.

Ted shook his head. The faint wrinkles on his face had deepened considerably in the last fifteen minutes. "Compulsion is something fictional that vampires or magicians can do. No, if Adya felt her soul was threatened, she would've rather died than let Myra take it."

Paxton agreed with a nod. "We don't know for sure if she's dead or not."

"Don't say the 'd' word. Ady's still alive. She has to be," Ashley insisted. She hadn't stopped shaking since the ritual.

"We're moving forward with our plan. Adya will be presumed as alive until we find out otherwise," Ted insisted. "Pax, please take Ashley to see Gaia. I will let both of you know as soon as I know anything."

Paxton nodded and escorted Ashley out of the office.

"She isn't dead," Ashley insisted in a somewhat erratic tone. "She's not."

"I know she's not," Paxton consoled as she led Ashley to the infirmary to see Gaia. Paxton hoped they were both right, but he wasn't so sure that it was the truth.

CHAPTER THIRTEEN

"She's alive, but barely," Maggie explained to Dhruva as the head of the Institute paced wildly in the infirmary.

"I didn't give you gifts just to have you let her die. Fix this or I'll make sure you never see a garden in any lifetime," Dhruva threatened.

"It would be immensely helpful if she didn't have the blockers stopping her elements from healing her," Maggie pointed out.

"Fine, stop the blockers for now, but keep her sedated. I don't have time to deal with her," Dhruva ordered. "I'll be back in the morning, and I *expect* to see improvement in her."

"Of course," Maggie said compliantly and checked on the IV that was delivering blood to Adya's depleted body.

Maggie breathed a sigh of relief and visibly relaxed when Dhruva and her two guards left the infirmary.

"You're going to be okay," she said softly to the unconscious girl and lightly washed her face with a cool washcloth.

Maggie had been horrified when she got the news that Dhruva captured Adya. Several times, she tried to see her friend, but Dhruva had explicitly ordered that Adya not receive visitors. In her free time, Maggie was sending text messages and crafting a plan to free Adya when the thirteen-year-old arrived in the infirmary almost dead. Now that Adya was with her, the escape was either going to be easier or much more difficult; everything hinged on Maggie healing her. "You did quite a number on yourself," she whispered to the slumbering affinate and softly brushed hair off the prone girl's forehead.

The weeks hadn't been kind to Adya. As she changed the bandage on her patient's neck, Maggie noticed that the already slender girl had lost quite a lot of weight. Dust and dirt from the room she was locked in coated her hair, skin, and clothes and was embedded under her short nails. Her face and lips were pale from the loss of blood; if it weren't for her chest scarcely rising and falling, Maggie would've thought Adya was dead.

Several long hours passed before the color began to return to Adya's cheeks. In addition to the blood transfusion, Maggie made another IV that would help restore Adya's strength and remove the blockers.

"My sweet Ady," Maggie whispered as she stroked the girl's hair. "I'm so sorry for all of this. I hope to tell you the story of how I got here someday, but for now, I need you to wake up so we can get you out of here."

Adya's elbow bent, and she grasped Maggie's arm. "You brought Lir here, and now he's one of those monsters," she whispered. A tear fell from Adya's eye and trickled into her hair. "I loved him, Maggie, and you took him from me." Adya's eyes remained closed.

Tears formed in Maggie's eyes. "I know you'll probably never forgive me, and there's nothing I can do to make up for what happened to him, but I'm going to get you out of here. Darius is on his way now. I can—"

Adya cut Maggie off mid-sentence and opened her eyes for the first time. "You should've let me die," she snarled.

Maggie furiously shook her head. "There is no way I'll ever let you die, nor will I let Dhruva take your soul. I swear on the elements, I swear on what's left of my own life that you will be free from this."

CHAPTER THIRTEEN

"Your word means little to me now," Adya replied and looked away from Maggie. "Tell me, can this soul extracting procedure be reversed?"

"I don't know much about it, but I don't think so," Maggie admitted.

"Do you know who took his soul?" Adya continued while staring at the clock on the wall.

"Does it matter?" Maggie posed. "If it can't be returned—"

Adya's head snapped back to stare at Maggie. "It matters because that's who I have to kill to release his soul so he can start a new life," she said with a clenched jaw and fist.

"You need to calm down, Ady," Maggie warned.

"Or what? You'll throw me back in that room?" Adya scoffed.

"If you make shit start flying around this room, the guards will come in, followed by Dhruva, and then I'll lose my chance to get you out," Maggie warned in a harsh whisper. "They will drug you again, and Dhruva will get what she wants—your soul."

"She'll never get my soul," Adya said, but relaxed her fist.

"That's my hope, too, Ady." Maggie sighed and appeared to Adya like a shell of the person she used to know—but at least not a soulless one. "I've been in secret contact with Darius through texts. He's not far from here, ready to take you home. When you and he are safely away, I'll text him the answer to your question."

"Fine," Adya replied and tried to get in touch with her elements again to no avail.

"I'm going to remove the IVs. Dhruva will be back to check on you soon, and I would highly suggest that you act like you're still asleep," Maggie warned.

Adya would *prefer* to murder Dhruva as soon as she entered but silently agreed to do what Maggie suggested by closing her eyes, lying still, and steadying her breathing.

About ten minutes after their conversation, Dhruva did return.

"She has improved," Maggie reported, "but I want to keep her here tonight to monitor her. She should be ready to return to her room in the morning."

"I have other plans for our dear Adya. Please make sure she receives another injection of the blockers tonight. I'll return in the morning to retrieve her. Perhaps a heavy sedative can be given beforehand to prevent any more willful outbursts like this morning."

"As you wish," Maggie replied as Dhruva left the room again.

Maggie checked her phone while Adya watched through the slits of her eyes.

"Was it worth it?" Adya asked quietly.

"Having an affinity again?" Maggie shook her head. "I haven't had any desire to use the affinity they gave me. I've lost everything important to me, and I will likely not make it out of here alive. But if I can save you, there will at least be some value to what my life has become," Maggie said sadly. She returned to Adya's side and checked her vitals. "Are you ready to go?"

Adya nodded.

"When you return to North Shore, give this note to Ted." Maggie tucked a piece of paper into Adya's pocket. "In five minutes, the guards' shift will change. No one will be back here for the rest of the night. I am going to inject them with something that'll knock them out. As soon as you hear them hit the floor, leave out the back door." Maggie motioned with her head to the far side of the infirmary where there was a wooden door blocked by a table. "About fifty yards straight out from that door, there's a chain-link fence with a hole cut into it. You should be able to squeeze through. Darius will be there waiting."

Adya was furious, but a part of her forgave Maggie for the series of mistakes that led to the stealing of Lir's soul. That small part of herself is what spoke next. "You can come with me," she said.

Maggie squeezed Adya's hand. "My oldest sister and Lucas are here. I couldn't leave without them, and there's no way to get them both and safely make it out. No," she continued, "you must go alone. We'll see each other again." The unshed tears in Maggie's eyes said something different than her words.

Adya squeezed Maggie's hand back. "I'll be back for everyone who can still be saved," Adya promised.

Maggie patted Adya's hand and went to retrieve the shots she'd prepared for the guards. "Are you ready?" she whispered.

Adya nodded and listened for the sound of the bodies collapsing.

"Go with balance, my sweet Ady."

Adya heard Maggie say something to the guards, and within a few moments, the sound of their bodies hitting the floor sent Adya scrambling out of bed. With one last lingering look at Maggie, Adya ran to the back of the infirmary and exited the building.

"Elements guide her," Maggie whispered and sent a final text to Darius with the answer that Adya was seeking.

Adya felt like a zombie going through the motions as Darius led her to the awaiting aircraft. While he had occasionally been around North Shore, they hadn't spoken in this current lifetime. Once Awakened, she knew who the tall, muscular man was. His name may have changed over the years, but his dark brown hair that swept across his forehead and his emerald green eyes always stayed the same.

"It has been quite a long time since I had to rescue you, Ady," Darius said in his usual deep voice with a distinctly

British accent and his proper speech. "I suppose that is a good thing."

Adya stared out the window, gripping the armrests a little tighter than usual. His words weaved into her empty thoughts, and she experienced a soul memory from their past.

It was the summer of 1789. The tension in the air was palpable, and Lir and Adya had been preparing to leave France even before the rioters stormed the Bastille fortress. They were lucky to escape before the mass exodus of nobles, but many citizens of the Third Estate angrily questioned them as they attempted to cross la Manche. The welcome in Great Britain wasn't much better. While many in England sympathized with the emigrants, many more harbored a distaste for the French and the nobility. Their distinctly French attire drew stares on the streets of London, and on more than one occasion, commoners threatened them and refused to allow them in their establishments.

Lir and Adya mostly found other affinates and noble sympathizers to board with on their trek to London, but on several occasions, they curled up together in an alleyway to sleep for the night. An alley like this is where Darius found the two, huddled against a discarded barrel, with their fine silks covered in dirt.

"Ahem," the Englishman said as he kicked Lir's shoe with his boot.

Lir immediately jumped up, nearly matching the height of the soldier that had awoken him.

Adya sat primly, waiting for Lir to offer her a hand up and studied the peculiar man that hovered over her. He wasn't an affinate, but there was something odd about him, she decided.

The man narrowed his eyes as he studied Lir and his frazzled wig that could use a new dusting. "I am Geoffrey, head of the Royal Guard. What business do you have here?" He placed his hand loosely on the hilt of the sword attached to his waist.

CHAPTER THIRTEEN

"We aren't here to cause problems," Lir said as he brushed some of the dirt and hay from his blue and pink striped waistcoat. "We're simply seeking refuge from Paris."

Geoffrey continued to glower at Lir. "You do not sound French. Now speak the truth. Why have you come?"

"We aren't French, sir, but we have been enjoying ourselves in Paris for some years." Adya craned her neck up at the two men while holding onto her wig so it wouldn't topple off her head. Finally, sick of waiting for the men's help, she attempted to rise to her feet despite the difficulties in doing so with the large hoop under her French silk dress.

Both men immediately offered their hands to help her stand, but Adya accepted Geoffrey's.

"I have heard of the troubles there," Geoffrey said and continued to hold Adya's hand after she'd risen. "I have no love of the French, but if you are as you say, I could escort you to my home to stay until you find your bearings."

Adya blushed and curtsied. "You are too kind."

Lir grumbled but followed behind the two as they spoke like old friends and strolled through the London streets without a care of the stares they were drawing.

Days turned into weeks, and Adya was quite comfortable in Geoffrey's house. Lir, seeming not as happy, left after the first week to speak to the head of the Academy in Birmingham—the epicenter of the start of the Industrial Revolution. He remained absent until the letter of Adya's marriage to Geoffrey arrived.

"What are you, if not an affinate?" Adya asked of Geoffrey one evening as they lay in bed beside each other.

"I am the head of the Royal Guard," Geoffrey began and continued before Adya could interrupt. "As I have been for over a thousand years."

Adya jolted up in surprise. "But you don't have an affinity. How can that be?"

"I am not reborn like you, Ady. I simply cannot die." Geoffrey reached up to caress his wife's cheek. "We are all influenced by magic, but not always in the same way."

Adya's brow's furrowed as she tried to grasp the meaning of his cryptic words. "So, you're saying that magic made you immortal, and you just stay here forever?"

Geoffrey readjusted himself to sit beside the bewildered Adya. "Yes."

Adya breathed out a heavy, frustrated breath. "Why? How? Help me understand. I've told you all about my affinities and my lifetimes, but I still don't know this about you."

Their white cat, Beautiful, jumped up onto the bed and demanded attention while Geoffrey explained his life to Adya.

"I wish you didn't have to," Adya lamented, her eyes still focused on the fluffy white clouds below the jet.

"We all have things we wish for, Ady. Things are as they are, and we just have to push forward." When Adya didn't reply, he left her to her thoughts and started reading through messages on his phone.

Adya didn't want to push forward, though. She wanted to go back to having Lir with his soul intact in her life.

Adya sat quietly in Ted's office, staring at the food that was brought for her while Ted and Darius spoke outside. Adya had no appetite and was still recovering from her near-death experience. She placed her palm against her bandage-covered wound on her neck and closed her eyes. Nausea swept through her body as unwanted memories of the past three weeks invaded Adya's mind like a nightmare she couldn't wake up from.

"Your friends are anxious to see you," Ted said as he reentered his office and closed the door.

Adya's eyes shot open, and her hand fell into her lap. "I don't feel like seeing anyone right now," Adya admitted.

"Would you mind if I went for a walk? I think I need to be close to my elements right now."

"I'd prefer you not be alone," Ted said as he eyed Adya's neck.

"I'm not suicidal, nor do I intend to sneak away," Adya replied defensively. "I've just spent three weeks locked in a room by myself, stripped of my affinities, and *really* need to feel them again." A desperate tear ran down Adya's cheek.

"I'm not worried about you leaving or hurting yourself, Adya. But for the very reason that you've been isolated for weeks, I would like you to have someone with you," Ted explained.

"Paxton," Adya whispered. "Pax can walk with me."

Ted nodded and squeezed Adya's shoulder as he walked past her. "Tell Huo that I need to see Paxton in my office," Ted said to the person—presumably Darius—in the hallway. Ted returned and sat on the desk in front of Adya next to the untouched plate of food. "The Council should've listened to you," he began. "Eli and Myra pose a bigger threat to the world's balance than we ever imagined."

"Dhruva," Adya corrected Ted. "Myra is now Dhruva. I don't know if it's a name she made up or if she completed the Awakening. I really don't care, either." Adya reached into her pocket and retrieved the letter Maggie had given her. "Here," she said flatly. "Maggie asked me to give this to you."

Ted took the note but didn't read it. He placed it down on a stack of papers, ready to listen to anything else Adya was willing to share at that moment.

"I tried to get her to leave with me, but she said one of her sisters is there. Maybe the note explains that. I don't know. I didn't care to read it."

A soft knock preceded Ted's door opening. He lifted his hand and shook his head, warning the person not to rush in. "Paxton is here now if you're ready to go on your walk."

Adya nodded and stood, glancing for only a second at Ted before her gaze went to the floor, and she walked towards the door.

"When you're feeling up to it, I'd like to have a longer conversation with you about your time there," Ted said softly.

Adya nodded. "Sure," she mumbled and walked past Paxton into the hallway.

The two walked in silence outside and towards the lake. Paxton understood from the mood in the room that Adya wasn't herself and didn't desire a joyful reunion with anyone.

"I know you and Ash were there," Adya finally said as they neared the tree. Adya stood under its bare branches and gazed out at the lake. "You shouldn't have risked it."

Paxton leaned against the tree and followed Adya's gaze to the water. "We felt helpless," he admitted. "We wanted you to know that you weren't alone and that we still cared."

"I know," Adya said, "but you saw what I did. There wasn't anything anyone could do at that moment to help me."

Paxton cringed at the memory of Adya stabbing herself. "I think what you did was brave," he admitted. "Although I probably would've tried to stab her instead."

"She'd taken my affinities away. If I had tried—" Adya sighed and didn't try to stop the tears from pooling in her eyes or cascading down her cheeks, nor did she care to wipe them away. "She stole everything from me. I don't think it was brave what I did; it was out of fear of becoming one of her soulless monsters or having to live knowing that's what Lir is now. . ." Adya trailed off for a moment. "That's what made me do it. I didn't consider what it would do to you or Ash or Sierra or anyone here. It was a completely selfish act."

"She didn't steal your soul from you—you stopped that. And she didn't steal your friends from you, either. We're still here and ready to fight with you to stop her," Paxton admitted.

"I don't have much fight left in me right now." Adya frowned and dropped her eyes to her clasped hands. "I don't know what I care about anymore. I think I need to be away from everything and everyone for a while."

Paxton frowned, too. "There's nothing you could say or do that will stop us from caring about you, Ady. So, if you need time alone to figure this all out, I'm sure Ted will allow it."

Adya scoffed and sniffled as she looked at Paxton again. "Ted didn't want me walking around here alone. I don't think he'll be supportive of any idea that involves me going off somewhere by myself." Adya took a deep breath. "But I think I need to go to Ava's old house. It's far away from everything and everyone. Maybe I'll find some version of peace if I can be near where she last was." Adya swallowed hard. "This is the first lifetime that I haven't had Ava to turn to. I miss her." Adya covered her face and sobbed.

Paxton stepped close to Adya and pulled her against his chest. He knew there was nothing he could say to take away her heartache, so as she cried that deep, nonsensical crying that comes from a profound loss, Paxton just held her and stroked her hair.

"Hey," Ashley said softly as she cautiously approached the two.

Adya squeezed Paxton before releasing him and turned to Ashley, immediately embracing her.

"You scared the hell outta me," Ashley whispered as she held her friend. Paxton shook his head for Ashley to see, hoping she wouldn't continue talking about what Adya obviously didn't want to discuss, but Ashley continued anyway. "Don't you *ever* take off like that again without me knowing."

Adya released her friend and wiped away some of the moisture from her face while she sniffled. "Okay," Adya replied remorsefully. "I'm going to be going away for a while."

Ashley frowned. "You just got back. Give yourself time before you go charging back there," Ashley advised.

"I'm not going back there," Adya corrected. "Not yet, anyway. I think I just need some time alone to find my balance again."

"Where will you go?" Ashley asked with concern. "Back to Switzerland?"

Adya chuckled. Of course, Ashley was thinking like a teenage girl and only considered what had made her friend happiest in this lifetime. "No," Adya said. "I don't see myself returning to Switzerland for a very long time." She sighed, feeling the familiar ache in her soul when she thought about happier times with Lir. "No, Ava's home is in West Virginia. Since she Ascended, the Elders took ownership of the property, but as far as I know, no one has disturbed it. It's a huge piece of land surrounded by trees, grasses, mountains, and a river. I think that's where I need to be."

"And a house, too, I hope. Not that I'm discounting your camping and survival skills, but you having the ability to take a shower that didn't involve a river would make me feel a whole lot better about you going."

Adya smiled reflexively, but it didn't reach her eyes. "There is a house with electricity and running water. I'll be fine."

"And you'll have your phone, so I can tell you all the gossip, right?" Ashley asked with hope.

Adya shook her head. "My phone is gone, and I don't think I'd take it anyway. You know I love you and our gossip, but I need some time."

Ashley nodded sadly and thrust her arms around her friend. "Please don't be gone long."

While startled by the suddenness of Ashley's embrace, Adya fiercely hugged her friend back. "I'm sorry you saw what I did," Adya whispered. "And thank you for trying to help." Adya reached out and grabbed Paxton's hand and squeezed. "Thank you, too."

CHAPTER THIRTEEN

After her brief reunion with Ashley and Paxton, Adya went to see Gaia in the infirmary. Adya never fully appreciated the care that had gone into creating the infirmary at North Shore until she'd been in Maggie's clinic at the Institute. The room at the Academy was bright and cheerful, even at night, and smelled of fresh flowers and earthy scents. It was reminiscent of Adya's grandmother's home in a lifetime long since gone, unlike Maggie's, which felt like a laboratory in a mental institution, filled with metal countertops and chemical smells. Nothing as sinister as an affinity blocker would ever be among Gaia's shelves of remedies.

"How are you feeling?" Gaia asked as Adya sat on the edge of one of the triage beds.

"I think you're the first one who's been brave enough to ask me that," Adya commented. "A little sore, a little tired, and very empty is the best way I can explain how I feel."

"I can help you with the sore and tired, but the empty part is something you'll have to work through yourself," Gaia kindly explained as she handed Adya a cup of tea. "I'm going to redress the wound on your neck," she warned.

Adya nodded. "I figured." She tilted her head to the right and brushed her hair aside, exposing the thick bandage on the left side of her neck. "Maggie did what she could to make sure it didn't get infected," Adya began, "but she refuses to use her new affinity, so it was just whatever medicines she had there to use." Adya flinched when Gaia peeled off the gauze.

"Yes, she did a good job stitching you up, but it looks a little infected." Gaia stood and went to her cabinet, returning with a fresh bandage and an ointment. "I will remove the infection, and the ointment will help it heal without a scar," she explained.

"No," Adya said unexpectedly and grasped Gaia's forearm. "I want the scar to remain," she insisted.

Gaia looked at the girl with confusion but nodded. "How's your ankle feeling?" she asked as she placed her fingers against Adya's skin around the puncture mark.

"Not awful," Adya said, "but it's a little achy. Probably because I walked about fifteen miles on it after I took off the cast."

Gaia retracted her fingers from Adya's neck after she'd used her affinity to withdraw the infection. She shook her head in disapproval at Adya. "That was a foolish thing to do."

Adya shrugged. "It seems I've done a lot of foolish things lately."

"It was stupid of you to run off by yourself like that," Gaia agreed, "but anything that happened there was not your fault. You possess traits I wish more people still had."

"And what traits are those?" Adya asked dubiously.

Gaia was an old enough soul to recall how things were in the old world when survival depended on protecting the people around you. "Loyalty to friends and family and a willingness to make the hard choices for the greater good and balance."

Adya looked down, feeling ashamed. "What if I did this because I couldn't live with the thought of not having Lir in this life?"

Gaia rested her hand on Adya's. "That sounds to me like a genuine lament of Emily. But if that was your only reason, why did you wait for—what's her name now?"

"Dhruva," Adya said.

"Yes, why did you wait for Dhruva to be in the room?"

Adya nodded and understood. "Because I wanted her to know that she wasn't going to steal my soul and also for her to know the extent I would go to keep the elements in balance."

Gaia smiled. "You're allowed to think and feel as Emily would. Trust your soul to guide you through the normal ups and downs of being a teenager." She patted Adya's hand. "Is there anything you need tonight?"

Adya thought about it for a moment and nodded. "I'm planning on taking a little time away from the Academy. I know I'm not balanced, and I can't see how being here, pretending to be a student, is going to help me. I was hoping you could give me some tea and herbs to take with me when I go away."

Gaia looked concerned. "Where do you want to go?"

"Ava's old house," Adya replied. "I'm hoping to find clarity and peace within myself."

Gaia seemed to approve of her answer and gathered some supplies for Adya. "This should last you a few months, but I hope you're not gone that long."

Adya stood and hugged Gaia before taking the items. "Thank you, Gaia. I don't think I'll be gone that long."

"Go with the elements, Ady," Gaia said as Adya left the infirmary.

"I know you don't want me to be alone right now, but I believe that's the best thing for me. I'm hoping you'll ask the Elders permission for me to—" Adya was desperately trying to convey what her soul needed when Ted held up a hand to interrupt her.

"You want to go to Ava's house. I know. Paxton came in and pleaded a case for you," Ted explained.

"And? Will you go to the Elders for me?" Adya begged.

"I already did. And the Elders agree with me that you shouldn't be left completely alone right now," Ted began.

Adya's face dropped. "I see," she said sadly.

"Which is why if you decide to go, you will need to check in once a week with an old friend of Elder Tama's that lives in the area. You don't have to talk with her about anything, but you will have to deliver her groceries to her weekly so we can vicariously keep tabs on you," Ted said with a grin. "How does this compromise sound to you?"

"I just have to take this woman groceries once a week, and I'll be left alone in Ava's house?" Adya thought it was a generous compromise, and she did understand that with all the threats getting ready to boil over, that they would want to make sure she was okay.

Ted nodded. "Just groceries. So, is it a deal?"

Adya smiled again and shook Ted's outstretched hand. "It's a deal."

CHAPTER FOURTEEN

The waning days of winter were in the air. Bittersweet memories flooded back to Adya as a man in a black suit drove her in a modern sedan from the airport to Ava's house. It didn't come close to comparing to Adya's memories of the early autumn days when she had driven down the same roads in Ava's brand new burgundy 1945 Cadillac Sixty-Two convertible with the top down. Those post-war weeks before Ava's Ascension were some of Adya's favorite memories, but the outcome of those memories was making her feel utterly alone.

Adya tipped the driver for the ride and carrying her bags to the porch of Ava's three-story house. When the dust settled, and the car was out of sight, she finally went inside.

The inside was not as she expected, but exactly as she remembered. The Elder's must've sent someone to prepare the house for Adya's arrival because there wasn't a hint of dust or cobwebs anywhere. Adya could practically hear the radio playing Doris Day singing *My Dreams are Getting Better All the Time* as they played cards and sipped iced tea in the living room, laughing together as though they had all the time in the world. But Adya knew now that Ava had already made her decision to Ascend at that time.

Adya left her bags by the front door as she explored. Books filled the shelves in the library, but none of Ava's journals remained; they were probably in the vault in Geneva. As she exited the library, Adya lamented as she brushed her fingers across the keys of the grand piano, "Lir and I used to play songs together on this."

She made her way into the kitchen, which stocked with fresh fruits, vegetables, and other perishables that weren't seventy years expired. A note was on the kitchen table with Adya's name written on it. It was a brief message with the address of the woman who she would visit weekly:

Please give Sophia our best wishes, and may you find peace with the elements during your stay.

-Tama

Beneath the note was an old journal, the one that Adya fell asleep reading at Elder Tama's estate the year prior. It was apparent, now that Adya had completed the Awakening, that the journal belonged to Ava. Still, she had wondered for a long time afterward about the heartbroken woman whose memories kept her company the night that her mother had died.

"Sophia," Adya said aloud, but she couldn't recall this woman from any other lifetime and was mildly curious about how she knew Elder Tama. With a shrug, she set aside her curiosity and made a simple salad with ingredients from the fridge; finally, a bit of her appetite had returned.

After picking at her salad—her stomach was still accustomed to the small meals served at the Institute—Adya made herself a warm pot of tea and took a cup of it and a blanket out on the back patio to watch the fading sun and to listen to the sounds of nature. From the wooden porch swing, she could feel and hear the gentle trickle of the river in the distance while a soft, cool breeze danced around her. Her elements were welcoming her back, and a bit of her internal peace returned.

Crickets began chirping while the birds returned to their nest for the night. A single black and white bird perched on the handrail of the porch in front of Adya.

"Hello there," Adya said and sipped her tea.

The bird cocked its head and studied Adya while she looked on with quiet revere.

"You're a beautiful magpie, aren't you?" Adya said softly. "It's getting late, though. Shouldn't you be finding your home?"

The bird hopped down to the wood deck and dropped a rock at Adya's feet before flying away towards the trees.

Adya watched the bird disappear and then picked up the gift it'd left her. It was a shiny black rock. Holding it in her hands, she called upon her earth affinity to identify it.

"Jet?" she said aloud, even more confused than she was when the bird left the gift. "There isn't any of that around here." She knew from her many lifetimes with her earth affinity that jet was for grounding and purification. Why would a bird bring a stone to her that likely wasn't found anywhere within a thousand miles? Still baffled, she caressed the smooth stone with her thumb as she watched the stars appear in the sky.

The chamomile-spearmint-lemongrass tea that Gaia gave Adya before she left North Shore was a perfect end to her day. She grew sleepy while gently rocking on the porch swing and decided to grab a pillow from the couch and sleep outside for the night. The warmth of the blanket, along with the sweet melodies of her elements, lulled Adya to sleep.

Over the next five days, Adya spent time slowly exploring the three-story house and the property outside the home. Each night, the magpie returned to the porch with another jet stone for Adya before it flew away.

On the morning of the sixth day, Adya gathered the stones and placed them in a circle in Ava's old garden. She spent an hour in the bare soil paying homage to her earth element. During her meditation, she heard the bird land nearby. After some time, Adya opened her eyes, and the magpie was watching her.

"Would you like your stones back?" she asked and held one in her hand, her palm lying flat.

The magpie, which Adya named Yiny—short for Yin Yang—due to her beautiful black and white feathers, hopped closer to Adya and squawked, but didn't try to take any of the stones.

"No? Well, if you want them back, I'm leaving them here in the garden. I think they look lovely here, but I still don't know where you're getting these. I will get some birdseed when I go into town today to thank you for your gifts." When Adya stood, the bird flew up onto a branch of the old oak tree that grew next to the house. She smiled up at Yiny before going to the shed to see if the bicycles were still there.

"Hmm, it doesn't look like they cleaned everything." Adya scrunched her nose as she dodged old spider webs to get to the three bikes that were leaning against the wall. "I'm glad I decided to go to town early today. It looks like I'm gonna have to walk with the bike and hope there's a bike shop that can replace these tires." Adya grabbed the red Schwinn—the only one with a basket on the front—and tugged it out of the shed. Seeing the bike in the morning sun, she knew it would need more than new tires to function. "Walking it is," she resigned and leaned the bicycle up against the shed before securing it closed.

Inside the house, Adya opened her duffle bag, which was still by the stairs inside the front door. It wasn't that she didn't have time to unpack, but instead, she had better ways to spend the previous six days than taking all her clothes out and hanging them up, a trait distinctly belonging to Emily. Inside the duffle bag, she knew there was a backpack that would come in handy if she was going to buy food for herself and still have hands free to carry Sophia's groceries. When she tugged the backpack out from the bottom of the duffle bag, a note and the present from Lir fell onto the floor.

172

CHAPTER FOURTEEN

In the almost full week that Adya had been away, she hadn't felt the sadness and emptiness that had driven her to Ava's house. Tears filled her eyes and spilled out when she bent over to pick up the note: *I thought you might want to open this while you were away. Love & balance, Ash.*

"Damn you, Ashley," Adya said and crumbled up the note. She knew her friend meant well, but Adya honestly didn't know if she'd ever open the gift from Lir. Feeling the strong desire to ignore it completely, she left it where it fell on the floor, grabbed her backpack and the directions to Sophia's house, and went for her five-mile walk to town.

Adya used the time getting to town to compose herself, wipe away the moisture from her eyes, and reclaim the fragments of balance she'd worked hard to achieve during the preceding days. By the time she arrived on the small stretch of the town's main street, she had composed herself. It seemed that not much had changed in the seventy years since she'd been there, and she effortlessly found the market.

"Yer not from 'round here," the red-haired boy scanning her items commented with an easy smile. The boy spoke with what Adya could best describe as a hillbilly accent. But he was polite, and Adya didn't think anything less of him when his smile lacked a couple of teeth.

"No, I'm just visiting for a while," Adya replied casually. "Hey, is there a bicycle shop anywhere around? I'm staying just outside of town, and my bike needs some work."

"Naw," the boy replied. "There's a Wal-Mart about thirty miles from here, though."

"Thirty miles," Adya repeated and crinkled her nose. "That's a little farther than I want to walk. Thanks, though."

"No problem," he replied.

When Adya finished paying for her groceries and the birdseed for Yiny, she packed everything in her backpack and slid it on her back. "I'm also supposed to pick up groceries for Sophia. Is this where I get them?"

"Ahh, so yer the one livin' in that old house out thar. I s'pected someone older to be pickin' these up," he said and walked around the counter.

"Yeah, I get that a lot," Adya commented.

The boy shrugged indifferently and disappeared into the back of the store. He returned shortly with five bags of groceries and started handing them to Adya; she barely managed to circle her arms around the full paper bags.

"Do you think you could give me directions to Sophia's house? I can't look at my map and hold these," she asked lightheartedly.

"Sure. Turn right at the street, go 'bout a mile, then turn left. The house is half-mile that way. Can't miss it," he said.

"Thanks," she said and managed to exit out of the store without dropping anything.

While she'd been pleasant to the boy in the store—it wasn't his fault, after all, that she had to carry a week's worth of groceries to a house a couple of miles away—Adya grumbled as she started on her way to the destination. Several people stopped what they were doing to watch her walk by, but no one offered to help her.

"No, it's fine," Adya muttered sarcastically to no one as she stopped at a corner to cross the street. "I got this, no problem."

"No one'll ever offer to help you if you keep talkin' to yourself," a boy with a somewhat deep voice said from behind her.

The grocery bags blocked Adya's view of the boy when she turned around. She muttered a curse in French to herself as the shadow of the boy approached. "Yeah, well, I really didn't expect anyone to help the strange girl in town anyway."

"I guess that makes me a bit of an enigma."

Adya turned slightly sideways so she could see the boy as he approached. He looked about Adya's age—although, with his voice that had clearly already changed, he was likely a couple of years older. He was slightly taller than her with dirty blond hair and bright hazel eyes. By the looks of his muscular arms and tan skin—even though it was the middle of winter—she guessed he did some sort of manual labor outdoors. "I don't know about that. The guy at the market talked to me, too."

"Were you mutterin' to yourself in foreign languages around him?" he asked.

"Well, no," Adya admitted.

"See? So that does bring me back to my original conclusion that I must be an enigma." The boy smiled. "You look like you need some help. Where ya headed?"

"I'm taking these to Sophia," Adya said as he took hold of three of the bags.

"Ahh, so you're the one stayin' in the witch's house," he said while nodding his head.

"Ava wasn't a witch," Adya protested. "And if you're going to stand there and insult her, I'll manage to carry these bags by myself." Adya readjusted the bags in her arms and tried to take the ones back from him.

"Whoa," he protested. "I know she wasn't a witch, but that's what all the town folks think an' that's just what they call it. I'm headin' to Sophia's house myself. I know you don't know me an' I just insulted your friend, but can I offer you a ride?"

Adya glowered at him. "You're right. I don't know you, so I'd just prefer to walk."

"Tell you what. I'm gonna get in my truck with these three bags of groceries." Adya started to protest, but he continued. "I'll drive real slow next to you while you walk with your two bags to the house. That way, you can save face by not gettin' in a vehicle with a stranger an' I keep my title as the most helpful guy in town. It's a win-win."

"Fine, but I *am* capable of doing this myself," Adya argued.

The boy chuckled and walked to his old Chevy pickup in the parking lot of the diner. After placing the grocery bags in the rusty bed of the truck, he got in the driver's side and started it up. Before he backed out of the spot, he leaned over and rolled down the passenger side the window.

Adya watched him for a minute before turning and walking in the direction the boy at the market told her to go. It didn't take long for the truck to pull up beside her and slow to match her pace. "Are you seriously going to drive two miles an hour next to me the rest of the way?" she asked, slightly annoyed.

"That's what our deal was. Do you want to put those bags in the back with the others?" he said out the passenger window.

"I guess," she conceded and waited for him to pull over next to the curb before she added her two bags to the other three in his truck bed and then resumed walking towards Sophia's house with only her backpack to carry.

The truck moved slowly with Adya. "So how do you know Ava?" the boy asked as they moved slowly towards their destination.

"She's an old friend," Adya replied and instantly regretted not having a better story to explain her relationship to the former owner of the house.

"An old friend? Didn't she die a long time ago? My grandma knew her way back in the day when she was probably your age. Well, she's not really my grandma, but that's not important."

Adya raised a brow at him as he babbled on. "Do you always talk this much?"

"I'm just tryin' to keep you from talkin' to yourself," he said with a shrug. "So, how's Ava an old friend?"

"She was an old family friend. Cousin of a cousin type of thing," Adya lied.

The boy nodded and then turned on his radio. "Do you like country music?"

Adya shook her head. "Not really," she said.

"What do you listen to then?"

Adya shrugged. "Mostly classical, some trance, alternative, and occasionally pop music. But I don't spend a lot of time listening to music."

"That's about all we have to entertain ourselves 'round here. Helps the work go quicker. Too bad we can't listen to it at school," the boy lamented.

"Shouldn't you be in school right now?" Adya asked.

"Naa, it's a field day, so we only go for a couple of hours in the mornin'. I could ask you the same. Do you do some smart person home school or somethin'?"

"Something like that," Adya replied vaguely.

"If it's not home school, what is it?"

Adya sighed. "I go to a private school. I'm taking a break, though."

"I knew it was somethin' fancy like that. You can just take breaks whenever you want?" The boy shook his head in disbelief.

"Look, I really don't want to talk with a stranger about why I'm here, okay? Just turn up your music, and I'll walk in silence."

He shrugged. "Okay, but I'll continue to be a stranger if we don't talk an' get to know one another."

Adya smiled falsely. "I'd prefer to walk in silence."

The silence lasted for about five minutes until commercials monopolized the radio station. "I've got two older brothers," he said and startled Adya out of her thoughts. "You got any siblings?"

Adya gave him an exasperated look. "No, I'm an only child."

"I'd never want to be an only child, but I bet your folks spoil you."

"My mom died almost a year ago, and I don't stay in contact with my father anymore," she said flatly.

"Aw, damn. I'm sorry," he said.

And there it was—the gut-wrenching pain caused by a recollection of Lir and the conversation they'd had about saying 'I'm sorry' when she had just returned to the Academy after her mom died. Adya wrapped her arms around her stomach and frowned at the ground.

"You're not lookin' too well. Are you feelin' alright?" the boy asked with genuine concern.

Adya waved her hand at him. "I'm fine. Are we almost there?"

"It's that house 'bout half a mile down the road. C'mon an' get in. You really don't look well."

Adya took a look at the dusty road ahead, and with a long sigh, turned towards the truck. "Fine, you can drive me the rest of the way," she said and slid in the passenger's seat after he pushed open the creaky door. For as beat up as the outside of the truck appeared, the inside was immaculate. Adya leaned back against the vinyl seat and stared out the open window while a cold breeze kissed her face.

"I'm sorry I upset you by talkin' 'bout your momma," he politely offered as they drove at an average speed towards Sophia's house.

It wasn't you talking about my mom that upset me! I look like I want to vomit because you brought back the memories of the man I loved who is now a monster thanks to my mortal enemy! Adya wanted to scream but opted for an uncomfortable silence that now hung in the air instead.

When they pulled up to Sophia's house, Adya and the boy walked around to retrieve the bags from the back. Adya liked the look of Sophia's house from the outside. It was a quaint country home with sheep and goats milling about in the fenced area behind it. She could see a field for crops behind that but didn't know what they were growing. Further back on the property, Adya noticed a tractor sitting in the doorway of a red barn.

"Grandma! Your groceries are here," he yelled at the house.

"Grandma?" Adya asked in surprise. "You didn't tell me Sophia was your grandma."

"She's not really my grandma, but that's what I've always called her," he explained. "An' you never asked." The boy walked past Adya with three bags of groceries to greet the older woman who exited the house.

"Oh, Jace. We were beginnin' to worry 'bout where you were. I thought Adya was bringin' my groceries today," the woman said as she kissed the boy on the cheek.

Adya stepped out from behind the truck and smiled at their interaction. "I'm here, too," Adya said and walked towards the older woman who was wearing blue jeans, a plaid shirt, and nothing on her feet. Sophia's white hair curled on top of her head, reminiscent of Betty White. Deep lines on her face told a happy story of a long life.

"Oh, my darlin' child. It's so good to meet ya finally," Sophia said with outstretched arms. "Here, let me take those from you. Jace put these on the table with the others an' get out to the barn before your brothers try to supercharge the tractor's engine 'gain."

"Yes, Grandma," Jace replied and tilted his head to Adya before disappearing into the house and out the back.

"Come inside with me, Adya. I'll make us some tea an' we can chat a bit," Sophia said hospitably.

Adya smiled and followed but frowned internally. What happened to just delivering groceries without talking? All she wanted to do was get back to Ava's to feed Yiny and forget about the reminders of Lir she'd had that day.

"You have a lovely home," Adya commented as she looked around the living room filled with trinkets, hung photographs, and floral-print furniture.

"It suits me just fine," the woman said as she carried two mugs of tea to the table.

Adya took off her backpack and sat at the table, accepting the tea with an appreciative smile. "Mmm," she commented after taking a sip and enjoying the subtle tingle on her tongue. "This is a very nice blend. Echinacea and mint?" she asked.

"With a dash of lemongrass an' a generous amount of honey," Sophia added. "I thought it might help with any possible lingerin' infections you might have," she said as she motioned with her nose towards Adya's neck.

Adya reflexively touched her healing wound and frowned. "Yes, well, I've been applying a balm to it. It should be fine."

"I'm sure it will, but a little extra boost never hurts," Sophia responded with a thoughtful smile. "It's been a long time since I saw you, Ady. You probably don't 'member, but I was 'bout your age now." Adya frowned in confusion, but Sophia continued. "Ava was teachin' me more 'bout my affinity, but I 'member seeing you with her in town. She thought the world of you, told me herself."

"You're an affinate?" Adya asked and searched the woman's face and eyes for recognition. "I don't know your soul," she finally admitted.

"I wouldn't 'spect you to," Sophia said after taking another sip of her tea. "I haven't lived many lives, an' my soul seems content with livin' right here."

"But you have grandchildren. Oh, right. He said you weren't really his grandma," Adya quickly corrected herself.

Sophia smiled. "Jace an' his brothers are my great niece's kids. My sister died in the war an' I raised her kids as my own. 'Grandma' became the title I inherited with Jace's mom's generation, even though they know I'm not theirs, an' I've always 'cepted it proudly."

"So, you have an earth affinity?" Adya asked, momentarily setting aside her desire to retreat to Ava's house.

"I do, 'though I 'magine it isn't as strong as yours," Sophia commented. "We don't have an Academy 'round here. Aside from what Ava taught me, I've had to do all my learnin' myself."

Adya gazed out the sliding glass door towards the livestock and fields. "You seem to be doing a great job of it."

"Jace an' his brothers are good kids," Sophia replied. "I don't have it in me anymore to get out there like I should.

But I taught them ev'rything 'bout respectin' the land. They do good by it."

"They know about your affinity?" Adya asked in confusion. Since learning about her own, she'd only interacted with other affinates and never even considered sharing that information with non's—aside from Maggie, of course. And her past lives had taught her many times over that sharing that knowledge freely often led to persecution.

"Didn't ev'r think not to," Sophia admitted like it was a novel idea to keep it a secret. "Some of the townsfolk avoid me, 'fraid that Imma witch or somethin' of the like, but we do right by each other an' get along just fine."

"Are there any other affinates around here?" Adya asked, truly fascinated.

Sophia shook her head. "None that I've ev'r met, but I don't travel too far. Tama comes for a visit when she's out this way, but not many others do. Met her the first time in her previous life when your Elders came after Ava left. Hoped I'd see Ava 'gain." Sophia retreated into a memory.

Adya nodded sadly. "She Ascended. I miss her, too. This lifetime is my first without her." Adya wiped the tears from her eyes.

Sophia reached across the table and rested her hand on top of Adya's. "Doncha be cryin' for Ava. She left us in peace on her own terms. An' her spirit remains in our hearts an' in the elements 'round us."

Adya offered a shrug. Sophia's kind words didn't take away sadness from the absence of her old friend. "You're probably right. But I should start walking back to the house. Thank you for the tea, Sophia." Adya took her empty teacup to the sink in the kitchen.

"Nonsense," Sophia said, rising with Adya. "You're gonna stay for supper. The boys'll be done in a few hours an' they start fightin' with each other if I don't distract 'em with food."

"Thank you, but I should really get—"

"You can help me in the kitchen," Sophia continued without listening to Adya's excuse to depart. "Maybe I'll teach you somethin' today."

Adya sighed in resignation. She was beginning to think that Elder Tama agreed to allow her to stay at Ava's house because she knew Sophia would be so insistent on keeping Adya from doing the one thing she came on this sabbatical to do—be alone. "Alright," she replied. "What do you need me to do?"

Sophia instructed Adya on where to put the groceries away while she began washing vegetables. "I usu'lly grow these myself, but hafta get 'em from the market this time of year."

Sophia talked almost nonstop while Adya helped her prepare a vegetable stew and make cornbread. Adya was able to keep mostly to her thoughts as she worked, offering the occasional "uh-huh" and "yes" to the one-sided conversation, but found a strange kind of peace with working in harmony with her earth affinity in Sophia's kitchen.

"Could'ya get the bread from the oven, dear?" Sophia asked while setting the table for dinner.

"Of course," Adya replied. When she placed the hot pans of cornbread on the counter next to the stove, she noticed the tile backsplash on the wall had tiny flecks of black rock in it. It reminded her of the stones Yiny brought. "Have you heard of any jet stones around here?"

"Hmm?" Sophia asked, but then responded anyway. "Jet stones. . . no, there aren't any 'round here. Ava gave me a necklace with a jet stone pendant, but I haven't worn it for years." Sophia rejoined Adya in the kitchen and touched the top of the loaf with her fingers. "No, this needs couple more minutes still," she remarked and slid the pans back into the oven. "I think I know where it is. Lemme grab it," Sophia said and left the room before Adya could protest.

Several minutes later, Sophia returned with a necklace draped over her fingers. "Yes, Ava gave it to me for healin' an' protection after my sister died."

Suddenly, hands slammed against the glass of the back door. Both Adya and Sophia jolted in surprise.

"Beat ya!" Jace yelled back at his brothers as he pushed the sliding door open.

"Yeah, only 'cuz you cheated an' left the keys in the tractor," one of the older boys who followed complained.

"Hi Grandma," the three said in unison, and each kissed Sophia's cheek in turn.

"You're gonna break that door one of these times," Sophia scolded. "Go get cleaned up for dinner. We have a guest."

The three boys followed Sophia's gaze to Adya in the kitchen while taking off their hats.

Adya offered a small smile. However, the three boys were already racing upstairs. Their commotion unnerved Adya, but Sophia didn't react like it was anything unusual and continued to approach Adya with the necklace. Turning her attention back to the piece of jewelry, Adya studied it closely, admiring how beautiful and delicate it was.

"It's lovely," she commented. "I have a magpie at Ava's house who keeps bringing me jet stones. I can't figure out why or where she gets them from."

"Maybe Ava sees that you need healing an' protection now an' is sendin' them to you," Sophia offered.

"How could she—" Adya started, but then remembered Murchadh and his cat and answered the question herself. "Oh," she said and released the necklace back to Sophia. "You think Ava sent Yiny—the magpie—to look out for me?"

"I told ya that her spirit is still with us," Sophia said as she started to return the necklace to the other room. "Check on the bread 'gain will you," she called out from around the corner.

Adya once again removed the pans from the oven and set them on the counter. When she turned around, one of Jace's brothers was standing in front of her with his hand held out and a goofy grin on his face.

"I'm Luke," he said abruptly.

"Hi," Adya said and hesitantly shook his hand. He looked like an older version Jace, with his blond hair, tanned skin, and muscular arms, but was a couple of inches taller and bore signs of an attempt to grow out facial hair. "I'm Adya."

"Oh, the girl stayin' in the witch house," the other brother said as he entered the room.

Adya scowled, but before she could defend Ava, Jace joined his brothers. "She gets feisty when you call it the 'witch house,'" he warned.

His brother rolled his eyes. "Whatever. I'm the handsome middle brother, Dusty." He was the tallest of the three, identical in appearance but had a faint scar down the right side of his face.

"Yeah, he's only called 'Dusty' 'cuz he's always rollin' 'round in the dirt," Jace commented.

Dusty forcefully hit Jace on the arm, prompting Jace to capture Dusty in a headlock. The two bumped into the couch and then the table as they wrestled, causing all the dishes to clank.

"Boys," Sophia scolded as she reentered. "You'll be eatin' out in the barn if you don't quit actin' like animals."

"Sorry, Grandma," the two boys said together.

"Good, now thatcha've met my grandboys, we can eat."

The three boys sat at the table while Adya brought the bread over, and Sophia took each a bowl of stew. "How yer folks doin'?" Sophia asked as she joined the five at the table.

"Busy with inventory," Luke said around half a mouthful of stew.

"Momma said they'll be 'ere for supper on Sunday," Dusty added.

"I'll make her favorite then," Sophia replied with a smile as the three boys groaned.

The family of four sat around and chatted nonstop—which Adya was grateful for—while she stared out the window at the setting sun. Her mind wandered to Yiny, to Ava, and the upcoming anniversary of her mother's death. So much had happened to Adya since previous the year; she could barely remember what it was like to be Emily. That girl wouldn't have traveled to Switzerland and drank warmed wine, nor would she have found herself living by herself in a home of her dearest friend from a past lifetime. While the constant talking and laughing at the dinner table wasn't anything she was familiar with in this life, it almost reminded her of meals at the Academy. She missed Sierra, Ashley, and Paxton, but she wasn't anywhere near ready to return to that life.

"So how long you stayin'?" Dusty asked the distant Adya.

"Oh," she said and brought her mind back to the table. "I don't know. A few weeks, a couple of months—I haven't decided yet."

"You can just up an' leave school like that?" Luke questioned.

Sophia watched on silently as her grandsons questioned their guest.

"Not really, but I have my reasons for being here," Adya replied without intending to sound mysterious.

"I bet she's on suspension. Got in a good fight, from the looks of that mark on her neck," Dusty commented.

Adya's hand flew to her neck, and she scowled as she pushed herself back from the table.

"I think that's enough interrogatin' our guest, boys. Luke an' Dusty can clear the table. Jace, why don't you drive Ady home," Sophia suggested.

"It's fine. I'd prefer to walk," Adya insisted, still angered by Dusty's comment.

"It's dark an' cold an' I'd feel better knowin' you got home safely," Sophia insisted.

Adya took a deep breath to calm herself. "Thank you for dinner, Sophia. I'll see you next week when I bring more groceries. It was nice to meet you all." Adya walked towards the door, prepared to walk back to Ava's, but knew Jace was likely going to follow.

Adya stood outside Jace's truck and looked at the dark landscape around her. The night was cold and quiet except for the animals making soft noises in the back of Sophia's house. The stars were out in full force, too. Some headlights moved on the distant main street, but otherwise, it was a quiet, beautiful night for Adya to be connecting with the elements.

"Go on, get in," Jace instructed Adya as he came out of the house.

Adya resigned to her situation and tried to open the truck door, but it was stuck. "Am I supposed to crawl through the window?"

Jace joined her and effortlessly opened the door. "You can't use force with this lady. Gotta have a gentle touch." Adya rolled her eyes as she got in while Jace walked around to the other side. "I was purdy sure I'd have to chase you down to get you to 'cept the ride home."

Adya shrugged. "Guess I'm full of surprises. Besides, if I'm going to enjoy a walk at night, I prefer it to *not* be with a stinky truck driving next to me. Sorta ruins the whole 'calm and peaceful' feel."

"You sure do have a lot of fire in ya," he said while dust kicked up behind them as they drove away from Sophia's house. "Let's see, can't talk about the house, your family, the reason why you left school, an' your neck. Why doncha lead the conversation, so I steer clear of bad topics."

"Actually, fire is the only thing I don't have in me, elementally speaking," Adya offered.

Jace slammed on the brakes, and the two of them jerked forward. He looked over at Adya with confusion. "You mean you can do things wit' all the other elements 'cept fire?"

Adya was glowering at him for the abrupt stop. "Yes. Earth, water, and air are my three elements. And before you say anything, yes, I'm a freak. Most other affinates have a single element they work with. I have a very old soul that's lived hundreds of lifetimes, and I believe I could've walked back to Ava's in the time you've wasted questioning me instead of driving."

The truck started forward again. "I think it's cool. Grandma has taught us a lot 'bout the earth, but we just don't see it the way she does. I wish I could."

"They encourage us at the Academy not to talk about our affinities with non-affinates. So, it's a little bit weird having a conversation with you about this," Adya explained. She could feel every tiny rock the truck bounced over in the road but had surprisingly relaxed some.

"Have you ev'r made it rain outta nowhere?" Jace asked curiously.

Adya smiled. "No, but I thought about it a few times. I got so angry once that my headmaster had to pull me in his office because he was afraid I was going to take out half of New Orleans with a tornado. Those were his words, not mine."

"Wow, and would you've?" Jace asked as he turned a corner.

"Probably not. But in this lifetime, I seem to struggle more than any other with controlling my temper. The teachers at the Academy tell us we have to let our personalities from this lifetime become part of our soul, but that doesn't always end well for me. This lifetime's personality is a bit. . . chaotic," Adya admitted with a chuckle.

"That's a lot to wrap my brain 'round: this lifetime, that lifetime. I prefer a simple life, not worrying much 'bout what came before or what'll come after," Jace admitted.

"There's a charm in living life like that, I'm sure. I wouldn't ever want to live a life where I didn't have my affinities and my soul memories, though." *Like Maggie*, Adya mentally added.

"Did you just call me charming?" Jace teased.

Adya laughed. "Not remotely," she said.

"So, did you just wake up one day an' you suddenly knew you lived all these other lifetimes?"

"No, not suddenly. It was a slow process to Awaken. Did Sophia ever tell you about hers?" Adya asked.

"She nev'r talks 'bout her old times. She likes to stay in the present life like me, I think," Jace admitted. "So tell me 'bout yours."

Adya shook her head. "Nope. I'm here to get away from that."

Jace pulled up to Ava's house and shut off the engine. "When I was eight, I threw a rock and broke Mrs. Humphrey's window. Soon as it shattered, I ran. I ran an' ran an' hid in the loft of Grandma's barn. Luke brought me meals an' I stayed there for almost a week, scared as shit. When my daddy found me, he whipped my ass an' told me that I hafta face what I'd done. He said you can't run away from the past 'cuz someone would always be there to beat you for your mistakes. Better to face 'em than run scared an' hide from 'em."

Adya nodded as she opened the truck door to get out. "Remind me never to throw rocks at Sophia's house," she smiled coyly and then suddenly realized she was missing something. "Oh, no. I left my backpack at Sophia's."

"Can you get inside your house?" Jace asked.

"Yeah, it was just food for Yiny and me," Adya explained.

"Yiny?" Jace questioned as he looked across the seat at her.

"Just a bird that's been keeping me company," Adya said.

"Lucky bird," Jace smiled. "I'll bring your backpack by in the mornin'. You good 'til then?"

Adya nodded. "I'll be fine. Don't you have school tomorrow?"

"Yeah," he said and started up the engine. "See you tomorrow."

Adya waved and watched the boy leave before stepping onto the porch. Yiny squawked at her from the same tree she was sitting in when Adya left.

"Good evening to you, too, Yiny," Adya said, totally comfortable with talking to the bird now. "I bought you birdseed, but I left it at Sophia's house by mistake. I'll put some out for you in the morning. Sleep well, my friend," Adya said. Her foot twisted as she stepped on something near the door. She bent down and picked up a small stone. While Adya couldn't see what it was yet, she knew it was another gift from Yiny.

"Thank you," she called to the bird and stepped inside.

With the lights on, she noticed Yiny had brought her something different than the usual jet stone. It was a smooth rock with a hole going through it—a hag stone. Adya smiled at the gift and searched for something to hang it with. Upstairs in one of the bedrooms, Adya found some old hair ribbons in a vanity drawer. She picked out a blue, lace-trimmed ribbon, threaded it through the hole in the stone, and hung it on the outside doorknob of the front door before retiring for the night.

CHAPTER FIFTEEN

Adya awoke midmorning and felt refreshed. She opened the window in the bedroom that was once hers while she stayed with Ava and shivered. Frost covered the ground, the sky was a beautiful shade of blue, and the air was uniquely fresh.

Yiny flew on the windowsill and squawked at her. "Good morning to you, too," Adya said happily. "Did you see that I hung up the stone on the door? I'll find a better place for it today." Adya stretched. "Let me get dressed, and I'll join you outside." Yiny chirped and flew away before Adya closed the window. Afterward, she went and took a quick shower before going downstairs to where her clothes were still lying next to the steps.

Adya was searching for an outfit to wear when something leaning against the living room wall by the front door caught her attention. In some ridiculous instinctive manner, Adya tightened the towel around herself. "Hello?" she called out, but no one answered. She was able to breathe again when she realized it was just her backpack, and no one else appeared to be in the house—but Jace had been.

Adya picked up the note on the top of the backpack.

Here's your bag, as promised. Nice rock hanging on the door, but I think you should fire your decorator for putting it there.

Also, you really should lock your doors. -Jace. PS - I took that bike that was leaning against the shed.

"For fuck's sake," Adya muttered and tossed the note aside. She opened the backpack and pulled out the birdseed, deciding it was only polite to feed Yiny before she ate.

After enjoying some fruit and tea for breakfast, Adya went outside and got to work in Ava's garden. The ground was frozen, but she laid her hands on the soil and heated the water within it until the garden area had completely thawed. It was not the ideal time of year to be planting seeds, but with any luck, the weather would start warming up soon. Until then, Adya would have to take extra care of the earth there so her plants could thrive.

"It's therapeutic," Adya explained to Yiny as the bird watched her from the tree. "Working with my elements to bring new life in a harsh environment will help heal those things in me that feel impossibly difficult to overcome." Adya felt it was symbolic, too, and decided when her plants began to flourish, she'd be ready to return to her regular life.

It wasn't an easy job to prepare a garden in late winter. The weather was constantly fighting her, anxious to overtake the ground she'd painstakingly prepared, and she frequently had to ask her elements to help her thaw the soil again. But it was a labor of love. Yiny flew away around noon after she'd eaten most of the birdseed, but the bird's absence didn't bother Adya; she was sure the animal would be back, especially now that she believed Ava had sent the bird to her.

By sunset, Adya finally felt good about her progress in the garden. She grabbed a white sheet from one of the spare bedrooms upstairs and secured it over the freshly planted seeds. "There, that should help them not to freeze completely." Adya asked the elements once more for their balance and assistance to keep the garden safe. She was satisfied with her day's work when she felt the balance of the elements around her.

While inside was warmer than outside, it blocked Adya from connecting as closely to her elements as she would have liked. So as soon as she made herself a small dinner, Adya sat on the back porch to eat. She admired Yiny's latest gift that was now hanging on the ribbon from a small hook on the patio's eave.

While appreciating the steam rising from her orange noodles, Adya heard the distinct rumble of Jace's truck's engine approaching from the distance. She sighed as she tucked the blanket around her legs that were curled up under her in the deck chair and ate her macaroni and cheese.

Adya remained unmoved when she heard the truck turn off out front and when the subsequent knocking occurred. "I'm out back," she yelled before running her fingers through the remnants of cheese sauce in her bowl.

"Whatcha doin' out here?" Jace asked as he rounded the corner with his jacket pulled tight around him.

"Eating dinner. What are *you* doing out here?" Adya fired back.

"It's a bit cold to be sittin' out here," Jace pointed out.

"I happen to appreciate the elements in all their forms. And now, back to my question—why are you here?" Adya didn't say it rudely, but she couldn't fathom why Jace would've driven out to Ava's house. She hadn't been the friendliest person to him, and he already had to trek out there once that day to return her backpack.

Jace shrugged. "It's Friday night. My friends are at some party an' I didn't feel much like gettin' drunk with 'em tonight."

"Is that what you do on Friday nights around here? Drink with your friends?"

"Purdy much. 'Cept next Friday there's a carnival in town for Valentine's Day. I'll prolly be there."

Adya wrinkled her nose at the mention of the holiday.

"Not a fan of love?" Jace asked.

"Love is fine, I just don't enjoy celebrating that day," Adya admitted.

"Oh," Jace replied. "Hey, you got any more of those noodles?"

Adya nodded and unfolded her legs to stand up. "Yeah, I was about to get myself some more. Come on in."

"I like where you decided to hang that rock," Jace commented as he followed Adya inside.

"Mmhmm," Adya replied. "It's kinda creepy that you came inside my house this morning, by the way."

Jace shrugged. "The door was unlocked."

"Yes, well, that has been remedied." Adya got another bowl out of the cabinet and scooped some of the remaining macaroni and cheese into it for Jace, and took a little more for herself. "Here you go."

"Thanks," Jace said and immediately started eating. "I would've 'spected you to eat fancier in this house. Is this whatcha eat at your school?"

"No, they'd never serve this at my school. We have a professional chef and kitchen staff that make our meals. It's exquisite, honestly. I guess that's why I'm choosing to eat from a blue box now," Adya added with a laugh.

"I don't get you, Ady. You're the strangest person I've ever met," Jace said with a smile.

"Not the worst thing anyone's called me. Have you met many tri-affinates in your time?" Adya countered.

"Very funny. You're almost tolerable when you're not fightin' everyone," Jace teased.

"So, what is it you want to know about me?" Adya asked and hopped up onto the counter to eat the few noodles she'd gotten as seconds.

"Is this a trick question?" Jace asked.

"No, let's call it payment for returning my backpack and not stealing anything this morning."

"Okay. Hmmm. There are so many good questions to ask." Jace pondered for several minutes and finally settled on one. "What were you like before you knew 'bout your affinities?"

"Starting with the easy questions. . . alright, I can appreciate that. Let's see. The name my parents gave me was Emily. I was an only child and did normal kid stuff. I'd go to the mall with my friends, pass notes in class, complain about Mondays, and usually go to a sleepover on Fridays. I was never tidy—a trait that's stayed with me, which you can see from my clothes scattered in there." An amused smirk danced on Adya's lips. "And I loved spending time with my mom in her garden."

"So, you became this grumpy, sulking person when you— what did you call it?"

"Awakened. And I'm not grumpy or sulking, I just. . . have complicated things I have to work through." Adya shrugged. "Alright, now it's my turn to ask a question."

"I don't owe you answers for anythin'," Jace insisted.

"I gave you my macaroni and cheese," Adya reminded him. "Besides, you like talking."

"What's your question?" Jace asked, setting down his bowl.

"Why did you *really* come out here tonight?"

Jace leaned back in the barstool chair and gazed at the wall with a contemplative look. "When I was here this mornin', it just felt kinda sad an' lonely. I know you don't have any friends here, an' I already know that you aren't one to admit you need help with nothin'. Figured if I showed up, you'd either chase me 'way with a tornado or you'd chat. I was 'spectin' the tornado," Jace answered with a grin.

"One day, and you think you have me all figured out, huh?" Adya mused. "You have two brothers. Haven't you ever just needed time away to think?"

"No, not really," Jace said thoughtfully. "I think while I'm workin'. I think in school. I like to spend my time doin' stuff, not thinkin' 'bout it."

"That makes sense," Adya said with a nod. "Hmm, how can I make this relatable?" Adya thought for a few minutes while Jace gathered the bowls and took them to the sink. "Okay, you like running, or at least racing your brothers, right?"

"Yeah, I s'pose." Jace started washing the dishes in the sink.

"What if you broke your leg, had to sit out of working and wrestling with your brothers for weeks. When it healed, do you think you'd be running around with them right away after your cast came off, or would you need some time to get your leg back in shape before you competed with them again?"

"I did break my leg two years ago," Jace nodded. "Yeah, Dusty made fun of how small my calf got in that cast. Took me a while, but I beat them now."

"That's kinda what this is for me. I lost something, and I just need some time to feel like myself again."

"Was it your mom dying?" Jace asked.

Adya chuckled softly. "No, although you might want to stay away from me next Wednesday. That's the first anniversary of her death, and I don't know yet how I'm going to react."

"So, what was it?"

"I'm afraid you already used up your one question. I guess you'll have to wait until you have something else to bargain with." Adya smiled and tossed Jace the towel to dry the dishes he just washed.

"I fixed your bicycle," he volunteered. "Got it in my truck right now."

Adya blinked in surprise. "You *fixed* it? I thought you probably sold it to a scrap yard."

"That beauty? Naw, she's a classic. Had offers from people to buy it from me, but I told 'em it wasn't for sale." Jace smile proudly.

"Thank you. I didn't think I had any chance of getting it working."

"Is that payment 'nough for you to answer my question?" Jace asked as he hung the damp towel on the stove handle to dry.

"What was your question again?" Adya asked with a smile.

"What did you lose that you need healin' from?"

Adya sighed. "It's a complicated mess of things I lost. But to answer simply, I lost almost everything in this world that's important to me."

"You know I'm itchin' to ask a follow-up question," Jace said playfully.

"Without you understanding soul lives and affinities and all that, it'd be hard for you to appreciate fully. Geez, that sounded condescending, but I swear that wasn't how I meant it." Adya frowned.

"Fair 'nuff. Why doncha tell me about these soul lives."

"You may wish you were drinking for this conversation," Adya joked.

"I'm sure we could find somethin' 'round here. C'mon," Jace said and held out a hand to help Adya jump off the counter.

"You realize that I'm thirteen in this body, right?" Adya asked.

"No, thought ya was at least fifteen, but no matter. Been drinkin' since I was nine. Like I said, not much to do 'round here. Besides, you could do with some loosenin' up."

Adya felt Jace was suggesting something. She narrowed her eyes. "We need to get something straight right here, right now. I do not need or want a boyfriend. I'm in a very complicated situation right now and can't have a winter fling with some hot guy in West Virginia."

"You said I was hot," Jace pointed out with a laugh. When Adya threw him a withering look, he verbally retreated, but his eyes were still bright. "I most certainly have no intention of doing anythin' romantic or otherwise with a thousand-year-old girl. Happy?"

"More like seven thousand, give or take a century, but yeah. It's better to have that out in the open." Adya led Jace into the living room where some old bottles of gin and brandy were stored. "I can't attest if these are even good anymore, but here you go."

"Hmm," Jace said as he studied the bottles. "Sealed and stored in a dark, cool place. They'll do just fine." Jace jogged back to the kitchen and grabbed two glasses with ice in them while Adya sat on the floor with her back to the couch.

"This should be interesting," Adya commented as she watched Jace prepare two glasses of gin.

Jace, who sat a couple of feet away on the floor next to Adya, reached over and tapped his quarter-full glass against Adya's. "Bottom's up."

Adya hesitated, watching Jace swallow his first.

"That means you're s'posed to drink it," Jace urged.

Gin had never been a preferred drink of Adya's in any life, but in the spirit of "loosening up," as Jace as put it, she tilted her head back and swallowed all the liquid in her glass in one gulp. That, of course, resulted in her coughing until tears streamed from her eyes.

Jace laughed and poured them both more gin. "It gets better," he encouraged.

Adya slapped her hand on the couch, trying to catch her breath. "I'll wait," she managed to say, holding up her hand to turn down the drink.

Jace downed another glass and set it on the coffee table next to where they were seated. "Alright, so soul lives. Educate me."

Adya started at the beginning, explaining her early lives and then how she met Ava. Jace listened intensely and consumed another drink every ten lifetimes or so. By the time Adya got up to the lifetime when she had met Lir for the first time, she had drunk two more glasses of gin.

Jace held up his hand at one point to stop Adya's story. "Lemme get this straight," he said. "You knew *the* Julius Caesar?"

Adya shook her head. "Not personally, but I was in Rome during his rule. And let me tell you," Adya said with a slight slurring of her words as she leaned in closer to Jace as if what she was about to say was a secret, "his death wasn't as dramatic as the stories make it sound." Adya nodded. "I'd never wanna rule anything ever. They always have targets on their head." She less-than-soberly poked the center of her forehead with her pointer finger.

"Damn, you're like a walkin' talkin' history book," Jace commented.

Adya shrugged. "Better than any history book. I've got soul magic," she said with a giggle and created a gust of wind that swirled around the living room. "Did you know that I can pick people up off the ground with this?" She focused the air and created a weak vortex around Jace.

Jace grabbed hold of the table with a look of absolute horror. "No, no. Don't do me. I'm 'fraid of heights!"

Adya teased him for a moment longer and then let the air in the room return to normal. "I'm sorry," she managed to say between fits of uncontrollable giggles.

Jace glowered at her as he grabbed another bottle of alcohol from the cabinet. "You have a very mean streak in you, Ady." But he smiled again and raised a refreshed glass of gin in salute to Adya. "Go on with your story," he encouraged.

The giggle fit slowly subsided, and Adya continued telling Jace about her lives, all of which from that point forward involved Lir. Thankfully, the alcohol took away most of the sting when talking about him.

"So, do you know these Pax and Lir guys now?" Jace asked at the end of Adya's story, which concluded at the end of her previous life.

Adya's relaxed expression tensed. "Yes," she said. "Pax just completed his Awakening and is back at the Academy."

"Are you gonna marry him again?"

The tense expression turned into a frown. "Not likely," Adya admitted. "Don't get me wrong," she added, "I will always and forever love him."

"But?" Jace prompted.

Adya looked down at her hands and the ring on her finger. "It's complicated."

"That's a shitty cop-out of an answer," Jace replied. "You went from 'leave me the hell alone' to tellin' me the stories of your lifetimes an' now you're shuttin' down 'gain? That's horse shit, Ady." Jace poured a healthy amount of gin in Adya's glass. "Take 'nother drink an' tell me the rest."

Adya's gaze didn't shift from the ring on her hand. "What do you care most about in your life, Jace?"

Jace pushed the glass closer to Adya as he answered. "I guess my family, my truck, and my dog," he replied.

"You *guess*?" Adya's temper flared for a moment, but then she sighed and picked up the glass. "Sorry. See? This is why I'm here by myself. I *know* what I care about most, and I've lost it." Adya took a large gulp of the gin and continued, "I can manage every lifetime except this one. I've been physically beaten, starved, persecuted, threatened, tortured, and every other unimaginable horror at various times throughout all those other lifetimes and can talk about them no problem. But this one—" Adya looked down at the disintegrating ice cubes in her glass and swallowed hard. "I can't make peace with what's happened."

"Stop pushin' it down inside you an' let it out," Jace said.

"You wanna know what happened to my neck?" Adya said before finishing the drink. "I stabbed myself."

"On purpose?" Jace asked.

Adya nodded, threw all abandon out the window, and dove into the story of Myra/Dhruva. "Now she's stealing souls and putting them in other people's bodies. People tell me that what I did was brave because it was to stop her from taking my soul."

"Sounds purdy brave to me," Jace commented. "Couldn't you've just used your soul magic stuff to stop her?"

"She injected me with a shot of something that blocked my affinities when I gave myself up to her, when I thought I could save Lir. You see, me and Lir were finally gonna get our lifetime together. And then Dhruva took his soul." Emotion streaked Adya's cheeks with wet tears. "We promised ourselves to each other," Adya showed off the ring on her right hand, "and then she turned his body into a soulless sentinel. His beautiful soul is in someone else's body, trapped until that person dies." Adya gazed sadly at the ice melting in her glass and then made the cubes freeze again.

"Do you know who has his soul?" Jace hesitantly asked, sensing Adya's fragile mental state.

Adya shook her head. "Maggie knows. She told Darius, the man who came to rescue me from Dhruva's hell hole, but he didn't tell me who, and I didn't ask. I'd already sunk too deep into the pit that brought me here. I can't even touch that murderous rage that's inside me. All I want right now is to talk with Ava and find my balance again."

"I'm not Ava or even an affinate, but I'll help you if I can an' if you let me," Jace offered.

Adya shrugged. "I don't know what anyone can do to help," she admitted.

"Tomorrow, you an' I are gonna go on a hike. You can tell me more 'bout Ava or Lir or anything else you wanna, an' you'll get some time with your elements, too." Jace smiled and then yawned.

"I think it's already tomorrow," Adya said lightly and motioned towards the windows and the dull light overtaking the night sky.

"Go get sleep, an' we'll talk 'bout it again when you wake," Jace said.

"There are plenty of rooms and beds in this house. Take whichever one you want," Adya said as she forced herself to her feet. She took a minute to balance as her head spun from the alcohol and exhaustion.

"I'll be just fine here on the couch. Sweet dreams, Ady," Jace said as he crawled onto the couch.

"Sweet dreams, Jace," Adya replied and then made a slow, calculated ascent to her temporary bedroom.

Yiny woke Adya later that morning by incessantly tapping at her window.

"Ugh," Adya complained as the bright midday sun shone through her window. Her head was pounding, and she still felt a bit drunk.

Adya practically fell out of bed and wobbled her way over to the window to open it. "Good morning, Yiny. I'll be down in a few minutes to give you some more seed." The bird seemed to accept her answer and flew down to the ground to wait.

With her long hair pulled back into a messy ponytail, Adya made a slow descent down the stairs. The room reeked of gin, and with Jace still passed out on the couch, Adya quietly made herself a cup of tea before going outside.

Yiny eagerly ate the birdseed that Adya provided and then flew away almost as quickly. Adya sat on the back porch and tried to cure herself of the hangover using her knowledge of water elemental healing. Several minutes later, she felt mostly better and finished her cup of tea before turning her attention to the garden.

It was there that Jace found her half an hour later. Adya was kneeling on the cold ground with her palms flat against it. "My loving earth, I ask of you to bring life back in this lifeless season, to extend your gracious gifts to this soul so that I might find balance within again and extend it out."

"Is that how you always talk to your plants?" Jace asked and peeked under the white sheet protecting the seeds. "It's too cold to be plantin' now."

"Precisely why I'm doing it," Adya said as she stood up and brushed the dirt off her legs. "If I can do the improbable with my elements, maybe there's a chance that I can do other things that don't seem so likely."

"Like savin' your boyfriend?" Jace inferred.

Adya shrugged. "I was looking to save myself first, but yeah, that's definitely a goal."

"Maybe you're just settin' yourself up for guaranteed failure, so you have verifiable excuses." Jace shrugged as Adya threw him an angry look. "But what do I know? I've only got sixteen years of experience compared to your seven thousand, give or take a century," he mocked.

"You should go." Adya's steely retort was cold.

"Alright," Jace said with a shrug and started walking away. "I'm not afraid to tell it to you as I see it," he called back as he pulled his truck keys from his pocket. "But maybe you're afraid to accept the truth. Gotta suck to always be livin' in the past." Jace took the bike out of the back of the truck and leaned it against the railing of the front porch before driving away.

"He's so stupidly wrong," Adya said as Yiny flew next to her and watched Jace disappear down the dirt road. "My past makes me who I am in the present. And that, beautiful one, is the truth."

Yiny squawked to bring Adya's attention to the pink and white flower she'd placed at Adya's feet. "An alstroemeria? It's beautiful, Yiny. A symbol of devotion and friendship? I already consider you my friend, though." Adya smiled at the bird and held the flower up to her nose.

Yiny squawked again at Adya and flew towards the spot vacated by Jace's truck, looked back at her, and then down the road and yelled at Adya again.

Adya chuckled. "He's just a normal kid, though. He doesn't understand, and I'm sure the only reason he came last night was to see how far he could get with me. Probably a bet with his brothers or friends or something. When I shut him down, he stayed for free alcohol. It's fine, though. I feel a little better after saying out loud all the things that I'd been keeping inside."

The bird made a sound that remarkably resembled a grunt and flew off in the same direction Jace had driven.

"Fine then," Adya said, taking playful offense. "Maybe I'll give the bike a test run."

CHAPTER SIXTEEN

Adya hadn't heard from Jace since she told him to leave four days earlier. While she kept reassuring herself that it was better to keep him at a distance than to accumulate another potential loss in her life, she truthfully missed his almost-friendship. Talking through things with Jace that night had loosened the vice-grip of some of the turmoil she felt inside, just as Jace suggested it might. Despite vowing to let Jace live his own life without her troubles to worry about, she found herself looking for him and his truck whenever she rode into town, which happened to be more frequent than necessary.

On this day, however, Adya had no other option than to ride into town. It was the anniversary of her mother's death. She had mixed emotions about how she should or would feel as the day progressed. It was also the anniversary of the beginning of her Awakening.

It was the warmest day since Adya arrived at Ava's house, with the late morning temperatures in the upper forties. She took her time riding the bicycle into town after tending to her garden and enjoying her morning breakfast with Yiny, who continued bringing her alstroemeria flowers—stubborn bird. Adya's mood was better than she'd anticipated, and smiled at the few cars that passed her on the main street in town.

She pulled up to a quaint flower shop with blooming window boxes and parked her bike by the entrance.

"I'd like to buy some white lilies," Adya said politely to the middle-aged woman behind the counter.

The woman brushed her dark blonde bangs out of her eyes as she spoke to Adya. "Do you want an arrangement in a vase or individual flowers?"

"I don't need a vase," Adya replied as she appreciated the sweet aroma in the shop.

The woman nodded and guided Adya to the selection of individual flowers grouped by type in the refrigerated section of the store. "Pick out the ones you like, and we can box them up for you." The woman walked away before Adya could explain that she didn't need a box.

Adya leaned over and inhaled. One of her favorite perks of her earth affinity was the euphoric feeling inside her when she breathed in the aroma of flowers. "These are lovely," Adya complimented. She handpicked a dozen white lilies and took them to the register.

"Yes, they are lovely. Are you giving these to someone special for Valentine's Day?"

Adya shook her head. "No, I'm holding a small memorial for my mom today. It's the anniversary of her passing."

"Oh dear, well, I'm sure your mother would've loved these," the woman said kindly.

"Thank you for saying that, and also for not saying 'I'm sorry,'" Adya replied with a chuckle. "Oh, and if you just want to wrap them in some paper, that'll be fine. I'm going to find a nice spot to place them."

"Shouldn't you be in school? I don't recall my boys telling me it was a short day," the woman said as she gave Adya her change.

"I don't live around here. Just visiting for a little while," Adya explained.

"You're the girl staying in Ava's house, aren't you? Adya, right? Grandma Sophia was talking about you at supper on Sunday."

Adya nodded. "Yes, I'm Adya. Are you Jace's mom?"

The woman laughed and nodded. "Yes, Jace, Dusty, and Luke are my boys. It's nice to finally meet the girl I've heard so much about. The boys might've mentioned you, too."

Adya felt her face heat up. "Well, thank you for the flowers. I might be back in some time just to enjoy the scents in here."

"I look forward to it, Adya. And if you're not doing anything Friday night, you should come to the festival," she suggested as Adya situated the flowers carefully in her backpack.

"I'll think about it. Goodbye," Adya said and inhaled deeply once more before leaving the shop.

Adya's next stop was the post office. She had written letters to Ashley, Sierra, and Paxton, letting them know she was okay and missed them. She told Ashley about Yiny, hoping that her friend would find humor in her new animal friend and the gifts she brought to Adya. She also mentioned Jace in the letter to her roommate, figuring she would enjoy a little gossip.

After dropping the letters in the mailbox, Adya noticed an elderly lady sitting on a bench feeding birds. Adya watched the woman for a brief while—she looked both sad and content if that was at all possible. An idea popped into her head, and she walked over to the woman. "The birds seem to enjoy you being here," Adya voiced softly, hoping not to startle the woman.

"I come here ev'ry mornin' I can to feed 'em," she said.

Adya pulled a lily from her backpack and offered it to the woman.

"What's this fer?" the woman asked in confusion.

"It's for having a kind soul. Enjoy your day," Adya said and left the woman to feed her birds.

Adya handed out three more lilies before she reached the diner, where she'd already planned to eat lunch while riding into town. Besides gardening, one of her unforgettable memories with her mom was sitting down together on a cold winter day and eating grilled cheese sandwiches with tomato soup. While she was waiting for her lunch to arrive, Adya handed out flowers to the four other customers in the small diner and one to the only waitress working.

"Thank you," Adya said politely as her food was delivered. The waitress seemed to be smiling more after receiving the flower. Something inside Adya told her that her mom would've liked her daughter's kind gesture.

While Adya was eating the second half of her sandwich, a group of teens around her age walked into the diner, instantly transforming the once calm establishment into what sounded like a noisy night club. Three of the other patrons paid and left almost immediately, and the smile on the waitress's face faded. It almost reminded Adya of the chaos that surrounded Jace and his brothers when they were together, except this group wasn't glued together by sibling love. Demanding, loud, and utterly oblivious that anyone other than themselves existed, Adya's harmonious mood was quickly deteriorating.

No, Adya's old soul told herself. *Don't give these kids the power to take anything away from you.* But when their obnoxiousness targeted Adya, the Emily part of her threatened to put them in their place.

"Hey! Aren't ya that weird girl livin' in the witch house?" one of the boys yelled at her. The girls in his group all giggled.

Adya did her best to ignore them and continued eating her food without responding.

"I think she's deaf, or mute, or somethin'," one of the girls replied to Adya's silence.

"Hey Mel!" a third one called out to the man in the kitchen. "I didn't think you served witches an' freaks in here."

"Behave you guys," the waitress warned.

The boys mock-saluted the waitress and then rolled their eyes collectively as she walked away with their orders.

"Hey, witch girl," a boy from the group called out and sidled over. "There's this hot girl I wanna take out. Can you give me one of those love potions?" The boy looked back at his friends and laughed as he stopped at Adya's table.

"You should probably go back and sit with your friends," Adya warned in a calm voice.

"Or what? You gonna hex me?" he said boisterously, wiggling his fingers at Adya like he was doing magic.

Adya had three choices: get pissed and let her affinities teach this kid a lesson, ignore him completely and leave, or mess with his head a bit. Adya grinned when she decided on the third option.

"Yes," she said matter-of-factly and closed her eyes. She hovered her hand over her glass of water and said what basically amounted to "you smell like a dog vomited on you" in Gaelic, which sounded to the boy like she was casting a spell. She used her water affinity to freeze the glass of water and then opened her eyes to stare at the boy, who was noticeably startled. "I'd be careful where I stepped, if I were you," Adya warned in a menacing whisper.

The boy jumped away from Adya's table and moved quickly back to his friends. "Holy shit, did ya see that? She *is* a witch!"

Adya returned the ice in her glass back into regular water and dabbed the corners of her mouth. She paid for her food, leaving a generous tip, before walking out of the diner. Adya got on her bike and rode away without looking back—even when she thought she caught a glimpse out of the corner of her eye of Jace's truck pulling into the diner.

Despite feeling satisfied with how she dealt with the kids at the restaurant, Adya's good mood that had persisted most of the day started waning. She decided to ride home and find somewhere around Ava's house to leave the flowers she'd bought to honor her mother.

Adya walked around the acreage of Ava's property for over an hour, not finding a suitable place to pay a fitting tribute to her mother, until Yiny showed up and guided her to the small river that flowed through the far edge of the property. Adya had been down there once when she first arrived at Ava's home but hadn't been drawn down to her primary element until now.

"This is a perfect spot, Yiny. Thank you."

Adya finally took off her backpack and set it beside her as she knelt on the river's bank. Out of her bag, she withdrew the remaining three lilies, a white candle, and a lighter. With the candle lit, Adya placed the flowers in the flowing water one by one while speaking aloud to the elements. "The elements guide us and protect us in life. Please follow the ones we love into their afterlife and provide balance and harmony to their souls." Adya remained kneeling on the shore with her lit candle, making peace with the elements until the stars were bright in the night sky.

As she walked back to the house, Adya half expected to see Jace's truck parked out front. After all, he had an annoying habit of doing the opposite of what she asked of him, and she had warned him to stay away on the death anniversary day. But it seemed like he had finally taken Adya for her word and was really staying away after she told him to go.

"It's for the best," Adya said to Yiny as she flew beside Adya. "I know you keep insisting that he's a friend, but after the scene at the diner today with his classmates, it's in his own best interest to keep his distance from the crazy witch girl." Adya chuckled, but if she allowed herself to admit it, she did miss having a friend to talk to—one that would actually talk back to her.

"Goodnight, sweet Yiny. I think I'm going to sleep early tonight. See you in the morning, my friend." Adya waited for the bird to depart before she went inside, double-checked that the doors were locked, and went upstairs to sleep.

The following morning, Adya woke up early and followed her usual routine of feeding Yiny, drinking a cup of tea, and tending to her garden. The sheet was helping to keep the frost off the planted seeds, but Adya still had to warm the earth each day.

Her next stop was the market in town to pick up a few items for herself, along with Sophia's groceries. With the help of the basket on the front of the bicycle, Adya had no problem carrying the bags. She looked around in town for Jace's truck, but she didn't see it nor any other high school-aged people and assumed it wasn't a field day. Adya felt a small amount of disappointment, but her focus shifted when Yiny flew up alongside her.

"Coming to visit Sophia?" Adya asked her companion. In response to a chirp from Yiny, she added, "Yeah, Sophia misses Ava, too. I'm sure she'll like meeting you."

Adya parked her bike against the front porch and knocked on the door. "Sophia, I'm here with your groceries," she called out, but there was no sound coming from inside. Adya went around to the back of the house and called out again, "Sophia! Are you out here?" Still, there was only the sound of the goats playing.

Yiny squawked at the back door, prompting Adya to see what the bird was trying to draw her attention to. As Adya peered through the glass door, she saw Sophia lying motionless on the dining room floor. Smothering her panic, Adya quickly went around the entire house and tried to gain entry through doors and windows alike, but to no avail. In a desperate attempt to reach the unconscious woman, Adya picked up a rock and threw it at the window embedded in the front door. She thrust her arm inside, gashing it on the jagged window, and opened the door.

Adya rushed over to Sophia and felt for her pulse. "Still beating," she said, feeling a brief moment of relief. Her hands rested on Sophia's face, and Adya called upon her elements to help her find the imbalance in Sophia—it was her heart.

Yiny jumped frantically on the patio outside the sliding back door, screeching out in concern. "I'm trying, Yiny," Adya said to her bird and then moved her hands to Sophia's chest.

Adya calmed her heart rate and took slow breaths as she used her earth and water affinities to stop the erratic rhythm of Sophia's heart. The older woman's water was out of balance, too, which may have triggered the heart's behavior. She also hit her head in the fall, which would be the third focus of Adya's healing.

It took more than five grueling minutes for Adya to balance Sophia's elements and return her heart to a comfortable, steady beat, and another two for her to mend the wound inside the woman's skull. Adya shifted from kneeling over Sophia to sitting back on her heels and waited for the woman to awaken.

Slowly, Sophia's eyes fluttered open, and she looked around in confusion.

"Your heart wasn't beating correctly, and you hit your head when you collapsed," Adya explained as she knelt beside Sophia. "I healed you the best I could, but you should probably see a doctor about your heart." Adya grabbed a tissue from the end table behind her and wiped the blood from Sophia's face. "I think I ruined your shirt," she admitted and looked down at the gash on her arm.

"Doncha be worryin' 'bout that. I have more shirts." Sophia paused to catch her breath. "I've seen 'nough doctors. They want to do some crazy surgery on my heart, but I'm just old. I've made peace with this lifetime," Sophia said and slowly sat up.

Adya frowned and helped Sophia get to her feet. "I also might've broken a window to get in," she admitted as she supported Sophia to the couch.

Sophia waved her hand dismissively. "The boys'll fix that when they come by." Sophia looked at Adya sitting next to her and nodded. "You have a remarkable soul, Ady. Ya know, when the kids would scuff themselves up, I would try to heal 'em. Nev'r could do much more than fix the scrapes. Tried mendin' Jace's leg when he fell outta that tree back there but couldn't do much for 'im. But you fixed my heart an' my head."

Adya smiled shyly. "It helps that I have three affinities on my side."

Sophia nodded. "True, but it takes more than havin' a gift to be able to use it well." Sophia took Adya's hand in both her hands. "Why're you here?"

"It's Thursday, so I brought your groceries," Adya said in confusion and worried that maybe she didn't do such a good job of healing Sophia's head.

"No, no, child. I know what day it is. Why are ya *here* 'stead of back at yer Academy?"

Adya gazed down at her hands. "Because I'm broken. A little over a month ago, I had everything: a love that'd taken lifetimes to happen, three affinities, friends, and a guardian who I loved like a sister— " Adya paused to let the wave of emotion to pass. "Except for my friends, I lost it all. And it scared me. If I wasn't strong enough to save everything that was most important to me, what's the point of even trying anymore?"

"You just saved me," Sophia reminded her. "And yesterday, yes, I know all 'bout yesterday. You turned one of your losses into somethin' beautiful for people you don't even know." Sophia rested her hand on Adya's leg.

"How do you know about me handing out flowers?" Adya asked, her brows drawn together in confusion.

"Child, this is a small town. Ev'ryone knows ev'rythin'. Also helps that my granddaughter is the florist," Sophia said with a wink. "But you, Adya, are not broken by anythin' you can't fix. Ya jus' hafta want it. I know there's comfort in removin' yourself from all the things in this world that can hurt you.

Why d'ya think I keep to myself in this small town? But the world needs ya. The elements need ya."

Adya smiled at Sophia's kind words. "I'm not going to hide away forever."

A tapping sound came from the back door, and Adya looked back to see Yiny anxiously awaiting an introduction. "Oh right, Yiny wanted to meet you. She's been waiting so patiently outside. Are you feeling up to an introduction?"

Sophia smiled. "I wondered when I'd get to meet her. Just help this old woman up." She held out her hand to Adya.

Adya grabbed onto Sophia's forearms and pulled her upright. She hovered over the older woman as she walked to the back door.

"I'm not that fragile, child," Sophia scolded pleasantly as they walked outside together to meet Adya's magpie companion.

"I don't feel good leaving you by yourself," Adya insisted as the two drank tea on Sophia's back porch. "Are you sure you don't want me to stay until your grandkids get here?"

"I'm fine," Sophia insisted. "Besides, Yiny will stay an' keep me company."

"Alright then," Adya said as she stood. "If you need anything, send Yiny for me." Adya turned to the bird that was happily enjoying some seeds Sophia put out for her. "Come get me right away if you think Sophia needs help."

"I'll be seein' ya 'gain soon, Ady," Sophia said with a smile. "An' if ya see Jace. . . just make good by him. He's been broodin' since he last visited you." Adya thought she saw Sophia roll her eyes.

"I'll try, but I don't usually go far enough from the house to see anyone."

"He'll be at the festival t'morrow evenin'," Sophia hinted.

"I wasn't going to—"

"He'll be there," Sophia added sternly.

214

"See you later, Sophia," Adya replied and hopped onto her bike. She took her time riding home, keeping an eye and ear out for Yiny, just in case anything happened to Sophia.

"No, I'm not going to go to the stupid Valentine's Day festival," Adya told Yiny as the bird hopped back and forth on the porch the afternoon following the visit with Sophia. "I know, Sophia expects me to go, but she's not my mom. I make my own choices," Adya insisted. "Okay, yeah, I feel bad that Jace is moping around, but he knows where I live. If he wanted to talk to me or yell at me, he knows where to find me."

Yiny continued to give Adya the stink eye.

"I don't even have anything to wear to a festival. It's Valentine's Day, and I'm sure they're all dressed up in their Sunday best," Adya argued. "Besides," she continued, speaking more logically than emotionally, "I tend to ruin special events. Everyone from the high school and probably their parents think I'm a witch. How well do you see it going over if I show up at their little party? They'd probably try to burn me or throw stones at me or something."

Yiny ruffled her feathers at Adya, the bird equivalent of an eye roll, and flew off in what Adya perceived as a huff. "I'm not going," Adya repeated as she went inside.

"No, I'm not going to go," she said to herself as knelt to go through the clothes Ashley had packed for her in an attempt to find something to wear to the festival. Meanwhile, the unopened gift from Lir seemed to be silently beckoning her. "You are *definitely* not getting touched tonight," she said and placed the package on the fireplace mantel, out of the way.

Adya uncovered the makeup she'd bought in Switzerland. "Hmmm, I guess if I *have* to go tonight, I can at least look the part." That gave Adya a great idea. She ran upstairs to Ava's old room and opened her closet. Ava's fabulous wardrobe—she had great taste in all her lives—was still there, and most of it looked to be in good condition, too. Adya sorted through the clothes one by one, considering each, but finally decided on a light blue dress with a white lace collar and decorative buttons that were the same shade as the dress going down to mid-chest. The skirt of the dress flared out from a high waistline, which was a typical style in the 1940s. What made it even better was when Adya tried on the dress, and it fit perfectly—Ava was quite petite in her last body.

After she applied makeup like Elena had shown her in Switzerland, she admired herself in the mirror for a moment before putting on a navy-blue pair of Ava's Mary Jane-style shoes. "I really shouldn't go," Adya said while taking one last look at herself in the mirror.

Since there was no way she was going to ride a bicycle in her dress, Adya put on her white coat and started the walk towards town. It didn't take long for her to come to hate the shoes—at least for walking in—and carried them by her side as she walked the rest of the way to town barefooted. The ground was cold, but Adya never complained about being in physical contact with her elements.

The location of the festival wasn't hard to find. The lights and music could be seen and heard when Adya was still miles away. There was also a steady stream of cars driving in the same direction towards the lights down the main street. Adya paused just outside of town and considered going back to Ava's house. "What do you think, Yiny?" Adya asked the bird as it landed beside her. The bird made an encouraging noise and then flew off into the direction of the festivities. Adya sighed, brushed off the bottoms of her feet, and then slid them into Ava's shoes. "Here goes nothing."

Walking up to the bustling event, Adya already felt out of place. Everyone was wearing jeans and coats, probably more appropriate for the weather than the dress she'd picked. Still, if she was going to do this, Adya was determined to hold her head high and attempt to enjoy herself.

The event was in the park in the middle of down. Twinkling white lights decorated the trees, and there were larger lightbulbs on strands stretching from tree to tree. It created a well-lit area for the venders, refreshment tables, and dance floor. In the distance, a live band was playing while people—both young and old—danced.

Adya paid the entrance fee—a nominal amount of money that was supposedly going to the town's historical society to preserve a building on the far side of the municipality that Adya had never traveled to. Just inside the entrance fee table, Jace's mom was handing everyone a carnation.

"Good evening," Adya said politely to the woman she only knew as "Jace's mom."

"Adya, it's good to see you again. How did your memorial for your mom go?" she asked kindly while continuing to hand out carnations.

"It was very nice, thanks to your flowers," Adya replied.

"Oh," the woman met Adya's eyes with affection, "and thank you for helping out Grandma. I don't know what we would've done if you hadn't gone to see her. We were all at the shop until late last night, getting ready for all the deliveries today."

"I was more than happy to help," Adya replied graciously. "I'm going to go find some food and let you get back to handing out your flowers." She brought the pink carnation to her nose, inhaled deeply, and continued her quest to find something to eat.

Adya wasn't oblivious to the random groups of people whispering and looking at her as she walked around. Whether it was because she was overdressed or because of the incident in the diner, Adya didn't know or care. She kept her head held high, smiled at everyone, and eventually made her way to the table that was selling barbequed hamburgers. "One burger and bag of chips, please," she asked the middle-aged woman who was working.

The woman narrowed her eyes at Adya. "We don't serve yer kind here," she said flatly and crossed her arms.

"You don't serve hamburgers to thirteen-year-old girls wearing blue dresses?" Adya questioned. "That seems like a very specific discrimination," she pointed out.

"Give 'er the damn burger, Sarah," the man at the grill yelled.

With a scowl, the woman that Adya had never met dropped the paper plate with the burger on the table, causing the buns and patty to separate. Adya picked up the plate and politely discarded her money in the same fashion. Coincidentally, it happened at the same time that a gust of wind swept through, and the dollar bills went flying.

"Damn witch!" the woman yelled at Adya as she was walking away.

Adya shrugged at Yiny when she noticed the bird watching Adya from a nearby branch and meandered around the park, looking for an open table to sit at to eat her hamburger. She spied a table on the far side of the gathering, but Adya would have to quickly weave through the crowds congregating close to the stage if she wanted to claim the spot before someone else got it.

Adya was doing a great job of dodging people and not dropping her food until she was about ten feet from her goal, and someone seemed to step in front of her purposely. Adya's plate crumpled, and her burger fell to the ground before she had a chance to react.

"Whatda we have here?" the boy, whose face she recognized from the diner, sneered at her.

"Normally, people apologize when they run into someone," Adya insisted.

The boy who'd approached her in the diner stepped up and had a sling on his right arm. "Take the curse off me, you witch," he demanded.

Adya couldn't stop the giggle that came out of her mouth. Before she could respond to the obviously accident-prone boy, a cupful of liquid splashed against her chest.

"Whatda ya doin', Becky?" the first boy demanded, equally as surprised as Adya about the liquid attack.

"I thought she'd burn or melt or somethin'," Becky replied.

When Adya wiped her face, she realized it was a soda. She could feel a circle of the obnoxious high schoolers surround her, and her mind started to come up with solutions to get her out of it. There were far more people at the festival than there had been in the diner, so striking back at them with her affinities wasn't her ideal defense.

As the circle started closing in on her, someone pushed through it from behind. "You should probably go back to dancin' an' enjoyin' yer night."

Adya looked over, and Luke was standing beside her.

"She's a witch, Luke! Look what she did to Joe," the original instigator argued.

"You're tellin' me a little girl beat up Joe? Not sayin' much for yer star quarterback," Luke fired back.

"She cursed me! She put a damn curse on me," Joe yelled.

Adya shrugged at Luke. "I told him he smelled like dog vomit and to watch where he stepped. Guess he doesn't do a good job of taking suggestions."

Luke laughed while Joe looked utterly embarrassed. "I'm tellin' ya nicely one last time to go back to dancin'." Luke, who was noticeably older than the teen posse and much stronger than them, seemed to get his message across the second time, and the group of kids dispersed. "Sorry 'bout them, Ady. You okay?"

"It was just a little soda," she shrugged. "It's probably time for me to head home anyway. I don't exactly feel welcome here and don't want to cause any problems that would ruin your fun party."

"Shoot, Ady. There's always fights at these things. This was nothin'," Luke said.

"Yeah," Dusty chimed in unexpectedly. His face appeared from behind Luke, and he winked at Adya. "It isn't a festival without a few punches thrown. B'sides, you can't leave w'out dancin'." Dusty put on his most charming smile.

Luke pushed his brother to the side. "She's dancin' with me first."

While the two brothers pushed each other back and forth, Adya watched on in mild amusement. "I don't know how to country dance, so I'm afraid you're both outta luck."

"Aww, it's easy. C'mon," Luke said and grabbed Adya's hand, pulling her to the nearest open spot on the dance floor.

Everyone was executing the same dance moves, and Luke joined right in while Adya stood and watched.

"Just follow the steps. They repeat. Like this," Luke encouraged, prompting Adya to follow the lead of everyone around her.

Adya bumped into a few people but was laughing by the time Dusty joined in on the other side of her. Luke threw his brother a playful warning look, but the three of them eventually managed to dance together peacefully. Somehow, Adya managed to only step on their toes three times.

When the band slowed the music down, Adya tried to excuse herself. "I think I'm going to go catch my breath," Adya said and took a step towards the edge of the dance floor.

Luke grabbed her wrist and shook his head. "Ya owe me a dance," he insisted.

"Isn't that what I just did? Dance?" Adya pointed out.

"What 'bout me?" Dusty chimed in.

"Your girlfriend wouldn't like that much," Luke reminded Dusty.

Dusty rolled his eyes. "Darlene won't care. 'Sides, she's got her feet up. Somethin' 'bout swollen ankles."

Adya raised a brow. "Your girlfriend is pregnant?"

Dusty grinned. "Yup. Due next month."

Adya had to remind herself of what Jace told her—there wasn't a lot to do around there. "Well, congrats?"

"Thank ya," Dusty said proudly.

"Alright, Luke. One dance, and then I'm heading home," Adya conceded. She placed her hands on Luke's shoulders and let him lead.

"I wanted to tell ya thanks for helpin' Grandma," Luke said as they danced.

"Is that why you stood up for me back there?" Adya asked.

"Naw, woulda done that anyway. I know how folks 'round here are. Grandma has been mistreated on occasion, too. Whatcha do is really cool an' I don't think people should treat ya bad just cuz you're different."

Adya shrugged. "It's not the first, nor will it be the last time something like that happens. You get used to it after a few hundred lifetimes."

"Jace was sayin' that you've been 'round for a long time. Thought he was makin' it up."

"Nope. He wasn't making it up. How is Jace, by the way? I haven't seen him tonight," Adya asked.

"He's helping daddy clean up the shop while momma is here with the flowers. I dunno. He's been moody lately. Somethin' upset 'im an' he's not talkin' 'bout it."

"Yeah, that's probably my fault," Adya admitted. "I was going to apologize tonight, but if he's not here, I'll catch him another time."

When the song ended, Adya curtseyed to Luke and giggled. "Thank you for being there for me tonight. I'm sure I'll see you again at Sophia's sometime."

"Do ya need a ride home?" Luke asked.

Adya smiled. "No, I enjoy the walk. Have a good night, Luke. And thanks again."

While Adya couldn't avoid the cautious stares of some as she was leaving, she managed to exit the park without another incident.

The night was overcast, which meant it was a little warmer than most other nights had been since Adya arrived. Before reaching the dirt road that led towards Ava's house, Adya took off her shoes and looked around for Yiny. With no sign of the bird, Adya started her walk solo, assuming Yiny returned to her nest for the night or was enjoying the party more than she had and decided to stick around for a bit longer.

It was a long walk back to Ava's, but still early enough in the night that Adya didn't want to go right to bed when she got home. As she walked, she considered pulling out Ava's old journal, lighting a fire in the fireplace, and reading it until she fell asleep, as she had at Elder Tama's house. Despite her ruined dress and the random rude people at the festival, Adya was in good spirits. She thought about Ashley and Paxton and hoped they were enjoying their Valentine's Day and whatever activities they ended up doing at North Shore.

With the moon and stars hidden by clouds, it was utterly dark around Ava's house. Adya was practically home when she finally noticed the truck sitting out in front of her house. She picked up the pace and walked quicker, expecting to find Jace in the cab, but it was empty. Adya mentally thought back to when she left the house and was sure she locked the door.

"Hello?" Adya called out as she neared the front door. She checked the doorknob, and it was indeed locked.

The wood boards on the porch creaked as she cautiously walked around on it to the back of the house. Jace was sitting on the porch swing, staring off into the dark distance.

"Hey," Adya said softly.

"Wasn't expecting you back so early," Jace commented.

"Were you planning to be gone before I returned?" Adya said and joined Jace on the swing.

Jace shrugged. "Wasn't plannin' to be here at all, but when I got in my truck to go to the festival, I just kept on drivin' an' ended up here."

"Sounds like it could be a serious medical condition," Adya joked. When he didn't respond, she invited him inside.

Adya opened the back door and turned on the kitchen light. "Sophia said you've been brooding around. I'm sorry if that was because of me."

"I haven't been broodin'," Jace said defensively.

"You're brooding right now," Adya pointed out. "Are you hungry? My burger at the festival kinda fell to the ground." Adya was looking through her cabinets for something to make, but when she turned back to face Jace, she noticed he had a black eye. "What happened?"

Jace shrugged. "Ran into a door," he lied. "What happened to you?" He motioned to Adya's dress.

"Nothing, just a little misunderstanding," Adya said dismissively. "Now, what *really* happened to you?" Adya walked around the kitchen counter and stood in front of Jace.

"Heard some kids from school sayin' stuff that wasn't true. I tripped one of them, but the other took a cheap shot at my face before I could defend myself," Jace explained.

Adya couldn't help but smile. "So, that's how Joe ended up in a sling?" Adya chuckled. "I may have let him believe I cursed him. Sorry that you got mixed up in that."

"I got myself mixed up in it. Wasn't gonna let those assholes talk bad 'bout you," Jace insisted.

Adya smiled and brought her hands up to his face. "Will you let me heal it?" she asked before touching him.

Jace shrugged but didn't retreat from Adya, so she placed the tips of her fingers around his eye and focused on restoring the health and balance of the injured tissue. After a minute, she relaxed her hands back down to her sides. "All better."

"Thanks. You didn't have to do that," Jace replied. "But I should probably get goin'."

Adya frowned and grabbed Jace's hand. "I'm sorry for telling you to leave. You were right about most of it. I *do* live in the past; what I've learned in my past helps me be better in this life. I won't shut that out. And maybe I *am* looking for actual excuses for my failures. Everyone keeps telling me I'm special, and while I understand that a little better after my Awakening, I just feel like I'm falling short of what I'm supposed to be able to do. This life, unlike any other, I'm having pieces torn from me and can't do anything about it. I'm caught in limbo between this person everyone expects me to be and not being able to do a damn thing about anything." The surge of emotion caused Adya's chest to heave after unloading her pent-up feelings.

Jace calmly listened as he stood and held Adya's hand. "I don't know what to say to you, Ady. Most of us get one life an' hafta survive on our instincts an' a process of trial an' error. When we fail, we dust ourselves off an' try again because we don't all get a second, third, or three hundredth chance." He didn't sound angry and wasn't condescending, but he almost seemed sad.

A week ago, when Jace had said nearly the same thing, Adya had thrown him out. At this time, at this moment, Adya wanted to absorb everything he was saying so she could understand better. "The girl who captured me—Myra or Dhruva or whatever you want to call her—for her, everything is about power. She wants to be stronger and better than everyone. For me, all I've ever wanted is to bring balance, but I don't think I can do that and defeat her without giving in to the need to be more powerful. So aside from my grief and PTSD, I'm facing this tremendous internal conflict. Me being here isn't about giving up, Jace. I have to make peace with a whole slew of demons so I can dust myself off and try again."

With a shrug, Jace responded, "Why do you want me to be here if there isn't anything I can do 'bout any of that?"

Adya thought about it for a minute before she replied. "Maybe I need help to dust myself off from someone who sees the world differently than I do. And maybe I could really use a friend who isn't afraid to tell me the truth about myself that I don't necessarily want to acknowledge." Adya was surprised that she was able to articulate her thoughts so well because she'd spent two weeks trying to figure out why she was there, other than the need to feel close to Ava. "And now your turn. Why would *you* want to be here to begin with when you know I'm a complicated, hot mess who might very well erase your town off the map if I get too frustrated?"

"'Cuz this would be the safest place to be if you tried to do that," Jace replied in a deadpan manner, after which both broke out into a much-needed laugh.

CHAPTER SEVENTEEN

A month passed in what felt, to Adya, like a blink of an eye. It was mid-March, and spring was alive in the air. The seeds Adya planted in Ava's garden began to sprout while Adya and Jace's friendship blossomed, too. The two spent time together every day. Sometimes Jace tagged along while Adya worked to strengthen her affinities, while other days, she hung out with Jace and his brothers at Sophia's. Their friendship was both complicated and straightforward. Adya knew that if she encouraged it, their relationship could be more, but she also knew that she would never use Jace like that; their futures were heading in very different directions.

"Weekly progress report," Jace said as the two hiked in the nearby mountain on a late Saturday morning. "First, how do you feel?"

"I feel," Adya began as she pushed herself up the mountain beside Jace, "that I should've broken in these new hiking boots before today's hike."

"Rub some tree sap on your blisters an' quit complainin'," Jace replied with a smirk.

Adya glared over at her friend. "Tree sap won't help with blisters, weirdo."

Jace grinned at her as they continued to hike. "You're the expert," he said. "So, what 'bout your affinities? Did you strengthen them this week?"

For the previous four weeks, Adya was given the task by Jace to find ways to grow her affinities. Sometimes Adya would spend days working on a new way to manipulate an element, while other days, she'd work on finding new ways to combine the three to create something greater than the sum of their parts. "Do you remember that rainstorm last week?"

Jace nodded. "Yeah, did you create that?"

"I wish." Adya chuckled. "No, but I did simultaneously redirect all the raindrops I could see. Did you notice the new pond that appeared next to the road on the way up here? Yeah, that was me," Adya boasted. "I used both my water and air affinities to move it where I wanted the water to land."

"Not bad, D," Jace said, clearly impressed. "D" was his new nickname for Adya—an even shorter version of her previous nickname, Ady. "An' the present from Lir? Still on the mantel?"

Adya scrunched her nose at him. "Yes, but I swear I'll open it soon." Jace had pointed out in the weeks prior that he believed the best way for Adya to heal completely was to open all wounds and deal with them directly. The present from Lir—and really, the whole Lir situation—was still something Adya couldn't bring herself to face.

"It's like a bandaid. Gotta rip it off fast an' the pain will be intense, but over quick," he reminded her. "You know, it could be a piece of fruit an' it's completely rotten now 'cuz you refuse to open it. It'll start stinkin' here real soon an' then you'll get bugs."

"Who gives fruit as a present?" Adya asked, genuinely baffled by Jace's logic. "Besides, even if your insane theory was correct, it would've rotted months ago."

He shrugged. "We make fruit baskets for people as gifts all the time when it's in season," Jace countered.

"It's not a fruit basket," Adya said and rolled her eyes. "Hey, hold up a minute," she said and diverted from the path they were taking.

Off to the side, Adya felt with her affinity a tree that was not balanced. She followed her element and came to a group of trees that looked like a disease infected them.

"What's up?" Jace asked as he followed Adya to the trees that looked like they were bleeding amber. He watched as Adya placed her hands on the first tree, and slowly the vertical crack disappeared.

Adya kept her hands on the tree, healing the external wound. She could still feel an imbalance caused by a lack of nutrients and water. It took another minute to restore the balance before she moved onto the next oak tree.

Jace sat under a healthy tree and drank water as he watched Adya work. Despite seeing everything she was capable of doing over the past weeks, her gifts still amazed him; he enjoyed the literal life she restored to the world. He couldn't help the feelings he had for Adya, even though he knew she loved another. Adya would be leaving Ava's home to go back to the Academy eventually, but he thought she was simply the most amazing person he'd ever known. Jace couldn't fathom how anyone couldn't be mesmerized by her. Even his brother and soon-to-be-father, Dusty, and Luke—who was surrounded by college girls most of the time—couldn't deny that something was alluring about Adya. Of course, none of them would admit that to Adya.

"There," Adya said as she interrupted Jace from his thoughts. "All bet—" Adya suddenly wrenched herself to the side and vomited what looked like the same amber sap the trees had been oozing. "Damnit," Adya cursed.

Jace offered her a drink of his water. "I dunno what you expected when you took in all that disease," he pointed out.

Adya frowned. "I expect to be able to absorb things without suffering the effects. There's gotta be a way to do it that doesn't involve me getting sick," she said.

"You'll figure it out," Jace encouraged as he took Adya's hand and squeezed it. "I believe in you."

"Thanks," she said appreciatively and squeezed his hand back.

"We're almost there. You feelin' up to hikin' a little ways further?"

"Almost there?" Adya repeated. "I didn't know we had a destination with this hike."

Jace smiled and wagged his eyebrows. "I always have a plan. C'mon."

The two resumed the trail they were following before Adya's tree incident and veered off from it when they were approaching the mountain's summit.

"Not much farther," Jace said as he weaved between trees to reach an opening in the side of the hill.

"A cave?" Adya asked with uncertainty.

"C'mon. There's somethin' inside here I want you to see." Jace pulled out his phone and tapped on the flashlight as they entered the ominous cave.

"There'd better not be a bear in here," Adya warned.

"There probably isn't," Jace teased and stopped about twenty feet inside the cave. His flashlight illuminated the back wall, which had ancient etchings carved in it. "Petroglyphs," Jace said.

Adya tilted her head and walked towards them. As her fingers ran over the engraved stone, she said, "Ogam. These are found in Ireland, too." Adya tilted her head to try to decipher what they said.

"Ogam? Never heard of it. I thought Indians did this," Jace said, clearly confused.

Adya nodded. "Yes, Ogam; it's an old Irish language. These engravings say something about the 'right hand of God.' There were a lot of religious scripts in ancient Britain and Ireland written in Ogam, but it isn't a language I studied, so my translation isn't going to be the best." Adya looked at them in wonder. "I don't know how these got here, though," she admitted. "I heard rumors in the 700s about some affinates who converted to Christianity. They supposedly sailed from Ireland to the west. I never put much faith in rumors, though."

Jace was even more awed by Adya and walked up behind her. He set his hand on hers as she traced the ancient letters. "How are you feeling now?" he asked softly as his head dipped towards her ear.

Adya froze for a moment and then turned to face Jace. "Confused," Adya admitted as her gaze shifted between Jace's eyes.

"What are your options?" Jace asked.

"I could crack a joke and get out of this tense moment we seem to be in," Adya said.

"Or?" he prodded.

"Or do something we both agreed not to do."

"What would Emily do?"

Adya closed her eyes for a moment and smiled. She considered what her normal thirteen-year-old self might do in a situation where she was all by herself staring up into the eyes of an attractive—both physically and intellectually—sixteen-year-old boy. When her eyes opened again to Jace's eyes studying hers, she bit her lip. "Probably kiss you," she admitted, intending to give in to the moment.

Jace smiled softly and leaned in to kiss her, but Adya turned her head away at the last second. "We agreed," she whispered and rested her head against his shoulder while Jace rested his cheek against the side of her head.

"I know we did," he said with a sigh.

Adya wrapped her arms around Jace and stroked the nape of his neck with her thumb. She felt the deep ache in her soul and knew she still loved Lir. Even though Lir was lost to her in this lifetime, Adya continued to wear her Claddagh ring. As long as Lir's soul existed in some form in this life, Adya determined that she would keep her promise to him, even if that meant she would deny herself every opportunity like this one. "Please don't hate me," she said softly.

Jace's body shook with a silent chuckle. "Couldn't hate you if I tried," he admitted. Their brief moment was interrupted by Jace's phone buzzing in his hand.

Adya broke away from Jace to allow him to read the message.

A smile broke across his face as he turned the phone for Adya to see. "I'm an uncle," he said proudly, and any hint of disappointment instantly vanished from his tone. "A li'l girl they're naming Dani."

"She's adorable," Adya gushed. "Do you want to head back so you can go meet her?"

Adya saw a new light in Jace's eyes as he nodded. "Yes. Would you come with me?" he asked.

"I will, but maybe it would be better if I waited," Adya offered as the two started hiking down the mountain. "I'm sure the families want to spend time with the new addition before they have some strange outsider come and visit."

Jace raised a brow at Adya. "You're not an outsider, D. Strange, yes, but definitely not an outsider."

"Gee, thanks," Adya laughed. "Alright, let's go meet your niece." Adya silently thanked the elements for their intervention and their strength to help her stay true to her promise to Lir.

"Your parents are okay with Dusty being a dad?" Adya asked on their half-hour drive to the hospital in the next town over.

Jace shrugged. "Don't think they're thrilled 'bout it, but they weren't much older when Luke was born. Jus' kinda the way things are 'round here."

Adya nodded thoughtfully. Her parents were in their thirties when she was born, and since she would never have typical high school experiences, she wasn't exactly familiar with modern teen pregnancies. Sure, in past lives, she'd helped deliver babies of mothers who were only slightly older than she currently was, but those were different times. "Do you want kids?" she asked.

"Yeah, gonna have me a big family, I think," Jace said confidently. "At least four kids, maybe more. What 'bout you?"

Adya chuckled. "I can't have kids. Endless reincarnations, yes, but we aren't able to have kids of our own."

Jace glanced over at Adya with a poorly veiled pity. "Do you ever wish you could?"

"And give up lifetimes of worry-free sex?" Adya giggled. "There have been times where I wish it were different, but I made peace long ago with the fact that I would never be a mom."

Jace blinked in surprise at Adya's candor. "Do you, umm, remember your, uhh—, sex from other lives?"

"Have we finally arrived at a topic that embarrasses the tell-it-like-it-is Jace?" Adya teased.

"Naw," Jace replied coolly, recovering from his previous stutter. "Jus' didn't know if it was somethin' you'd wanna talk about."

"Talking about sex doesn't bother me. Emily, on the other hand, would've been mortified by you asking." Adya laughed. "Yes, I remember making love in past lives," she answered plainly. "I don't recall every moment of every day I've ever lived, but the special ones stick with me."

"Have you ever. . . in this lifetime?"

Adya smiled. "No, not in this lifetime. I'd never even had a boyfriend until a year and a half ago. I seem to have shitty luck when it comes to relationships in this life," she added with a shrug.

"So you and Lir didn't?" Jace asked with surprise.

Adya shook her head. "Our physical age difference makes that an incredibly questionable situation, so we were going to wait a few years," Adya admitted. "There are many ways to share your love with someone that doesn't involve sex." Adya realized for the first time that talking about Lir wasn't bringing tears to her eyes. "Maybe it's because I've known him for so many lifetimes, but Lir and I had a connection that I've never known with anyone ever. We could literally share thoughts and memories, ones that the other hadn't been a part of, without saying a single word. It was a deeper intimacy than any physical connection."

Jace continued to drive and let a thoughtful silence hang between them. As he pulled into a parking spot at the hospital, he reached for Adya's hand to pause her from getting out of the truck. "Can I ask you something without you gettin' mad at me?"

Adya eyed him curiously. "Probably."

Jace chuckled. "Okay, just don't go breakin' my windows when I ask."

"Uh, oh. This sounds serious. I promise not to break your windows," Adya vowed.

"If your connection with Lir is so strong, couldn't you just, I dunno, connect with 'im in the body his soul got put into?" Jace flinched in preparation for Adya's reaction to his suggestion.

Adya wasn't upset at all by Jace's question. In fact, she was intrigued by the idea and spoke aloud to herself, "If I could connect with his soul, maybe I could figure out a way to separate it from the host's body. . . " Adya frowned and cocked her head sideways in thought. "But I still wouldn't have a way to transfer it back to his body. It was a good thought, Jace." It was an idea that would swirl around in the back of Adya's mind. "So, are you ready to go and meet your niece?"

Adya remained in the waiting room while Jace joined his brothers and parents in the hospital room, where they all gushed over the baby girl that had just entered their lives. The time alone allowed Adya to mull over the idea that Jace had brought up in the truck. She thought about how every soul entered a body at some point. She tried to remember—if that was even possible—how her soul found Emily's body. Obviously, it happened in the womb before there was conscious thought. After all, she experienced the memory of accepting her twin brother's soul in the womb, which she knew was given freely to her, not by force or manipulation. So, if it required an unconscious mind—or at least a mind that wasn't fully aware—to receive a soul, and Dhruva received her second soul from a brain dead affinate, why wouldn't it be possible to transfer Lir's soul back? She would just need his body, the body of his soul's host, and. . . Adya sighed. She still needed a way to separate his soul from whatever tangle of souls the host body had.

"You seem deep in thought. What's on yer mind, child?" Sophia sat beside Adya in the waiting room.

"I'm just pondering how our souls choose our bodies," Adya said with a smile. "How are you feeling, Sophia?"

"Not too bad for an old woman," Sophia replied, patting Adya on the knee. "I sometimes forget that your mind is older than that body of yours. I 'spected you were thinkin' 'bout boys an' such."

"Sometimes, I wish my life could be that simple, that I could let myself fall in love with someone like Jace and have a family of my own," Adya admitted. "I guess you sorta have the best of both worlds with your adopted kids and grandkids while still having your affinity."

"You could have that, too," Sophia suggested. "I see the way Jace looks at ya. He could give ya that simple life."

Adya smiled at Sophia. "I know he could, but even if I pushed aside the responsibilities I believe are mine in this life,

I would never want to rob him of the future life he's striving for. He wants kids and a family, neither of those I can provide him. Besides," Adya added, "I made a promise to someone, and I refuse to give up until his soul is free."

Sophia reached into her purse and handed a letter to Adya. "This came for you late yesterday," she said and patted Adya's hand once more. "I'm gonna go down an' see my new grandbaby." Sophia rose from the seat with difficulty and shuffled towards the room with the rest of her family. She paused briefly and looked back at Adya. "Doncha be thinkin' 'bout leavin' us without sayin' goodbye."

Adya opened the letter from Ted and began reading. It wasn't the "how are you feeling" letter she was expecting, and she was glad she was seated when she read it.

"You're in a hospital," Adya whispered aloud to herself before she reread the news. The Elders were meeting at Elder Tama's estate to discuss strategies when Dhruva and her army attacked them. Two were dead, and Elder Tama was in critical condition in a hospital in South Carolina. Ted apologized for asking, but they needed Adya's help. She rubbed her forehead and scowled at the letter. She wasn't upset about being needed; she was both relieved and concerned that the full force of her hatred had finally returned.

"Hey, D. Come down an' meet l'il D," Jace called out happily as he ambled down the hallway towards her. "Uh oh," he said as soon as he saw Adya's expression. "What's wrong?"

"I need some air," Adya said and darted towards the staircase. She made it down one flight of stairs before Jace opened the door and yelled down to her, "Wait up!"

Adya didn't wait, though. She knew she needed to ground herself before the fury inside erupted. She practically jumped down one more flight and flew through the door. When Adya burst outside, she fell to her knees in a patch of grass under a tree.

"Stay away!" she yelled back at Jace, who was jogging to catch up with her.

"No," he replied and knelt beside Adya. "Breathe an' hear me out," Jace demanded. "I dunno what's happened, but I know that this is the moment when you get to see just how powerful you are."

"What are you talking about?" Adya said. She was shaking as she struggled to hold in the rage boiling inside her.

"I can feel it in the air 'round us, D. You're 'bout to lose control. So, decide not to. It's just like whatcha did with those sick trees. Your anger is the disease. You just hafta absorb your rage an' hold onto both the power an' the balance."

"I don't think I can do that," Adya said desperately and dug her fingernails into the grass.

Jace positioned himself closer to Adya despite her shaking her head at him and wrapped his arms around her. He could feel her trembling and hoped his plan would work. "If you release your rage now," he whispered to her, "you'll hurt me. I'm hopin' you don't wanna do that."

Adya adjusted herself and held onto Jace tightly, trying to redirect her fury into her desire to protect Jace—even if that protection was from herself. Images flashed through her mind: she envisioned Dhruva and her path of destruction and then saw Lir's soulless eyes. Adya could feel herself shaking like she was going to explode. . . And then a strange sort of peace washed over her. The horrific images switched to beautiful ones of equal intensity: she and Lir's restrained passion in Switzerland, the fiery kiss from Paxton, bonding with Ashley over boys. Finally, she felt Jace's strong arms wrapped around her, supporting her when she thought the world was going to implode. Her elements' energy coursed through her body with an intensity that made her gasp and open her eyes. She looked around her and saw the earth's energy reaching outward from the ground like fingers. The invisible air around them had a soft glow, and she could see the direction it was moving. Minute molecules of water danced in the air like a grand performance. Adya could feel the connection between her mortal body and the energies swirling around. Despite the euphoria, or perhaps because of it, Adya began weeping.

Jace continued to hold onto Adya, not knowing what was happening within her and not knowing if he was about to be flung across the parking lot if she wasn't able to control herself. When Adya gasped for a breath, he loosened his hold on her and allowed her space to breathe. Jace watched Adya look around in confusion. As he was about to ask her if she was okay, Adya began weeping again.

"D? What's wrong?" Jace asked as he pulled Adya into another tight embrace and stroked her hair.

"Nothing," Adya replied. Suddenly, her sobbing turned into laughter. She leaned back and stared into the face of the confused boy in front of her. "You were right," she said, now smiling. "I didn't have to release my anger; I had to accept it. That power that comes from all my emotions, good and bad, doesn't have to explode out from me. Having that passion makes me stronger." Adya knew she probably wasn't making sense to Jace, but never having experienced anything like that in any of her lives, it was hard to put into words. Adya thought back to when she was reading Ava's journal at Elder Tama's house, how Ava said that she had to accept her lover's decision to lead a different life. Ava wrote that she would carry that sorrow with her as she continued. It wasn't the heartache she was accepting, but an emotion that she would use to make herself stronger. Ava had known for centuries what Adya had only just now discovered. It wasn't the age or wisdom of the soul, or even the number of affinities one was gifted with that gave them strength; it was the strength of the soul itself to harness the passions within that fueled a power that was in balance with the elements.

Adya leaned forward and kissed Jace's lips, not in a passionate way, but in a manner befitting someone who had encouraged her to be the version of herself.

Jace blinked in surprise at the unexpected kiss. "Wow. Umm, I'm not sure what to do with that." A look of serious confusion governed his features.

Adya caressed his cheek. "Accept it as my promise that I'm forever indebted to you. I don't think I would've bridged the gap that has been eluding me the entire time I've been here if you hadn't stepped in and forced me to pick myself up and keep trying."

Jace smiled and removed Adya's hand from his face before he kissed the back of her hand. "I was just hopin' with all that shakin' you were doin' that you wouldn't explode yourself into tiny pieces that I'd have to scoop up off all the cars out here."

"That would've been gross," Adya said with a laugh and stood up. "I could use a drink of water, and then, if you're not too scared that I'll explode, I'd like to meet your niece."

Jace stood and smiled. "I think we can make that work, but if you start shakin' again, I'm getting' you far away from her."

"You can push me out the window, and I wouldn't blame you," Adya agreed. "Can I use your phone real quick? I need to get in touch with Ted."

Jace handed over his phone. "Sure. I'll go grab you some water."

"Thanks," Adya said sincerely.

Ashley was ecstatic to hear from Adya. After being interrogated about using Jace's phone and giving her friend a brief rundown of what was going on with her, she pleaded for Ashley to get Ted.

"I take it you got my letter?" Ted asked as he took the phone from Ashley.

"Yeah, and I handled the news probably about as bad as you expected," Adya admitted, "but after that, I figured everything out. I know how we can stop Dhruva and maybe a way to return people's souls to their bodies."

Jace returned with a bottle of water for Adya when she was in the middle of explaining her idea to Ted.

"We are at a disadvantage because we see her soulless army as the people we knew and loved. What we need to do is remove them from the equation," Adya explained.

"Are you suggesting that instead of going after Eli and Dhruva, we kidnap her drones?" Ted questioned.

"Exactly. If we can face off against Dhruva and Eli by themselves. . ." Adya paused and decided to rephrase. "If I can go up against Dhruva alone, I will win."

"I don't want you to go in there alone, but we can fine-tune the plan when you return. You are coming back soon, right?" Ted asked.

"Yes, I'm catching a plane back in the morning. I have some things I need to finish up here before I return." Adya smiled at Jace. "Will you be able to put together a team to capture her sentinels? I think if we take a systematic approach and are subtle enough about it, she might not even realize they've gone missing."

"I'll get to work putting something together. Be safe, Adya," Ted said and hung up the phone.

Adya handed Jace's phone back to him. "Thank you for the water and the phone. I honestly can't remember the last time I was on a phone call," she said lightly.

Jace frowned and tucked his phone back into his pocket. "So, you're leaving tomorrow?"

Adya nodded. "I need to go back and be a part of this fight. Dhruva attacked and killed some of the Elders. She needs to be stopped." Adya looked at Jace, sadness heavy in her heart. "Don't think that me leaving tomorrow is *adieu*. But we'll talk about that later, okay? Can I go and meet Dani now?"

CHAPTER EIGHTEEN

"**D**ani is lovely," Adya commented as Jace parked in front of Ava's house. "Please look out for her. She will likely struggle with her fire affinity for a long time." When Adya visited the baby, she knew the child's soul and knew that she was a fire affinate. Dani had gifted Adya with something else, too. She was going to ponder that knowledge for a while before sharing it with anyone else.

"So, keep her away from matches an' lighters? Got it," Jace replied with a sad smile. "I don't want you to go," he admitted.

"Technically, you will be the one going when you leave me at the airport," Adya said with a smirk before she exited the truck. "Would you come inside with me?"

Jace smiled, although there was a definite sadness to it. "Lemme guess. . . you need help packin'?"

"No, silly," Adya said as she opened the door. "Maybe I want to be selfish just a little while longer."

"Ahh, an' I thought you might make me some more of your famous mac n' cheese." Jace followed Adya inside and chuckled at the mess of her clothes all over the living room. "Yeah, you'd make a terrible housewife."

"I'll happily make you macaroni and cheese if you quit insulting me," Adya said, although she was already in the kitchen preparing a pot of water to boil.

"The truth is a hard pill to swallow," Jace replied and sat on the barstool to watch Adya.

"That's kinda one of the reasons I wanted you to stay," Adya admitted. "I don't want to be alone when I open up Lir's gift."

"I knew it!" Jace declared. "You're afraid it's gonna be bug infested."

"You figured me out," Adya said with a roll of her eyes as she walked to the fireplace to retrieve the gift off the mantel. Blue and white paper wrapped the medium-sized square box, and a green bow sat in the center of the top.

Jace followed Adya to the couch and sat beside her as she stared at the present. "Unless you have telekinesis, I don't think it'll open by staring at it."

"I know," Adya insisted and took a deep breath before picking it up again.

"Did you at least shake it?" Jace asked.

Adya threw Jace a look that said it all—of course not. "I hope you have a mop ready to clean up in here after I explode," she warned.

"You're not gonna do any such thing. Just rip into it," Jace offered.

Adya tore the paper off with her eyes closed, peeking out of her nearly closed eyes after getting through the wrapping.

"It's not gonna bite," Jace teased and then rested his hand on Adya's knee for support.

Adya lifted the lid and saw a handwritten note. On one side, it said, "*Mo chéadsearc*" with an arrow indicating to flip the letter over.

"What does that say?" Jace asked.

Adya licked her lips as she fought back the tears. "It says, 'my true love.'" She wiped away the tears streaming down her cheeks.

"At least I was wrong about the fruit theory," Jace said lightly. "Or was I? C'mon, finish opening it."

Adya chuckled and elbowed him. "I'm going as fast as I can." Adya's hand was shaking as she turned the note over. "*An bpósfaidh tú mé?*" she whispered as she revealed the ring Lir had shown her in the vault in Geneva. Adya felt her heart wrench like a knife was stabbing and twisting in the center of her upper body. She clenched her chest and fell over against Jace's arm, sobbing as she held the ring in her fingers.

Jace removed the box from Adya's lap and circled his arms around her. He didn't exactly know what the note said but got the gist of it. Without saying anything humorous as usual, he decided to let Adya cry without words. Jace stroked her hair while she soaked his shirt, but he didn't care; he just wanted to be there for his heartbroken friend.

"You know," Adya said eventually when the tears slowed, "there was a time when I thought he was using the present to break up with me." She chuckled.

"But he asked you to marry him?" Jace asked hesitantly.

Adya nodded with a sad smile. She told Jace the story of the first lifetime that Paxton proposed to her and how Lir had been planning on doing the same later that same day. "He showed me the ring when we were in Switzerland—it was in his vault. I thought he put it back." Adya frowned again. "I broke his heart so many times," Adya continued. "I guess it's fair that mine finally shattered, too." She sighed as she relaxed out of Jace's embrace and sunk into the couch. "I don't know what to do with this now," she admitted.

Jace reached around to the back of his neck and unfastened a necklace he was wearing. It was a gold rope with what looked like a hawk pendant on it. He removed the charm and offered the chain to Adya. "Put it on this an' you can keep it with you. Maybe you can draw strength from it or somethin'," he offered.

Adya looked at him wistfully. "I can't take your necklace. It looks important to you."

"Not as important as the ring is to you," Jace countered as he took the ring from Adya and threaded it onto the necklace before affixing it to Adya's neck. "Besides," he said, "now you'll never forget me."

Adya smiled softly. "I wouldn't forget you regardless." She leaned over and kissed Jace on the cheek. Adya's eyes suddenly went wide. "Oh, no! The water!" She jumped up and ran to the kitchen but ended up breaking out into laughter as soon as she arrived. "It boiled away! All of it! Some water elemental affinate I am."

Jace cleaned up the paper in the living room and joined Adya in the kitchen. "There's only one thing to do now," he said and reached for the pot.

Adya smacked his hand away. "Maybe only one option for *you*, but I can fix this," she insisted. Adya gazed into what would look like empty air to anyone else, but she could see in the air all the droplets of water that had evaporated. Focusing on them, she slowed their rapidly moving molecules and delivered boiling water back into the pot. "It's like it never even happened," Adya announced happily, but inside, her voice was telling her that the pain she felt was real, and it was going to take a lot more than redirecting water to fix her loss.

Jace stayed the night with her, sleeping on the couch again while Adya spent one last night in her old room. In the morning, Adya fed Yiny and visited her garden one last time, enjoying the flowers that had started blooming.

"I don't know if it's possible, but I would like you to find me at the Academy, Yiny. I know Ava sent you to watch over me. With what I'm doing next, I could use all the strength and help that Ava and any of the other Ascended souls can offer. If not, please look out for Sophia and Jace and their families, especially little Dani, who will need lots of guidance." Adya picked up one of the jet stones from the garden, tucked it into her pocket, and returned inside to get the rest of her things.

CHAPTER EIGHTEEN

"I gotta ask this one last time, D," Jace said as she entered the house. "Progress report time: how are you feelin'?"

Adya smiled at her dear friend. "I'm okay, but if you make me think about it, I'm sad about leaving you."

Jace nodded as if he was a therapist keeping notes. "And your affinities? Have you made progress on strengthening them?"

Adya giggled and pulled Jace into a bear hug. "I've never felt stronger or more balanced."

Jace savored the embrace, hugging Adya back before kissing the top of her head. "You were such an angry girl when we first met. Who'd've thought we'd become such good friends?"

"I'm still an angry girl," Adya pointed out, "but have had a lot of help in redirecting it positively and getting back up on my feet again." Adya picked up her duffle bag, but it was immediately taken from her hands by Jace. "Will you keep the bike you fixed and give it to Dani when she's old enough to ride it?"

Jace shook his head. "Nope. Auntie D has to come back an' give it to her."

"Does that mean I'm officially part of your family?" Adya said with a big smile.

"Yup. You're stuck with us now," Jace said, returning the smile.

"Oh! I almost forgot one thing," Adya said and ran out the back door. Using the energy in the air, she masterfully unhooked the hag stone from its spot on the back porch and took it into Jace. "I'd like you to have this."

"You're givin' me a rock?" Jace blinked in confusion.

"It's not a rock—it's a hag stone. In Ireland, they're symbols of good luck. In other places, they are protection stones, keeping you safe from magic and nightmares. Plus, you're supposed to be able to look through the hole and see into the fairy realm."

Jace held the rock up to his eye and looked through the hole at Adya. "Sure 'nough. There's a feisty pixie right here in this room."

Adya rolled her eyes and laughed before the two left Ava's house together for the last time.

"Please take care of yourself," Adya said as she hugged Sophia for the third time. "I'm coming back to visit as soon as I can, and I expect to see you chasing Dani around."

Sophia laughed. "I dunno 'bout that, but I'll take care as best as I can."

Adya hugged Luke next. "I know I don't have to ask this, but please look after Jace for me. Make sure that the girl who's lucky enough to win his heart is worthy and ready to have lots of little ones." She kissed Luke on the cheek. "And the same goes for you, too. Find someone who brings you infinite happiness and can put up with this crazy family."

Dusty stepped up to give Adya the next hug. "I'm still the best lookin' of them all," he joked.

"I hope you have so much fun with your daughter, and I expect to receive an invitation to the wedding eventually," Adya said sternly. Then with a smile, she added, "When Dani is older, she'll have a place at North Shore if you want to send her there. I might be able to talk my fire elemental friend to come out and give her a few pointers, too." Adya kissed the baby on the forehead and hugged Dusty's girlfriend, Darlene.

"Tell your parents I said goodbye. I'm gonna miss you all so much," Adya said tearfully.

"Your jet's gonna leave without you if we don't leave. Everyone'll be here when you get back," Jace urged Adya.

Adya smiled at them all from the doorway and waved as she retreated to Jace's truck.

"That's one of the perks of having a private jet at your disposal—they aren't gonna leave without you," Adya explained to Jace as she remained unwilling to exit his truck.

"You are feisty an' stubborn," Jace informed her. "Besides, you told me yourself that you'll come back to visit."

"I meant that as a threat," Adya joked. "I expect Ava's garden to be alive when I get back, too."

"You're gonna text me your number when you get a new phone, right?" Jace asked.

"Of course. And you guys will be able to get in touch with me if you need anything." Adya stared out the truck window at the jet that was ready to take her back to reality.

Jace got out of the truck and carried Adya's duffle bag to the aircraft and then returned to open Adya's door. "It's time, D."

Adya smiled at the hag stone that Jace had hung from the rearview mirror before conceding to the inevitable end of her sabbatical. "You know," Adya said as she wrapped her arms around Jace and held on tight, "the Emily part of me will forever be kicking my ass for not kissing you." Adya placed a soft kiss on Jace's cheek.

Jace smiled sadly and caressed Adya's cheek. "It wouldn't really be fair to my future wife if we'd kissed. How could anyone possibly live up to what it must be like to kiss a seven-thousand-year-old tri-affinate," he said with a wink.

Adya rolled her eyes dramatically and lightly smacked Jace on the chest. "You are the friend I never knew I needed. Thank you for not giving up on me."

After one final long hug, Adya broke away from Jace and boarded the plane. She waved to him from the window and then began preparing herself for the battle looming on the horizon. "Let's go home."

Adya busied her mind on the return flight by reading through Ava's journal again. It amazed her how differently it read in the wake of Adya's personal growth. Ava, whether knowingly or not, left hints throughout her diaries of the hidden strength in passion. When Adya read entries that Ava wrote during times of anger, there was power and beauty masked by what seemed like raw emotion on the surface. Her balance within and control over her elements was nothing short of powerful and graceful. Adya didn't think she could admire her longtime friend any more than she already did.

"I wish I could talk to you now that I know," Adya whispered in revere to her Ascended mentor.

It was the early evening hours when Adya's car drove into North Shore. The students were at dinner, but Ted and Gaia were awaiting Adya's arrival.

"How are you feeling?" Gaia immediately asked as Adya was stepping out of the backseat of the car.

Adya looked around the Academy with her new eyes and smiled at Gaia. "I am better," she replied.

"Come and see me after you and Ted chat," Gaia requested and hugged Adya before walking away towards her infirmary.

"How have things been here?" Adya asked Ted as they walked towards his office. "And how is Elder Tama?"

Worry and stress marred Ted's features. "Elder Tama is making a slow recovery, but it's looking hopeful that she'll come through this."

Adya followed Ted into his office. The two continued walking to the round table in the corner—dim light shined through his large window onto a mass of books and papers.

"We've been discussing your plan for capturing Dhruva's soldiers, but I've had to fight some who don't see the value in this tactic," Ted admitted.

Adya looked around the office at the energies of the elements present. Before responding to Ted, Adya rested her hand on the table and used her new abilities to slow down and balance the elements.

CHAPTER EIGHTEEN

Ted felt the change and looked questioningly at Adya. "You've grown a lot since you left," he commented while feeling the tension in his body subside some.

Adya smiled and nodded. "I figured out a lot when I was gone," she admitted. "As far as the plan goes, I want to save all the affinates. They aren't the soulless creatures I thought they were—they are our friends and part of the balance of this world. We can't harm them, and we can't get to Dhruva with them in our way," Adya explained.

"What do you think we can do with a group of soulless affinates? They don't have a mind of their own anymore," Ted argued.

"We return their souls to them," Adya said simply. In response to Ted's questioning expression, she added, "Look, if Eli has a way of moving souls between bodies, why can't we simply use it to restore them?"

"How are you going to separate the original soul from the stolen one?" Ted questioned.

"I'm still working on the process, but my idea is simple. Eli is a scientist, right? So, whatever his original intention was with this whole thing, we can trust that, like a good scientist, he kept records. We will know who received whose soul. That is our starting point," Adya explained. "We will also know what the affinity of each of the stolen souls was, so it will simply be a matter of seeking out that element that's foreign to the host."

Ted nodded thoughtfully. "What about the people who have absorbed more than one soul?"

Adya sighed and nodded. "Like Dhruva, I know. It gets more complicated with multiple souls, but I think it still can be done. We just need for the minds of the people with the souls to be unconscious. And this also means that we can't kill anyone in our attack on the Institute." Adya bit her lip. "It's not going to be easy."

"Where do we even start? There are huge risks in every part of this plan, Adya."

"There are huge gains with this plan, too," Adya countered. "My thought is we do this in waves. First, we get her sentries out of the way—they are just cannon fodder to her, so she won't feel their loss immediately. Next, we need to get the people out who Dhruva intends to use as donors. If we can remove the blockers in their systems, they will add to our numbers. After seeing how Lir was treated in the holding cell and then living through that myself, I bet that those awaiting the procedure will gladly opt-out of helping Dhruva if they were ever there voluntarily to begin with."

"There's no scenario where she'll be oblivious to us at this point. Dhruva will fight us, and I'm not confident we can win if we're going in with the mindset that we can't kill anyone," Ted said.

Adya smiled like she knew the punch line of a joke Ted told. "I think I can disrupt the abilities of the false affinates," she said.

Ted raised a questioning brow at his student.

Adya explained her epiphany at the hospital to Ted and how she can not only feel her elements now, but she can see their energies. "When the elements are imbalanced like they are around the Institute and within those who received the stolen souls, I can manipulate the energies in the direction of balance, just like I did in this room when we entered. If I'm right about this, bringing balance to those that are existing outside that balance should disrupt their abilities to use their false affinities."

Ted nodded thoughtfully. "I felt the change when you did that, like you lifted a weight from me. But this is all speculation. You don't know with certainty that they will lose their affinities."

Adya shook her head. "No, I don't know that this will work for sure. What are our other options?"

Ted thumbed through the papers on the table. "Aside from plans to obliterate them, we didn't have anything else until you proposed your idea."

"We can't let them kill those people, Ted," Adya warned.

"I agree," he replied. "In the letter that Maggie had you give me, she roughly outlined the layout of the Institute. I'd like for you to study it while I contact the remaining three Elders who are calling the shots."

Adya nodded as she took the paper. "This will help a lot," she agreed. "I would like to head back to my room and catch up with Ashley, if that's okay."

"Of course. We're glad you're back and seemingly much better than you left us, Adya." Ted smiled and motioned towards the door. As she was about to walk out, Ted added, "Darius told me who has Lir's soul."

Adya shook her head adamantly. "I don't want to know until after this is over. I need to believe that every person could have it so I can save as many people as possible." The irony of Adya's change in attitude didn't escape her. Two months prior, all she could focus on was killing whoever had Lir's soul, saving him through releasing his soul to the universe. She was glad she found another way. As she made her way to her residence hall, Adya pressed the ring hanging around her neck against her chest.

Adya entered her empty room and smiled as she looked around. Nothing had changed in the two months she'd been away— three if you include the weeks she was held captive. In an attempt to be a little more considerate to Ashley, Adya decided to put her things away. But while she was unpacking, her door flew open. Without thinking, Adya turned and flung her would-be attackers against the wall, pinning them in midair.

"Oh, no!" Adya cried out as soon as she realized it was Ashley and Sierra, and carefully used the same air to set the two startled girls down on the ground.

"Holy shit, Ady. What was that for?" Ashley protested angrily.

Sierra stood in place, blinking in confusion and terror.

"I'm so sorry, guys. You can't sneak up on me like that, though." Adya immediately went and hugged Sierra. "Are you okay?"

Sierra nodded but was shaking and a paler version of her beautifully dark self.

"I'm fine, Ady. Don't worry about your best friend," Ashley said sarcastically but was already smiling with open arms to hug her roommate.

Adya made sure Sierra was stable before running over to Ashley and hugging her fiercely. "I missed you, Ash. So, so much."

"Yeah, yeah. I missed you, too, but that little trick of yours is new," Ashley replied.

Adya sat down with Ashley and Sierra and told them both about her time away. Despite her missing Jace, Yiny, and Ava's house, she was glad to be back with her friends.

"A fire affinate baby?" Sierra said with amazement. "I guess she's lucky to have Auntie D to watch out for her," she said with a giggle.

"She's lucky to be born into a family that knows about and accepts old souls and all that they bring to this world," Adya replied. "There are too many people in that small town, though, that think we're witches. Dani will have a rough time living with that legacy, but I'm hoping to convince them to allow her to come to North Shore when she's older." Adya turned her attention to Ashley. "And you. . . I'm so angry with you."

Ashley already looked guilty. "What did I do?" She visibly gulped.

"Sneaking Lir's gift into my bag. Do you know how much that tormented me?" Adya scolded. With a sigh, she added, "And also, thank you for that. It was the last piece of the puzzle I needed to solve before I returned."

Ashley relaxed some but still looked concerned. "What was in it?" she asked, but her voice still had an uncertain tremble to it.

Adya pulled the necklace out from under her shirt and showed her friends the ring. "This," she said. "It was the ring Lir was going to give me in that same lifetime when Pax and I were first married."

Sierra moved closer to look at it. "It's so pretty," she said.

"The pearl is for my earth affinity and the blue sapphire for my water. I only had two affinities back then." Adya smiled softly.

"So, was it a proposal?" Ashley asked.

Adya nodded sadly. "It was. It is. Now, all I have to do is figure out how to return Lir's soul to his body so I can tell him yes."

"So, you're sure Lir is still who you want?" Ashley asked.

Sierra flashed a look to Ashley and then moved quickly to the door. "That's my cue to leave," she said.

Ashley feverishly shook her head at Sierra. "You should stay," Ashley insisted.

"Nuh-uh. You saw what Ady did when we scared her. I'm *not* sticking around to see what she does when you tell her that." Sierra quickly disappeared down the hall.

Adya's brows furrowed as she watched the odd exchange between her friends. "What's going on? What do you have to tell me? Did something happen while I was gone?"

"Nothing bad, if you look at it from one perspective," Ashley explained, skirting around what she really had to tell her roommate.

"Okay, so if it's not bad, why are you both acting like you killed my proverbial puppy?"

Ashley drew a pillow up to her chest, partially hid behind it, and took a deep breath before spilling, "Because Pax and I started dating while you were gone, and I'm really, really, really sorry if it hurts you, but we kinda grew close because you left us, so it's all your fault."

The speed at which Ashley said that made it difficult for Adya to understand it completely. Adya blinked a couple of times and then rose to her feet and began pacing the room. "So. . . you're telling me it's *my* fault that you and Pax are dating now so I can't be mad at either of you? Interesting." Adya continued pacing the room, her index finger tapping her lip in a contemplative way.

"Please don't hate us, Ady," Ashley begged, still cowering behind the pillow. "It's just, we spent a lot of time together after you left, working on ways to help you, and it just kinda happened."

"You were trying to help me?" Adya asked, raising a brow at her terrified roommate. Secretly, of course, she was enjoying torturing Ashley, but not because she was angry.

"Yes, that's all we wanted to do was help you." Ashley nodded her head very quickly to make her point.

Adya stopped pacing right in front of Ashley. She rested her hand on her hips and narrowed eyes at her friend. "I couldn't be happier for you guys." Adya laughed as she watched Ashley's face twist in confusion.

"You're *happy* for us?" she repeated.

Adya nodded and plopped on the bed beside Ashley. "No one has a claim on anyone, no matter what happened in other lifetimes. I love Pax and always will, but I made a different choice for this life. My choice kinda sucks right now, but I am hopeful that I can remedy it. I'm glad you two got close, but I'm sorry that it was out of worry for me."

Ashley appeared to be breathing again and relaxed. "Wow, that went so much better than I could've hoped."

Adya shrugged. "I'm marginally a better person than I used to be. No one has to worry anymore about me destroying cities or causing chaos because I'm angry. My world has shifted for the better. I draw strength and balance from my passions—and fury—instead of creating a larger imbalance with it." Adya continued to explain to Ashley about the elemental energy she sees now and how she can tap into the ebb and flow of that energy at a higher level than just manipulating the elements as she'd always done.

"But that won't stop me from using my elements to protect myself if I feel threatened," Adya concluded, narrowing her eyes again at Ashley. "So, don't plan any surprise parties for me, or you might find the entire room struggling to breathe."

Ashley giggled and rested her head on Adya's shoulder. "Any version of you is better than the zombie you became when you returned in January. I'm glad you're back."

Adya's eyes went to the tree outside. She withdrew a spring blossom from one of the branches and delivered it to Ashley's lap with a gentle breeze. "I love you, my sweet friend, and I am so happy that you're happy. Do me a favor, though."

Ashley picked up the flower and smelled it. "What is it?"

"Let me confront Pax before you tell him that I'm cool with everything. I would enjoy seeing him squirm a little." Adya smiled deviously.

With a giggle and nod, Ashley agreed. "I'm supposed to meet him near the trees that caught fire last year. That's kinda been our spot."

Adya kissed Ashley's cheek. "Don't you dare text him while I'm walking there. Pinkie swear it."

Ashley locked her pinkie with Adya's. "I promise."

Sierra peeked her head around the doorway. "Is everyone still alive in here?" she asked cautiously.

Adya laughed. "It's safe. No broken bones or windows or anything." She winked at the younger girl on her way out the door. "See you both in a bit."

It took nearly the entire walk to Paxton and Ashley's meeting spot for Adya to decide how she was going to torture him. Upon seeing him pacing beside a tree, Adya broke out in a full run with her arms open to embrace Paxton. "Pax! I'm so happy to see you. I've missed you so much." She wrapped her arms around his chest and rested her cheek against his shoulder.

"I'm, umm, happy to see you, too. Are you okay?" Paxton asked with genuine concern.

"I'm so much better now. And I realized while I was gone how stupid I was with the whole Lir situation. Of course, it's you I want in this life. Can you ever forgive me?" Adya leaned back and looked at Paxton with big doe eyes and a hopeful smile.

"Listen," Paxton said nervously. He rested his hands on Adya's shoulders to control the space between them.

"Yes?" Adya said and batted her eyelashes at him.

"We, umm, can't really, umm, you know," Paxton stammered.

"What do you mean?" Adya said, feigning surprise.

"I'm seeing Ashley now," he blurted out and immediately flinched.

Adya stepped backward with a dramatic gasp but couldn't hold the amusement in anymore. Her outburst of laughter resonated off the trees.

"What's so funny?" And then Paxton realized. "You already talked with Ash, didn't you?"

Adya calmed her outburst to a soft giggle. "Of course I talked with her. She's my roommate and best friend."

"Is she still conscious and breathing?" Paxton asked, still wary of Adya's reaction.

Adya sighed and rolled her eyes. "Of course. I would never hurt her or you, for that matter. Not intentionally anyway."

"You know," Paxton admitted, "while we were both thrilled to hear that you were coming home, we were pretty scared about how you'd react."

CHAPTER EIGHTEEN

"I know, which is why I asked Ash to let me mess with you a little bit." Adya smiled brightly. "I'd like to try to show you something. I had to explain it to Ashley, but I think I can share this memory with you." Adya offered her hand to Paxton.

He looked hesitantly at her. "What do you mean, share a memory with me? Like a memory we didn't share?"

Adya impatiently grabbed Paxton's hand and pulled him towards the nearest tree. "I've only done this with Lir, but I'm hopeful it'll work with you, too. I'm going to show you a memory of how things have shifted for me. If you can see it, it'll make so much more sense than me trying to explain it. And honestly, I'm tired of all this talking I've had to do since I got back." Adya lowered herself down to her knees and waited for Paxton to follow.

"This is a little weird," Paxton admitted as he knelt in front of Adya.

"It's only weird if you make it weird. Look, we both know our pasts were intimate and full of love. We aren't those people in this life." Adya shrugged nonchalantly. "And nothing will ever change the fact that I will always love you, Pax. You and Ash deserve a chance to be happy together in this life if that's what you both want."

"What about you? Are you happy in this life?" Paxton asked with genuine concern.

"I'll manage just fine whatever the outcome is," she said confidently. "Now, are you ready to try this?"

Paxton nodded and placed his hands with Adya's as she instructed. As he relaxed, he had a flash of a semi-intimate soul memory with Adya and immediately opened his eyes. "Are you sure about this?"

Adya nodded. "Wait for me to recall the memory in my mind." She breathed in deeply through her nose and slowly out while recalling the moment everything changed. "Okay, ready. Follow my energy into my mind. Find your element inside me and use it to guide you to my memory," she instructed.

Several minutes passed, and the two remained connected at their palms, slowly breathing, and experiencing Adya's memory until Paxton let his hands fall to his lap. "Is that really what you see when you look around now?"

Adya nodded. "Fire is invisible to me, but I can see the empty spaces as its energy mixes with the other elements. Like right now, you have what looks to me like an invisible aura around you from your element radiating out. Pressed up against that, I can see the earth, air, and water energies interacting with it. I suppose you'd light on fire if they weren't," she added teasingly.

Both stood up and brushed off their knees. "So that guy—"

"Jace," Adya inserted. "He's just a good friend. The whole reason we were at that hospital in the memory was because his niece was just born. She's a fire elemental affinate. Do you remember Shula?"

Paxton searched his memories and nodded. "I think I met her once."

"Baby Dani has Shula's soul. I thought that maybe in a few years, you might be willing to help her with her affinity? I know that seems weird, but Jace's family became my family over the past couple of months. Their town is small, and while I could handle the shit the locals wanted to throw at me, this little girl doesn't deserve that."

"Hey guys," Ashley called out as she approached them. "Is everything alright?"

"I'd be happy to help, Ady," Paxton replied to Adya before his smile brightened at the approaching Ashley. "Yeah, everything's great. Ady was just telling me about a new fire affinate that might need my help when she gets a little older."

Adya smiled as the two linked hands. "I'll leave you guys alone. I have unpacking to finish, and, yeah." Adya waved at the two and left them to do whatever it was they usually did in the trees off to the side of the school.

CHAPTER NINETEEN

C lasses continued as usual, but Adya had missed so much of the semester, she didn't bother attending. The teachers had agreed to give her leniency due to her unusual circumstances and the fact that she was the mastermind behind the upcoming rescue mission.

"You realize that I could teach many of these classes now," Adya argued to Ted as she sat in his office on a sunny afternoon in mid-April. She had been back at North Shore for just over a month and was feeling a bit stir-crazy waiting for the powers-that-be to make decisions on her plan.

"Except for Maggie, we thankfully don't have any openings for instructors at the moment," Ted replied wryly. "Besides, regardless of everything you already know, it's not going to harm you to continue learning—or reviewing."

Adya rolled her eyes. "Speaking of Maggie," she said to divert the conversation from the forever-surfacing debate about Adya's continuing education, "has Darius or anyone else heard from her? I was going over the layout she had me give you, and there are a few areas I'm unclear about."

Ted shook his head while typing something on his computer. "No, nothing from her since the end of January when she helped get you out." Ted furrowed his brows at the computer screen.

"What about the Elders? Have they been able to rally people to help?" Adya tried reading what was on Ted's screen but couldn't make out the small words from where she sat.

"Come here and look at this," Ted said, temporarily ignoring Adya's questions.

Adya walked around the desk and leaned over to read the email Ted was reviewing. Her brows furrowed, too, and she stood with a baffled look on her face. "Are we sure that's really from Eli?"

"I don't know this email address, but the Elders have an encryption code for their emails. While it was changed after Eli left, this is definitely an authentic code from when he was on the Council," Ted explained.

Adya shook her head. "This feels like a trap. Why would he give us this information?"

"We have to assume it's a trap, but I think we should try to verify if any of this is true. Eli is a scientist, and his intentions with this project were pure. Maybe Dhruva's pushing him beyond his ethical limits with these seemingly trivial wars she's creating."

Adya rolled her eyes dramatically. "So after almost a year of stealing souls and kidnapping affinates, which was somehow ethical in his mind, suddenly after nearly eliminating the Council and Dhruva's little crusade to start World War III, it's now 'going a little too far'? I don't trust him at all."

"Those two Elders that died were his friends. Everyone has their limits. Everyone has that moment when their eyes open up to the truth." Ted shrugged. "You don't have to trust him entirely, but if we can verify Dhruva's flight out of the country, at the very minimum, it would give us time without her there to do a recovery mission. Eli is smart, but he's not the strongest affinate. If your plan to deactivate the stolen affinities works, they shouldn't have strong enough defenses to counter us. Adya, this might be our best opportunity."

Adya paced the room as she considered their options. Ted was correct; this might be their best chance of getting the upper hand on Dhruva. "As long as we have absolute certainty that Dhruva is away, I think you're right. Were there any objections to my idea to shoot the sentries with tranquilizer darts?"

"Only a few that still don't see value in saving the soulless affinates. Thankfully, the majority appreciate the hopeful option you laid out for us. With the non-affinate powers of the world that are still on our side, we have a team of elite soldiers ready to assist." Ted picked up his cell phone and sent a text message. "I'll let you know when we get external confirmation of Dhruva's trip."

Adya didn't chat much with her friends at dinner that night. Ashley and Paxton had a side conversation going while Calder, Sierra, and Sierra's classmate from the air elemental house, Nadia, discussed the significance of the lunar cycle on their elements. Adya's thoughts were thousands of miles away, wondering if this was really going to be her chance to get Lir back and to save all the other affinates. She needed to know more about Eli. Without saying anything to her friends, Adya stood and followed one of the wait staff into the kitchen.

"Where's she going?" Ashley asked, anxious at the sight of Adya's retreating, but the rest of the group was as clueless as she was.

Inside the kitchen, the staff was busy with their assigned duties that coincided with the end of a meal at North Shore. Dishes were carried in by waiters, while others were appointed to scrape off the plates before handing them to the dishwashers. Extra unserved food was being divided between plates and placed in a salamander to stay warm until the staff had finished and could enjoy a meal, too.

Adya spotted Chef Caroline in the far corner, talking to members of her kitchen staff between bites of her dinner.

". . . and see what berries John can spare. We're running low, and I want to avoid using the frozen ones," Chef Caroline instructed one of her subordinates.

"Excuse me, Chef Caroline?" Adya interrupted politely. Unlike her familiarity with Lucas, Adya hadn't spent any time in the kitchen during her second year. She didn't know what to expect of the head chef. Chef Caroline did, Adya noticed, have a much calmer way of dealing with her staff than Lucas, who was regularly shouting in Italian. "Do you have a moment to chat with me about Eli?"

Chef Caroline issued a few more orders to her staff before inviting Adya into her small office that was next to the walk-in freezer. "It's been a while since I thought about him," she admitted. "What is it you want to know—Adya, isn't it?"

Adya nodded. "Yes, I'm Adya, and I'm sorry to bother you with this, but I need for you to tell me the kind of man he was before—"

"Before he ran away with that horrible girl who's hell-bent on starting a revolution?" Chef Caroline smiled at Adya. "Yes, I know quite a bit about what's going on in your world right now. I knew a lot about Eli, too, or thought I did," she explained. "He would work in his study until the early morning hours most days. He believed affinates should be more and do more for the world. Science was his answer to everything, and he believed technology was what affinates needed to help restore balance."

"So, his involvement with stealing affinate souls surprises you?" Adya asked.

Chef Caroline nodded. "Yes. He was frustrated with the other Elders, sure, but he didn't want to overthrow them."

"Do you think the Eli you knew would feel remorse for the chaos his technology has created?"

"Undoubtedly, and I think if he were on this side, he'd be inventing some clever piece of science to stop what's going on." Chef Caroline finished her food and stood from behind her small desk. "I have to get back to my staff. I hope that was the information you were looking for," the woman said with a smile.

Adya stood, too, and nodded. "It helps. Thank you, Chef Caroline." She left the kitchen and opened her new phone to send Jace a text. *Can you call me when you have a minute?* Continuing on her way, Adya tucked her phone into her pocket and walked outside.

The mid-April night was cool and calm. Adya watched the energies of the elements dance in harmony. It couldn't have been more peaceful, but the balanced energy didn't help Adya as much as she'd hoped. She was anxious to put her plan into action, but mostly, she really wanted to see Lir's soul returned and have him back in her life.

Her casual meanderings led Adya to the piano in the banquet hall. With her free time over the past month, she spent a lot of time listening to music and translating it to the keyboard. Her current favorite song was *The Way That I Feel* by Danielle Parente. If passion was her strength, this song had become Adya's anthem. With her fingers splayed on the keys, she began playing the slow, jazzy music and sang:

Grass on the ground is as green as can be
Birds in the sky flying so free
And that taste in my mouth is as sweet as can be
But it still don't change the way
No, it still don't change the way
The way that I feel

Adya answered her phone when it rang and switched it to speakerphone so she could continue playing the song. "Hey, Jace. Thanks for calling me back," she said.

"No problem. Is somethin' wrong?" Jace asked, sounding concerned.

"Not really. I just wanted to hear your voice," Adya said while continuing to play the song on the piano

"Are you at a jazz bar or somethin'?"

Adya smiled, even though he couldn't see it. "No, I'm just playing the piano. Trying to get my mind off stuff."

"Ashley an' Paxton?" he inferred.

"Nah, I'm okay with them. Probably better than I ought to be, but I have enough other things to worry about," Adya admitted. "We might have an opportunity to get in and save the affinates at the Institute."

"Oh? Is this like some super-secret hush-hush type of mission?"

"Kinda, I guess. I don't know. We got an email from someone on the inside. I just don't know if I trust what this guy told us." Adya started playing another song. "The piano isn't bothering you, is it?"

"Not at all. I didn't know you could play," Jace admitted.

"I have many talents you don't know about," Adya teased. "But in all seriousness, I'm worried that I'm going to let everyone down again. This is my plan, using my theory that I don't know will even work."

"So you wanna talk to me 'cuz I'm the seer of futures?" Jace asked.

"I wish. Then I wouldn't have to worry about any decisions I made. I could just talk to you first. Tell it to me like it is, oh all-seeing, all-knowing Jace." Adya giggled.

"Here's what I see. . . You're teasin' an' jokin' with me, so I think you're a lot more confident than you're pretendin' to be. I also know how strong you are. But I can't be the only one believin' in you, D. You gotta do that for yourself, too."

"She's not alone," a voice from behind Adya said.

Adya whipped around to see Paxton and Ashley behind her. "Hey, Jace. I'll give you a call back in a bit," she said immediately. "And Jace? Thank you."

"Talk to you later, D."

Adya clicked her phone off and looked at her two friends approaching her. "What's up, guys?"

"Ted was looking for you," Paxton began.

"He said that you should get ready to leave in the morning," Ashley added.

"Alright," Adya replied and turned back to the piano. She started playing the first song again, but Ashley stepped up and rested her hand on Adya's forearm.

"We're really," Ashley started.

"Worried about you," Paxton interjected. "What can we do?"

Adya looked between the two. "You could stop finishing each other's sentences, for one." She sighed and shrugged. "There's nothing you can do. My plan will work, or it won't."

"It will," they both started at the same time, but Paxton motioned for Ashley to go ahead.

"It will work," Ashley said confidently. "You know, you didn't have to phone-a-friend to get a pep talk. We're right here." Ashley sounded a bit hurt.

"I know you are," Adya said. "I know it's been a month since I got back, but I still feel disconnected from everything here. Life went on without me, as it should. I guess I'm just used to chatting with Jace about things." Adya was trying hard not to blame their relationship on the distance she felt from them now; it had very little to do with their closeness. "This year has really sucked for me, guys."

"It hasn't been all picnics and parties for us either," Ashley replied.

"I know, and I'm sorry I've made you guys worry so much. I'm glad you have each other, though," Adya said sincerely, but the smile didn't reach her eyes.

"You have us, too," Paxton interjected.

"I know," she sighed. "I don't know what I'd do without you guys. I love you both so much." Adya couldn't stop the tears from leaking out of the corner of her eyes.

Ashley sat on the piano bench beside Adya and hugged her friend. "We're not going anywhere. Even when you leave us physically, we're still there with you."

"And that brings us to the other reason why we came." Paxton reached into his pocket and pulled out a small chain. "Since they aren't going to allow us to go with you," he began.

"We argued with Ted for about twenty minutes to try to convince him to let us join you," Ashley interjected.

Paxton cleared his throat so he could continue uninterrupted. "We wanted you to have a little something for you to draw strength from, or at the very least, to remind you that we're there with you in thought and energy." Paxton placed the bracelet on Adya's wrist.

Adya smiled tearfully as she read the inscription on the round charm, "'Earth my body. Water my blood. Air my breath. Fire my spirit.' Thank you both," she sniffled.

"We infused it with our elements, too. I got the idea from the snowflake necklace," Ashley said as she proudly showed off the necklace around her neck. "I wear it everywhere."

Adya sat in quiet revere, looking at the gift they gave her. "You guys are the best. Thank you," she whispered.

The three remained in quiet contemplation until Paxton broke the silence. "Hey, Ash. Could I have a few minutes with Ady?"

"Sure," Ashley said without hesitation and hugged Adya once more. "You know where to find me, Pax," she said and lightly kissed Paxton. "I'll see you back in our room," she added to Adya before waving to the two and leaving the building.

Paxton took over the spot on the bench that Ashley vacated. He leaned forward, resting his elbows on his thighs as he gazed towards the opposite wall. "I know you better than you want to believe. You don't have to put on an act for me, Ady. I know you're worried about your plan, but I also know that you're terrified of not being able to save Lir."

Adya spun around in annoyance and faced the piano again. "You don't have to talk with me about Lir. I know you could care less about what has happened to him." She started playing the aggressive *Requiem* by Verdi.

Paxton sat patiently, at first, while she played the forceful tune, but as she continued, he turned towards the piano and grabbed her left wrist, pulling it away from the keys. "I care because he's important to you. You have been overwhelmingly supportive of Ash and me. She and I have known each other in other lives, but never romantically. This is new and different, and who knows how this will end, especially after she's Awakened."

Adya connected with the uncertainty of the unknown that Paxton was sharing, but she remained quietly listening.

"I know if Dhruva had taken me, you would be fighting just has hard to get me back as you are for him. I might not ever be friends with Lir—and maybe I can't fully appreciate how deep your feelings are for him—but I want you to know that everything inside me wants to help you get him back. . . for you." Paxton released Adya's wrist. "I want you to be happy and feel loved."

"I can't even begin to internalize what happy and loved feels like right now. For me, I just want everyone to return," Adya finally said after the brief silence when Paxton finished. "When I was there, and Maggie was trying to heal me, the only thing I wanted was to know who had Lir's soul so I could kill them and free his soul. Maggie texted the answer to my question to Darius, but when Ted tried to tell me who has it, I told him I didn't want to know. I want more than just Lir saved—I want the elements and the energies balanced, too. I want to go in with the passion I have to save Lir and apply that to everyone."

Paxton listened thoughtfully. "I know things have changed for you with everything you've been through this year, but I can see the good change in you. Your friend, Jace, had it right;

you just gotta believe in yourself." He swiveled around on the bench and stood. "For what it's worth, Lir is very lucky to have you and to have you fighting for him. I've gotta catch up with Ash, but I'll see you before you leave in the morning, okay?"

Adya nodded. "Thanks for the pep talk."

CHAPTER TWENTY

Adya played with the jet stone in her pocket, nervously rubbing it between her thumb and first finger while her gift from Paxton and Ashley rested against her wrist. Of all the places she'd dreamed as her un-Awakened self that she'd be at age thirteen, riding in a military convoy in the dead of night to rescue soulless people was not even in the top hundred on that list. Yet here she was.

It was around eleven o'clock at night when Adya was escorted from the airport to meet with the mission teams. Despite the soldiers receiving the mission report beforehand, Adya noticed the concerned looks on their faces when she walked to the front of the room to lead the meeting. She ignored their questioning looks and went over the details of the plan. On the large drawing of the Institute, she illustrated where the guards and affinates would be.

"Shouldn't you be texting boys or planning your outfit for tomorrow instead of leading a military mission?" one soldier asked as they sat in the back of a troop transport on their way to the Institute.

"Yeah, I have a niece your age. She's pretty much on her phone all day and night," another chimed in.

Adya looked calmly at the ten men who waited for her to answer. "If I wasn't the best person to lead this, do you think

I'd be here? These are *my* people, *my* elements, and *my* plan that won't work unless I'm there."

The tension around Adya was as palpable as it was visible to her. She removed the jet stone from her pocket and placed it in the middle of the floor. With a deep breath—and ten sets of eyes still on her—she transferred some of the grounding and protective energy from the stone into the air around the group. She watched the energies swirl and dance around them until they achieved balance.

The men collectively sighed, and Adya bent down to retrieve the stone. "I assume you all feel a little more focused now?"

"That little rock did that?" the first man who questioned her asked.

"No," Adya replied. "I did that with the help of the stone."

"No shit," the soldier said with an easy laugh.

Adya allowed herself to smile but soon reorganized her face into a solemn expression. "Your job is to protect me so that I can protect you from others like me. There will be a lot of kids my age, but don't mistake them for the child you think me to be. They will try to do something like what I just did—manipulate the elements—only they won't be trying to relax you. Those kids are receiving training to be powerful and to fight and kill, if necessary." Adya looked at the faces of the men in her company. "If any of you have doubts that I can do this or if you still think I should be back home texting boys or posting selfies, then I will politely ask you to stay behind."

The group rode the rest of the way in silence, giving Adya time, once again, to reflect on her elements and draw strength from their energy. To Adya's relief, all the soldiers in her vehicle exited upon arrival and circled her as planned.

There were four other vehicles like hers that carried troops with different assignments. The first team that would go was responsible for tranquilizing the external guards. They would clear a path for the second wave, the tactical squad with EMP jamming devices, to enter and target the Institute to disable all electronic devices. In other words, Dhruva wouldn't know anything was happening while she was on her way to Egypt.

Won't that also damage Eli's soul-sucking machine? Adya had asked Ted in his office that morning as they discussed the plan before flying to New York.

It might take Eli some time to fix it in the aftermath, but it's the only way can ensure that we complete this as stealthily as possible, Ted explained.

Adya tried to push this snag in her ultimate plan of getting Lir back to the back of her mind—she needed to be focused.

"Here, you'll need these." One of Adya's soldiers handed her a pair of night-vision goggles so she could see where they were going on that very dark night.

Adya adjusted them to fit her face and then pushed them up on the top of her head until it was their turn to enter the encampment.

Team three waited for two minutes before they followed the EMP carriers. Their task was to tranquilize any remaining external guards and begin removing the unconscious, soulless sentinels. Finally, Adya's team—team four— and team five would go into the buildings. The primary responsibility of Adya's team was exactly what she explained to them: guard her while she put her theory to work against any would-be defenders. Team five would be tranquilizing anyone that moved.

When it was about time for Adya's troops to move in, she knelt to the ground and placed her palm on the dirt. She took a moment to breathe in the cool night air and to feel her elements around her. She closed her eyes, calmed her mind, and spoke aloud to the elements. "To the earth that grounds me, the air I breathe, the water that gives me life, and the invisible fire I know is within me, I ask that you give me your energy to bring everything back to balance here. I beg the Ascended souls to give me the courage and strength to do what I must to restore our elements, and also that you protect these men who are working to protect our elements."

Adya opened her eyes. Her entire company had knelt with her, and everyone held a gloved palm to the ground. She smiled at each of them and then pulled down her goggles as she rose to her feet. "Let's do this."

It was only about a minute into their walk to the Institute property that Adya removed the night vision goggles. While she could clearly see her surroundings, the goggles completely blocked her ability to see the elements' energy. It was essential to her that as they moved along, she also did what she could to bring balance to the chaotic stream of energies.

Her soldiers were in a tight formation around her, and by the time they arrived, Adya could hear members of the other teams removing the unconscious guards from the area. *Please let one of those be Lir*, she said in her mind as they approached their first target building. According to Maggie's map, the building they were entering was one of three that housed the recipient affinates.

Two soldiers entered in front of Adya, quickly shooting the darts at the four guards they encountered inside the door. The group of twenty-one stepped over the bodies and continued down the first hallway, where a girl poked her head out the door.

"What the—?" she shouted.

Adya felt her heart racing but harnessed the feelings of fear and uncertainty inside her to focus on the elemental signatures around the girl. She was an air affinate, but the energy of water flickered destructively around her. Just like when the water had boiled away in Ava's kitchen, and Adya manipulated the water's molecules to restore it to the pot, she disrupted the energy around this girl, mentally holding her breath that it would work.

Before the girl could finish her sentence, a look of shock took over her features, and she fell against the doorframe. One of the soldiers fired a dart, and the team moved onto the next room.

Adya took a moment before she walked forward, her mind screaming in exhilaration, *holy shit! It worked!* The soldier behind her prompted her to continue moving.

Teams four and five cleared the first building without incident. They were fortunate that the majority of the affinates were sleeping. Thanks to their stealth, Adya didn't have to do much; the soldiers were fast to shoot and very accurate. The second building proved to be a bit more complicated.

There was a group of eight in the common room in the second building. A few in the group had been alerted when the TV they were watching cut out with the EMP blast. They had gathered to defend the Institute and attacked the lead soldiers with fireballs as soon as the door opened.

Adya diverted water from the air to extinguish the small fires on the men's chests. Thankfully, they were wearing body armor and didn't suffer any significant injuries. Those two men flanked to the sides of Adya, who had already begun manipulating the energies in the room. First, a man in the group of affinates tried to charge the invaders, but Adya quickly used her earth affinity to root him, which allowed the soldiers time to shoot him with the tranquilizer. Air was the most imbalanced element in the room, so with a subtle motion, she pulled the air towards herself. As her hair flew back, four of the remaining seven affinates gasped and grabbed their throats, but then quickly were neutralized by the soldiers. When one of the fire affinates attempted to hurl another fireball them, Adya flooded the room with water energy, absorbing the ball of flame and knocking the girl backward three feet, where her body went limp from the tranquilizer. The remaining two were caught in a wind vortex of Adya's creation. Once they'd been shot, she lowered them gently to the floor. While this felt like a massive victory to Adya, there was no time to pause and celebrate. She quickly refocused and moved on with the rest of her team to finish their job.

The entire operation took just over an hour. When Adya returned to the base camp, she was exhausted. But her night wasn't over yet. She tried to make her way through the returning soldiers as quickly as possible. Unfortunately, it was slower than she would've liked because many stopped to offer her congratulations.

Adya generously thanked each soldier she passed, too. "Thank you," she repeated more times than she thought possible. "Has anyone seen Ted?"

The transport trucks were leaving with bodies of the unconscious. Adya was concerned that Ted was on one of the vehicles, too. Fortunately, she found him after about fifteen minutes of searching, talking with the head Commander of the troops.

"Ted?" Adya said as she neared the two men. "Do you have a minute?"

"Your plan worked, Adya," Ted said proudly.

"My men said you were a sight to behold," the Commander added.

"Thanks," she said again. "We couldn't have done this without your help. Thank you for not giving up on the Elders and us," Adya added with more sincerity.

Ted and Adya stepped away from the Commander, but still heard him marvel to one of his officers, "I still can't believe a thirteen-year-old girl led this."

"You did really well tonight, Ady. I can feel the elements returning to balance already," Ted said as they walked away from the gathering.

"That was the plan," she replied. "We didn't kill anyone, right?"

Ted shook his head. "No, there was a small skirmish in team two, but everyone has been subdued and is on their way to the military base where they will remain sedated until Eli can fix his machine."

"So, the machine was damaged?" Adya said solemnly.

"We knew that would happen. The Elders are debriefing Eli. They'll get him working on the machine as soon as we get it removed from the property," Ted explained.

"What about Lir and Maggie—and Lir's soul?" Adya finally got to ask the question that concerned her most.

"Lir's body was in the second convoy to the base. We have both his body and soul. Maggie—" Ted paused and sighed. "She's suffered a lot since helping you leave. Most of the affinates waiting to have their souls extracted were also in depleted health. We're going to take Maggie and those others to a private hospital and hopefully get them healthy again."

A wave of relief and new worry washed over Adya. The rage she felt for Maggie faded a long time ago. Guilt for her friend's suffering as payment for Adya's freedom replaced the anger.

Ted placed his hand on Adya's shoulder. "What happened to her isn't your fault. You risked your life to save her. There was never a question in her mind that she would do the same for you."

Adya nodded. "I know, but that only takes away a small amount of the guilt I'm feeling. Maybe capturing Dhruva will ease that a little more."

"That could take a while, although I question the Elder's decision to put it off. I have a feeling she won't exactly be happy to return to an empty compound," Ted admitted.

"Why don't we take the fight to her right now? We still have the element, so to speak, of surprise," Adya suggested. "We know approximately where she is, so put me on a plane, and I can finish this before she takes revenge on us."

Ted looked at his student with sadness in his expression. "You look like a gentle breeze could knock you over right now. Get some rest. In the morning, we can have another discussion with the Elders about a team going to Egypt to retrieve Dhruva."

Adya nodded compliantly. "Okay," she submitted, "but I'd like to visit Maggie. Maybe there's something I can do to help her and the others."

"Until the blockers leave their bodies, we are hesitant to use the elements to heal them. But I will arrange for you to get transportation to the hospital," Ted conceded. He wasn't sure if it would be a good idea for Adya to see Maggie in her current condition, but also appreciated that the girl had more than earned the right to be granted a simple request.

After speaking with the Commander, Ted secured a spot for Adya in one of the transport vehicles. "A car will be waiting at the hospital to take you to the hotel afterward. We can talk more in the morning about plans to take a team to Egypt. Please, for the love of the elements, get some rest tonight, okay?"

Adya nodded. "I'll see you in the morning."

The walk down the hallway in the hospital to visit Maggie brought back memories of Adya visiting her mom for the last time. Although Adya was a stronger version of herself now, she still felt anxious. Death, while it was still sad, was seen as a release of the soul and a chance for rebirth. Maggie had an old soul, even if her baptism took her affinity away. And while Adya didn't wish to lose her guardian just yet, a part of her considered it might be for the best so she could come back and have her affinity the natural way.

Maggie was in a room by herself. When Adya entered, the woman she loved like a sister was unconscious. Remnants of healing wounds—old burns, scabbed over and infected cuts, and white lines scarring her flesh—covered much of her visible skin. Her body looked unhealthily skinny and frail, and her hair was visibly thinning. Most of the elemental energy that Adya could now visibly see around affinates seemed like the element radiating out from the person. But when she looked at Maggie, there was only a faint aura of water energy hovering around her body, akin to a small child walking around in adult clothes—it didn't fit.

Both the look of it and the actual affinity itself came as a surprise to Adya. She knew Maggie refused to use her artificial affinity, but in the short, angry time that Adya had been in Maggie's care, they didn't discuss her new gifts at all.

"Maggie," Adya said softly, leaving the water-energy hovering around her undisturbed. "It's me, Adya. You're safe now, and we're going to get you healed." Adya held Maggie's hand, and a memory immediately took over her mind's eye:

"You don't have to do this, Maggie," a man said as Maggie kept her eyes closed. She knew if she opened them, the tears would spill out, and she might physically get sick.

"This isn't what they promised me," Maggie whispered to the man. "You were supposed to be insurance."

The man's hand reached over and squeezed Maggie's hand reassuringly. "Adya came to find me last night," he began, "but Dhruva sensed her there with me. Her psychotic mind flipped to revenge mode and saw value in this change of events. But you can stop this. I know Adya and her stubborn soul won't be able to stay away. Just give her a little more time," he begged.

Maggie turned her head to the side and finally opened her eyes. The tears flowed freely, and her body was shaking as she helplessly stared into Lir's eyes. "Dhruva's going to kill my sister if I don't go through with this. My sister just wanted to understand what I had when we were kids. She wanted to be like me."

Lir released Maggie's hand and nodded. "Adya is going to be in over her head when she shows up, especially if she sees what they're going to do to me. Just promise me you won't let Dhruva do this to Ady," Lir begged.

"I will make this right somehow, Lir. You don't deserve this," Maggie said tearfully.

"Tell Ady that I will love her for always," he said and closed his eyes to wait for the inevitable.

The memory played in Adya's mind instantly, and she immediately withdrew her hand from Maggie's as soon as it ended. Adya paced like a caged animal inside Maggie's hospital room. Lir's soul. . . Maggie was the one with it trapped inside her body. And if she died now, Eli wouldn't have a chance to restore Lir's soul to his body, even if he was able to fix and modify the machine. Adya knew that was a selfish way of looking at Maggie's well-being, but until she had adequate time to process the slew of emotions she felt, this would have to suffice.

"I'm not going to let you die," Adya vowed and rested her hand against Maggie's frail chest.

There was so much going wrong inside Maggie—from an imbalance of elements to a lack of nutrients to. . . a will to die? "No, no, no," Adya begged and began to work on healing Maggie, despite Ted's warning that the blockers needed to wear off first.

The wounds on Maggie's skin began to improve as Adya worked with her elements to fix all that was going wrong with Maggie. Beneath the exterior surface, Adya felt the effects of the blocking serum along with some minor poisons she had absorbed. Had Maggie been consuming lead from the old paint in her room?

Adya reeled back and started coughing, which alerted a passing nurse to enter. "What's going on in here?" the nurse demanded to know.

Adya shook her head and placed her hand back on Maggie's chest. "She's dying. I have to keep going," Adya insisted.

"Guards!" the nurse yelled as she struggled to pull Adya away from Maggie's body.

"No!" Adya yelled and stood upright, voluntarily releasing her touch on Maggie. Adya conjured up a force of air, pinning the nurse to the wall and slamming the door closed. "I don't have much time before that damn serum takes over." Adya channeled her rage and determination into her elements, twisting in and out of Maggie, healing the internal and external damage, until finally, she couldn't.

The nurse rushed to grab Adya as soon as the air released her. Guards immediately stormed into the room and restrained Adya. There was nothing more Adya could do—the absorbed blockers were affecting her now.

As they dragged Adya away, Maggie's eyes fluttered open. "Adya," she whispered as loudly as she could. Maggie was still weak and not out of danger of dying, but Adya couldn't help her anymore. "You wanted me dead," Maggie said. "I tried."

Adya tried screaming back to Maggie as the guards escorted her out. "Please don't die! I can save you both!" But Adya didn't know if Maggie heard her.

Ted showed up at the hospital to pick up Adya from security. He apologized to the staff and assured them there'd be no other interruptions to their facility.

"You knew all this time," Adya said exhaustedly in the car on the way to the hotel.

"I did, but you said you didn't want to know," Ted reminded her.

"I told Maggie I was going to kill the person who got Lir's soul. She was trying to kill herself," Adya said, still stunned by the encounter.

"In the letter she had you give to me, she told me she would find a way to free Lir's soul. Why do you think we rushed her to a private hospital for treatment? Do you honestly think anyone wants her dead?" Ted asserted.

"She thought I did. I don't know how many of her wounds were self-inflicted, either." Adya hung her head in exhaustion and shame. "They were going to kill her sister if she didn't take Lir's soul. Even if she refused and sentenced her sister to death, his soul would've gone to someone else that day, maybe even Dhruva herself. I saw a soul memory of hers when I first touched her; it was the last moments before Lir's soul was transferred."

"We won't let her die," Ted said and pulled something from his jacket pocket as they pulled up to the hotel. "Take this pill when you get back to your room. Eli said it should counter the blockers. We are administering them to the ones we saved. I imagine you probably absorbed whatever was in Maggie's system."

Adya accepted the pill and held it in her clenched fist. "Thanks. I promise not to cause any more problems tonight. Tomorrow is a different story," she said with a tired smirk as she exited the backseat of the car.

Ted chuckled and followed her out. "I want you to know," he said as he grabbed her arm before going inside the lobby, "that with or without the Elder's consent, we will get you and whatever you need on a plane to Egypt before Dhruva leaves."

Adya was visibly taken aback by Ted's promise. She nodded her head. "It's our best option."

The two entered the lobby and rode together in the elevator. After Adya parted from Ted to go to her room, she finally felt the full magnitude of the night's events. She entered her hotel room, made it just past the bathroom, and broke down crying. Without being able to manipulate the elements because of the blockers she'd absorbed from Maggie—nor was she able to draw on their energy when she was so obviously lacking—the emotions burst through unhindered. Every thought circled back to Lir—from the small, ordinary room she was in that lacked the forethought Lir had put into their hotel rooms on their trip, to the vivid soul memory of his final moments before he had his soul ripped from him. He was thinking about her through it all. And now there was nothing she could do anymore to save him except wait for a scientist who had just been working against them to come up with a plan to give people their souls back.

For the foreseeable future, Adya thankfully had a distraction. After she cried herself out, she grabbed a bottle of water from the mini-fridge in the room, drank the neutralizing pill, and laid on the bed, thinking about strategies to capture Dhruva until she fell asleep.

CHAPTER TWENTY-ONE

"**T**he Elders voted two-to-one against the trip to Egypt," Ted told Adya as they sat in the tiny café in the hotel lobby, eating breakfast. He could already see the objection on her face and held up his hand. "I told you that I supported this idea, so I called Elder Tama, and she agrees with us." Nearly a month and a half had passed since the attack on the Elders. While Elder Tama was recovering in the hospital, she had taken a step back from most of the usual Council business.

It surprised Adya that Elder Tama had stepped in to voice an opinion on this, and even more surprising that she agreed with herself and Ted, given that she was a strong opponent against every part of Adya's attempts to stop Dhruva. "What happens when there's a tie?" Adya inquired.

Ted responded with a shrug. "It doesn't usually happen because there are supposed to be seven Elders. Between the two that Dhruva killed and Eli leaving, only four Elders remain. Regardless, we will continue to move forward with our plan to get you to Egypt. How are you feeling today? Did the pill work?"

"Was dreaming about the dead supposed to be a side effect?" It felt like Adya had one long dream where she visited with Ava. Adya got to talk to dream-Ava about her new abilities and so many other things, including what she believed was the final piece of the puzzle they needed to restore the souls. She had woken up feeling like herself and in complete control of her emotions and abilities.

"There shouldn't be any side effects." Eli walked up and joined Ted and Adya at their small table.

Adya narrowed her eyes at the man who was responsible for the entire mess they were attempting to clean up. Her pettiness got the best of her; she touched the glass of water that was placed in front of Eli and froze it solid. "I'm doing just fine today," she said with a clenched jaw, "unlike the others who are being forced unconscious or recovering in the hospital."

"I didn't mean for it to happen like this," Eli said remorsefully.

"We're not meeting to point fingers at each other," Ted interrupted. "Adya, Eli wants to ask you questions about the modifications he'll have to make to return the souls to their proper bodies."

Adya stared blankly at the man and waited for his questions.

"Okay, then," Eli began. "Your theory is basically the same theory I had about transferring souls. It wasn't an easy device to design, but—"

Adya cut him off. "You shouldn't have designed it at all. You aren't a god or the director of the universe, so why the hell did you invent it?"

Ted remained quiet, drinking his tea, obviously waiting for an answer as well.

"It felt like we were losing our fight to keep the balance. With everything going on in the world, and it was only looking like things were spiraling out of control, I just wanted to give the elements the best chance. Ava felt it, too, all those years ago, and got tired of fighting what felt like an inevitable loss. It's only gotten worse since then," Eli explained.

"Don't you dare talk about Ava in the same breath as this monstrosity you created. She would've *never* been okay with this," Adya scolded.

"Be that as it may," Eli continued, "I had pure intentions going into this."

"How far 'into this' did it take for you to realize what a psychotic, destructive, power-hungry bitch Dhruva is?" Adya demanded.

"I was mostly in my lab, so I didn't pay Dhruva much attention until the attack on the Elders. My intention for the Institute was to have students who could master all the elements, teach them how everything works together, not against each other. Believe me; I know the dynamics of the Academies. So much of the emphasis is on mastering the affinate's element that it becomes a competition between the elemental houses about which one is stronger, better, and has more affinates. I wanted what you want: peace and harmony for the elements."

Adya was about to fire back at Eli, but Ted interrupted the banter. "What is it you need to know from Adya, Eli? We have other things we need to attend to today."

Adya was silently grateful that Ted didn't share their plans with Eli; she still didn't trust him or his intentions.

"I didn't design the machine to return souls to their original bodies. I can't understand how we could separate the guest soul—for lack of a better term for it—from the original soul of the host," Eli admitted.

Adya took a slow sip of her tea, watching Eli the entire time. She didn't mind making him wait for the answer he seemed anxious to know. Finally, she set down her cup and began explaining her epiphanies. "I have three affinities because I absorbed the souls of a dying twin in the womb. This integration was able to happen because both minds were unconscious, and the soul of the dying twin desired to go somewhere."

Both men nodded at Adya's explanation.

"Those souls became part of my soul because my soul was able to accept and absorb theirs, and those souls willingly gave themselves to me. I can tell when I am around the people who have received a soul from your machine because theirs are not in harmony. I understand now that there are literally two souls sharing a body. Instead of creating a balance, it actually does the opposite. Exactly what you said you don't like about the Academies, this procedure inflicts—it forces their souls and elements in conflict with each other. The energies surrounding those people are extremely erratic. I'm sure you saw evidence of that when the recipients tried using their new abilities. So, to put the souls back into their proper bodies, you need to identify the soul by its affinity and move the affinity back into its correct body. The soul should gravitate with the elemental energies. The affinity should act like a fingerprint or a signature, unique to each soul. You did keep records of whose soul you gave to whom, correct?"

Eli looked intrigued by Adya's theory. "If I modify the machine to look for the elemental signature and transfer that between the bodies. . . yes, I think that could work. Oh, and yes, I have records of everything. Or at least I did. Were all my files removed from the lab, Ted?"

Ted nodded. "Yes, they are on the base along with your equipment. I want to make it very clear to you, Eli, that reversing the souls does not pardon you from your involvement in the attacks against the Elders and the elements."

"I understand," Eli said, remorse evident in his voice and his slumped posture. "I will start working on repairing and modifying the machine as soon as I'm back at the base. Thank you for sharing your insights, Adya." Eli stood from the table and was escorted out of the hotel by a pair of soldiers.

Adya raised a brow at Ted. "Did you want to punch him as much as I did?"

Ted chuckled. "There have been many times in my lives when I wanted to hit that man. I hope he can make good use of your theory, Adya." Ted placed money on the table to cover their meal and stood. "Now, it's time to move onto the final part of your plan. What do we need to get you for your trip?"

Preparing for the trip to Egypt to capture Dhruva didn't take much time. Adya knew her affinities were more potent than they had ever been. After successfully interrupting the energies of the affinates at the Institute, all Adya needed was to be able to find Dhruva—the rest should be easy.

Adya spent a brief amount of time shopping in New York before departure. She wanted to be able to blend in with the native people in Cairo and not stand out like an American tourist. With the help of an earth affinate, who also happened to be a high-end fashion designer, Adya dressed in a brown, teal, and light blue wrap dress. Not only was it fresh off a fashion show in Cairo, but it was a beautiful blend of the colors representing her elements.

The team assembled for Adya's trip included two American soldiers who would fly with her to Egypt. They would be joined in Cairo by three Egyptian Medjay—an elite paramilitary police force that supposedly disappeared from Egyptian society over three thousand years ago. The final member of Adya's team was a member of an army RSTA unit and would act as the team's eyes and ears. Adya was fitted with an earpiece and a communications device that would help her give and receive intel during the mission.

The private jet made one stop in London for fuel before the final six-hour flight to Cairo. The long plane ride provided the team with ample time to study maps of the city. They highlighted places where Dhruva was likely to conduct meetings and stay, along with routes in and out of those locations.

As Adya's eyes moved across the map of the now-modern city she hadn't visited in millennia, she focused on an oasis outside Cairo. "Faiyum," she said, bringing three sets of questioning eyes upon her. "That's where I lived in my first life," she explained. Adya looked at the three men and asked, "Would there be any possibility of luring Dhruva there?"

"That's about an hour and a half from Cairo," the tactician explained. "It would be inadvisable to take the chase there."

"I could be bait," Adya explained. "There is no question in my mind that Dhruva will drop everything to hunt me down. If we could feed her information somehow about the attack on the Institute, she would have even more reason to come after me than she already does."

"We have orders to not acknowledge the mission at the Institute, ma'am," one of her soldiers said.

"In all due respect, this is my mission. If we confront Dhruva in the city, there is a high probability that people and structures will be compromised. In Faiyum, the population is considerably less. More importantly, I believe returning there for me will make me stronger." It was just a theory that crystalized in Adya's mind with shocking clarity. Whether or not the birthplace of her soul and her water affinity would benefit her in any way was a gamble, but it was one Adya knew she had to take. "Do we know who she is meeting with?"

"The Medjay should have that information," the tactician replied.

"Let's give the people Dhruva are trying to recruit against the Elders information about the dismantling of her army, and that the Elders would like to meet with them to discuss reaffirming their alliance." Adya was thinking out loud, trying to come up with a way to make her revised plan happen. "After we speak with the Medjay in Cairo, we can take a helicopter ahead to Faiyum and set up there. The Medjay could deliver the information and then tail Dhruva." Still facing resistant looks from the men, Adya pressed her hand in the middle of the map and demanded they take her plan seriously. "We will shift our strategy from chasing her to force her to chase us. We will completely control where and how this happens, giving us a strategic advantage. You have to see that," she argued.

Two of the men stepped away from the table to make phone calls, leaving just one soldier with Adya. "How'd you get to be such a strategist?" he asked her.

"Lifetimes of experience, of seeing things done, of having things done to me." Adya shrugged. "How'd you get roped into this mission? Lose a bet?" she joked.

"I volunteered," he said plainly. "I was in team five on our raid last night. I saw what you did. Never would've thought a kid could take down all those people like that." He reached into one of his back pockets and pulled out a photograph. "I have kids younger than you at home. I felt it was my duty to protect you like I would protect my own."

Adya leaned in and looked at the picture of his family. "They're adorable, but they look more like your wife than you," she added with a grin.

"Luckily for them, yes," he said with a smile. "Do you really think this Dhruva girl will be so easy to trick into chasing after you?"

Adya nodded with certainty. "I trained with her when she first got her second affinity. She has always wanted to be the most powerful affinate and has always seen me as a threat. Considering that, I don't doubt that she will know she's being followed and possibly set up, so I'm under no false assumption that we are going to be a complete surprise to her. Still, she will be thrown off kilter by news of the Institute, and that will give us an even bigger advantage."

"Are you stronger than her?" he asked.

Adya smiled and looked down at her hands for a moment to think of an easy way to explain something that most non-affinates wouldn't be able to comprehend fully. "That's complicated to answer directly. The pure strength of her elements defines her idea of power. I have to believe she has all four affinities now, which by her definition, she is stronger than me with only three. However, it's always eluded Dhruva that the power of affinities doesn't come from the number you have; it stems from your ability to balance them and work within the natural energy of the elements. My affinities are natural, something gifted to my soul, but hers were forced inside her body through technology. They don't act as one soul, but rather she has presumably four souls inside her, each fighting the artificial union of the elements."

"Oh," he replied because what else really could he say to that.

The other two men rejoined them. "The Commander has approved this deviation, but I will remain with two of the Medjay operatives in Cairo, and one will go with you in my place," the soldier informed Adya.

"That'll be good," Adya agreed. "The Medjay operative can help with the locals in Faiyum and hopefully find us an advantageous spot to wait for Dhruva."

The four shifted their focus for the rest of the flight to the new map of Faiyum, discussing strategic positions of advantage and disadvantage.

Adya peered out the helicopter window as they flew to Faiyum. She let her soul take her back in time when she lived there in her first life. So much had changed—the flow of water, the shape of the sand dunes, the roads—yet there was a familiarity to it all, too, and that was because of the elements. Adya thought back to the nine months at the Academy before her Awakening and knew that flying to Faiyum would've brought on a major case of *déjà vu* for that girl. Now, at least for a piece of her soul, it felt like she was coming home.

There was a fierce breeze blowing sand at them when the helicopter landed. To protect herself and the team, Adya created a bubble of air around them that diverted the sand away. The sun was high overhead and hot, but Adya only felt the overwhelming call of her native element.

"Do you need my help to set up?" Adya asked as they neared the building they decided to make their base.

"You got a hot date with an old boyfriend?" the soldier who was talking with Adya on the plane asked.

Adya chuckled. "Nothing quite that interesting, I'm afraid."

"We need you back in twenty minutes. Wear your earpiece so we can communicate with you," the RSTA soldier said and went inside to set up his equipment.

Adya affixed the small device in her ear and headed out on foot towards the oasis. It wasn't the most comfortable thing to wear, but at least it didn't inhibit her interactions with the elements and their energies like the night vision goggles had.

At the water's edge, Adya knelt and put both of her hands in the water. She marveled at the sensations of touching it again at the place that was her first home. Lifetimes had passed like the grains of sand flying through the air. The work she did with her water affinity in that first lifetime felt so rudimentary compared to what she could do with three elements in this one. But even now, she could appreciate by looking at the life that still existed in that hostile environment that her contribution to the elements back then helped life thrive here. There was power and beauty in that.

Adya wanted to immerse herself in the waters that bound her to her primary affinity and her first lifetime. "Hey, guys? Umm, over?" Adya said to the device on her that allowed her to talk to the team.

"Is there a situation?" someone replied over the radio.

"No, I just wondered if the equipment is waterproof," Adya said.

There was a brief pause before someone replied, "Did you get it wet?"

"Not yet, but I was going to go a little deeper in the water and didn't know if I should take it off," she explained while removing her sandals.

"Don't submerge the equipment. And we're going to need you back soon so we can all be in position. We have confirmation that Dhruva is in a car heading in this direction."

"I'll be back shortly," Adya said and waded into the water up to the bottom hem of her dress. She could feel the energies of her element infusing her body—it was unlike anything she'd ever felt. In the year and a half that she mostly lived at North Shore Academy, whenever she returned, she could feel her elements welcome her back. But this was undoubtedly tenfold that sensation. "I told Lir revisiting old places would be amazing," she said aloud to herself.

"Could you repeat?" a voice in her ear said.

Adya cringed, not used to having people listen in on the conversations she had with herself out loud. "Nothing. I'm on my way back." She slowly, and somewhat reluctantly, made her way out of the water, put her shoes back on, and returned to the base to prepare for the battle to come.

"A black car with four occupants is approaching from the northeast," one of the soldiers assigned to lookout reported over the radio. The entire team did a final ready check on their equipment and waited.

When Adya returned to base camp, she convinced the team to place her on the far side of the oasis. From that position, she had the water on one side and sand dunes as far as the eye could see on the other. She would be in a location that balanced her three elements within her.

The entire team of seven was assembled and in their assigned places, but there was hardly a moment of radio silence. The noise in Adya's ear made it difficult for her to concentrate on her ritual to the elements.

In frustration, she removed her earpiece so she could honor the elements and ask the Ascended to guide her in this fight. "I will need all your strength and all your energy to be successful in restoring your balance," she whispered in reverence.

Adya didn't hear the voices in the earpiece warning her of Dhruva's approach, but Adya could feel it. The frenetic, violent energy that radiated from the girl was palpable. Despite knowing Dhruva was approaching, Adya didn't stand from where she had knelt to touch the earth—she could feel the girl's approach like Dhruva was walking on a drum.

"Who's the predictable one now?" Adya said as she turned and stood in one motion.

Dhruva said nothing with her words and expected the wave of fire she sent towards Adya to speak for her. But Adya had already mentally prepared for any possible attack from her nemesis. Before the flames could reach Adya, she extinguished them with water pulled through the air from the oasis. A sizzle vibrated through the dry air as the water and fire consumed each other.

"I knew this was a trick," Dhruva said and pushed wind and sand towards Adya, but that, too, was blocked by the same simple bubble of air that she had created for her team when they exited the helicopter. "The Institute hasn't fallen; you just wanted to get me out here," she insisted.

"No," Adya said as she calmed the wind. "That was the truth. You have nothing to go back to," she added with a shrug.

"Lies!" Dhruva accused and pulled a branch off a distant tree. It whizzed through the dry air and landed in a substantial blow to the back of Adya's skull.

Adya swayed and felt a wet spot of warmth on the back of her head. She needed to be focused, which was a little bit more difficult with the stars dancing across her vision. Dhruva attacked again immediately and pulled air from around Adya, causing her to gasp for breath.

It reached the point of near panic in Adya's oxygen-deprived body before she shifted the fear into power and pulled the air back. To keep Dhruva busy while Adya caught her breath and stopped herself from almost blacking out from the concussion, she used both air and water elements to create a water vortex and wrapped it around Dhruva.

"I thought… that you might… have gotten smarter," Adya struggled to say. "You've lost."

Even if Dhruva believed she had lost everything, she wasn't going to go down without a fight. "I am stronger than you!" she shouted. "I'm stronger than everyone!" The vortex burst, and water pooled on the sand at her feet. Immediately, she countered and brought forth a fiery vortex that encompassed Adya.

Adya could feel the heat absorbing into her body, burning her flesh and hair. She cried out and stamped her foot hard against the earth, sending waves of energy outwards. The fire vortex vanished when the vibration knocked Dhruva off her feet.

"Stand down," Adya commanded and walked towards the girl scrambling to get to her feet.

The earth reached up at Dhruva's command and rooted Adya in place, stopping her forward momentum. "I will finish you off, just like I did to those Elders, and then go after the remaining Elders, wherever they're hiding around here." Dhruva whipped around wildly and began destroying nearby buildings—the first with a strong gale of wind that caused the structure to crumble, the second with fire, and a third was buried in sand before Adya freed herself from the earthly grasp.

Adya was bleeding, burned, and the grounding trick happened at the precise time she was stepping with her formerly broken foot—she heard a resounding snap, but at that moment, she felt none of the pain. Adya centered all of her focus on the chaotic energies that enveloped Dhruva's body. Fire, water, and air energies were shooting out from her body. Adya mused in the back of her mind if she'd be shocked by them if she tried to physically grab Dhruva. But she wasn't going to touch the girl—she was going to disable her.

Water affinity was the last one Dhruva had received through the soul transplant, so it was the weakest and most natural energy for Adya to control. Using her new ability to manipulate the elements' energy, she pulled the water-energy away from Dhruva and sent it towards the body of water.

Dhruva's body twitched, and she shook her head, not realizing that Adya had effectively stolen Dhruva's water affinity, or at least disabled it for the time being.

Next, Adya focused on the air element's energy. Dhruva was actively using the air affinity when Adya stole that gift from her. The sand that was being carried through the air as a destructive dust devil immediately fell back to the earth.

"Give up, Dhruva," Adya ordered and attempted to take a step forward, but she could felt the freshly broken bone grate painfully and couldn't put weight on it.

Dhruva stumbled backward, trying to recreate the wind vortex despite the distressed look on her face. Whatever was happening to her was obviously very painful. "I will *never* surrender to you!" she shouted.

Adya focused on Dhruva's fire affinity, which was difficult because she couldn't see the energy in the air like the other elements. She used the cues from Dhruva's earth energies to pull the fire from the shattering girl. This one took longer to manipulate. While Adya worked on that, Dhruva managed to focus hard enough to hurl another tree branch at Adya. This time it fell short of its mark, falling to the ground a few feet behind Adya.

"You can tranq her anytime now," Adya said in hopes that her team was still listening.

A scant moment later, three darts from three different directions struck Dhruva's body. The girl collapsed to her knees and stared with confusion at Adya, who limped closer.

"I told you—it's over."

Dhruva's eyes struggled to focus before they rolled back into her head, and she collapsed onto the sand. It took less than a minute for Adya's team to show up and apprehend the unconscious girl.

"We're taking her to the helicopter along with the other two that were with her. The Medjay are questioning the driver," the leader of the two soldiers informed Adya.

"Got a little singed out there, did you?" The other soldier wrapped a supportive arm around Adya's waist and helped her to the helicopter. "We're taking you to the affinate hospital in Cairo, and then we're going to rendezvous with the Commander in New York. The three will remain sedated," he told Adya.

"Thanks," Adya said wearily. As soon as they lifted off, Adya could feel the throbbing pain of her injuries but was too exhausted from her battle with Dhruva to heal herself. While she was flying back to Cairo, Adya stared at the unconscious girl. She knew she should feel happy about the victory, but instead felt a mix of pity for Dhruva and a desperate longing to take an extended vacation with Lir.

CHAPTER TWENTY-TWO

"You're coming to the end of year celebration, aren't you?" Ashley—now Lydie—asked as Adya as the two got ready for bed. In the two weeks Adya was away on the two missions and in the hospital in Cairo, Ashley completed her Awakening and was excited to get to stand up on the last day of school at the celebration and announce to everyone her soul name.

"I'll be there, crutches and all," Adya replied. She admired her roommate's simple life, especially when she compared it to her own previous five months. And now that Lydie had completed the Awakening, Adya felt their bond would strengthen. They had already spent most of Adya's first day back reminiscing on the four lifetimes they'd had together.

"Any news on how Eli is doing on getting people their souls back?" Lydie asked hesitantly. Without Adya evening mentioning it, Lydie knew that in the aftermath of the missions, the main focus of her best friend's thoughts was on her boyfriend and if she'd ever see him again.

"Ted didn't have any news to share with me except it could take a while for Eli to get it right," Adya replied with a shrug. "I'm going back to New York after the ceremony to stay with Maggie while she recovers. She and I have a lot to talk about."

"Yeah," Lydie agreed. "Oh, I almost forgot. You got mail while you were away." Lydie grabbed the envelope she'd placed in Adya's desk. "It looks kinda fancy. Maybe you're getting a Presidential award or something for taking down Dhruva."

Adya laughed. "I highly doubt that." She carefully opened the thick letter-sized envelope and smiled as she read the invitation that was inside. "Dusty is getting married," she said affectionately. "On my birthday, it seems."

"Oh! That's awesome! Are you going to go?" Lydie asked.

"Dusty, Jace, and Luke are like brothers to me. I wouldn't miss this for anything. Well, unless Dhruva somehow freed herself from her induced coma and got past the armed soldiers guarding her. But I don't think that'll happen."

The soldiers took Dhruva to a military base where she was being monitored and guarded around the clock until Eli could remove the three souls that didn't belong to her. She was once again going to be Eli's guinea pig and be the first one to be tested with the new procedure. There was speculation about what would happen to Dhruva after Eli removed the three foreign souls, both to her body and to her person. She would have to answer to the Elders for her crimes against the elements and affinates, that is if she awoke from the coma. No one knew what to expect since the first implanted soul brought her out of a coma initially.

"Don't even think things like that, Ady. I want to close the chapter on Dhruva and her insanity forever," Lydie said.

Adya took a minute to read over the letter she received from Jace with the invitation and then felt a sting when the RSVP asked for the number of guests attending. "Hey, are you going on another outdoor adventure with your family this summer?" Jace was dating a girl from the next town over now. While Adya was happy for her friend, it meant that she wouldn't have a buddy to hang out with at the wedding.

"Thankfully, no. My parents are going to Europe for their anniversary, and my brothers are all off doing college stuff.

I'm going to spend a couple of weeks with Pax and his family when they go to Hawaii in July," she replied with a dreamy quality to her voice.

"That should be a lot of fun," Adya said. "I've never been to Hawaii. But anyway, would you consider being my 'plus one' to Dusty's wedding? I know you don't know them, but I am going to feel like a third wheel around Jace and his new girlfriend. Besides, we know how well it goes when I'm friends with an attached guy." Adya shook her head sadly but laughed.

"Guys are stupid," Lydie commiserated. "Would it be okay if Pax came along, too?"

Adya rubbed her face with her hands in a semblance of frustration. "That sorta defeats the whole idea of me not being a third wheel." She sighed. "Fine, Pax can come, too. Besides, I want him to meet Dani and fall in love with her, so he'll help her out with her affinity when she's older."

"I can't wait to see Ava's house again. Do you think the Elders will let us stay there for a few days?" Lydie asked with excitement.

"I think the Elders will pretty much agree with anything I ask of them, at least for a little while," Adya said somewhat smugly while sealing the return envelope with her RSVP inside.

"Goodnight, Ady," Lydie said as she yawned. "I like your shorter hair, in case I didn't mention that already."

"You did, and thanks," Adya said and stifled her own yawn. One of the results of Adya's few moments in Dhruva's fire vortex—besides the second-degree burns covering about forty percent of her body—was a good portion of her hair that previously hung to her mid-back was singed. When Adya looked back on the stand-off now, there was a small amount of humor she could find in the resulting hairdo that looked like a three-year-old child got a hold of a pair of scissors and a Barbie doll. But thanks to a creative and talented hairstylist, she now looked more like Rapunzel in *Tangled* after she cut her hair.

"Goodnight, Lydie," she added as she rolled to her side. Adya held onto the ring that was fastened around her neck as she fell asleep.

The end of the year celebration thankfully went off without a hitch this year, except Lydie nearly tripped on her way up to the podium to present her soul name. Ted, Gaia, and Adamina all asked Adya to give a speech at the ceremony, but she declined because, honestly, she felt disconnected from the Academy with her semester-long absence.

Adya said her goodbyes to Lydie, Paxton, Sierra, and Calder before the ceremony started so she could slip out quietly after Lydie's introduction—although leaving any quiet room with the aid of crutches was not as stealthy as Adya had intended.

Paxton caught up with Adya outside before she got into the car waiting to take her to the airport. "Leaving so soon?" he asked as he approached her.

Adya shrugged and leaned her crutches against the open door. "Yeah, I thought I'd beat the rush out," she said.

"You're not staying here this summer?" Paxton asked.

"No, I'm going to do some traveling, I think. Maybe revisit some past life haunts and maybe go to some new ones." Adya didn't have a concrete plan, but she knew she wanted to experience more of the feelings that surfaced in Faiyum.

"You'll be back in the fall, right?"

Again, Adya shrugged. "I haven't decided that yet. Elder Tama wants me to consider joining the Council. It isn't my first choice for things to occupy my time, but I'm not sure where I'm going to end up. Just know that I am always here for you and Lydie, whatever it may be." Adya felt the moment was getting too emotional, so she attempted to lighten it up. "Besides, I'll see you both in West Virginia next month. Just don't overthink what to wear; dressed up to that town is more casual than what you and I consider it to be." Adya leaned in and kissed Paxton's cheek. "Take care of yourself and Lydie, okay?"

"You, too, Ady." Paxton helped Adya into the car after hugging her goodbye and watched as the car drove away.

Adya asked Ted to contact the hospital before she arrived to ensure that she wouldn't be immediately escorted from the premises when she tried to visit Maggie. It seemed to have worked, but while she wasn't getting kicked out, many were eyeing Adya with caution as she walked down to Maggie's room.

After an unanswered knock, Adya invited herself into the room. The curtains were open, making it naturally bright, and along with the numerous vases of flowers decorating the room, the hospital room gave off the appearance of being a happy, cheerful place to recover.

"Hello?" Adya asked cautiously to the empty room and then moved to the flowers on the windowsill, enjoying their aroma.

The toilet flushed, and Maggie reentered the room, surprised to see Adya. "Hello," she said softly and walked back to her bed.

Adya turned to watch her friend as she shuffled to her bed wearing cozy pajamas and slippers, which seemed to Adya to be better suited for lounging at home than recovering in a hospital. "I hope I'm not bothering you," she said and sat in the chair by the window. "You've received so many beautiful plants and flowers."

Maggie tucked the blanket around her legs and reclined back in the bed. "Yes, and thank you for the ones you sent. They told me you'd visited on the night I was brought here, but only have a vague recollection of that."

Adya nodded and chuckled. "Did they also tell you that they had to drag me out of here?"

Maggie motioned to the whiteboard on the wall where a picture of Adya hung with the words "No Admittance" written beneath it. "Doesn't look much like you anymore. I like your new haircut," she said with a smile, which instantly faded. "I'm guessing you found out about Lir's soul and came to free it?"

Adya shook her head and sighed. "I told Ted I didn't want to know who had it. When I came to see you that night, I intended to just be with you and to heal you, if I could. Then I touched your hand and saw your memory of the moments before they gave you his soul. That's when I found out." She paused for a moment and continued. "I was desperately trying to heal you when they entered. I *may* have pinned a nurse against the wall and held off security while I tried to save you and Lir."

"Why would you want to save me?" Maggie asked.

"Didn't they tell you about the modifications Eli is making to the machine to put the souls back?" Adya asked. It had been two and a half weeks since they rescued Maggie, and it surprised Adya that she would be in the dark about what was inevitably going to happen to her.

"They told me I'd be in the hospital until Eli's machine was ready," Maggie admitted. "But how did you know that night that he was going to do that?"

Adya smiled softly. "Because it was my idea. I figured out the transferred souls didn't combine with the soul of the new host's body. My working theory was they could be separated without causing a problem to the host." Adya watched Maggie process the news and then added, "I wanted to save you *before* I knew about Lir's soul and even more so after. I'm sorry for the anguish I caused by telling you I was going to kill the person with his soul."

"I was trying to do right by you," Maggie said softly. "And I never used his affinity," she admitted.

Adya smiled gently. "I know. I can tell by looking at you that you didn't. The water-energy around you is hovering there, not projecting from your body."

"You can see elemental energies?" Maggie asked in surprise. "When did this happen?"

"I've had an interesting six months," Adya said and told her friend about everything that happened to her after escaping from the Institute.

Maggie shook her head in amazement. "From all that I've read from affinates' journals, there has only been a small handful that could do that."

Adya nodded. "I know. After reading through Ava's diary, I can see now that she could do it, too."

"You said you were able to see *my* memory?" Maggie said, backtracking the conversation.

"Yes. While in Switzerland, Lir and I worked on seeing soul memories that we weren't a participant in. I swear I didn't try to see your memories—it just flashed to me when I touched you."

"Maybe Lir was trying to reach out to you," Maggie suggested.

Adya shrugged off the idea. "It was your memory I saw."

"But I don't have soul memories. I'm stuck with regular memories," Maggie countered. "What if Lir's soul helped orchestrate that memory you saw?"

"It's possible," Adya conceded. "It was a pretty specific memory. Maybe he wanted me to know that he loved me to the end and didn't want me mad at you for taking his soul." Adya pondered the possibility of it while Maggie stared off distantly, apparently doing the same.

"Maybe you could connect with his soul now?" she suggested with her focus returning to Adya.

"I don't know," Adya replied hesitantly. "What if I ended up seeing one of your memories again? I think we'd both be embarrassed if I saw something—ummm—private like your debit card PIN or you having sex with Lucas."

Maggie's face flushed. "Well, I can almost guarantee that you've accumulated some sensual soul memories over the lifetimes, so I'm not too concerned about that. But if you'd rather not, I understand."

Adya considered it for several moments as she looked at the flowers and plants decorating Maggie's room. "You know, without the thoughts of taking down Dhruva occupying my every thought, it's been hard to not think about Lir," Adya admitted. "As long as you're okay with me seeing random events of your life, I think I would like to try to connect with Lir's soul."

Maggie held out her hand to Adya, who hopped on her uninjured foot from the window seat to the round stool that the doctors use when they're in the room. Adya clasped Maggie's hand with both her hands, focused on the water-energy hovering around Maggie, and closed her eyes. Nothing happened immediately, but as Adya focused on Lir's water energy, she was finally able to find his soul.

Everything was extremely bright, like a cloudless summer day when you have to squint to be able to see when you step outside. As Adya's eyes adjusted, she could see an endless green field with wild daisies growing. "Ireland," she whispered and marveled at the scenery.

She didn't notice him at first because he didn't embody his mortal form, but as she neared the brilliant glow, she immediately knew that it was Lir's soul. "My darling," Adya whispered emotionally. Awe overcame her as she gazed at his glorious, naked soul, and by being able to communicate with him again.

The energy wrapped around Adya. "I've missed you, mo ghaol." Lir's soul spoke directly to her mind.

CHAPTER TWENTY-TWO

Adya embraced his soul and allowed it to entangle with her projected body. "I've missed you so, so much." She could feel the raw emotions vibrate within her. "Are you okay? Where are we?"

"Don't be sad, Ady," Lir comforted as he struggled to find words to explain where they were. "This is. . . my home. It's the place where my soul gravitates to, a place where my soul first entered the world. I suppose this is where I return to when my body dies. Did I die?"

Adya longed to kiss him and feel his arms wrapped around her again. "No, my love, you aren't dead. Your soul is apart from your body, though. We're working on a method to return you, but the how isn't important right now. I just need you to know that I've been fighting to get you back."

"Of course you are, my stubborn darling. I'm at peace here, though, so don't worry about that," Lir said. "But I feel this isn't a place you can stay with me."

"No," Adya replied. "I already see signs that reality is pulling me away from you." Adya noticed the colors around them that were once vibrant were starting to fade. "We will be together again soon," Adya promised. "I love you, Lir."

"I love you, too, Ady."

Adya remained silent and unmoving when the connection to Lir was lost. Maggie only realized she was back when Adya had released her hand.

"Did you find his soul?" Maggie asked cautiously.

Adya nodded but remained silent. She felt the pain in the back of her throat, that choking feeling when sadness is threatening to make you cry, but you really don't want to. "His soul is undamaged," she managed to whisper before the tears began to fall.

Maggie retook Adya's hand and pulled her onto the bed. She wrapped her arms around the emotional girl and just held her for the duration of the afternoon. "I'm so sorry, Ady," Maggie repeated several times throughout the otherwise quiet hours that passed until both fell asleep and remained undisturbed throughout the night.

Adya visited Maggie every day for the following three weeks. The two chatted, played board games, and watched about every rom-com that existed. The hospital staff also removed the warning photo of her from Maggie's room and even helped Adya remove her cast when the time came.

"Ted told me that Eli's finished with the modifications, and they've started putting souls back in their original bodies," Maggie said as Adya entered the room that day. "They're coming to transport me to the base this afternoon."

Adya's eyes widened. "This is great! Did Ted say if there were any problems with the process?"

Maggie smiled sadly. "Not all of the people who had the soul extracted survived. Which is one of the reasons why they didn't call me in right away."

"There has to be a way to save both people," Adya insisted. "If I could go and talk with Eli, maybe I can come up with an adjustment he could make."

Maggie stopped Adya from standing. "None of the people without affinities before the transfer have survived. I know Ted is demanding Eli find a workaround, but I'm one of the last non-affinates—" Maggie paused and sighed. "It's okay, Ady. I prepared myself to die months ago. I want you and Lir to get your chance in this lifetime. Maybe Lucas and I will get our chance in the next."

Adya studied Maggie's face and saw the struggle in her eyes not to cry. She knew that Lucas must not have survived the procedure. "Maybe it'll be different for you because you didn't use his affinity," Adya suggested, but her mind was still working on a strategy to save Maggie.

"Adya," Maggie said sternly. "Whatever happens to me, it'll be okay. Dying won't be so bad. I'll have another chance at a life *with* an affinity. Besides, I want to make things right for you and Lir. It was my fault he lost his soul. I owe him this."

"He wouldn't want you to die for him, though," Adya insisted tearfully.

"This isn't something you can talk me out of doing, Ady. From what Ted tells me, the original bodies are accepting their souls back, but it's taking time for them to readjust. I would venture to say Lir could be back to himself within the next week or two."

"I take back what I said to you at the Institute. I don't want you to die. Please, Maggie. Wait until they can save both of you," Adya pleaded.

"I know you don't want me to die. I'd prefer to stay around for a while longer, too. If I don't survive, I'm asking you to make peace with this. We'll see each other again." Maggie smiled at Adya and released her hand. "Aren't you supposed to be getting ready to head to West Virginia for that wedding?"

Adya rolled her eyes at the apparent topic change. She felt like there was more she should say or do to help ensure Maggie survived the procedure. "Yes, I'm getting ready to leave for the airport as soon as I saw you this morning. I wanted some time alone at Ava's before Lydie and Pax arrive. They're supposed to be there next Thursday, the day before the wedding. And I'm also going to help Jace's mom with the floral arrangements for the ceremony. It was nice that they offered to let me help."

"I'm sure they will be beautiful arrangements with you helping. I hope you have a great time. Jace and his family seem to be good for your soul," Maggie said.

"They are," Adya agreed. "I will introduce you to them someday."

Maggie chuckled and gave Adya a heartfelt hug. "Forever the optimist. Whatever the outcome, know that I love you, Ady. I have enjoyed watching you grow into your magnificent self."

Adya refused to acknowledge that this was their final goodbye. "Some journals are waiting for you at North Shore, and I'm hoping to uncover some more this summer. I'll talk to you soon, okay?"

Maggie smiled and squeezed Adya's hand. "We'll talk soon."

Adya was tending to the neglected garden at Ava's house when she heard the familiar sound of Jace's truck approaching. She'd debated on whether or not to tell Jace that she was arriving early for the wedding, but since she wanted to help with the event that was taking place in the barn at Sophia's house, she gave him a head's up about when she'd be there.

Adya listened and only heard one door shut, which meant Jace didn't bring his girlfriend with him.

"Hey," he said as he strolled around the side of the house where he knew Adya would be.

"Hey yourself," she said and didn't stand up. "Didn't I tell you to take care of this garden?"

Jace chuckled and walked over to Adya. "Between school, workin' Grandma's fields, workin' at the flower shop, an' my girlfriend, I've barely had a moment to myself," he said.

"You made time to come up here today," Adya pointed out as she stood, unable to mask her smile any longer. She wrapped her arms around Jace and hugged him tightly. "I've missed these hugs," she whispered.

Jace held her tight until the hug felt like it was over and leaned back to look at Adya with his hands still resting on her shoulders. "Your hair looks awful," he said plainly. "Who took a butcher's knife to your hair an' where are they now so I can return the favor?"

Adya glowered at Jace. "It looked worse after the fire tornado wrapped around me. This haircut was the best they could do with what was left. Besides, my friends tell me it's cute."

"You need some new friends," Jace commented.

"Did you drive out here just to insult me?" Adya demanded.

Jace made a thoughtful face as he took the time to consider his answer. "I thought one of the many reasons you liked me was 'cuz I tell it to you like it is." He smiled and then laughed. "Now that I'm done with that, why doncha tell me how your mission thing went."

The two spent the afternoon on the porch swing drinking lemonade. Adya and Jace took turns catching the other up on what had happened in their lives over the previous three months. Jace shared with Adya a few details about his girlfriend and how they met. *Boys*, Adya groaned and rolled her eyes internally at the lack of valuable information in Jace's story. Then, Adya told Jace about the missions and about the idea that was inspired by him that they were using to return souls to their original bodies.

"But Maggie doesn't believe she's going to survive it. I should've stayed with her. Maybe I could've done something to help," Adya admitted.

"It sounds like she's a purdy strong woman an' has made peace with dyin'. So, whatever the outcome, I think you need to make peace with it, just like she has." Jace squeezed Adya's leg and stood from the swing. "I gotta get goin', though. Supposed to take Clary to the movies tonight."

Adya stood, too, and took his empty glass from him. "You realize that's the first time you've said her name?" She chuckled. "Enjoy your movie, Jace. I'm sure we'll run into each other again before the wedding."

Jace kissed the top of Adya's head. "I'll be buggin' you again before the weddin'. Doncha worry."

Adya walked Jace out to his truck and waved goodbye before returning inside. She tried not to watch her phone obsessively for news on Maggie, but she turned the volume up to maximum and set it in front of her while she played piano. Before going to bed, she sent a text to the new phone that she'd bought Lir, hoping he would receive when he woke up from the procedure.

Despite texting and calling Ted frequently, Adya didn't receive any news about Maggie and Lir for three days when Ted finally returned her phone call.

"Why didn't you call me sooner?" Adya demanded as soon as she picked up the phone.

"I didn't have any news to tell you," Ted admitted.

"But now you do?" Adya was pacing on the back porch while Yiny watched her from the handrail.

"Eli made some adjustments before the procedure with Maggie. He returned Lir's soul to his body without complication. Maggie put up a good fight. Her vitals were low but stable."

"Were? You mean—" Adya was too choked up to even say it.

"Maggie passed away this afternoon," Ted said solemnly. "She left instructions for me, and there are some things of hers that she wants you to have. I know you're busy helping to prepare for that wedding, but I'm hoping you can return to the Academy afterward."

Adya plopped into a deck chair when Ted told her the news and sobbed. "Okay," she managed to say eventually.

"Do you have someone that can come be with you right now?" Ted asked, concerned.

"No, I'm. . . I'll. . . be. . . okay," Adya insisted, although it was challenging to force words past the lump in her throat. "Is. . . Lir okay?" She swallowed hard and said a silent prayer to the elements.

"Lir is doing fine. They are keeping him in an induced coma for a little while longer to make sure there aren't any issues with the bonding of his soul. Are you sure you're going to be okay by yourself?"

"Lydie. . . and Pax will. . . be here. . . in two days," Adya pieced together. "I'll. . . be okay."

"I'm going to check in with you in the morning. If anything changes or if you just need to talk, I'm here," Ted said.

"I will. Thanks, Ted."

Adya texted Jace as soon as she got off the phone with Ted and then set her phone on the kitchen counter. Within fifteen minutes, Jace was knocking on her door. There wasn't much that Jace could do except be there for Adya and listen to her stories about Maggie.

When Adya was feeling a little better, the two broke out a bottle of gin, and Adya played songs for Jace on the piano. "How long have you been playin' piano?" he asked after Adya had finished her third song, and he had finished his fourth glass of gin.

"Roughly four hundred years," Adya said with a giggle. Her eyes were bloodshot and puffy from crying, but she felt markedly better after talking with Jace and drinking two glasses of gin.

"Damn, why doncha play professionally?" Jace asked.

Adya shrugged. "I prefer to play for myself or friends. Hey, your girlfriend isn't gonna be mad that you're here, is she?" Adya began playing another song.

"Naw," Jace replied. "I've told her all about you. She's cool with me havin' friends that are girls."

Adya threw him a doubtful look, but let it go. The two finished the bottle of gin and sang a few songs before Adya was too exhausted to stay awake any longer. Adya pulled herself all the way upstairs before she realized Jace was following her. "You're not gonna sleep on the couch?" she asked, holding onto the doorframe of her room for balance.

"I was thinkin' of takin' one of the extra beds tonight," he replied.

Adya nodded. "Knock yourself out. G'night, Jace."

"'Night, D."

Adya heard Jace crash into something in a bedroom down the hall before the house went quiet, and she passed out in her bed.

"*Hello?*" Adya heard a voice downstairs calling out.

"Ugh," she groaned and rolled out of her bed to see who was in the house. "I'm coming," she called out.

Jace stuck his head out the door. "Everythin' okay?"

Adya could see his bare shoulder and knew he was shirtless. "Yeah, someone's downstairs. I'm going to check it out."

"Wait for me," Jace said and then closed the door again.

Of course, Adya didn't wait and walked towards the stairs while looking at the energy in the air. As soon as she saw the familiar auras, a smile broke out on her face, and she ran down the stairs. "Lydie!" she exclaimed and hugged her friend. "I didn't think you were coming until tomorrow?"

"Hey, Ady," Paxton said as he entered from the back patio.

"I thought I said to wait for me," Jace scolded as he hopped down the stairs, buttoning up his jeans—and still shirtless.

Lydie and Paxton shared the same shocked expression. "Umm. . ." Lydie pursed her lips, not knowing what to say.

Adya looked between her friends and burst out laughing. "Oh my god. You guys don't think. . . him and I? No, no, no."

"Aww, c'mon sugar bear. Can't hide it now," Jace said and kissed Adya on the temple.

Adya returned his joke with a loud smack to the chest. "Knock it off, Jace. Guys, this is Jace. He was sleeping in a *separate* room than me. I just needed someone to chat with last night after I found out about Maggie." A small frown returned to Adya's face. "Oh, and Jace, this is Lydie—she was Ashley when I was here last—and Pax."

Paxton and Jace shook hands while Lydie checked out Jace's abs.

"Ah, the past-life husband an' the best friend," Jace recalled. "You two are—"

"Dating now? Yes," Paxton said and took Lydie's hand in a very 'she's mine' way.

"Ted called me last night after he talked with you. He thought you might need us to come early, so here we are," Lydie said with a smile. "This house hasn't changed a bit."

Adya smiled. "There are some very good memories in this house." Adya was trying not to think about the sad memories of the house—and the current state of her life.

After a somewhat awkward moment of silence, Jace said, "So Pax, what can you tell me 'bout your fire affinity that'll help me help my niece?"

"I'm going to go for a walk with Lydie to show her the garden and stuff like that. You guys play nice, okay?" Adya warned.

Adya linked arms with Lydie and walked outside with her without bothering to put shoes on or change into clean clothes for the day.

Once outside and out of earshot of the house, Lydie started in with her interrogation. "You didn't say he was that hot."

Adya rolled her eyes. "Yes, well, I don't tell you how hot Pax is, either, but that doesn't mean it's not true. Jace is my friend, and that's all I see when I look at him." Adya paused for a moment and then added, "Well, sometimes I see him as an annoyance, too, especially when he's telling me things like how awful my haircut is."

"Your haircut is amazing! Sheesh, boys don't know anything about that stuff," Lydie said with a huff. "So honestly, how are you doing? You look much worse than you're sounding."

"Gee, thanks. I'm okay, not great, but I'll be fine. I only look this awful because Jace and I drank a bottle of gin last night."

Lydie blinked in surprise. "You *drank* with him last night?! Are you *sure* nothing happened between you two?"

"I'm positive. We talked about Maggie, I played songs on the piano, and then we went to sleep in *separate rooms*," Adya emphasized again.

"So, when do you get to see Lir?" Lydie asked, quickly changing topics.

"I guess it depends on when they think it will be safe to start gradually waking him from the coma. Ted said it would probably be a few days, so I'm crossing my fingers that I can go see him after the wedding on Friday." The more Adya thought about seeing Lir again, the slower time seemed to go. Thankfully, she had plenty of distractions keeping her from ruminating.

"Are you planning any trips with him for the summer?" Lydie hadn't lost the Ashley part of herself after the Awakening and still thrived on gossip.

"I'm not planning anything. It all depends on what Lir's up to doing. I'm thinking about staying in New York for a couple of weeks with him to give him time to recoup. I really don't know what to expect, though. And Ted wants me to go back to North Shore to go over some of Maggie's affairs."

The two girls wandered the property for about an hour, casually chatting. When they returned, the boys had prepared breakfast.

"Wow, I'm genuinely shocked. Thank you," Adya said as she took a plate of eggs, toast, and pancakes.

Paxton pointed at Jace. "He's to blame if it's bad. I just kept the food warm for you."

Jace—who was wearing a shirt again—smiled and shrugged. "Thought you might be hungry."

"Oh, and Ady, Ted called to check on you. I told him you seemed alright and were out gossiping with Lydie." Paxton winked at Lydie.

Jace raised his brow at Paxton but didn't say anything.

After the four ate breakfast, Adya took a quick shower and left with Jace to help his mom with the arrangements for the wedding. "Behave, you two," Adya said as she walked out with Jace.

CHAPTER TWENTY-THREE

The day of the wedding finally arrived. Adya, Lydie, and Paxton had been busy over the previous two days helping Jace and his family get everything ready for the at-home ceremony. Paxton bonded with Jace, Luke, and Dusty while they cleaned out the barn. Lydie helped Sophia in the kitchen while Adya helped Jace's mom with the flower arrangements and decorating the barn.

"I love that they're having the ceremony outside at Sophia's," Lydie gushed while Adya zipped up the back of her friend's yellow sundress.

"It looks like it's going to be a perfect day, too," Adya commented as she admired her now fourteen-year-old self in the mirror. She'd picked out a light blue sundress with subtle white daisies patterned all over the dress; it reminded her of the place where she visited Lir's soul.

"*Are you two ready to go yet?*" Paxton called from downstairs. "*The car will be here to pick us up any minute.*"

With Jace being his brother's best man and dealing with all that entailed—not to mention his truck couldn't fit the four of them in the cab—the three decided to hire a driver to take them to Sophia's for the wedding.

"Are you sure I shouldn't wear the blue dress? I mean, if we are standing up to invite and welcome the elements to the ceremony, shouldn't I look the part of water?" Lydie turned to the wardrobe where she'd hung the ten dresses she'd brought in preparation for one event.

Adya put her hand on her friend's shoulder. "You radiate water energy, Lydie, no matter what color you wear. I adore that dress on you, and I think Pax is gonna love it, too." She turned to the window and asked her magpie companion for her advice. "You agree with me, right, Yiny?" The bird danced happily on the windowsill. "See? You can't argue with Yiny about these things."

"Thank you, Yiny," Lydie said to the bird. "Alright, I guess I'm ready."

The two girls descended the staircase, Adya following Lydie so Paxton would see her first.

"Wow," Paxton said as he watched the two enter the room. He was waiting by the door wearing black slacks and a white button-up shirt with the top button left undone.

"Wow yourself," Lydie said as she kissed Paxton tenderly. "I was worried that the smell of hay and dirt wouldn't wash off you."

Adya stood back and smiled at her friends as they doted on each other. "Alright, you two. Don't forget that I'm still here."

Lydie giggled, and Paxton opened the door for the girls as the car pulled up to the house. "You look amazing, too, Ady," Paxton whispered as she walked past him.

"Thanks," Adya said graciously.

Sophia's house was buzzing with excitement when the three arrived. Guests were already milling around, enjoying lemonade and iced tea on the back patio while Sophia hustled in the kitchen with Jace's mom to finish the cake and food.

"Do you need any help?" Lydie asked as they entered Sophia's house. Lydie enjoyed spending time with Sophia, probably because the two could carry on non-stop conversations about anything and everything. They had only met once—the day before—and were carrying on like they'd known each other for lifetimes.

"Sure, hun. I can always use your help," Sophia replied. "Oh, Pax, honey. Luke can use your help gettin' the band set up in the barn."

"I'm on it," Paxton said and kissed Lydie's temple before heading out to the barn.

"I guess I will go check on Jace and Dusty," Adya said, excusing herself upstairs. She knocked on the only closed door and cautiously turned the knob. "Is it safe for me to come in?" she asked.

"It's fine without the tie," Dusty argued as Jace stood in front of him, holding a blue and brown striped tie. "I don't need to match the weddin' colors."

Adya watched the brothers argue back and forth about a tie and finally stepped in when it looked like they were about to start throwing punches. "It's his wedding," Adya said. "If he doesn't want to wear the tie, he doesn't have to. But I think you would look better with the tie on," she interjected.

"See?" Jace said. "She's a girl an' thinks you should wear it."

Dusty rolled his eyes and snatched the tie from his brother. "Fine, but it's comin' off after the ceremony. Damn thing feels like it's chokin' me."

"Crisis averted," Adya said with a smile. "How are you feeling, Dusty?"

"Nervous as shit," he replied rather grumpily.

Adya could see the agitated energy in the room and took a moment to calm it down.

Both boys noticeably relaxed. "Thanks, D," Jace said.

Dusty nodded, "Yeah, thanks. Hey, Jace said you were good at playin' the piano. I know I shoulda asked sooner, but would you play the first dance song for me an' Dar? Luke an' his band are good at the fast stuff, but she's worried 'bout the song they picked for our first slow dance together."

Adya shot Jace a look of annoyance but then nodded with a sigh. "I'd be honored to, Dusty. I'm sure I can come up with something perfect for you." Adya glanced over at the green candle burning on the dresser. "Isn't that for the ceremony?" she asked.

"Jace, you were s'posed to take that outside already," Dusty snapped.

Adya calmed the energies in the room again but felt like it was an act of futility. "I'll take it down with me. Just stay calm and try to relax. Today will be perfect." Adya smiled at the two and then picked up the tray with the melting candle on it. "I'll see you both in a bit," she said and exited the room just as their dad was entering. Adya was hopeful that he'd have better luck at controlling his sons than she had.

"Where do you want their candles?" Adya asked Sophia when she returned downstairs.

Sophia was too busy to even look up from the food she was preparing. "Darlene's is already out there," she answered. "I told those boys to have that out there an hour ago."

"I'll take Dusty's out there now. Anything else I can help with?" Adya asked.

"No, we're managin' fine in here," Jace's mom replied. "Maybe you could check on Luke while you're out there."

"Alright," Adya replied and exited through the patio door.

Chairs set up for the ceremony were to the left of the barn just on the other side of the fields. Yiny joined Adya as she carried the lit candle—which she protected from going out with a small bubble of air—to the altar where the other candle was burning. "Looks like you've been doing a good job watching over them, Yiny," Adya complimented the bird. "Thank you," she said.

Adya placed the green candle beside the red one that Darlene chose to represent herself. The combined wax from the candles was a symbol of the two lives that were about to be joined. Adya didn't know what Darlene's beliefs were, but she loved and appreciated that the couple decided to incorporate elemental marriage traditions into their ceremony. A lot of the influence, Adya imagined, was because Sophia was officiating the wedding. Regardless of Darlene's beliefs, with her daughter being an old soul and fire affinate, she was officially swept into the world that Adya lived in—a path that was guided through and with the elements.

"There you are," Paxton said as he approached Adya from behind. "Luke needs for you to make sure the piano will work for you."

Adya was mesmerized by the candles and melting wax. "Do you remember our first wedding?" she asked distantly.

"I'll never forget it," Paxton said and placed his hand on top of Adya's as she rested them on the table selected to be the altar. "You wore the ivory lace dress and had a crown of jasmine, bluebells, and orchids. It was a beautiful afternoon in that field, but it paled in comparison to how radiant you were."

"That dress is in a vault in Geneva along with a few of my other wedding dresses. Lir saved them after I died." Adya smiled and looked down at Paxton's hand on hers and took a deep breath. "I'm sorry for all the hurt and frustration I've caused you in this life."

"There's no need to apologize. Lydie and I are very happy together. I would've never thought to give her a chance if it wasn't for you." Paxton noticed Adya's brow raise and realized that might've sounded harsher than he intended. He quickly added, "You were right when you said that we have to make our own choices in each lifetime. I sincerely want you to be able to be happy, too."

"Hey! Ya comin' to check out the piano?" Luke yelled at them from the barn. "This thing's s'posed to start in fifteen minutes!"

"I'm coming!" Adya yelled back.

Adya turned and hugged Paxton. "I will always and forever love you, Pax."

Paxton squeezed Adya in his arms. "I'll love you for eternity, Ady."

Dusty and Jace stood in front of the altar with Sophia standing behind it as Luke carried baby Dani down the aisle. The guests let out a collective "aww" as the baby went by dressed in a tiny pink lace dress. Luke took a seat with Dani and his parents on the left side. The bridesmaid followed Luke, preceding the bride and her father down the aisle.

When the bride met with the groom at the front, Sophia began the ceremony. "We would like to begin by calling on the elements to join us and bless this union."

Paxton, Lydie, and Adya joined Sophia as she walked around the altar and stood between the wedding party and the audience.

"We call upon the earth to join us in celebrating the union between Dusty and Darlene. May it provide them grounding throughout their lives and serve as a strong and fruitful foundation for their life together." Sophia closed her eyes to call upon her element. Immediately, the vines on the archway over the couple bloomed with flowers.

Adya heard some gasps from the guests who weren't familiar with the gifts of affinates. With Sophia and Lydie representing Adya's other two affinities, she stepped forward and offered a blessing for air. While holding up a wooden windchime, engraved with the couple's names and the date, she said, "We ask the air to join this couple and bless their union. May it be with them through every breath they take together, soothe them when tempers rise, and bring a freshness to each of their united days." Adya lifted her free hand, and a gentle, sweet-smelling breeze blew over the guests, lightly jostling everyone's hair and creating a soft melody with the chimes.

Paxton stepped forward next, holding an unlit candle. "Fire is behind all the passions we feel in life. We invite fire to bless this couple with its strength and warmth, and to remain bright with love throughout their years." Paxton closed his hands tightly around the pillar candle and made the wick light using his affinity.

Finally, Lydie stepped forward, holding an empty glass bowl. "We call upon the element of water to join with Darlene and Dusty. Let it quench their thirst and forever give them life with its blessing." The empty bowl filled with water as Lydie called upon her affinity. The four turned to face the bride and groom.

Adya walked forward with the hauntingly beautiful wind chime. After an appreciative nod, the two placed it on the altar behind them. Next, Paxton handed the couple the lit candle, which Dusty and Darlene held together and set in the middle of the altar, forming a triangle with the two that were already there. Lydie then stepped up and offered Darlene the bowl. She took a sip of the water before handing it to Dusty to do the same. They added the bowl to the other offerings. Finally, Sophia took the bouquet the bridesmaid had been holding and gave it to the bride before taking her place between the altar and the couple. Adya, Lydie, and Paxton retook their seats to observe the rest of the ceremony.

Adya smiled at Lydie and Paxton as they held hands and watched, but she noticed Paxton continually checking his phone. When she threw him a questioning look, he offered a smile and refocused on the ceremony.

After the couple slid wedding bands on each other's ring finger, Sophia tied a ribbon around the couple's joined hands. She began reciting the traditional words of an unknown author used in many handfasting ceremonies. "Please face each other as you hold each other's hands so that you can see the gift they are to you." Sophia sounded more formal in her speech than she did in everyday talk, but her accent remained thick. "These are the hands of your best friend, young an' strong an' full of love for you, that are holdin' yours on your weddin' day as you promise to love each other today, tomorrow, an' forever. These are the hands that will work alongside yours as together you build your future. These are the hands that will passionately love you an' cherish you through the years, an' with the slightest touch will comfort you like no other. These are the hands that will hold you when fear or grief temporarily comes to you. These are the hands that will countless times wipe the tears from your eyes, tears of sorrow an' tears of joy. These are the hands that'll tenderly hold Dani an' your other children, the hands that'll join your family as one. These are the hands that'll give you strength when you need it, support an' encouragement to follow your dreams, an' comfort through difficult times. An' lastly, these are the hands that even when wrinkled an' aged like mine, will still be reachin' for yours, still givin' you the same unspoken tenderness with just a touch."

Adya wiped away a tear that trickled down her cheek and noticed how equally touched many others were by the words Sophia spoke. Adya's hand rested on the ring that was hanging from her neck, and she wondered if she would get a chance to have a ceremony like this in this lifetime.

With Dusty and Darlene's hands still wrapped in the ribbon, the two read in unison from the script that Sophia held for them. "My love, you are the one person with whom I can share all that I am. I promise to trust you an' to be honest with you. I promise to listen to you, respect you, an' support you. I promise to laugh an' play with you, an' grow an' bend with you. I promise to cherish every day we have together. I promise to do all of these through whatever life brings us: riches or poverty, health or illness, through good times an' bad, until the end of my days."

"As the elements have blessed this union, so do I. May you carry forward in balance as husband an' wife." Sophia kissed both on the cheek before the couple sealed their marriage with a kiss. Everyone in attendance cheered and threw rose petals at the couple as they walked down the aisle to start their new lives together.

Lydie sighed happily. "That was so beautiful."

Adya noticed Paxton checking his phone again. "Everything okay?" she asked.

"Yeah, I just have a last-minute gift that I need to go pick up," he replied mysteriously.

Both Lydie and Adya raised a brow at him. "You're leaving?" Lydie asked.

"I'll be back before they cut the cake, okay?" Paxton kissed Lydie and rushed towards the car.

"Do you know where he's going?" Adya asked Lydie.

Lydie shrugged. "No clue," she said, looking just as baffled as Adya.

The girls joined the other guests in the barn for snacks and drinks while they waited for Darlene and Dusty to finish getting pictures taken.

"I loved what you girls added to the ceremony," Darlene's mother said as she approached Lydie and Adya near the refreshment table. "Is that what my grandbaby will do someday, too?"

Adya nodded. "Yes, she is like Paxton, the guy that had the candle."

"That seems dangerous, havin' a child play with fire. How'd you fill that bowl with water?" the woman asked Lydie.

Adya smiled at the two and left them to discuss affinities while she wandered over to where Jace and his girlfriend were sitting. "That went well," Adya commented.

"It was a beautiful ceremony," the girl agreed. "I'm Clary, by the way."

Adya shook the girl's slender hand and admired her delicate beauty: long, fiery red hair, pale, flawless skin, and soft blue eyes. "Nice to meet you. I'm Ady," she responded politely.

"I feel like I know you already. Jace has told me so much about you," Clary said sweetly and then playfully hit Jace's shoulder. "Her hair is cute."

Jace chuckled. "I'm feelin' a little outnumbered here. Gonna go check on Dusty to see if they're close to bein' finished out there." Jace excused himself from the table and kissed Clary before exiting the barn.

"So, you don't think his family and, well, me are strange?" Adya asked after Jace departed.

"Jace and his family are a good kind of strange," Clary said without any hint of the accent that everyone else around there had. "When you grow up in San Francisco, strange becomes the norm. I have to admit, though, that I've never seen anyone do what you guys can do. Did you go to school to learn that?"

"There's a school that teaches us how to use our affinities, but it's something you're born with," Adya explained.

"Oh, right. An old soul, that's what Jace said. So, your soul is reincarnated, right? Do you remember your other lives?" Clary was entirely at ease with the seemingly crazy conversation they were having.

"I remember all my lifetimes, but obviously not every moment of every day of those lives. The important things stay with me," Adya explained. "Pax, the guy with the candle at the beginning, he and I have been married in past lives. And Lydie, his girlfriend, has been my best friend in my past four lifetimes."

"You remember being married to him? Why aren't you together now if you don't mind me asking?" Clary said apologetically.

"I don't mind. Pax and I made different choices in this lifetime despite loving each other still." Adya shrugged. "I'm happy that my friends chose each other."

Through the twenty minutes Adya and Clary talked after Jace left, Adya concluded that she really liked his girlfriend. Never in any other lifetime had Adya enjoyed so easily sharing the knowledge of her affinities with a non-affinate. Even the first conversation with Jace about it didn't feel as natural or comfortable as it did to talk with Clary.

Jace rejoined the two as they continued to chat. "Don't mean to break up the party, but I think they're ready for you to play the first dance song, D."

"It's been very nice to meet you, Clary," Adya said as she stood from the table. "I'm sure we'll talk again."

Adya walked up to the microphone and addressed the crowd. "It's an honor to be asked to play the first dance song for Darlene and Dusty. I decided to play a song called 'Kiss the Rain' by Yiruma. I hope you enjoy it." Adya sat in front of the electric piano and began playing the romantic melody while Dusty and Darlene embraced in the middle of the empty dance floor.

A soft smile graced Adya's lips as she watched the two dance. She noticed all the people watching them shared her same adoring expressions. About halfway through the song, Adya noticed Paxton enter the barn. Not seeing him holding a gift, she gave him a confused look. He smiled at Adya and stepped to the side, allowing Lir to walk in beside him.

Adya had a hard time concentrating on the rest of the song with tears blurring her vision and her heart nearly beating out of her chest. She couldn't know for sure, but it felt like the tempo of the song increased with her heart rate. When the song concluded, and the audience applauded the kissing couple, Adya quickly exited the stage and ran to the back of the barn, leaving Luke to announce the next song the band would be playing.

While she knew she should've said something to Paxton, who was still standing there, all Adya could think about doing was embracing Lir. Adya wrapped her arms around Lir and held him like she was afraid he might disappear.

Paxton leaned close to Adya and whispered, "Happy birthday," before walking with Lydie to the dance floor, which was now alive with couples dancing to the songs of Luke's band.

Adya looked up into Lir's eyes while she rested a palm against his cheek.

"Checking to see if it's really me?" Lir joked softly and moved Adya's hand to kiss the center of her palm.

"Just making sure your soul is there," Adya said, happy tears still streaming from her eyes. "Please tell me this isn't a dream."

Lir pinched Adya's backside, prompting a startled squeak. "Nope, you're not dreaming. But just to make sure—" Lir touched the bottom of Adya's chin, tilting her head back, before pressing his lips against hers. The kiss lingered for nearly half a song and then ended with their foreheads pressed together.

"How did you know where to find me?" Adya whispered.

Despite the loud atmosphere of the celebration around them, Lir heard her with perfect clarity. "Paxton picked me up from the airport and brought me here."

Adya leaned back and blinked in confusion. "Pax arranged this? Since when are you two speaking?"

Lir grinned. "I called you the other day. I guess you were out on a walk with Lydie. Pax answered because he didn't want me to think that you were mad at me or something. Anyway, we settled our past grievances, and he came up with the idea to surprise you here today."

"This was Pax's idea?" Adya repeated and continued to blink in disbelief. "I'm sure I'm dreaming now."

Lir chuckled and kissed Adya again. "When you wake, I'll still be here. In the meantime, would you like to join me for a dance?"

"Can't we just make everyone disappear for a while and make up for the time we lost over the last almost six months?" Adya said with a smile.

Yiny flew down and interrupted the two with a squawk. Adya laughed. "Yes, Yiny. We got Lir back," she said to the magpie. "Lir, I'd like you to meet Yiny. Ava sent her to watch over me for a while. Now she's tasked with keeping an eye on a new fire affinate that recently joined this family."

326

"Nice meeting you, Yiny," Lir said to the bird. "I guess Murchadh might've been correct about Muriel being sent to him."

Yiny did what appeared to be a bird's equivalent of a happy dance and then flew off.

"We have all the time in the world to catch up on everything I've missed out on," Lir said while taking Adya's hand. "But the music and celebration will be gone at the end of the night. Let's enjoy tonight."

"Promise you're not leaving at the stroke of midnight?" Adya said, eyeing him cautiously.

Lir laughed and tugged Adya towards the dance floor. "I promise," he said as they found an empty spot to dance near Lydie and Paxton.

Jace and Clary were dancing nearby, too, and moved closer when Lir and Adya joined the crowd on the floor. "I wager a guess that this is the famous Lir? I was there when you and Pax were talkin' 'bout you coming and surprising D," Jace said with a grin.

"Mmhmm," Adya replied with a huge smile. "Lir, these are my friends, Jace and Clary."

"Nice to meet you," Lir said to the couple and then whispered in Adya's ear. "Did he call you 'D'? And non-affinate friends? We definitely have some catching up to do."

"You're the one that insisted on dancing," Adya said teasingly.

"Some things just can't wait," Lir teased back and pulled Adya closer. "Interesting choice with your hair. I'm sure there's a story behind that, too."

"You don't like it?" Adya asked with a faux pout.

"Didn't say that," Lir said as he ran his finger through her short locks.

The two continued to dance close together and chat, only interrupted by the occasional praise offered to Adya for her piano piece, until it was time for the cake cutting.

"Let's take a walk," Lir suggested as everyone else stood around the cake table to watch the newlyweds feed each other cake.

With locked hands, the two left the barn for a walk in the fresh summer night air. "I should've texted you when I was going to meet Maggie," Lir confessed as they meandered around Sophia's property.

Adya squeezed Lir's hand and shook her head. "Let's not talk about regrets right now," she requested. "I have so many of my own, too." She could feel the emotions creeping up on her but wanted to remain in the blissfulness that had engulfed her since Lir walked into the barn.

Lir nodded, and they continued walking with a comfortable silence hanging between them.

Finally, out of seemingly nowhere, Adya stopped and brought Lir to face her. "Yes," she said.

Lir raised a brow at her. "Yes, what? Yes, I should've texted you?" he asked.

Adya pulled the ring from where it rested hidden under the top of her dress. "I know, I was supposed to wait for your call to open the present. To be fair, I was *forced* to open it about three months ago. It broke my heart, something that I'm sure I've done to you too many times. But the answer is yes."

Lir studied the ring with a subtle look of confusion like he was trying to remember wrapping it for her. Finally, his eyes cleared, and his features softened, and he reached around behind Adya's neck, unclasped the necklace, and carefully unthreaded the ring. "I know we have years to wait, but I knew when I gave this to you that my feelings for you aren't going to change. Are you sure that this is what you want in this life?" Lir held the ring in his fingers in the space between him and Adya.

"Just put it on my finger already before my bazillionaire French fiancé, Pierre, comes and steals me away," Adya said with a grin.

"Tá mo chroí istigh ionat. Mo chuid den tsaol." Lir whispered words of love as he slid the ring onto Adya's left ring finger and kissed the back of her hand.

Paxton and Lydie left the following afternoon, but Lir and Adya decided to stay in Ava's house a little while longer before they had to go back to North Shore and address Maggie's belongings with Ted.

"Did you ever think you'd be back here?" Adya asked while resting her head in Lir's lap on the porch swing as they watched the sunset together.

"Let's see. . . which 'here' are you referring to? Ava's house? Being together with you? Or being alive in general?"

"I meant Ava's house, but any and all of those are fine to answer," Adya said with a grin while playing with Lir's fingers in their grasped hands.

"Ava's house makes me sad," Lir confessed, "but I guess it's the good kind of sad. I didn't think I'd come back here, no, but the new memories here are taking away some of the sadness. As far as being alive and with you again. . . are you sure you want to get into that now?"

"There's one more bottle of gin left inside, if that'll help," Adya teased.

"You've been drinking Ava's gin alone?" Lir asked in surprise.

"Not alone. Jace and I shared a couple of bottles while I pretty much told him the history of me," Adya admitted. Sensing some form of jealousy in Lir, she added, "Nothing ever happened between Jace and me. We have this kind of brother-sister love-hate thing going on, but that's it."

"You wore your promise ring this entire time?" Lir asked.

Adya nodded, looking up into Lir's face. "Not even near-death can come between me and a promise I made." Adya sat up and positioned her body to face him. "I know a part of you still sees me as a child, but my old soul is stubborn, and it's made its decision—you, Lir. There is and will be no one else for me in this lifetime. I think I've lived enough lifetimes for you to know that I'm not acting as the child that everyone sees me as being right now."

Lir caressed Adya's cheek and looked at her with adoring eyes. "You know it's your soul that I'm in love with and have been for centuries. I'm sorry I don't have my Claddagh ring anymore."

"It's just a ring," Adya replied and leaned into Lir's touch. "I know where your heart lies."

Lir admired Adya with loving eyes. "As for the other two, no, I didn't think I'd be alive in this lifetime to hold you like this. Dhruva broke me and then stole my soul. I don't remember anything about that time except I have this vague, dreamlike recollection of Dhruva capturing you."

Adya recalled that, too. "A tear fell down your face when your soulless body locked me away. I held onto that for a long time, believing you were still in there somewhere, until Dhruva broke me, too." Adya tilted her head to the side and showed Lir the scar on her neck. "I didn't want to live in a world without you, and I didn't want Dhruva to take my soul, so I tried to take my life. I go back and forth between feeling selfish and brave for my actions."

"What did you finally decide?" Lir asked tenderly.

Adya paused to stare into Lir's eyes. "In the end, all I know is that I did it out of love for you," she finally admitted.

Lir traced Adya's neck, feeling the scar, and closed his eyes. "I think you were brave," he said softly, "although I never wanted this for you." He opened his eyes and tried to blink away the tears that had pooled in them.

Adya reached up and caressed his cheek. "It's over now. And we have a lifetime of 'what ifs' to explore together. For example," Ayda said and sat up, "what if I straddled your lap right now?" She slid into his lap, one knee on each side of him. "And," she continued while kissing the corners of his mouth, "I could fill in all the missing gaps in your memory," she finished very quickly before pressing a passionate, longing kiss against his lips.

Lir enjoyed her aggressive lips against his but ended up tickling her ribs to break her free. "I think you're bound to have a lot more than 'missing gaps' filled in if you keep this up," he teased. He looked up into Adya's adoring eyes and ran his fingers through her short hair. "Maybe I should ask them to put me in a coma for the next three to four years, and we try this again."

"Don't you dare even think about leaving me for the next three to four years," Adya replied with a pout.

Lir playfully bit Adya's jutted out lip. "I wouldn't dream of it, *mo ghaol.*"

EPILOGUE

What's left to say? Upon returning to the Academy, Lir and I opened the letter from Maggie, willing us her journals and wishing us both happiness in this life. I decided not to return to North Shore because the things I needed to learn in this life wouldn't come from an Academy. I turned down the Council seat, too. Instead, I opted for an advisory role to the Elders during times of need—and there seemed always to be plenty of demand.

Lir stepped down from his research position—an obvious decision after his six-month hiatus—and we traveled the world, seeing places we once lived and creating memories in new ones. We continued to devise and test new theories to help affinates relate better to each other and with the world. Oh, and of course, we found new ways to share our intimate desires—in appropriate ways.

On my mortal eighteenth birthday, Lir and I were married by Sophia in a very intimate ceremony at Ava's house. Lydie was my maid of honor, of course, and in a surprising turn of events, Pax stood as Lir's best man. Despite some rocky moments, Lydie and Pax were still together and looking to get married in Hawaii in the distant future. . . probably. Jace and Clary were in attendance, too, newly engaged, and preparing for their first child to be born.

Dhruva never woke from her coma. After two years, the Elders made a decision (with my input) to take her off life support and let her soul return to the universe. We keep a constant vigil to look for signs of her in new affinates. We hope that we can intervene early on and help mold her into a positive force for the elements. Truth be told, I have my doubts, but it has opened research into identifying affinates earlier in their life.

I continued to see signs that the Ascended were trying to contact us for a reason, but we haven't been able to determine how or why they wanted our—or my—attention. The world was, as usual, determined to destroy itself, but the affinates were once again unified to maintain balance.

And what have I learned from this body, mind, and soul altering experience? That my perspective of happiness and fulfillment is mine alone. To truly be me, I have to do what's right by me and have to carve my own path to achieve my perspective of happiness and fulfillment.

So, until I'm needed again, I will continue to live what is possibly my favorite lifetime with the man I've loved for so many lifetimes.

Peace and balance always,
Adya

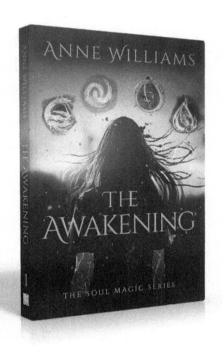

The Awakening, book 1 in the Soul Magic series, is available from Amazon, Barnes & Noble, and other major online resellers. Or order directly from https://thesoulmagicseries.com.

Coming summer 2021

Book 3 in the Soul Magic series:
The Ascended

Visit https://thesoulmagicseries.com for the latest info on everything about the Soul Magic series.

Interested in publishing a book? Need an editor or ghostwriter? Visit https://thepneumaproject.com for more information.